KYNWULF

M. R. KANIA

Snow River Press

SNOW RIVER PRESS
Ogden, Utah

3 mph Publishing
Ann Arbor, Michigan

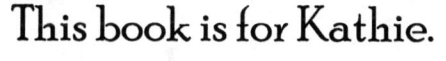

This book is for Kathie.

KYNWULF

M. R. KANIA

1

It would have been a safe bet on that sun-flecked morning that if Alex Kynwulf had suspected the long, strange trip that lay in wait for him on the other side of the Idaho state line, he might have turned that truck around right there in Atomic City and high-tailed it back to Altoona with all the speed that those four half-worn-out Michelins could have mustered.

But then again, when the heart cries out lonely, it takes more than geography that stretches past memory and mind, more than the threat of facing physics in real time and space to turn your back on possibility and promise.

....

Alex felt he must be on the loneliest highway in America. He hadn't seen one vehicle in over an hour. The last car he'd seen was in the ditch, and it looked like it had been there for some time. The sun- scalded "Pray for me, I drive 93" bumper sticker was almost white. The numbing effect of the long road spawned an unnatural calmness, and his mind wandered in time to an endless progression of electric poles and fence lines. The new topography spawned mountainous daydreams. Alex dreamed about cowgirls, long-legged, All-American cowgirls with lots of blonde hair and shiny teeth. It was a pleasant series of thoughts, like pictures in a magazine, and it seemed to match the mountains as he sped his old Chevy past the derelict Ramshorn Café.

Ahead to the northwest, the Lost River Range ran like a line and rolled into a fading perspective of snow-capped peaks, unending mountains against a cerulean sky. This is what the west looks like in my daydreams, Alex thought. Just like this. Just like Idaho.

There was a strange message painted on the surface of the highway, in long extended letters, three rows, faded white road paint. Alex slowed down, read, "DON'T.....BE A.....GUBERIF". He was certain he didn't see it right.

Not many things one could aspire to be began with the three letters G U B. As he began to climb the grade below Leatherman Pass, there it was again, road paint faded, almost gone, "DON'T....BE A....GUBERIF", sprawled right across his lane. Alex laughed out loud and decided then and there that he would never become a GUBERIF, especially as he was going to be working for U.S. Forest Service.

Alex pondered the thin line of disconnected events that all seemed to bundle together at once. He reflected back on two-hundred-and-thirty-seven job applications, fifty-three telephone interviews, twelve face-to-face interviews, and forty-six unsuccessful medical school applications.

He thought about home.

His father could not understand how Alex could not have a real job nine months after graduating from Penn State, and he constantly goaded him by bringing up his close ties to the local asphalt industry. "Just give me the word, and you'll have a job on the paving machine," his dad would lament each time Alex opened another rejection letter.

It wasn't just the fear of a cancer-causing-suntan that pushed Alex in his military-like job march across the continent. A deeper desire also drove Alex, pulled him away from his mother's breaded pork chops and pumpkin pies. Alex needed a woman, and he needed one soon; a best friend kind of girl, a steady Saturday night date, a long-term prospect, his own hugger. This longing for a female friend was fueled by a biological clock running in overdrive. It was the desperate hunt of a twenty-three year old that had finished a college career without ever having had a steady girl.

And it wasn't for lack of effort. At Penn State he had taken his minor interest in art and enrolled in a series of art classes: watercolor, figure drawing, oils, print-making, all just to try to meet women. He calculated his chances, counted his rejections, didn't give up. Alex learned to dance, joined every club that he could morally justify; and somehow, he had managed to spend four years at a major party school without ever having had a long-term relationship with a girl.

After graduation he had desperately searched the single's bars, the dance clubs, the concert scene, even started going to mass, and had come to the uneasy conclusion that he had exhausted the generational supply of women in Altoona.

As his search for work lead him westward, a small germ of an idea, an unlikely weed of a thought, began to sprout and take root in the deep, dark soil in the back of Alex's mind. Maybe, just maybe, against all the odds, a woman

2

waited for him in the high country. He tried not to think about it, but this tickle of a thought of a woman in the west kept tugging at him and tried to get his attention. But Alex had played the long shot at love for too long and didn't believe in luck, or at least not good luck.

The net result of his job quest was one job offer from a most unlikely source far, far from home. With an almost religious conviction of predestination, Alex began to pack his few possessions into his battered Chevrolet pickup. Hope and anxiety shared equal portions of his thoughts as he prepared to accept his one and only offer of a white collar future.

His mother was concerned. His father was flummoxed and told him so. "Turn down a good union job just to go gallivanting across the country. You must not have a God-damn brain in your God-damn head."

"Dad, this is a professional level job opportunity."

"Yeah, but they're paying you peanuts."

"I know, it isn't much, but it's full-time work, and - - ."

His father interrupted. "I give you a year, a year and half at most, and you'll come dragging back, begging to get on down at the Union Hall."

Alex took a deep breath. "Thanks for the pep talk, Dad."

Following Alex out on the porch, his father yelled after him, "Who ever heard of a career in recreation anyhow?"

A long convoy of doubts seemed to follow Alex from Altoona, clear across America.

The highway ahead formed a sensuous curve along the grain of the slope up Willow Creek, a ribbon of asphalt in the melting frost. Alex stopped the truck at the summit for a photograph to legitimize the occasion. Standing next to the "Entering Elkhorn County" sign, Alex could barely make out an outline, a vestigial mark across the landscape far to the north, a glimmer that could be Goldburg.

There was a deep, low, rumbling, sonic-boom sort of sound that started like thunder from the south. A line of dust at the base of the mountains raced toward him at the speed of sound, rocks cracked and broken on the wings of a jet. With a hard jolt the ground began to shake, short hard shakes. With a convulsive intensity, the shock waves deformed the roadway into sine waves of asphalt. Alex stood unbelieving, his arms straight out to keep balance, his mouth held open in an involuntary gasp in a desperate dance to stay upright as the earth betrayed him. At the point where surprise turned to terror, the earthquake slowed, the waves subsiding, the ground again firming, the noise pealing away in a race northward. Alex caught the scent of broken rock and the dust of deformed earth, a long forgotten, almost instinctive fear surrounding him. He had to force himself to lower his arms. Alex saw the crack in the asphalt that ran right between his legs, one shoe four inches lower than the other. A crack turned into a line, a fresh scar etched on the landscape. The earthquake scarp described an angry arc in the gravelly soil and created an impression of a long loop from where Alex stood all the way to a small aspen patch below the highway and back again, tracing a unlikely shape that more than suggested a heart.

2

"It was a redhead.
A redhead to make a Bishop kick a hole in a stained glass window."
Raymond Chandler (adapted)

Alex sat down right in the dirt and tried to force out of his head the unsettling fact that the earth can move hard and fast. His shoulder muscles bunched and twisted as tiny electric shocks ran down his arms. He was conscious of the hair on the back of his neck. He nervously clamped his hands and cleared his throat, again and again. Alex waited and listened, took seven long breaths in a row, talked to himself right out loud.

Back in his truck, Alex picked up speed as he raced across Antelope Flats. He was in a hurry now, a springtime breeze at his back, the highway curving through folds of sagebrush, seeming to disappear in a rust-red wall of rock. The small brown sign read "Grandview Canyon" in hand-painted white letters. He just had time to read it, taking the second curve a little too fast. The old pickup tried hard to stay in the appointed lane. Alex, alert now, on edge, gently braked, holding the steering wheel with both hands tight, willing the truck through the end of the curve. Then he saw the cows; lots of cows, and calves, stacked like brown and white cordwood right in the middle of the highway.

Alex stood on the brakes. Squealing like a banshee, the old pickup skidded right through the curve, somehow missing every bug-eyed Hereford in the front bunch, sliding past the cows like a kid on a sled. The truck bounced down over some lumpy sagebrush and plowed into a soft-bottomed gooseberry creek without hitting a rock.

It was shakes all over, and Alex could hardly stop until he had to remember to breathe. A quick once-over; he was still inside his seatbelt, the front end of the truck seemed smooth, he apparently hadn't hit anything hard. In a conscious effort to affirm life, he improvised on a few basic curses.

"Dirty damn, no good, piss-whore cows!" were the first words he said.

He liked the phrase, so he repeated it, almost verbatim, "Damn, no good, piss-whore cows!"

The cows didn't seem to mind much, since they began moving again, filing past the mired truck in groups of brood cows and calves. As Alex calmed down, he noticed that he wasn't alone. Three figures on horseback pushed along the cattle with whoops and yells, two men and a young woman. Alex could see her pretty well now, she was the closest to him, and what he mostly saw was hair, lots of it, red-brown in the sun. The girl rode closer, tall in the saddle, leather chaps and gloves, black duster and hat. They were only separated by about fifty feet of Herefords. One of the last in the herd, a thick-necked bull, shoved close to the truck and gave a quick kick as he passed by. There was a ringing of metal on rock, and Alex watched one of his baby moon chrome hubcaps bounce down some rocks and roll into the creek.

"Son-of a -bitch!" he swore just a little too loudly.

The girl followed the hubcap with her horse, a tall, roman-nosed pinto, mane all tied up in buckaroo braids. She slickly slid off the saddle, pulled off her gloves and plucked the baby moon out of the shallow water. She carried it like a war trophy, rolling it over just to watch it shine.

"Hey there," she said smiling, "look what I found."

Alex sheepishly slunk out of the truck and stepped right in two inches of water and four of mud, then tried to stand up straight.

The girl looked Alex square in the face and stopped still, dropping the hubcap with another loud ring on rock, her mouth and eyes both formed O's. She bent down quickly and scooped up the baby moon, started to say something, then stopped, cautiously extending her arm.

He often had made a similar impression, for Alex Kynwulf looked different from most people, a lot different. Alex was not handsome nor was he plain, but raw and rugged looking far beyond the normal range of expectations. Like his namesake, he had the look of the wolf, tall and lean with powerful arms and shoulders matched with strong facial features: a long nose and chiseled jaw, prominent brow ridges and a bushy head of blond-brown hair, strange mane-like hair, more like fur, that pushed out in all directions like he had just taken off his hat. But it was his eyes that were most noticeable, unique eyes, glass-gray, like the watch-eyes of a Malamute, set rather too far apart, cold eyes that always seemed to be staring.

"Ah, thanks." he said, trying to act what he hoped was more natural, accepting the hubcap like a birthday present, leaning his arm against the too-obviously stuck truck.

This girl's smile was back, but this time without any teeth showing. "Looks like someone was driving too fast down Little Grand Canyon," she said quietly. "Is your truck all right?"

Alex's attempts to minimize his unusual appearance had manifested two undesirable and opposite personality quirks, self-defeating social traits that he found hard to control. With great effort, Alex finally blurted out in a deep voice, almost a growl, "Yeah, I think so, didn't hit anything." He searched for more words, but he became more tongue-tied when he looked in her bright blue eyes. Sometimes Alex froze when he was nervous or excited, and he did it a little too often and held onto it a little too long. Long pauses in conversation combined with his steely-eyed stare often unnerved and frightened women, and many a promising match-up had ended with the girl slowly backing away into her group of friends.

The girl was trying hard now. "You're lucky you didn't smack a rock or two."

After some hesitation, Alex said, "Yeah, yeah, I sure am lucky." Witty remarks crowded his mind but couldn't make it to his lips. In situations like this, Alex had to watch he didn't let his other limitation show. Often Alex tried so hard to overcome his reticence that, once started, he went too far the other way, chattering like a school girl with way too many arm movements and facial expressions. If you didn't know him, it could be downright scary.

"You want some help getting it out of the mud?" she asked.

"Sure, sure," he said, still short of better words. Alex noticed her height, most of it in her legs.

Almost like an act of self defense, the girl said, "My dad and uncle will get up here as soon as they push a few stragglers through. Sorry about the cows on the road, but we're just moving them onto the spring BLM range."

"BLM?"

"Oh, Bureau of Land Management."

Alex thought he detected a slightly warm tone in her statement and a small shot of self-confidence stirred within him. "Right, right," he said, flustered and feeling dumber by the second. "You live around here?" was the best he

7

could come up with, and then added, "I'm new to town myself."

"Goldburg? You live in Goldburg? Since when?"

"Yeah." Alex noticed a small bump on the bridge of her nose. He was entranced by it for a second before he added, "I was just coming into town for the first time when I almost ran into your round-up," hoping he was using the right term.

A gleam of a silver belt buckle flashed from beneath her coat. "Oh, you must be the new guy for the Forest Service."

Alex was feeling better, somewhat bolstered by this small degree of recognition. God, she's pretty, twenty-one or twenty-two, no ring on her finger. He decided to take his chance at conversation. "Say, did you feel the earthquake, not even an hour ago?

"You bet, it was quite a rumble. We've been getting them the last year or so every once in a while. Now, Bucky, my horse, must have heard it coming. He just firmed up and wouldn't go, just stood there staring south with his ears up. I even put the spurs to him a little bit, and he barely moved. Then all of a sudden, all the cows were bellering. Then it started to shake like we were all standing on Jello. It was a little nuts for a while, and took a bit for everything to calm down."

"That's something, that the animals felt it first."

"Some geologist told me that something is going on under Borah Peak."

"Did he say what was going on?"

"Well, it could be aftershocks from a quake we had last year closer to Goldburg, or these could be foreshocks, a warning for something bigger that's going to happen."

Alex hesitated too long again, and even the two courses in geology he had taken couldn't seem to help him with words.

The girl filled in the pause. "I hear you're from back east somewhere?" she said in musical notes that only Alex could hear.

"Pennsylvania," he said, waiting just a bit too long to add, "my name's Alex, Alex Kynwulf. What's yours?" he blurted out, cringing a little inside at such a poor delivery.

The girl cocked her head to one side, like she was thinking about it. Another smile formed and she said, "Kin-wolf? That's a pretty different name, never heard it before."

Alex was embarrassed anew and squirmed in wet boots. "It's an old-English name. I guess it's sort of uncommon."

8

"Kin-wolf," she carefully sounded out the name, like she was getting prepared to write it down. "Well, I think Kin-wolf is a fine name. I'm Angie, Angie Kowalski."

"Nice to meet you," Alex held out his hand like he was meeting the president.

Her grip was firm, the hand cool, and a little spark jumped through Alex, jerking his head back just a degree. He worked on the edge of his thin blonde mustache, trying to catch the end of it in his teeth.

"Pleased to meet you," she replied, somewhat too formally, slightly disappointing Alex. "Hope you enjoy living in Goldburg."

"I'm sure I will." Alex was starting to feel a little better about his conversational skills.

Up rode two men, her dad and uncle. She introduced them, and Alex instantly forgot their names, as he was concentrating instead on Angie's oversized bright-silver belt buckle.

Angie got in the truck and started it up. With the help of Alex, her dad and uncle all pushing in time, she rocked the truck right out of the mud and onto the edge of the pavement.

"Hey, the truck looks good. Thanks, thanks a lot," Alex said, hoping for a little more conversation, but it was all business now, as dad and uncle didn't say much, their body language somewhat negative, and Angie fell in behind. Soon all three were up on their horses and following the cows out of Grandview Canyon. Alex watched the tall girl on her painted horse slowly move down the road, and just before the two of them disappeared behind the canyon wall, she turned around. Alex immediately waved, hand high above his head and held the pose, stationary, still, waiting, as Angelica Kowalski returned just the smallest of waves, almost like she was brushing away an insect from around her black hat, her hand fluttering slowly back to her side.

Alex watched the place where the red rock divided, imagining the girl, a smile pasted on his face as a germ of a summertime dream formed and followed him all the way to Goldburg.

3

"Romance at short notice was her specialty."
H. H. Munro

Goldburg, Idaho, county seat of Elkhorn County, population seven hundred and ninety, home of the Sleeping Deer Ranger District of the White Cloud National Forest. Horses and mules, at least thirty of them, stood behind a five-rail-high white pole fence,. It was almost four o'clock and Alex didn't see a soul about as he pulled into the parking lot next to the ranger station. He stepped out of the Chevy, stretched his hands high above his head, revolving his neck, took a deep breath, dropped his arms, and walked into the office.

Inside, it was all wood: knotty pine walls and ceiling; a scuffed-up hardwood floor; a long, curved oak credenza; oak chairs and desks behind; little nameplate signs made of wood and even a large wooden hand-carved map of the district with elf-like lettering and three-dimensional mountain peaks. It was like a strange Hobbit house of the wood people, Alex thought, as he walked up to the front desk, his introduction memorized, clearing his throat to alert the receptionist.

"Hi, my name is Alex Kynwulf. I'm the new recreation forester for the District."

The large green eyes went round, blinked several times, squinted as the woman said, "What was that?"

Nervous now, Alex repeated his name and his job title, soon to be a worn out phrase as he shifted from foot to foot.

"Kin-wolf? Oh, the new forester? We were wondering when the hell you were going to get here," the woman said in a strange-friendly way. "I hear you come from back east somewheres?"

"Well, yeah I do, Pennsylvania."

"Is that a fact? I don't think we've ever had anyone work here from Pennsylvania before," she said carefully, sounding out the syllables. "Oh I'm sorry. I'm Sandy, Sandy Spotts, nice to meet you." She reached her arm over the

10

counter and shook Alex's hand for what seemed an uncommonly long time.

Alex looked Sandy in the eyes; contact lens green eyes. She was thirty eight, maybe forty, brunette; hair cut straight at her shoulders, with the look of an aging showgirl, a big smile and lots of movement, a tight green uniform instead of pasties and g-string. Sandy was still a good looking package and was busy sending out signals.

"Never been east of Denver myself," she said. "Just never cared to go."

Not knowing what to say, Alex changed the subject. "Is the Ranger in?"

"No, no, Big Stan is out in the field. In fact, everyone is. I'm the only one in the office today."

As Alex measured the fifteen years or more that separated them, he watched her eyes dart around the room and then land back on him. "Is that what you call him, Big Stan?"

"Actually we call him Stan, or Stanley. Big Stan is sort of a town name."

"A town name?"

"Yeah, a town name."

"He's pretty big is he?"

"Oh yes, oh yes, Big Stanley is all of that. I think he must be the biggest ranger in Idaho, maybe even in the whole Forest Service."

An unsettling Paul Bunyan image formed among Alex's thoughts.

Sandy twirled her left hand through her hair. "But don't mention his feet."

"His feet?"

"Yeah, his feet."

More strange images zipped through the world behind Alex's eyes, a club-footed pirate boss perhaps? "Why, is something wrong with his feet?"

"No, no they're fine feet, just big."

"Big?"

"Big." More hair twirling, leaning slightly forward, a whiff of liquor on her breath. "He's sensitive about that."

Alex reminded himself not to mention anything about feet around the office. "So when do you expect the ranger back?"

No mistaking it this time, a breath of whiskey from the bottle, Sandy leaned way close to Alex and smiled with all her teeth showing, "Not until Monday."

Alex moved perceptibly away from the woman. He had run out of things to say from the prepared text in his mind. "Well, I'll come back Monday, I

11

guess."

"Is that your date when you officially start work?"

"Yeah, yeah, on Monday." Alex felt like he was in a movie and he was the stupid one that couldn't walk or talk straight, and promptly backed into a stuffed elk head, hitting his own head with a sharp brow tine.

"Watch out for Elky Summer." Sandy laughed.

"Who?" Alex said as he grabbed his head.

"Elky Summer, the elk." Sandy laughed another measured laugh.

"Oh yeah, the elk."

"That's Deer Abby on the wall over there," she said, pointing to a large, yellowed mount of a mule deer buck, glass eyes too large.

"Dear Abby, right, the deer." Alex wanted to leave, but since he hit his head and Sandy laughed so much, he figured he needed to make some shop talk before he went out the door. "So, ah, is this like a new job, or am I filling in behind someone?"

Sandy rolled her eyes and planted her elbow on the counter, chin in hand. "Oh, I don't think you want to hear a sad story, being new here and all."

"A sad story?"

"Oh my yes, poor Larry."

"What happened?"

"Got fired."

"Fired?" Alex was nervous now and down to one word questions.

"Well, not really fired, I guess. 'Let go' might be the nicer way to put it. About the same thing. Anyway, when his probationary period was up, he wasn't made a permanent employee."

Alex's cold, gray eyes were as wide open as they could get. "So, I'm not considered a permanent employee?"

"Not unless you've worked for the government before."

"Well, how long is the probation period?"

"Eighteen months."

"Eighteen months?" He was counting the months ahead, fast. "Can I ask what happened?"

"You don't want to know."

"I don't?"

"No, you don't. Trust me. It's better this way."

"Better?"

"Better."

Alex wouldn't let it go. "Was it a legal problem?"

"Oh, gosh no! Larry was a straight arrow all the way, never missed a day of work, came early and left late. Everybody liked him, well almost everybody."

Alex froze like a statue at the "almost everybody" statement.

Sandy looked at him, expecting Alex to say something more, but the best he could do were three deep breaths. "You feeling all right, soldier?" Sandy squinted again. "You don't look too good."

"Fine, fine," Alex finally stammered.

"Maybe I should get you a drink."

"No, no! No drinks, please. Don't make me a drink. I don't want a drink, really." The words poured out like water from a broken-down dam. "It's way too early in the day, and we're both at work, you know, it wouldn't look good. Maybe later, you know, maybe next week or something, after I have some time to settle in, get acquainted. Maybe then, you know, after work, one of these days after work, you know, we could get together for a drink or something."

"I was only talking about a glass of water." Sandy looked perplexed, her carefully plucked eyebrows furled. "Oh, oh, I get it now. This is all an act!" She laughed with her mouth held open and her head back. "Ho! you had me going there for awhile. You're a real comic, you are. I see I'll have to watch you close."

Alex had it bad. He had to bite his lower lip to help himself shut up, change the subject. "Well, I guess I should be going."

"Yeah, you better get out of here before you trick me again, you sly dog you."

Alex carefully backed toward the door. "See you on Monday, I guess."

"You bet, Monday it is," said Sandy, closing her left eye and pointing her finger like a pistol, dropping her thumb like the hammer, "but not unless I see you first".

4

Early Saturday morning, the April sun illuminated the long row of leafless Lombard poplars that paralleled the still-dry irrigation ditch. Angelica Kowalski sat in her father's twenty-year-old blue truck. She looked over the first calf heifers that had not yet freshened, the stragglers that had not been bred in time for February calving, kept in the small pasture next to the machine shed. She caught her eyes in the rear-view mirror, studied her face, thought herself plain, wished she was prettier. She glared at the bump at the bridge of her nose, a childhood souvenir from an unremembered accident, then sighed and tried to be more positive. Her thoughts poured in like waves. She began to think about going back to Idaho State, and then decided against it; maybe California instead. At least it was warm there. Then Angelica wondered why all the guys she knew were so dense. It wouldn't hurt Finn to read a book now and then, but then she knew that she and Finn were not much of a match. He didn't like music much, hated poetry and all things literary. He was fun and had a nice body, but he did drink too much. Even though he was five years older than she was, he still acted like a kid most of the time, another lost boy that would never grow up. Maybe she would get her guitar out and try to write a song about it. While she was wishing, she wished she could sing. She thought her voice too quiet and undistinguished, like the rest of her.

A long sigh and Angelica spied a heifer near the far fence that was more than ready. Two white front legs protruded from her hindquarters, stuck right out in the sunshine, waiting for the expectant mother to lie down. Angelica watched the heifer walking slowly in a circle, head smelling the ground. Biology finally forced the cow to lie down, front legs first. She had the calf puller in hand and was slowly approaching from behind. "Easy girl, I'm not going to hurt you."

The heifer turned her head and stared bug-eyed at the girl but did not attempt to get up.

14

"That's a good girl, easy does it." She knelt behind and carefully looked over the situation. The front hooves had been sticking out for a while. They were plaster-white and dry. The heifer was straining, but the calf was not moving. Angelica slowly worked the slip cord down over the hooves and pulled it tight up behind the hocks of the calf. "You just take it real easy."

Angelica settled in behind and waited for nature to assert control, waited for the next push. She wrapped the thick cord around her back and used her heavy boots to dig spaces for her heels to push against. The rope felt thick in her gloved hands. "Come on girl. I'm ready."

The heifer strained and Angelica pulled, but not much happened, maybe an inch or two more leg showing. Angie could tell from the size of the hooves that the calf was a large one. The heifer was undersized, and Angelica wished her Dad hadn't gone down to Salmon today. With a low moaning bellow, the cow pushed again, and Angelica pulled with all she had. The net result was eighteen inches of white forelegs and a pink, mucous covered nose beginning to show, barely peeking out.

"Okay girl, now this is the head, the hard part. You can do it," she said softly. The heifer, more bug-eyed now, stretched out her neck, her head out straight, and pushed as Angelica pulled, pulled hard.

But not much happened. The calf was stuck with the eyes still inside. Angelica could see a little red-colored hair showing on the front legs now. It went on like this for a little too long. The heifer was getting tired and the calf was still stuck right at the eyes. With each contraction, Angelica pulled, but it wasn't working. The calf was just too big.

"Come on now. Come on. You can do it. Come on now, you bitch!"

The little heifer's contractions were timed so they seemed to match the command. The cow let out a pitiful, mournful bellow, again stretching out her neck, this time her head almost flat to the ground. Right in time Angelica pulled, puffed and pulled, pulled so hard she went red in the face. "Come.....on......you.......b-b-b-bitch!"

And the calf's head slithered out, blue tongue hanging, eyes open, ears slathered back on its neck, wet with birth fluid.

Through gritted teeth, "Come....on... don't quit......just need the.........shoulders."

Animal instinct, involuntary contractions and the heifer strained again.

Angelica, angry now, could barely form words, boots kicked deeper in the dirt, "ah.....ah.........ah, ah.........come............on!"

15

The calf slowly emerged at the shoulders, inch by inch. The shoulders cleared, and then the calf just flowed out the birth canal. Angelica fell back on the grass, eyes open, panting, looking at the clouds. She blew out a hard breath and scrambled up on her feet. The calf wasn't doing anything. Angelica bent down and cleared the mucus from the calf's nose and mouth. Then she grabbed both front legs, pulling and rolling the calf from side to side, hard. The calf kicked and sputtered, and like time-lapse photography, came to life, the blue tongue turning pink with the flush of oxygen in the blood.

The cow looked back and let out a low bellow and stood up, hind legs first, the afterbirth trailing behind. The calf was all wet and sticky, the too-wide head wobbling on an unsteady neck, lying on green grass next to a pool of blood and water. The cow nuzzled the calf, drinking in the scent, then began to lick the calf's face and mouth with a long sandpaper-like tongue. Angelica stood aside. "Yeah, come on. You know what to do. Mother him up." Leaning forward she lifted a hind leg to check the sex. "A pretty bull calf, but too damn big for you." Angie smiled at the cow as if it could understand her, bent down with a burlap feed sack and helped dry off the calf. The mother cow, anxious, was smelling and licking the calf's hindquarters. "How about I put a little grain on him to keep you interested." Angelica sprinkled two handfuls of grain on the still wet calf and the mother cow licked with her strong tongue, roughly rolling the calf's skin from side to side. "Looks pretty good, girl." She wiped her gloves on her wet and bloody pants.

Angelica drew back now to let the mother cow finish up, watching from the fence line. The sun was warming, there wasn't any wind, the calf was drying off fast, and Angelica decided against putting the calf in the shed. It was better to keep the calf on dry grass, she thought, less chance of scours or other health problems.

Fifteen minutes later, the calf was trying to stand, falling over once, twice, three times. By twenty minutes, he was up and wobbling from side to side, four legs splayed out wide. Angelica wanted to go help, line the calf up with the teat, but decided not to butt in and just watched. Within ten more minutes, the calf stumbled along, face and mouth up against the mother cow's side, searching with a constantly bobbing head. Three little lurching steps later, he was at the bag, his head up bobbing against the udder, sucking now, searching, finding the front teat, slipping off, and finding it again. Angelica could see the calf's jaws moving, sucking, saw the pink-white colostrum milk foam on its mouth.

16

Angelica felt good. She put her foot up on the fence rail and pushed her hat back, face full in the sun. She smelled her hands, a sweet smell, smelled them again. Looking over across the river toward Goldburg, Angelica for some reason thought about the tall young man she had met yesterday in the Little Grand Canyon and said right out loud, as if she were talking to someone, "He sure is a different looking guy."

5

"Who loves not wine, woman and song,
Remains a fool his whole life long."
Johann Heinrich Voss

Saturday morning; two days to find someplace to live, get settled and get ready for work.   Alex made the rounds of Goldburg, introducing himself whenever he got the chance. Strangely, everywhere he went people all seemed to know who he was.

"You're the new fellow working at the Forest Service," said Gridley Jones, the cowboy-hatted realtor. "Come from back east I hear."

"Yeah, Pennsylvania."

"Pennsylvania? That's just great. Never been there myself, but I hear it's nice." Gridley lapsed directly into real estate speak. "So what can I help you with today?" He folded his hands into a little church-steeple shape and smiled the confident real estate smile of low money down, good financing, and low monthly payments.

"I'm looking for a place to rent for a while."

"Not much to rent in town. Sure you're not interested in buying? Lots of good properties on the market, but you need to act quickly." The thumbs began to twiddle.

"Not just yet. I was thinking I would find a place to rent for a year or eighteen months, and look around a bit."

"A good strategy, but don't wait too long. Opportunities like we have here today may not come around again. Many a potential buyer has let that dream property slip through their hands and had to live with the regrets." Gridley talked like he was reading from an instruction manual titled, "How to Be a Realtor."

"Do you have anything outside of town?" Again the image of the cabin in the mountains, surrounded by aspen trees and thigh-deep snow, the smoke from the chimney going straight up, his skis resting alongside the door.

"Matter of fact, a little place just came on the rental market. Part of a bigger ranch and the family wants to hang onto the place while they figure out what they want to do with it. Just a small house. It's up Garden Creek aways, right next to Chipmunk Hill."

"Chipmunk Hill?"

"You bet, Chipmunk is our local ski-hill. Got a nice rope tow, great place for the kids. Six miles right to town. It's just a small one-bedroom."

"Like a cabin?"

Gridley looked up and sensed the air, his nostrils flaring. His real estate bell was obviously ringing inside. "You look like a man that just might be interested in a cabin."

Alex tried to put on a poker face. "Oh, I might be interested in a cabin."

Gridley beamed a smile you could see a mile and said, "Well, this is your lucky day. This is just the perfect cabin, and right next to winter recreation."

It didn't take long for Gridley to reel him in. The house was small, painted red with a log veneer, but it was on Garden Creek, set in a grove of aspens right next to the Forest Service boundary. One look at the view out the small picture window, and Alex was caught, sinker, line and hook. He figured he probably paid too much, but the deal allowed him to move in that afternoon. Gridley drove Alex back to town in his white Lincoln Continental and drew up the lease arrangements.

As Alex took the pen to sign the lease Gridley said, "Just goes to show you that when a man gets up in the morning, it's always a new day and you never know what might happen."

Saturday night and Alex was the only male in The Wild Bunch not wearing a cowboy hat. Inside the tavern, mule deer heads lined the walls, all of them seemingly of ancient vintage, hair bleached almost white, eyes bulging, horns dark with varnish. There was a sudden commotion on the dance floor as two young cowboys got into a fight. Harmless punches filled the air but didn't seem to connect. There was a lot of huffing and puffing but not much else, until the bartender grabbed them both at once, knocked them around a bit to quiet them down, and then hustled them out the swinging doors. Alex smiled as he watched the show and thought that he'd been in the place only five minutes and already seen a bar fight.

A band was getting ready to play on the small stage, adjusting the amplifiers and tuning up their instruments. Alex noticed a cardboard sign above the bar, "The Letgo Brothers, Tonight." He also noticed that one of the three brothers was a girl, a big-boned blonde. The two Letgo brothers looked like the caricatures of hillbillies in the comics, with long pointed beards and big, black floppy hats. As soon as the music started, Alex knew that the brothers could play. The music was a mix of bluegrass, country and western, and even a few folk tunes thrown in. The harmonies were tight. The big blonde took the stage and knocked out Alex with "Leaving Louisiana in the Broad Daylight."

Alex was still sipping on his first beer when Angie Kowalski and a young cowboy came into the bar and sat at a table fronting the dance floor. Back in the half-dark and smoke, Alex watched the girl intently. She was dressed all in black, like a female Johnny Cash with a silver-oval belt buckle. The buttons of her blouse glistened when they caught the lights over the bar. Angie and her date didn't talk much, and Alex noticed the girl carefully scanning the room, like she was looking for someone. Alex wanted to catch her eye, and then he didn't, and couldn't make up his mind.

At the start of the next song, Angie's boyfriend led her out to dance like he was leading a calf. It was like she really didn't want to but did anyway. Alex rarely judged others on looks, but he jealously felt that Angie's friend was an odd-looking sort, squat and powerful looking, with a Neanderthal-like shuffle in his cowboy boots. Stiff, short hair completed the Pleistocene look. He danced about the same, Alex thought, flat-footed with exaggerated arm and leg motions.

Angie danced with smooth and supple motions, almost hypnotizing Alex as he tried not to stare. The next dance number was a slow one and Alex noticed a regulated reserve, a sudden stiffness in the girl as her date held her close. When the music stopped, Angie moved purposefully back to their table and again there was little conversation. Not five minutes later, the pair got up to leave, hand in hand, and it was easy to see that the girl kept the longest possible distance between herself and her date. The thought came to Alex that if there was a maximum distance one could separate oneself while still holding hands, these two were at it.

An offbeat group passed Angie on their way in. Not only were there no cowboy hats among these two odd couples, but three of them were wearing Peruvian wool caps, the kind with the ear flaps that tied under the chin, a mainstay of the environmentalist winter dress code. They were all about the same age, early to mid-twenties, and ended up at the table next to Alex, and he couldn't help but overhear their conversation.

The smaller, ganglier of the two men was clearly interested in the unusually tall, broad-shouldered girl he had followed into the bar. Now, Alex

20

was tall and looked at the world as a large man does, measuring and scaling to his own size. But even he was impressed at the size of this girl, at least six feet tall, with narrow hips and barely perceptible breasts. She looked every inch the Olympic athlete, with a sweet, feminine face. Alex listened to the strange and stilted discussion between the two, a conversation with an odd scientific bent. The gangly guy kept talking about plate tectonics.

"I guess the real question revolves around the assertion that the mid-Atlantic trench is spreading open, while at the same time, the ocean floor is plunging beneath the continental shelf at the same rate. It all seems too clean-cut for me."

The tall girl in the Bucknell sweatshirt edged closer and said, "I think the pulsing of the hot magma from the mid-ocean rift pretty well seals the argument."

The skinny guy stroked his thin beard like a precious stone. "I give more credit to mountain building and thrust-block faulting on a regional basis for local geomorphology."

The girl countered, "But Argo, if you can't believe in the symmetry of plate tectonics, how do you explain the need for the hot engine that drives the earth? What is the reason for the design of a molten, nickle-iron core; the changes in planetary magnetism; the basic attractive force?"

Smiling and trying not to laugh, Alex politely turned his back to the group and kept listening to the ongoing discussion on continental crust movement. After a while, he had the odd feeling that he was being watched. Alex hazarded a glance, and saw the four hunched over and whispering. Turning back, he could feel the stares at the back on his head. He had just decided to leave when he heard someone say, "Excuse me?"

Alex slowly turned. "Yeah?"

It was the tan, muscular guy from the group. "Are you the new guy at the Forest Service?"

"Yeah, yeah I am." Alex pushed his chair out and extended his hand. "I'm Alex."

"Oh, I'm sorry, I'm Howie. Good to meet you Alex." The two shook hands like brothers. "And this is my wife, Nedra."

Alex leaned over to shake hands with the girl. He thought her a looker; never seen such platinum-blonde hair, like a model in a shampoo commercial. He smiled, caught her eye, and saw her jump.

"And these two, arguing about structural geology are Argo and

21

Teffonie."

"Pleased to meet you." Alex said.

"Disney was right," the fellow called Argo said. "It's a small world after all. Two of us work for you."

"Really?"

"You bet," Howie interrupted. "Argo works on the kayak crew with me. Teffonie works for Buck on the fire crew."

"So, you're like summer employees?" Alex said.

"We call ourselves seasonals, but yeah, we won't start work until next week," Howie said.

"And I'm a kept woman," Nedra said. "I volunteer for the Idaho Conservation League in the central Idaho Chapter."

"Yeah, Nedra is busy saving the world so the rest of us can play in it. So, have you met Big Stanley?"

"No, not yet."

"You've got a treat coming then."

"So what's the story about this Big Stanley? Is there something I need to know?"

"Oh no, " Howie said. "He's a great guy, just - - "

"Different." Nedra completed the sentence for him.

"I did meet Sandy. I guess she's the clerk."

"Oh, Sandy," Nedra said. "You mean randy Sandy Spotts, M.A., ex-Texas showgirl, and currently Big Stanley's heart-throb."

Alex squirmed in his curved-back chair wondering aloud, "What's the M.A. stand for?"

Nedra smiled a knowing smile and looked sideways over to Howie, who answered the question for her. "Maintenance Alcoholic."

"Oh."

Howie sipped his beer but didn't offer anything more.

Alex tried to think of less alarming things to talk about. "So how long have you all been in Goldberg?"

Howie answered first. "This is our second season. We just came up from winter camp over in Maui."

"We're perfecting our windsurfing," Nedra chimed in.

Howie turned to face the others. "Argo, Teffonie, how long have you worked on the District?"

Argo rolled his eyes. "This is my third summer."

22

"Actually, I came late last summer, just to look around," Teffonie said. "So this is really my first field-season working."

"So when do you start work?" Howie asked.

"Monday," Alex said.

"Good, good. It's been a while since Larry left, and I was hoping I would have a new boss by the time I got here."

"I heard some about Larry."

"Yeah, a bad deal all around."

"Is this like something you can't talk about?"

Oh, no. Larry was a nice guy, a great guy. He just didn't fit in with management, I guess."

"Sandy said there was some kind of problem."

Howie tightened his jaw and said, "His only problem was Riddles, the Forest Supervisor."

"Chester M. Riddles," Nedra interrupted. "Don't forget the M. It's like a name cult around here or something."

"Is this Riddles a tough guy to work for?"

Howie rubbed his head but didn't say anything.

Nedra grinned like the Cheshire Cat. "I hear he's a mean little bastard. He's like this big." She held her hand up to her shoulder. "Supposedly hates anybody bigger than him, which is like everybody."

Alex was immediately conscious of his own height and felt the anxious feelings coming on. "But his office is like sixty miles away, in Salmon?"

"Right, nothing to worry about," said Howie.

Alex wanted to believe, but deep inside he calculated a complex algorithm involving sixty miles and eighteen months and didn't like the answer. He looked across at the reflection in the big mirror behind the bar. Alex saw himself acting happy, wanting to fit in with this crowd, an unlikely exotic mix of cowboys, wannabe hippies, and geology aficionados. He studied his reflection but had no thoughts at all. As he turned away, a flash of movement in the mirror caught his eye, right behind him. Startled, Alex turned quickly but was greeted by only an empty chair, pulled out from the table at that odd angle that suggested it was reserved for someone.

6

"I've lived through some terrible things in my life,
Fortunately, most of which never happened."
Attributed to Mark Twain

After tossing and turning all night, Alex found himself nervously driving down Garden Creek Road to his first day of work. He arrived too early. The office was still locked, and Alex had an awkward five minutes deciding whether to pace back and forth in front of the door, to try to appear relaxed and shift his weight from one foot to the other, or to just wait in his truck. He had just decided on pacing when he turned around and almost ran over a thin, hawk-nosed man in a Forest Service uniform.

"Whoa there," the man said with a smile, tilting back his sizeable hat with his hand. "You must be the new guy. I'm Kloyd, Kloyd Spurr. I'm the packer on the District."

Alex took hold of the outstretched hand. "Good to meet you, I'm Alex."

Kloyd opened the office door with one the dozens of keys hanging from a large carabiner on his belt loop. "Come on in Alex. I'll get the coffee on. What was your last name again?"

Alex felt embarrassed that he hadn't offered it. "Kynwulf."

"Kin-Wolf, huh? I seem to remember a Har-wolf back in the Ward when I was living in Malad City, but I never heard of any Kin-Wolfs." Kloyd shuffled his feet like he was in a hurry to get somewhere. "Care for some coffee?"

"No, I don't drink coffee."

Kloyd smiled a revealing smile and said, "I shouldn't be, but then you won't tell, will you?'

Alex wondered who he could possibly tell about this coffee drinking, still not getting the drift.

Finally Kloyd asked, "Just wondering and all, are you LDS?

Alex had to think what LDS was, decided it wasn't the drug; probably the religion. "No, I'm not."

"I'm only asking cause you got the look. Sort of on the Joseph Smith side with that blonde hair and all."

"Well, some of my ancestors were from Illinois. I don't know what religion they were."

"Could be one of the Prophet's own progeny," Kloyd said. "Jeez-O-Friday, wouldn't that take the rag off'n the bush."

"That doesn't seem too likely. It's a big state."

"Yeah, but thirty-six wives produce an awfully big family tree. I think I should know."

"I really don't know much about them."

"We can fix that. The church has got records on all the Saints, all the way back to Nauvoo and New York, even. I got a cousin works down at the temple in Salt Lake, and she can work on your genealogy. Figure it out in two shakes of a lamb's tail."

Alex didn't know what to make of such an offer and tried to change the subject. "How long have you been on the Forest?" He asked, hoping for a secular answer.

"Me? Oh, I been here forever, born and raised just down by the river, up from Bayhorse. Been working on the Forest, off and on, since I graduated high school, almost twelve years ago." Kloyd still held an empty coffee cup in his hand. "I heard tell you come from back east somewhere."

"Yeah, Pennsylvania."

"So, were you on the Allegheny National Forest back there?"

"No, this is my first job with the Forest Service."

A sense of wonder came into Kloyd's green eyes. "No kiddin'?"

Before Alex could stop himself he admitted, "I just graduated from Penn State last summer."

This time Kloyd's jaw dropped slack as he said, "Well, you must of worked for the Forest Service in the summers or something."

"I worked two seasons for Pennsylvania State Forests, on a fire crew, back in my sophomore and junior years."

'But never worked for the Forest Service?"

"Ah, no, I haven't," Alex said.

Kloyd was incredulous, as if he were witnessing a miracle, as if fishes and loaves were multiplying in front of his eyes. "Jeez-O-Friday, but that's a new one. I can't recall us ever hiring somebody for a permanent job that never worked for the Forest Service."

25

Once again, Alex tried to change the subject. "So, you're the packer," Alex said, not even sure what a packer was.

"You bet. The District has the best string of mules in the region."

Now that the packer term was defined, Alex felt a little more at ease. "I was hoping the District did a lot of horse work back in the wilderness."

"That's about all I do," Kloyd chuckled. "It's probably a little different than you're used to."

More confident now, Alex said, "that's what I was wishing for."

"Well, be careful what you wish for, it just might come true."

A quick little rush of an omen flew through Alex's mind. Then, shaking his head, he noticed a tall, lanky cowboy marching purposefully, head down, shoulders hunched, toward the white warehouse next to the office.

"Here comes Buck," said Kloyd. "You might not want to mention the first job deal with him."

"Why's that?"

"Well, Buck's Buck and all, and sort of set in his thoughts. He's been here a long time and don't like things to change much."

Alex had more of the anxious feelings now, "What does he do?"

"Buck is the District FMO."

"Fire Management Officer?"

"That's right, and he's a burning fool. Loves fire, and hates it too. Just don't ever call him Smokey."

"He doesn't like the nickname?"

"It ain't no nickname. It's just a town name, and he don't like it."

"A town name?"

"Yeah, a town name."

Kloyd didn't offer any more explanation and gave Alex an "of course" look. Sensing there was a story behind the name, Alex added one more note onto his mental list.

Tall, thin, and ready to face the day, Buck Twiddle, full of purpose and determination, opened the door, saw Alex, and stood up straight in his green uniform, the bronze badge polished bright.

"Buck," Kloyd said, "This here's Alex, Alex Kin-wolf."

"So this is the new Larry, huh?"

Alex stepped forward, extended his hand and said, "Hi."

Buck was almost as tall as Alex but impossibly thin by comparison. His handshake was firm and quick. "What was that last name again?"

26

"Kynwulf." Alex stretched out the two syllables as far as he could.

"Kin-wolf? What kind of handle is that for an American?"

Alex was turning his darkest shade of red. "It's a totally American name."

Buck seemed undecided about the name issue. "I hear you come from back East," he said.

"Pennsylvania."

"Alex just got out of Penn State, Buck," Kloyd chimed in.

"A college boy, huh," said Buck. "We've had plenty of them come and go."

Alex sensed the challenge and tried to act unaffected. "Oh?"

"Yeah, most of em' couldn't pour piss out of a boot." Buck fashioned a sardonic curl of a smile from his thin lips and reached for a cup, quickly filling it to the rim with black coffee.

"Anyway, Alex, look forward to working with you," and nodding his head, Buck moved back out the door.

Sandy Spotts drove her white Mustang convertible right up to the office door. Dressed again in a too-tight green skirt, she welcomed Alex like a long-lost brother.

"Alex, well, here you are," she said, acting surprised, as if she hadn't expected him to return.

"Yeah, here I am, "

'Yes, you are, " Sandy said. "And ready for work I'll bet."

Alex felt more confident with this line of discussion, and his brain synapses began to pop more in their usual rhythm. "Is the Ranger coming in today?"

Sandy formed her formidable lips into an exaggerated pout. "Oh, no he isn't. Big Stanley called in and told me he won't be in until tomorrow."

Alex quickly wondered where Big Stanley called in to Sandy, but pushed that line of thinking away as he watched her sway.

"But Big Stan told me to make sure you get your physical and get fingerprinted today before you can do anything anyhow."

"Where do I get that done?"

Sandy smiled her showgirl smile. "I'll get it all taken care of. And tomorrow Big Stan is taking you out in the field."

The portent of doom quickly passed overhead again, but Alex wouldn't look. "Out in the field?"

27

"Yes, out in the field." Sandy said the words slowly like they had hidden meanings. "He said to bring a lunch."

Kloyd sidled up to the conversation. "Big Stan said for Alex to bring a lunch, huh? Well, you better get yourself ready."

Alex felt flustered. "What's the big deal about bringing a lunch."

"Oh, I wouldn't want to ruin it for you," Kloyd said. "Sort of an initiation, you'd call it. Everybody on the District has had the 'bring a lunch' talk."

"I never had the 'bring a lunch' talk," Sandy said.

"Oh, well, it's different with women of course. Sort of a guy thing, I guess."

Sandy shrugged her shoulders. "More of your smelly, macho man stuff back in the wilderness?"

"No, no, nothing like that. Well, shoot, I went and said too much." Kloyd moved toward the door with quick little steps. "Alex, nice meetin' up with you. Here's hopin' everything goes well tomorrow."

7

"There are men that somehow just grip your eyes,
and hold them hard like a spell.
And such was he, and it seemed to me,
like a man who had lived in hell."

Robert Service

Big Stanley lived large, and he looked the part, with a head of wooly gray hair and bags under his eyes that did not suggest a monastic life. Built for strength, not speed, Big Stanley was six foot eight and weighed almost three hundred pounds. He was more than impressive in his size sixteen cowboy boots and tall hat. He was a monument. Ordinary men seemed to fade to the background when Big Stanley rolled into a room.

Swallowing repeatedly, Alex walked up to the ranger's office and knocked on the door frame. Big Stanley turned his head, flashed a disarming smile, and stood up to his full height. He offered Alex a baseball-mitt hand.

'Good to finally meet you, Alex." The voice had a surprising southern twang and was higher pitched than Alex would have imagined.

"Same here, sir." The sir came out by accident.

"Oh, let's not have any sirs here. Just call me Stan, or Pickens, if you want to get my attention."

Alex glanced up at the big-faced clock on Big Stanley's wall. It was 8:20, and he was late. He couldn't understand how, as he left for work in plenty of time. "I'm sorry I'm late. I know we were supposed to meet at eight o'clock."

"Ah, my boy, but you're right on time. All the clocks on the District run on "Our Time," twenty minutes fast. Got the idea from a documentary on Vince Lombardi." Big Stan rummaged in his shirt pocket, sliding out a red can of Copenhagen. "Alex, I thought we would head out in the field today. Talk things over, mano a mano, and I'll tell you about the District."

"Sure, sounds great."

"Now, did you bring a lunch?"

Alex remembered his instructions. "Yes, yes I did."

29

"Good man. Rule number one, never get separated from your lunch."

Alex shared the truck seat with Wanda, Big Stanley's German Shorthair, as Big Stan hurtled down the Salmon River road seemingly oblivious to the speed limit, the green Dodge truck negotiating the curves as if magnetized. The ranger talked incessantly.

"This Salmon River country gets in your blood, they say. I've been here for eight years, and it seems like only yesterday."

"So you like it?"

Big Stanley just talked right over him. "It's too early to get back into the Middle Fork, so I thought we'd take a spin up to Cape Horn, check out the Girl Scout camp. We've got a post-and-pole sale planned in Marsh Creek, and maybe the snow might be off the ground enough to get in there. It's been a warm spring, not like last year."

The Salmon River was still running winter low flow, and Alex could clearly see the boulders on the bottom, right down into the pools. It was another sunny April day, and somehow the scenery kept pace with Big Stanley. Alex was in a state of heightened awareness as he carefully watched the white line at the edge of the highway. He estimated the often long drop into the river each time Big Stanley stomped on the accelerator.

Big Stan got started on a long story about his last muzzle-loader antelope hunt. The story had a lot to do with him crawling through the sagebrush toward this trophy buck antelope. He had needed to get within a hundred yards for his open-sighted muzzle-loader to have a good chance of killing the antelope, but after hours of deliberate stalking on hands and knees, Stan was still way short, and with no way to get closer.

"And then I noticed that antelope would jerk his head up and look every time that a semi truck came down the highway. He wouldn't look at a car or a pickup; it had to be a semi. It was over a mile to the highway, but that antelope, he was smart and watching. So when I see this semi coming and that antelope's head turn, why I crawled about ten yards as fast as I could and then stopped. I did this like five or six times. Every time a truck came by, why I'd crawl for all I was worth. I got to the point I just needed one more truck to get to this little gully and could set up for my shot."

"So what did you do?"

"Well, I stayed crouched on my stomach until I thought I would die, and still no truck came by. It was just a car or a pickup every now and then. About drove me crazy. When you need a semi, there's never one around. Finally, far down the road, I hear a truck coming. But it didn't sound like no semi. I peeked up my head, and saw it was a dump truck. Now, I wasn't sure that a dump truck would do, but it was getting late. So I decides to give it a go. As soon as that antelope's head jerked up, I was on the move. I rolls into the gully just as the antelope looked my way."

"So you were ready to shoot?"

Big Stanley never broke stride, "Well, I would of been, except for the badger."

"The badger?"

"When I rolled into the gully, I neglected to see this big badger and rolled right on top of him. Well, this badger was as surprised as I was, and started to rip and snort the same time that I started yelling and headin' for the door. The trouble was, that badger had sunk his jaws into my Forest Service jacket and we were tangled up together. It must of taken me two rolls and one header to get that jacket and that badger off my back. I was bloody elbows and knees, but my ass was intact."

Big Stan paused a moment for breath, and Alex asked, "So what happened to the antelope?"

A smile crossed Big Stanley's face. "Last I saw that buck, he was hightailing it back to Antelope Flats, and he was going in high gear."

"And the badger?"

"Oh my, yes, that badger. Why I turned around when I got about ten yards on him, and he was just sitting on a mound of dirt, a ragged piece of my uniform jacket clenched in his jaws, looking at me as if to say, "I heard about these government programs, but this is ridiculous."

Big Stanley muscled the Forest Service truck around the last set of hairpin turns on the Salmon River Road, and Alex had his first view of the Sawtooth Mountains, gray granite spires, blue shadows on snow, aspen brown on the foothills, pine dark in the bottoms. There was still snow in the Sunbeam Basin, but the spring sun was cutting the big drifts down to size. Large open patches of sagebrush and brown wild hay peppered the creek bottoms and the southern slopes everywhere you looked.

"It's been a light snow year," Big Stan said. "I think we'll be driving over Fir Creek Summit and into the Middle Fork by the first of June this year."

"That goes to Boundary Creek, where the boat launch is?"

"You studied your geography I see. Yes, Boundary Creek is our main portal to the Middle Fork, the fabled land of Oz."

31

They turned off the highway just before Cape Horn on a dirt lane leading to a small lake still covered in ice. Getting out of the truck, Big Stanley began to wave his arms around. "We're going to do a little forest-health project here. Get rid of some of these buggy trees, reduce the fire hazard for the power line and the summer homes. This is all mountain pine beetle mortality."

Alex nodded and prepared to speak but never got the chance.

Big Stanley was in full flow, and as he spoke, it was as if a crowd of well-wishers were surrounding him, campaign banners waving in the air. Alex watched, mesmerized, as Big Stan told of the heinous mountain pine beetle burrowing his way through the cambium of the large, even-aged stands of lodgepole pine, effectively cutting off the tree's water supply. "And as the pines die of thirst," Big Stan went on, seeming to speak not of science but of evangelism, "the forest becomes a tinderbox of dead, red-needled trees, just waiting for the stray lightning bolt to ignite a conflagration." Alex easily pictured Big Stan as a gospel-tent apostle, or maybe even a snake handler clutching the head of the serpent and waving it over his head, speaking in tongues, charming the revival-tent throngs back in the ranger's native Tennessee. When he finished, Big Stan took off his Stetson and slowly waved it in front of the nonexistent crowd as if still hearing their cheers fill the air.

Wanda came over just as Big Stanley took his bow. "Kiss me," Stan commanded.

Wanda complied with an eager excitement usually only reserved for flushing pheasants, washing Big Stanley's face in adoration with furious laps of her tongue.

Somehow strangely satisfied, Big Stan stood up, and reached into the pickup truck for his ditty bag, a blue cotton sack festooned with small white daisies. Opening the sack, Big Stanley pulled out a small silver hip flask and offered it to Alex, who politely declined. Big Stan turned, tilted the flask, took a quick hit, and put it back in his ditty bag.

After a sandwich, Alex asked the question that had been bothering him. "I heard about this probationary period, eighteen months. Anything to it?"

"Oh, it's just a formality. I wouldn't worry about it. Doesn't affect your pay or benefits at all. Before you know it, it'll be here and gone, and you'll be a permanent employee like the rest of us poor fools."

Braver now, Alex asked, "So what happened to Larry? I mean, I heard about him and everything. I was just wondering."

Big Stan rolled his jaw from side to side. "Well, Larry got crossways with the Forest Supervisor. Let's say there was a difference of opinion on an environmental issue, and Larry got on the wrong side of it."

"What was the issue?"

"Wolves."

"Wolves?"

"The whole shitaree was over the reintroduction of wolves back in the Middle Fork. Larry really liked wolves. Said something to the local paper that the Forest Supervisor didn't like. The issue sort of escalated from there."

"The Forest Supervisor doesn't like wolves?"

"Hates 'em, I guess. Doesn't matter much now, as we've got wolves all over the place. They take a few deer, more elk, and the hunting is a little tougher, but it wasn't as big of a deal as everybody made it out to be."

"So he was let go, just for that?"

Big Stanley paused like he was sensing the air, looking straight ahead, not at Alex. "It had gone too far already. I couldn't help him." Anticipating Alex's next question, he said, "Some people just have a low tolerance for diversity of thought."

Alex didn't say any more. Big Stan got up from the tailgate and ambled over to a small garbage dump-pile. He started sorting through the historic refuse, picking out old pop bottles. Alex watched with growing interest as Big Stan set six pop bottles on six consecutive fence posts. Reaching into his ditty bag once more, he pulled out a pistol, a single action Colt revolver, with a black barrel and mother of pearl grips: the Peacemaker, the gun that won the west. After lovingly loading the gun, he offered it, handing it safely on its side to Alex, who understood what was expected and accepted it without comment.

Sighting carefully down the gun barrel, Alex cocked the old single action and arm extended slowly squeezed off a shot. The bottle exploded, the sound of the shot loud in his ears. The next bottle and the one after, he hit. After four in a row, he got careless, rocked the next bottle but didn't break it, and then cleanly missed his last shot. "I'm not really much of a shot with a pistol."

Big Stanley didn't say a thing, just began humming softly to himself. Alex couldn't catch the song, but thought it might be the "Banana Boat Song." Big Stan rummaged up six more bottles for the six fence posts, ejected the spent cartridges and reloaded, and then holstered the pistol at his side. He just stood still for at least a minute. All Alex remembered was that there was a blur as Big Stanley whipped the pistol from the holster and fanned the hammer. The shots were so close together it sounded like one continuous roar. Alex stood transfixed

33

as each bottle exploded; six in all, and it probably took less than four or five seconds.

Suitably impressed, Alex watched Big Stan eject the spent shells and put them in the pocket of his green wool cruiser coat. By now the humming had turned to song, as Big Stanley began in a quiet baritone, "Day-o, Day-o, daylight come and me want to go home."

Alex thought to himself, and not for the last time, I'm working for a crazy man.

8

"Let's do it; Let's fall in love."
                              Cole Porter

The Y café was as close to an institution as Goldburg had. This was where the real community politics took place, under the cover of cowboy hats and flapjacks. Local politics in Idaho had evolved like the first fish crawling out of the Paleozoic ocean, all scaled over and unadorned. The Y was a friendly looking place. The knotty pine paneling went around the walls and across the ceiling to the big picture window facing main street and the local tire shop, the mountains rising over the white cinder-block building and the "Tires, new and used" sign.

Alex was developing the habit of lunch at the Y café as part of his new town social calendar. Today was a full table with three of his employees, Fast Eddie, Harmon, and Argo. Only Alex, Eddie and Argo were eating lunch, while Harmon sat with them hoping for leftovers. Harmon was considered by many who knew to be the most frugal person in Idaho. Even among his kayaking buddies, he was the cheapskate of the crowd. Another peculiarity was Harmon's innate desire to exaggerate his skills, accomplishments, love affairs, and almost everything else. He constantly boasted of his attractiveness to women, but no one could recall him having a girl friend. Above all, he boasted of Kentucky. It didn't seem to matter what the topic was, but Kentucky had more or better of whatever it was.

Argo, the capable, assistant kayak crew foreman, was a different breed of cat, so different he might not even be considered part of the cat family. Argo started out star-crossed from birth, raised by hippie parents in California's Marin County, named after the ship that carried Jason on his quest for the Golden Fleece. Thin and fierce of face, Argo was what someone had kindly described as sort of bony-faced, like it was all put together wrong. Largely self-educated, with the help of over two hundred credits from the University of California, Berkeley, and no degree, Argo walked trails in life that few others could even

35

see. An ardent Born Again New Age nihilist, but only at times, Argo defied categorization.

As they were perusing their menus, Alex kept looking at Eddie's right index finger. The tip was conspicuously missing. Finally he asked, "Eddie, how did you lose the tip of your finger?"

Fast Eddie replied without hesitation, "It happened during my vision quest."

Alex pondered a moment, "What's a vision quest?"

"A vision quest is an initiation rite of manhood. I went out on the ice on Redfish Lake and waited for a sign, a recognition of my totem."

Now Alex saw where this conversation was headed, but he asked the question anyway. "So, are you like, a Native American?"

"I'm one-sixty-fourth on my mother's side."

"That's not what I hear," Harmon said. "I was told your mother is Irish, came right from Northern Ireland, like, and it wasn't that long ago, like when she was a teenager."

"Our genealogy is somewhat murky in places, but my great grandmother on my mother's side was one-quarter pure Cherokee."

"How can someone be one-quarter pure something?" Harmon wouldn't let it go. "Anyway, the way I calculate it, that makes you one, one-hundred-and-twenty-eighth at best, or maybe even one-two-hundred-and-fifty-sixth. That's assuming great-grandma went and emigrated over to Ireland to settle down."

Alex went back to the finger. "So what happened to your finger?"

"Well, this beaver bit it off."

"A beaver?" Harmon beat Alex to the mark.

"Yeah, while I was sitting on the ice, searching for truth, I saw this beaver over by the outlet, right on the ice. And somehow I just knew it was the spirit of my great-grandmother, and if I was ever going to break the family curse, I would have to kill that beaver."

"Kill the beaver? The family curse? That's the craziest thing I ever heard of," Harmon fumed, but Fast Eddie rolled right past him.

"Yeah, I had to kill the beaver, just knew it. I don't know how I knew it, but there it was, like staring me in the face."

"The beaver?" Argo finally joined in the conversation.

"No, my vision quest mission," Eddie said. "So I start sneaking over along the shoreline, trying to get close enough to kill the beaver. The trouble was I didn't have a gun or even a knife. All I had was my bare hands."

"Bloody Hell!" said Argo.

"So I sneak up on that beaver, all nice and quiet like, and just as I get ready to pounce on him, he looks and sees me. It was now or never. I jumped for that beaver and got a hold on his tail just before he made the water. That's when he bit me."

"Did it hurt?"

"Not too much. It was probably because I was sort of high at the time. Lost a lot of blood, though."

"So did you kill the beaver?" Harmon asked.

"Not really. After it bit off the end of my finger, that sort of took the fight out of me."

"Bummer," Argo said. "You need to get more zinc in your diet. Keep those hostile thoughts at bay."

Harmon lost interest in the story when he heard the beaver didn't die and asked Alex, "Are you going to use any of those coffee creamers?"

"No. I'm not much for coffee at lunch."

"Great," Harmon said, and promptly reached over and took the bowl of coffee creamers and began to drink them, one by one, right out of the little plastic-tub containers.

"Jesus," Alex said, more than somewhat surprised.

Harmon paused between coffee creamers, wiping the white smile off his upper lip. "Calories," was all he said.

Alex had the recurrent thought that he was in reality an anthropologist in a far-off land. Like a modern-day Margaret Mead, he was living on the borders of the known world, watching the strange rites of the natives.

"Calories?" said Alex.

"Free calories."

Alex shook his head, and as he shook his head, he noticed the tall red-headed waitress behind the counter. It was Angie Kowalski. Moments began to flow in slow motion, as a dreamlike intensity surrounded Alex. Copper-like, he could taste it on his tongue. Some of the feeling from The Wild Bunch was still there, and like waves, his thoughts flowed toward her. Something about her focused his thoughts and blurred them at the same time, like he had known this girl before and now he was remembering. Maybe it was the way her nose had that slight bump at the crown, or maybe it was that hair. There certainly was a lot of it. Those blue eyes were hot, and she had red-brown eyebrows that had a little bit of a wave at the end. She was tall, and Alex liked tall girls. But most of

37

all it was that face of hers. It just gave him an electric buzz when he caught her eyes. Except for her apron, she was dressed all in black again, a stark contrast with her white complexion. Alex thought there was a bit of a Goth look to her. Even though Alex knew the answer he asked Fast Eddie, "Who's the girl, the redhead?"

"Oh, that's Angie Kowalski."

"What do you know about her?"

"Well, let's see. She was going with Finn Fusco. He works up at the Double Spring Ranch. But they recently broke up. I hear she's been off work, visiting relatives in Salt Lake the past few weeks."

"Anything else?"

"You mean, like, is she available?"

"Yeah, sort of."

Eddie looked around with a smile, his coal-black hair jutting out at strange angles. "You'll just have to give it a try, I guess. Better men than you have tried and failed with that one. Even darlin' Harmon here couldn't make it with Angie Kowalski, and he's death on wheels with women."

Harmon felt he had to intercede. "I dated a Polish girl once. She and her whole family wanted me to marry her. After that, I swore off Polish girls."

"What happened?" Argo asked.

"It just didn't work out. I was off playing rugby for the New Zealand National Team at the time, and she had to help her family back in Poland run the farm and fight the communists."

"Harmon, communism is long gone in Eastern Europe," Fast Eddie said. "Been gone for years now."

"Well, not in their part of Poland," Harmon said defensively. "The communists held out a lot longer in the rural areas of Poland, near the border and all."

"Sort of like in Kentucky," Fast Eddie said.

"Now you keep your mouth off Kentucky. There ain't never been any communists in Kentucky."

The much-talked-of Angie Kowalski came over to their table, menus in hand. She looked right at Alex and smiled with just the corners of her lips. "Well, if it isn't the man with the pretty name. Looks like you weren't telling me a story about livin' in Goldburg after all. And how are you boys today? Have you decided?"

"I'll have the Goldburger."

38

"Me too."

Alex smiled back. He liked what she said about the pretty name, and was hoping that maybe some of what she said about his name trickled down to the rest of him. He cleared his throat three times like he was about to make a pronouncement, so much so that Angie and all the rest were waiting for him. Finally Alex said, "Hi" and after a moment added, "How are you doing?"

Angie Kowalski stood straight and tilted her head to the side. "I am just so in the moment that it isn't funny. So how are you, and how is that fine red truck today?"

This time Alex was prepared and the words came easily. "The truck is fine, and I'm doing all right. How about you?"

Angie assumed a thoughtful expression by pursing her lips and placing her fingers to her chin. "I think I just answered that question, but I'll try better this time. I would say I'm doin' fair to moderate, maybe even pretty good, depending on the tips today, of course. So, what can I get you?"

Alex noticed the accent on the word, you. "I'll have the Twin Peaks special."

"You want fries with that?"

"Please," he said in a whisper.

"How about you?" she asked Harmon.

"Oh, just some water."

"Just a little something to wash down that coffee creamer?" Angie Kowalski said.

The table erupted in laughter. Even Harmon gave a grin.

"Good one," Fast Eddie said. All of them watched her as she whirled her waist-long ponytail over her shoulder and sped back to the counter.

"So, Alex, you gonna make a play for her?" Eddie said.

"Maybe." Alex shifted nervously.

"Well, don't wait too long. An opportunity like this one doesn't come along every day."

"That's what the realtor keeps telling me."

Fast Eddie was playing with the silverware. "There's a dance this Saturday night at the Plywood Palace."

"The Plywood Palace?"

"Up in Sunbeam," Eddie said. "Right at the Salmon River road junction. The big building with the TX-111 siding."

"Oh, yeah, I've seen it."

39

"The Letgo brothers are playing."

A plan began to gel in Alex's head. "That's interesting."

"Ho, ho," said Eddie. "I see the tumblers moving. The boy's going to go for it."

Alex had trapped himself. He had to ask her out now, and everybody would know about it. The time had come to cast his net upon the waters of dating. God, how he hated this part of the ritual.

As Alex approached Angie at the cash register, he angled himself to be the last in line, hoping for everyone else to move on. Hovering near the door, Alex almost abandoned the quest. It was enough to be turned down, he thought, but to be turned down in public was too much to risk. Maybe he would call her up tomorrow. Can't be that many Kowalskis in the phone book. Hell, the whole thing is only ten or twelve pages. That would be the safest route, he calculated. She'd probably turn him down anyway, and this way he wouldn't have to worry about not knowing what to say. He could practice up tonight, before he called her.

But events transpired to push Alex along into a strange vortex. When it was his turn at the cash register, as he prepared to hand over his bill to Angelica, a furious dog fight broke out just outside the door. A husky-shepherd cross was mixing it up with a big brown dog of indeterminate lineage. A mighty struggle in the dirt and dust took place in full view, and Harmon, Fast Eddie and Argo joined the others at the broad picture window, effectively leaving Alex alone with Angie.

Alex smiled and looked Angie Kowalski full in the face just as she looked sideways at him. She gave a little smile back to him. He could tell that she knew that he liked her, but Alex could never read the return signs and was clueless if women were attracted to him. Like a coal miner lost underground, Alex searched in the dark.

She took the offered bills. "So how was your meal?"

"Great, great, it was, ah, real good, tasty. Cooked just right, liked it a lot, excellent. Man, just damn good food."

Angie was nodding her head in time to Alex's comments. "And to think, it was only a cheeseburger."

"Yeah, yeah, but it was a good cheeseburger."

"That's really good, I guess."

"Yeah, it was great." Alex looked up at the ceiling for help, found none, kicked himself mentally for talking like such an idiot. "Say, I hear there's a dance up in Sunbeam this Saturday." There was a noticeable pause before he added, "Would you like to go?"

There was a surprised look in Angie's eyes, like she really wasn't expecting it, a quick darting back and forth. "So, the new guy in town wants to go dancing, does he?" Angelica posed in a schoolgirl fashion. Outside, the dog fight intensified. "And this would be for the Fireman's Brawl, the Sunbeam social event of the year?" Angie smirked and said, "Oh, I don't know. Maybe."

Alex hung motionless, like a puppet on strings. "Might be fun. I hear they've got a good band playing."

"The Letgo brothers? Yeah, I guess you can call them a band."

"So what do you say?" There it was, all out in the open, his heart on his sleeve. The nanoseconds ticked by. Blood continued to course through Alex's body, sugars and water moved through his brain, billions of brain neurons directed trillions of synapses, all seemingly focused on Angelica Kowalski.

"All right, I guess so," she said, drawing out the phrase. "The dog fight is about done, and I guess you've suffered enough."

Alex had to fight the herky-jerky gratitude reflex. Try to stay calm, look cool, keep a real cool head, he reminded himself. "So, where do you live, and what time should I pick you up?"

"It's a ways to Sunbeam. How about seven thirty? You know the Kowalski Ranch?"

"No, no I don't."

"It's right at the turn off to the Goldburg Hot Springs. Big white house can't miss it."

Alex grinned. "I'll be there." He backed into the crowd returning from watching the dog fight and was shuffled out the door quicker than he would have liked. He lingered outside the diner door until Angie saw him and waved with just a flick of his hand as his eye caught hers. She saw the movement and returned the same small wave.

In the rest of Round Valley, the sun was shining, the grass was growing, the river still moved downstream, but Alex noticed none of this as he floated high above the sidewalk on his way back to the District office.

9

"Normalcy is overrated."
                                                    Author

The early morning rain had turned to a cold mist and the fog lay low on the valley rim, obscuring the peaks and saddles, painting the landscape in shades of gray like a Wyeth winter scene. Alex sat in his office of wood, hands folded at his ancient mahogany desk scarred from years of boots, pens and pocket knives, staring out the dirty window to the corrals, the mules, the fire warehouse, looking across the Salmon River to where the Kowalski ranch lay hidden by a line of cottonwoods.

His job as Recreation Forester made him the nominal head of the recreation department, supervising everyone except Buck, Kloyd, and the trail-and-fire crews. His primary responsibility was the administration of the Middle Fork Wild and Scenic River, a nationally known and prominent wilderness recreation program, something he knew painfully little about. His college experience wasn't helping much. He felt everyone on the District knew more about what was going on than he did, and he was right. But Alex soldiered on and hoped that management by osmosis would catch up to him before it became pitifully transparent that he was in a perpetual wondering-what-to-do mode.

Alex's office was sandwiched between Buck's and Big Stanley's offices. Big Stanley's door was always closed when he was in, which was seldom, and Buck's door was only closed when he was gone. When Buck was in the office, whether talking on the telephone or with his crew, there was an everyday string of profanities that rolled out his doorway, splattering and spreading like rain on parched clay.

"Son-of-a-bitch," Buck would say if surprised. "Fuckin' A" if he was not. These and other colorful sayings were common fare. Surprisingly, supposedly due to an ex-wife from the far religious right, Buck never took the Lord's name in vain. As a substitute, Buck mangled a few favorite curses and freely improvised others. Probably his favorite was "Clum Dummit" with the accent on the "Clum," a variation, it was understood, of "God damn it." And Clum Dummit was freely expressed, whether Buck was sitting in his office or scratching his back by rubbing against the loading chute. Whether the situation was happy, sad, or angry, a quick "Clum Dummit" often served as the final word. Alex tried not to eavesdrop but found it difficult not to count Clum Dummits in his head, especially when Buck and Kloyd got together.

"Clum Dummit, when the hell are we gonna get the stock truck back?" Buck exclaimed. "You know we're packin' into the Middle Fork the first of May."

"Just simmer down now, Buck," said Kloyd. "I'm sure it'll get fixed before then. I just talked to Gilmore up at the Esso station, and he told me he's just waiting for the parts."

"Waitin' for the parts? It's a Clum Dum Chevrolet!"

"Now take 'er easy. You know how it is in the government."

"You're Clum Dum right I do. But we're packin' into the Middle Fork with or without the Clum Dum stock truck."

The rush to field season was progressing like snowmelt, faster and faster. Buck was in a constant hurry, obsessed with the looming first of May. It didn't matter that there was still three feet of snow on Rabbitsfoot Summit. The plan was set. They would pack in from Cobalt, take some extra hay and pellets, and push snow if they must to get to Meyer's Cove. Kloyd scurried about with saddles and halters, checking the tack. Buck and Kloyd both worked on re-shoeing much of the stock. They were having problems getting shoes on one half of the team of Bob and Bill, the two half-Belgians workhorses that were used to pull the patrol grader on the backcountry airstrips.

"Clum Dummit, hold that dumb-ass horse," Buck said. "I can't get this Clum-Dum nail in right."

"Well Buck, if you ask me, you need longer nails for old Bob," Kloyd said.

"I ain't a askin. Now hold that fucker's head."

Alex watched the horse shoeing proceed in fits and starts as old Bob wouldn't let Buck hold his foot still. The heavy horse tossed his head, showing the whites of his eyes, flattening his ears and snorting his displeasure.

"Clum-Dum horse. He's just lucky the price of horseflesh is low in France right now," Buck said.

It wasn't meant as a joke, but both Alex and Kloyd laughed.

"Kynwulf, you think this is so Clum-Dum funny? We need another hand on the spring trip. You know anything at all about pack stock?"

Alex jumped upright from his spot leaning against the corral post. "No,

43

not really."

"I figured as much. Then you'll have to learn."

"Sounds good." Alex was talking in cowboy speech, short and to the point. "But what's the schedule?"

"First of May."

Kloyd explained. "We need to get the stock down to pasture at Little Creek before high water. There's no bridge at Little Loon Creek and she really booms with the runoff."

"That would be great. I probably should ask the ranger if he's got other plans for me."

"Big Stanley?" Buck laughed. "Don't worry about it. I'll tell him I need you. Tell you what, your first job is to buy the groceries. Kloyd will give you a list. You can charge it at the Wise Buy. We'll all settle up with you before we go and then you can pay the bill. There'll be five of us, you, me, Kloyd and the Gold Dust Twins."

"The Gold Dust Twins?" Alex had heard a few snippets about the Gold Dust Twins but didn't know who they were.

Kloyd said, "That's just their town names. Their real names are Charley and Darrel."

Alex had seen their names on the District temporary hire list. "Oh, yeah. Charley and Darrel."

Buck finished the last shoe on old Bob, stood up and adjusted his Stetson. "Now I got to go uptown and bust some ass on that Clum-Dum stock truck. He took off his shoeing chaps and gloves. "Just remember, Kynwulf, don't fuck up."

With that gentle reminder in mind, Alex tried to mask his growing excitement with a feigned nonchalance. "Got it down."

Buck smiled and threw down his shoeing gloves. "I'm sure you do."

The second day of rain in a row, a misty, moist morning and everyone was in the office. Big Stanley was firmly planted behind his oak desk, signing permits and drinking cup after cup of coffee from a Utah State mug. After a long, closed-door session with Sandy, Big Stanley ambled over to Alex's tiny office. "I hear you're packin' in to the Middle Fork with Buck and Kloyd and the trail crew."

Alex jumped at the tone of authority. "Yeah, Buck asked me to help move the stock. Sounds like a great trip."

"Oh, it will be. I just wish I could tag along, but someone has to do all this paperwork." Big Stanley held up a wad of permits in his hand for emphasis. "So, Alex, tell me, what do you know about horses?"

"Well, not much, I guess. I used to do some riding with a friend of mine once in a while, back on the farm." Alex's mind raced back to an adolescent image of Pinto Bill, the overweight Appaloosa owned by the neighbor girl, and remembered rides down to the ball field, slapping the old horse on the rear with a flat board to get it into a canter.

"Have you ever done any trail riding in the mountains?"

Alex was jerked back into the moment. "No, not really."

"Well, perhaps we better do a little training today." Big Stanley was in a rare mentoring mood, perhaps driven by altruism but more likely looking for an excuse to get out of the office. "Let's go out to the corral. Give me ten minutes."

"You bet." Alex answered with the standard western reply of strong agreement.

Alex was talking with Kloyd, who was working on some halter ropes, when Big Stan rolled up and asked, "Kloyd, why don't you catch old Major there and bring him over here for Alex."

Kloyd easily caught the horse, throwing the halter over his neck and leading him back to the gate. Major, a big bay gelding, almost sixteen hands, had been on the District many years and was considered an easy horse with few bad habits for a government horse, at least. Big Stan led Alex through the tack shed, selecting a saddle, bridle, blanket and pad.

"This saddle has good, long, adjustable stirrups and should work for you, since you're tall and all," said Big Stanley. "I've got the same problem, but I've got my own custom-made saddle for Stain."

Big Stan carefully led Alex through the process of blanket, pad, saddle, and bridle. He showed Alex how to loop the bridle behind the ears, carefully bending them forward, and how to squeeze the gums to get the horse to accept the bit at the edge of his teeth. "Now don't clank the bit against his front teeth, he'll shy for sure. Just sort of give him a squeeze and wait for him to unclench his jaws. When he does, just slip in the bit and slide the bridle over the ears."

Major stood unmoving while Alex tried to get the horse to open his mouth. It was no dice.

"Here, let me show you again." And Big Stan had bit in and bridle on in a moment.

Again Alex tried and Major wouldn't move. "Clum Dum horse," Alex muttered under his breath, and like hearing the magic word, Major accepted the bit.

"Good, good. Now this part is real important. I don't know how many horses I've seen with sores from having the cinch too tight. I like to get it so you can just barely get three fingers in there."

Alex dutifully saddled and unsaddled Major, taking extra care to get the cinch strap just right.

Then Big Stanley showed him how to mount and dismount, slipping up on the saddle with an athlete's ease. "Now you got to make him stand still when you put your foot in the stirrup. Turn that stirrup out, so that if the horse moves, the movement puts you into the saddle, instead of trying to catch up from behind."

Alex was better on this part, easily getting up and over on the big horse.

"Second important thing is to know how to load and unload a horse without getting hurt. You've got to watch the horse and particularly watch your feet. Most of the horses and all the mules we got are good loaders. I just hate a poor-loadin' horse. Hey Kloyd!, where's the stock truck?"

"Still in the shop, boss."

"Does Buck know that?"

"You bet, boss," Kloyd smiled.

"Well Alex, you'll just have to watch Kloyd and Buck load up when we get the truck back and stay out of the way, and don't get hurt." Big Stanley looked up at the low clouds hanging over Lone Pine Peak like a shroud. "Sure hope that stock truck gets fixed."

Alex, without thinking, honestly asked, "So what would happen if Buck wasn't able to pack in to the Middle Fork on the first of May?"

Big Stanley turned, and his eyes seemed to burn with a strange intensity. He made a quick sign of the cross. "Good God man, don't even think such a thing."

10

"Ends and beginnings. There are no such things. Only middles."
Robert Frost

Angelica Kowalski wasn't feeling up to par that Saturday morning. She wasn't sick, she knew that, but something was bothering her and she couldn't place what it was. A heightened sense of anxiety seemed to be the primary symptom, as if she was positioned and ready for the starter's pistol but the shot wouldn't come. Angie felt a little sad about Finn. He kept calling her to try and make up, but she didn't want those troubles anymore. And then there was that date coming up with the new guy at the Forest Service, the big, scary-looking guy with the funny name. How did she let herself get roped into that, she wondered? Well, it was only a dance date. No big deal, might even be fun. Maybe he could dance. Thinking of his size and the hulking look, she doubted it. Angie couldn't decide on his looks, different for sure, oddly attractive in a rough-cut sort of way; but then, those eyes of his. Never saw eyes like that.

Angie thought that maybe some music would cheer her up. She tuned up her guitar, admiring the curly maple sides, back and neck, the glossy-finished spruce top. She warmed up her fingers with a short blues run. Hit the blues notes hard. Wished she had someone to jam and sing with. But the blues weren't working that day. Even one of her favorites, Deep River Blues, wouldn't do the trick. Maybe it was too early in the day, she thought. Shouldn't play the blues in the morning, might jinx the day or something.

She didn't have a lot to do on the ranch. It was the relatively quiet time between calving and haying, and the cows were all out on the public range. Her Dad had switched two years ago to center pivot irrigation, two circular systems each irrigating a quarter section of alfalfa, so she didn't have to move sprinkler pipe anymore.

Her restlessness moved her toward the corral, and she decided to catch Bucky and take a ride in the hills. Before she picked up her saddle in the tack shed, she knew where she was headed. Her secret place. She hadn't been there for a while, more than a year. It was a long ride, but she had the time.

Up along the fence line she rode, to the BLM boundary, along a series of low ridges, sage-covered, broken by basalt rim rock, standing stones that looked like small men. She stopped at Hole-in-the-Rock Creek and let Bucky get a drink where a spring ran sandy bottom clear out from under a tilted red stone. She clicked up her horse, easy riding now, and worked her way across Spud Basin towards an inconspicuous saddle. On top of the ridge she rested her horse, looking over toward the Lemhi Range, all deep snow above timberline. It was the same looking south. Grouse Creek Point, clear around to Sheep Pen Basin, it was all white in the high country.

She found the game trail that led down off the divide on the Pahsimeroi Valley side and rode past Opal Spring and turned up a narrow slot of a canyon guarded by twin blocks of columnar basalt. Near the head of the canyon, she saw what she was looking for, a narrow band of limestone that seemed to grow out of the sagebrush, an exposed remnant of the last of the sedimentary rock of the Lost River Range. The banded limestone formed a rock shelter, almost a cave. She tied Bucky up to a big willow above the spring and crept out on the rock face. It was a bit of scramble to get there, on the broken rock above the rock shelter. Out where the rock formed a smooth wall, on the north face, hidden from view, there was a small space to sit, an almost perfect natural bench. Right at face level, close enough to touch, the pictograph panel began, red-ochre hand paintings of deer, stick men and crude mountain sheep. This was Angelica's secret place. She had found it all by herself, and never told another about it. There was a lithic scatter of broken arrowheads and atlatl points all along the rock face, rock cores of red and yellow chalcedony, flakes and chips everywhere. When she first discovered the rock shelter, Angie picked up dozens of arrowheads, brought them home and hid them in her dresser drawer. She felt guilty about it afterwards and couldn't say why, but ended up packing it all back and carefully burying the points one by one all along the rock face where she hoped that no one would ever find them.

Angie liked to sit up on the rock face and look out over the Pahsimeroi country, out past the head of Sulphur Creek. She had fanciful thoughts of people sitting and making arrowheads thousands of years ago, right where she was sitting now. She wondered what they might have been thinking, how they felt about life, their futures, their worries and dreams, as she carefully stood up small rocks and stacked them into figures like a miniature Stonehenge. Tired of sitting, Angie climbed up high on the outcrop, out to the end of the smooth rock, just

48

before the cliff broke over. She had to look a while to find it, had to actually get down on her knees and look in a small space between two stones. A burst of surprise, almost like the first time she saw it: a red outline of a human hand, looked like it was done yesterday, like someone had held their hand in place and spray painted red all around it. She could still hardly believe that it was real. She found out that these hand paintings were done with a hollow goose quill. They blew paint through it like an airbrush. She held her hand up against the pictograph. It matched perfectly. This gave her the strangest feeling; a feeling she never could remember or describe afterwards, and she held her hand in position and thought nothing.

A quick brush of air past her face startled her, made her snatch her hand back like she had burned it. She turned quickly and saw the raven, only a few yards away. Angie looked right at it and the bird just stayed in the same slip stream of air, tilting it wings slightly from side to side to remain in place, like it was a mobile turning in the breeze, not a living thing. She remained motionless watching the bird watch her, staring into the small black eyes fixed on her, and for some reason it made her afraid. She threw up her hands in response, and the bird darted away, but after a short minute it floated back down into a position level with Angie, but further away this time. Again, she threw up her hands and yelled "Get out of here!" The bird again moved quickly away, only to carefully return to its position, hovering, looking right at Angie. Angry now for being afraid of a bird, she bent down, looking for a rock to throw. The raven immediately flew up, banked high on the breeze, let out a rough rattle, a strange vocalization even for a raven, folded it wings tight and was gone behind the rocks in an instant.

11

"O, young Lochinvar is come out of the west.
Through all the wide border his steed was the best,
And save his good broadsword he weapons had none.
He rode all unarmed, and he rode all alone.
So faithful in love, and so dauntless in war,
There never was knight like the young Lochinvar."
                                            Sir Walter Scott

On the appointed day at the appointed hour, Alex found himself driving down the long lane of Lombard poplars that led to the Kowalski Ranch. In an exaggerated perspective of sorts, the clouds receded back toward the horizon like in a impressionist painting and dark shadows were beginning to move out from the mountains. A brown dog ran out from under the porch and barked furiously. Alex opened the truck door and let the dog have a smell, which set off fast wagging of a too-short tail. He stood still for a moment and framed the view of the white farmhouse with the line of trees and the mossy stream running down the irrigation ditch, the high red cliffs beyond. As Alex stood at the door, he saw it was exactly seven-thirty. He took a deep breath and knocked.

The door opened instantly, his hand still in position for the third and fourth knock. Angie stood there looking like a model in a Pre-Raphaelite painting, one of the best that Rossetti or Waterhouse ever painted. She wore a short black skirt and black blouse, again with the mother-of-pearl snaps. Her red hair was brushed long and straight, the tips of her ears showing through. Alex could taste the color and feel the wind that formed around the girl.

After an awkward moment, Alex came back to himself and said, "Hi, how're you doing?"

"Fine, fine, come on in."

"I've got some flowers for you." Alex held up the bouquet of white daisies he had just bought at the Wise Buy.

"Oh, daisies, I just love daisies! How did you know?"

"I'd hoped that you'd like them."

Alex was exceptionally polite when he met Leo and Sylvia, Angie's mom and dad. Leo was a big man, heavy in the middle, with big arms and a full head of brown hair brushed up high on his head. Alex could tell that her father really didn't like the idea of Angie going out with strangers she met in the café, so Alex tried not to act the part. Angie's mother was tall and thin, looking every bit the rancher's wife: tanned arms and face, rough hands, and hair graying at the temples. Alex told her a little bit about himself, not much, just enough to keep a mother satisfied. After a few minutes, Angie started moving toward the door, and Alex followed her lead, shaking hands with her father, refusing more cookies. Then safely seat-belted, he waved goodbye from the pickup truck. They pulled out of the driveway just before eight o'clock.

The highway from Goldburg to Sunbeam follows the Salmon River, the twists and turns flowing like sine waves one upon the other. He couldn't help but glance at Angie as she looked out the window, noticed the thin patina of freckles across her cheeks. An evening breeze, a canyon wind of clear skies and high pressure, blew the water from the wheel-line sprinklers into a curved mist, making rainbows where the last rays of sunshine poked into the canyon bottom.

Angie caught him watching her. She said, "So what do we talk about?"

"Well, you could ask me a series of really personal questions, just to make sure I'm not an axe murderer or some other kind of fiend."

"That could prove embarrassing."

"We could try the weather. I love climate and weather."

"How about not. That's all my dad talks about. If he's calving, he talks about snow. If he's haying, he talks about rain. Drives me crazy."

"Okay, truce, no weather related talk." Alex was searching now through his prepared monologue and not finding suitable material.

Angie picked up on the pause in the conversation. "Well, how about, how old are you?"

"Twenty-three."

"You seem older."

"It's this beard." He stroked the thin blonde goatee. "If I shaved it off, I don't think they would even let me in The Wild Bunch. It's not much, but it's the best I could do."

"So how old do you think I am?"

"About twenty-four," he lied.

"I just turned twenty-two last week down in Utah. Not the best place to turn twenty-two. Some friends took me out to a party. It was a pretty tame

51

affair."

"3.2 beer, I'm told."

"I take it you're not LDS."

"No, but I am on a mission."

Angie looked puzzled. "On a mission?"

"Yeah, I'm on a mission to dance, and I've got happy feet."

"Oh brother, happy feet. Like Goldburg is the home of happy feet," Angie said, secretly pleased. "Where do you get this stuff?"

"I read a lot." Alex hoped he wasn't overdoing it.

The Plywood Palace, the largest building in Sunbeam, sat prominently on the crest of a small hill directly above the junction of highways 75 and 21. It was after nine o'clock, and the gravel parking lot was jammed with pickup trucks or an occasional Subaru or Saab for the token environmentalists in the county. On this Saturday night, the population of Sunbeam had tripled at least.

The door to the Plywood Palace was a large, barn-like wooden portal with wrought-iron strap hinges and an elk antler for the handle. Angie brushed back her hair as Alex strained to open the door to a cavalcade of voices and loud music.

Inside the Palace was essentially one large open room with a long bar running the length of the back wall. Tables and chairs had been pushed back tight to reveal an unusually large dance floor of polished oak. Alex and Angie made their way to the back and squeezed into a small table next to a window. The cathedral ceiling, held in place by peeled fir timbers, created a feeling of space, a geometry of volume. The room had that pleasant feel that always precedes a good time, Alex felt.

A waitress in a white cowboy hat took their drink order. Alex had a Moosehead Ale and Angie ordered a rum and coke, a college-girl drink.

Alex felt a little dreamy, almost on the edge of deja vu, but he couldn't guess why. He waited a moment before he spoke his thoughts and blurted out, "You know, I just barely had the nerve to ask you out."

Angie sat up straight in her chair. "Why was that?"

"You're so beautiful, I couldn't believe you would be available."

"Oh, come on now. What a smooth talker." She blushed steadily.

No one had ever accused Alex of being a smooth talker, and he was smiling. "If you hadn't smiled just then, I would of never had the nerve. It's not easy walking up to some girl in a public place and asking her out."

"I thought you were acting kinda strange when you walked up to the register. You were staring a bit too much. Sort of funny lookin', really."

"Hey, it's the Gold Dust Twins." Alex pointed with his beer bottle at the stage.

"Didn't you know that Darrel and Charley play?"

"No, they never said anything about it. But then, they never say anything."

"Darrel is about the best fiddle player in Elkhorn County, and Charley is real good on the pedal steel guitar."

"No kidding?"

The Letgo brothers fumbled with the amplifier at each end of the stage. One had a harmonica attached around his neck on a brace.

"So are these Letgo brothers really brothers, or are they like the Gold Dust Twins?"

"Oh yes, they're brothers. They live up the Yankee Fork, about thirteen miles."

"They look like they live in the woods. Look at the beards on those guys."

"They've got a little cabin, no electricity or running water."

"That would explain the beards. Now, is Letgo like a real name or is it a town name or something?"

Angie laughed. "I think it's their real name, but in Elkhorn County you never know."

The crowd was merrily getting tuned up. Most tables had a copious number of beer bottles rounded up in the center as if they were trophies. The conversations were loud and getting louder.

The deja vu feeling sort of comfortably rested on Alex's shoulder as the evening unveiled itself. He searched the room for omens or portents and found nothing more substantial than the reflection in the long mirror above the bar. It reminded him of a Manet painting, the famous one of the bar scene with the big mirror.

The band was getting ready to play. Darrel tuned his fiddle, the Letgo brothers their guitars, while Charley sat impassively and picked a little run on the pedal steel. Adjusting the microphone, Buzz Letgo introduced his brother, Billy, and the Gold Dust Twins. The crowd was busy with its beer and didn't notice.

The band opened with a slow number, a country western tune that Alex remembered hearing once or twice, "The London Homesick Blues."

The crowd started to wake up. Some hoots and hollers and boot stamping started in the back. Buzz and Billy sang it pretty well and Charley made the pedal steel cry. Without a pause, Darrel's fiddle burst into a reel, a country swing dance number.

Alex leaned over and offered his hand to Angelica. "Do you want to dance?" His foot tapped in time, "I've got happy feet."

Angie glanced down. "I don't know how happy they are, but they certainly look big enough."

"Hey, come on now, don't go giving me a complex or anything. Let's dance."

Angie made a funny face and took the proffered hand, following Alex onto the dance floor. Only two other couples joined them and everyone was watching.

Alex was a little different in that he sincerely loved to dance and he was fairly good at it, able to pick up steps quickly. He didn't have to be liquored up to dance, but a beer or two didn't hurt, either. Alex had noticed early on in his college career that most women loved to dance and that most guys didn't. He had realized that he needed to use every advantage to overcome his appearance and personal limitations. This natural selection process validated his own personal belief in continued human evolution, and like Darwin's finches, he adapted to fill the niche. He had happily danced his way into a cultural ecosystem of bands, bars, beer, and hillbilly music with an ease that surprised him.

Alex grasped Angie's hand and looked her straight in the eyes. He led with his left foot and arm, walking her into an easy swing, a cowboy jitterbug, a series of picturesque twirls and drop moves, right in time with the music. He two-stepped Angie into an elegant walking sashay, side to side, the length of the dance floor.

It was obvious that Angelica knew the moves and there was little hesitation following Alex's lead. Her black skirt carved parabolic curves through the air. It was as if the dance followed a series of arithmetical equations, and Alex and Angelica knew all the theorems.

Alex ended the dance number with a series of fancy moves, including a walking twirl that ended with a behind-the-back drop, catch, and dip. The crowd erupted in applause. Angie and Alex stayed out on the dance floor.

"Hey, you really are a dancer," said Angie.

"Yeah, you're pretty good yourself."

Angie smiled. "I've got happy feet."

54

Sensing the opportunity, the band kept the music going with another good dance tune, "Oh Las Vegas." The dance floor filled in a rush of bodies and Alex and Angelica were hemmed in. Seemingly everybody in the joint was ready to dance.

Right and left, left and right, bodies twirled in abandon to the music as the cowboy swing went at full throttle. The frenetic motions once again gave Alex that anthropological feeling.

Whether by plan or for reasons of self-protection, the Letgo brothers changed the pace to a slow one.

"Oh man, 'Four Strong Winds,' this is one of my favorites," Alex said, pulling Angie back toward the dance floor. He took her right hand with his left, placing his right on the small of her back. He felt her spine, bumpy, right through the fabric. Angelica still kept a respectful distance apart but responded to Alex's lead as they smoothly circled the dance floor. When the music stopped Alex loosed his grip so quickly that Angie's hand stayed up in the air for a moment.

Back at the table, Alex ordered another round. This time Angie had a plain Coke.

"Sure you don't want something in that to spruce it up some."

"No thanks, I don't do a lot of liquor."

Alex immediately felt guilty but he didn't know why. "I don't drink too much either." He reluctantly pushed the bottle toward the center of the table.

They watched the dance floor fill to bursting as the liquor quotient had finally overcome the natural male shyness, and bodies were bouncing off each other as the cowboy swing hit its stride. The dance floor was covered in a sea of cowboy hats.

Alex took a deep breath and decided on a delicate route of conversation. "So besides liquor, what else aren't you into?" He moved closer to Angie to be heard above the din. "I just thought I should know, in case I decide on a new hobby or something."

"Well, let's see. I'm not into smoking, drugs, bull-shitters, braggarts, show-offs, liars, cheats and thieves, among others, I guess."

"Pretty good list you've got there, but so far, I'm still doing fine. How about guys from back east?"

"Especially guys from back east. God, I can't stand those preppy types, Oh, I forgot, momma's boys, too."

Alex decided he wouldn't mention that he had gone through prep school.

"I'm a bit more flexible. I like women that don't hit me. At least not right away. That's about it."

She laughed easily, leaning her head back on her neck. "Oh, I wouldn't worry about that. So how about you, what kind of things do you like besides dancing?"

"Oh, me, when I'm not working, you know the usual, saving my money wisely, volunteering at the old-folks home, working with disadvantaged youth, helping ex-presidents build houses for the poor, you know, the typical stuff."

"Oh, I see, just a modest guy."

"Yeah, that's me, you know, humble."

"Sounds like you're about ready for sainthood."

Alex blushed.

"But you like women, it appears."

He almost jumped up to attention. "Sure, sure, but, ah, only smart, red-headed ones."

"No blondes or brunettes for you, then?"

"No, oh gosh, no." He had taken it too far, and was having a hard time keeping the tête-à-tête going. Alex had run out of witticisms. The conversation ebbed out and stranded for a bit too long. He nervously decided to talk about music. "That sure was a good song, real good song." He looked up at the ceiling as if for guidance, "Four strong winds, man, that's just poetry."

"How do you know all these old songs?"

"In college, I got my uncle's old records, all on vinyl. He went to CD's and didn't want to store them any more, I guess. I had a hell of a time getting a turntable to play them on. Finally found one at a garage sale."

"You really seem to like music. Do you play?"

Alex was immediately embarrassed. "Oh, I like to sing sometimes, just sing to myself, you know. I tried the guitar. I'm pretty much a hack; about all I can do is chord along. You know, I just sort of like to sing."

"I bet you have a good voice."

"No, no, but it is loud, I guess."

"I play guitar."

"No kidding?" Alex got so excited at the prospect of possibly playing music with a woman that he could hardly form the words, and they came out all staggered and funny sounding. "May, maybe, we could like do some music, play together, or something, you know, maybe, yeah." Alex lost the thread of thought he was spinning and there was another awkward pause.

Angie smiled in his face. "Sure, might be fun."

Alex echoed the words. "Yeah, fun, might be fun." He was grinning so hard his face hurt.

The Letgo brothers had finished a quickstep dance number, and the crowd stayed on the dance floor. A rosy glow from the wagon-wheel light fixtures gave the whole place a mystic feeling.

A loud voice rang out from the back, "Hard Hat in my Coffin!"

Two others echoed. "Do the hard hat song."

"Hard hat, hard hat!" The crowd took up the cause.

"What's the hard-hat song?" Alex asked.

"Oh, it's their big hit. It was even on the radio for a while. The country radio stations in Idaho picked it up. It never went national."

There was loud applause as Charley laid down a melody on the pedal steel, and Darrel picked up his fiddle to play. Buzz and Billy sidled up to the microphone and waited for Darrel to finish his fiddle lick. Then Buzz began to sing in his benign baritone:

> "I've worked in the east, fought fire in the west,
> But it's time and a half that I like best.
> Working outside is just my cup of tea.
> I've fallen timber, I've built a dam,
> Worked on the highways all across this land.
> Never been to college or worked in a factory.
> Oh, but sometimes late at night, I wake up in
> such a fright.
> Wondering what's waiting for me on the other side.
> And though I'm mighty scared, I still want to be
> prepared.
> So put my hard hat in my coffin when I die."

Darrel did a quick riff on his fiddle and the crowd roared. Alex thought it was like temporary group insanity, a religious fervor, a fundamentalist hoedown.

Brother Billy joined in harmony on the chorus:
> "Put my hard hat by my side, and try to sympathize,
> with a worker bee whose wings have grown old.
> Just listen to me kid, before they close the lid,

57

Put my hard hat on my head and wave goodbye."

After three more verses and a double-end chorus, the song died out amid cheers and a rush to the bar.

"So what's your degree in again?" Angelica sat like a judge with her elbows on the table and her chin resting between her clenched hands.

"Biology."

"Biology?"

"Yeah. I was in pre-med, but med-school didn't work out."

"Then why are you working for the Forest Service?"

"Good question. I don't really know, I guess. All the time I was in school, I daydreamed about getting this great job somewhere. But now there aren't any good jobs anymore, or almost none, I mean; not many good ones for somebody with a biology degree just out of school." Alex finished the rest of the bottle. "I guess I was just too busy going to school to really plan on what I was going to do when I got out. Then one day, whammo! I was a senior in my last semester, heading for that real-world door I always kept hearing about."

"That famous real world. I know what you're talking about."

Alex fiddled with the empty beer bottle, tearing off the label for some unknown reason and smiled with just the corners of his lips. "Trapped in a world I never made."

Angie laughed like an actress, measured and clear. "You know, you're pretty funny when you want to be."

"It's that life-long ironic streak," he said. "Sort of sets up your brain for it."

Angie leaned forward. "So tell me, how did you get in the Forest Service? I've got friends that have tried to get on permanent for years, but they can't seem to; and here they bring you all the way from back east."

Alex scuttled his chair closer to sit by her side. "Well, I'll tell you, it's sort of a mystery to me. I didn't have any real knowledge of the Forest Service. I mean, I knew there was one, but never really thought about it much. Sort of like a sewage treatment plant. You know it's there, but don't really know how it works."

"That's an interesting metaphor."

"Well, maybe the Electoral College would have been a better example. Anyway, I saw the flyer for the job. It was called a "job announcement." Now get this. I didn't see this announcement on the wall or bulletin board or anything. I was on my way to class, just walking down the Penn State mall, just up from the Sackett Building, when I see this piece of paper on the sidewalk and I picked it up. It was just a loose paper blowing around."

As if on cue, Angie's eyes opened wide. "Wow, kismet!"

"That's what I thought. Anyway, the job market was lousy and graduate school wasn't looking too good, so I thought, what the hell. I daydreamed about it for a couple of days and then sent in an application. I barely met the educational requirements for the forester series. I had taken a couple forestry and forest ecology courses, and it must have been enough." Alex looked around the room, smiling at the thought. "Or else they didn't get any other applicants."

"And you got the job, just like that?"

"Yeah, but it was like nine months later, and I'd forgotten all about it. For almost a year I covered half the country looking for a job, any professional level job that I was remotely qualified for. Nothing, nothing at all, just some handshakes and smiles. Then this government job deal. I didn't have a job interview or anything. I spent months making a professional looking portfolio, and no one even asked to look at it. One day I got this call, this disembodied voice from human resources, in Ogden, Utah, offering me a job."

"That was it?"

"It was like job magic, I tell you." Alex felt the deja vu feeling hard now. It was sitting right there next to him.

Angelica looked at Alex, right square in the eyes. "So, now you're sitting in the Plywood Palace on a Saturday night in Sunbeam, Idaho, wondering how in the world you ended up here, of all places?"

Alex winced. "You're right on the mark."

"You are an interesting story, Alex Kynwulf, an interesting story."

Alex shifted around in his seat, a little nervously. "Well, thanks for the compliment, I guess. So what's your story?"

"Well . . ." Angie rolled her eyes. "Obviously I came by the more direct route, being born and raised here and tied to that ranch with a steel cable around my leg."

"I thought ranching is this great lifestyle?"

"As long as you like cows, fixing fence, making hay, and driving a tractor for all hours of the day and night, it's great, I guess."

"Sounds a little overrated."

"A bit."

"Are you going to school or anything?"

Now it was Angelica's turn to wince. "I went to Idaho State for two

59

years, down in Pocatello. Didn't go back last fall. Guess I still don't know what I want to do."

"So what were you taking?"

"I was enrolled in Elementary Education. Somehow I didn't picture myself as the schoolteacher type."

"Hey, you'd be my first choice for schoolmarm," Alex said smiling.

Angie smiled back. "You know, I just can't stand kids, especially the bratty, school-age types. Anyway, I might go back this fall. This waitress gig is starting to get old already."

Alex thought there was more to the story, remembering what Fast Eddie had told him about Angie's recent breakup. He also sensed that more school questions were not good ones to ask. He was rescued from more conversation when the band started to regroup on stage. The Gold Dust Twins were looking a little bright-eyed from their long visit to the bar, but it didn't seem to show in the music. The bow was on the fiddle strings, the pedal steel was running the scales, and the Letgo brothers were ready to retool. They were joined on stage by the big blonde gal that Alex had heard singing with them in The Wild Bunch.

Alex stood up and held out both of his hands towards Angelica. "Would you like to dance?"

"Boy, you weren't kidding about this happy-feet deal."

The big blonde held her Gibson jumbo up to the microphone, cocked her head to one side, and began to sing in a strong voice, another slow dance number called "Someday Soon."

Alex held Angie tight as they danced slowly in a small circle, his hand firm on the small of her back. Pressure. Felt the thinness of the dress. Smelled soap on her neck. This time, Angie responded to the hand and snuggled closer, both hands on his shoulders now. Alex began to feel warm all over, lost in the music as they moved in front of the speakers. He felt like they were the only couple on the dance floor as the lyrics came from all around him.

Alex didn't want the song to end and he held her tight for a few moments after the music stopped. She didn't try to pull away; rather, they both relaxed their bodies at the same time and gently moved apart.

Alex and Angelica stayed on the dance floor for the entire second set, barely speaking at all, doing most of their conversation with their eyes and their smiles. They carefully danced the cowboy swing with the rest of the loud, raucous crowd, and Alex kept a small space within himself waiting for the next slow dance with an anticipation that bordered on the manic. He was totally in the moment: the smell of her hair, the touch of her hand on his neck, life in her breath.

After the second dance set, back at the table, Alex felt he had never talked this easily on a first date. He felt confident enough to talk without rehearsing the words. "The word is that you like poetry."

"Yeah?"

"Oh, no, I sort of like it too. I meant that poetry is okay. I don't know if I like all the reference to death and dying."

"But then again, it is the human condition."

"Once in a while, these poets could crack a smile, and it wouldn't kill anybody." Alex realized he had made a rhyme, and was sort of proud of it.

"Well, it looks like I'm going out with a wordsmith."

Alex clutched the sides of the table with both hands and looked up at the ceiling. 'What's in a name? That which we call a rose by any other name would smell as sweet'."

Angie clapped. "Romeo and Juliet, how nice."

"We did the play in high school."

"And were you Romeo?"

"No, no, of course not." Alex shook his head at the impossibility of it. "I just liked the story."

"These violent delights have violent ends'," Angie said.

"Let's hope not. How about this one? 'We are such stuff as dreams are made on . . . . '."

Angie twirled her hair with her index finger and slowly said, 'and our little life is rounded with a sleep'."

"Wonderful, wonderful! I remember that one because it's often misquoted as 'Such stuff as dreams are made of'."

"Humphrey Bogart, 'Casablanca,' one of my favorite movies."

"Wow, the lady knows her classics."

"Here's looking at you, kid." She raised her glass of Coca-Cola.

Alex was desperately trying to remember the ending of the movie. Something like "the start of a beautiful friendship," but he couldn't quite put it together in time, so he just said, "Yeah."

Angie looked at her wristwatch and said, "We probably should be going. I've got to work the breakfast shift tomorrow. We've got a long drive."

"Right," Alex said, moving in slow motion, his thoughts locked, looking forward to a long drive home.

61

Out in the parking lot it was cold, the stars bright, the cat-eye crescent moon shining. At the doorway, Alex put his arm around Angie without thinking, and she responded by moving closer.

There was some background noise going around the parking lot but Alex ignored it. Somebody was angry about something and yelling. It wasn't any concern of his. From out of the corner of his eye, Alex noticed two men in cowboy hats moving toward him and talking loudly. The bigger one yelled at Alex to turn around. Alex reflexively turned in time to see him launch an overhand punch, right at his face. Alex saw the punch coming and just managed to roll his shoulder and head away, absorbing some of the power of the blow. Even so, Alex hit the gravel hard.

"Finn!" Angie screamed. "What have you done to him?"

"That son-of-a-bitch," Finn said. "He's lucky I didn't kill him. Why did you do this Angie? What's the matter with you?"

"What's the matter with me? With me? Finn, you're a fucking idiot!" She was crying now. "I told you it was over. Why don't you leave me alone?"

The ringing in his ears had lessened and Alex tried to get his legs under him. "You heard her, leave her alone." He managed the words in thick syllables.

"What's that you say?" Finn taunted him. "Didn't they teach you how to use your fists in college?"

"Finn, you stupid fuck, stop!"

"You God-damned hillbilly," Alex muttered.

Finn was dancing in front of him now, side to side, his fists held in front of his face. "Come on, come on. Stand up again, and I'll finish you off."

Alex was trying to stand when he saw Teffonie VanWinkle move in front of him, like some sort of avenging angel.

"Leave him alone," Teffonie said.

Finn laughed, his arms down at his sides now. "What are you going to do about it, big girl?"

Teffonie was as tall as Finn.

"What are you going to do about it?" Finn laughed again.

What Teffonie did about it was hit Finn with a left hook in the solar plexus. She hit him so hard that Finn's breath came out in a "whoosh!" and he involuntarily bent forward from the waist. Teffonie then clubbed him with her right fist, once, twice, three times between eye and ear, almost too fast to see. Finn went down face first and pitched on his head, his nose plowing a furrow in the parking lot gravel, his unconscious hands still clutching his stomach. His boot heels pointed to the sky until Teffonie kicked him in the ribs, hard, and Finn fell over on his side with a long, drawn-out moan.

Angie knelt down and held Alex's head in two hands, moving it back and forth like she was checking to see if it was broken. Teffonie, unclenching her fists, said, "He's got a pretty good punching-bag look. Let's get him out of here." She and Angie helped Alex onto wobbly legs and toward his truck.

"Thanks, Teffonie." Alex's voice was coming back. "Where did you learn to fight like that?"

"Just a little something I picked up at Bucknell."

Alex had a new-found respect for the Ivy League. "I owe you one, Teffonie."

"Not to worry," Teffonie said. "But you're acting a little ringy. Are you okay?"

"Yeah, I think so."

Angie said, "I better drive."

Teffonie followed Angie and Alex back to his truck as a small crowd began to gather and hover around the prostrate figure of Finn sprawled in the dirt.

"I'd better split," Teffonie said.

"Yeah," Angie said. "You better head out before Bang Bang gets here."

Frozen for a second at the door of the truck, Alex said, "Bang Bang?"

Angie explained. "The local deputy. He's sort of quick with his gun. He hasn't shot anybody yet, but we don't want to give him an opportunity now, do we?"

Alex blinked his eyes, clarity and feeling coming back, "God, it's like everybody has their own town name."

Angie looked at him seriously. "You better be more careful, or you'll end up with one too."

12

"I don't mind where people make love,
as long as they don't do it in the street,
and frighten the horses."

Mrs. Patrick Campbell

The brown hues of the spring landscape were reflected by the bruise on the right side of Alex's face as it healed and faded, now almost gone except for the brown under his right eye. There had been no repercussions from the parking lot battle at the Plywood Palace. No one in the office had even mentioned the fight, though Alex was certain that everyone in Goldburg knew about it.

It was the first of May, that long-prepared for day for packing into the Middle Fork. Alex surveyed his surroundings as a nervous excitement moved through him like series of electric shocks.

Kloyd had taken two loads of mules over to Cobalt the day before in the just-returned-in-time stock truck, and this was the third and final load. Alex was to follow with a pickup loaded to the top of the green-pipe stock rack with tack and supplies. To Alex it looked like they had enough gear and supplies to last the summer, not for just ten days.

Alex had spend most of Sunday buying and packing the food for the trip. Buck's list seemed endless, full of heavy canned goods, meat, and eggs. There were five of them going in: Buck, Kloyd, Alex, and the Gold Dust Twins, Charley and Darrel. The Twins were looking particularly rangy today, Alex thought.

He finally asked Kloyd, "They don't look much like twins?"

"Naw, they's brothers, but they ain't twins. Charley must be two or three years older."

"So, what's this Gold Dust bit about? Are they like miners or something?"

"Not that I ever heard of. Charley and Darrel been cowboyn' all their life. Grew up just down the road on Twin Creek, still live there with their old

64

dad."

"Then why are they called the Gold Dust Twins?"

"Don't really know, I guess."

Alex smiled, looking around at the horses, the mules, the white buildings. "Do you ever call them that in person?"

"God, no, not unless you want to get punched in the kisser."

On the road to Cobalt, Alex followed the dust of the stock truck up Morgan Creek, through the narrow rock-walled canyon, basalt reaching like dark brown fingers to the sky. Up on Morgan Creek Summit, the snow was deeper than the fences, and Alex slowed and down-shifted to follow Kloyd and the stock truck and his eight mules down the steep grade to Cobalt

Out in front of the old ranger station, it looked like a western movie with horses and mules lined up at the hitch rack, packs and mantas spread out on the brown grass, tools and feed bags stacked against the porch. Buck seemed to be everywhere at once, barking orders like a drill sergeant. Kloyd was busy putting the Decker saddles on the mules. Charley and Darrel, the Gold Dust Twins, were balancing out packs side by side.

Alex stood by, wanting to help but unable to decide how until Buck barked, "Kynwulf, get over here and I'll show you how to manta up a pack. This is even easy enough for a college kid like you." He pulled out a white canvas tarp and spread it out the ground in the shape of a diamond, then put his own soft pack containing his personal gear, in the center of the diamond. "You fold it up like this, with the fold in the front, on top." His movements were quick and precise. Standing the bundle on edge, Buck added, "You hold down the flap with your arm and you throw a loop around it. Tie off with a half hitch over a loop, then roll the line over the pack from top to bottom, tying off to the loop." His hands moved in a blur. "Got that?"

Alex, of course, had gotten none of it and was lost as soon as he laid the pack on the manta, but he said, "I think so."

"Good, you get this stuff mantied up, and try to match packs by weight," Buck said, then rushed off to kick the Gold Dust Twins into a higher gear.

Alex stared at the pile of unrelated elements at his feet - sleeping bags, pads, a chainsaw, gasoline, loops and loops of rope, the carefully folded canvas mantas - and tried to make some sense of it all. Fifteen terrible minutes later, Kloyd came by and said, "Here, I'll give you a hand. Why don't you go help Charley and Darrel saddle the mules?"

Remembering his recent training and glad for a task he might be able to do to satisfaction, Alex grabbed a pack saddle, pad and blanket, and headed over to the line of mules at the hitch rack. He settled next to Dun, an enormous buckskin mule with faded black stripes on his hindquarters. Alex looked at the mule while the mule watched him. He thought he detected a sighing sound, more like air escaping from a tire, but thought it must be his imagination. Alex successfully managed the saddle and was fiddling with the cinch strap, remembering Big Stanley's admonitions, hoping he didn't have it on too tight. He was just testing the cinch, inserting the required three fingers, when Buck came up, watching, head held askance. "What do you think, Buck, is the cinch strap about right?"

Buck didn't say a word, but he grabbed the cinch strap in both hands, put one booted foot against the mule's side, and gave a heave so hard that Dun expelled a belly-load of air with a loud "Wuuuuhhhh!". The mule's tongue shot out like a frog's. "That should be about right." Buck wore a sadistic grin. "You have to watch these mules. Give em' a chance and they'll suck in so much air the saddle will roll off as soon as you get on the trail."

"Old Dun seems to know what's going on." Alex said.

"Clum Dum but he should. He's been doing it for longer than I have," said Buck.

"How old is Dun?"

"Older than you. Better than thirty years old," Buck scratched a growth of beard. "Mules are smart animals. It takes them awhile to catch on, but once they do, they don't forget. Better than some people, I suspect."

Alex looked back from the mule and over to Buck, "So how long have you been doing this?"

"None of your fuckin' business."

Kloyd and the Gold Dust Twins had finished mantying up the packs, and Alex watched Buck matching the packs for weight, testing each one and arranging them in pairs. Alex led Dun over to the where Buck was hefting two large wooden boxes.

"Dun always carries the kitchen boxes, 'cause he don't mind the clink and clank of the pots and pans," Kloyd said, as he hoisted one of the canvas-covered boxes opposite Buck, clipping the belts on the kitchen boxes into the two steel rings of the Decker saddle. Then unloosing the lashing ropes on the steel rings, he tied the box down in a flurry of motion, loop upon loop, finally tied down to the cinch so that the box was held tight against the mule's side. "Tell you what, Alex, I'll show you how to throw the packer knot tomorrow when we

66

got a little more time."

Working in pairs, Kloyd and Buck, and the Gold Dust Twins didn't take long to load the fifty-two packs on the twenty-four mules and on Bob and Bill, the two draft horses. They built five pack strings in all, four with five mules each and one with four mules and Bob and Bill.

Buck strode over to his horse, a small Appaloosa mare, nervous in eye and foot, and said. "Alex, you come after Kloyd, and Charley and Darrel will follow you. Now remember, never tie off your Clum Dum lead rope, and don't get it tangled in your fingers. Anything happens, you just drop the Clum Dum rope. Last thing we need is a two fingered college boy on the District."

With that as his full set of instructions, Alex walked over to where Major was tied at the hitch rack, anxiously pawing the dirt. Alex led Major over to his pack string. With a deep breath, he held the lead rope in his right hand as he put his left foot in the stirrup and saddled up. So far, so good, he thought. The big mule, Dun, was first in his string, followed by four others, the last being a somewhat wild-eyed sorrel that Kloyd had warned him about getting too close to, as the mule had a tendency to shy away.

Buck was obviously the leader of this trip, and nothing happened until he mounted up and moved out with his pack string, saying a curt, "Three miles an hour," loud enough for everyone to hear. Kloyd moved in behind, Alex gave Major his head, and the big bay horse fell right in line behind Kloyd's string, his head buried right in the last mule's tail. Alex glanced back over his shoulder, and Charley and Darrel were right behind. They were on their way to Meyer's Cove.

The overgrown Forest Service road led up into the timber and started to climb. Major seemed to know what to do, and Dun and the other mules were content to follow. Alex constantly checked behind him that the packs were riding well. It wasn't long before the group was breaking through crusty snow. Alex buttoned up his Mackinaw and pulled the ear flaps down on his green wool hat as he watched a few snow flurries spitting from a leaden sky.

Kloyd had explained that the best way to prevent a wreck was to keep moving. Other than an occasional stop to take a leak, Buck kept the outfit moving at three miles an hour. The snow was up to the horse's hocks and blowing sideways, the wind had freshened, and they still were on the wrong side of Rabbitsfoot Summit. Alex's hands were cold in his sheepskin-lined gloves as he turned his face away from the wind.

Rabbitsfoot Summit was no more than a timbered saddle that marked the divide between the Middle Fork drainage and Cobalt. A small brown sign reading "Elevation 7200 feet" poked out of the snow. Alex could barely see Kloyd only fifty feet ahead of him. The snow was coming in squalls of big wet flakes, and the drifts were almost belly deep on the mules.

Half frozen, his head stuck in position watching his mules, Alex could feel the drop in elevation. The snow began to let up, turning into sleet. Major had his head up the mule's butt ahead of him. Alex watched Kloyd reach back into his saddlebags for a sandwich, and Alex, taking the cue, realized that this was as close to a lunch break as they were going to get. His jaw almost frozen, Alex had to consciously think to chew his rock-hard sandwich, balancing the reins and lead rope in one hand while he ate as quickly as he could. The cold turned into pain, and the ice on his thin beard thickened into an exaggerated goatee. Alex began to retreat into his own little world behind his eyes in an effort to think warmer thoughts. Major moved beneath him with a kind of military cadence, walking, walking, walking, three miles an hour.

The abandoned road broke out of the timber into the wide- open basin where Silver Creek dumps into Camas Creek. The snow stopped, the wind was lessening and brown grass popped up through crusty snow.

Buck led his pack string right past the trailhead and, with not even a hint of stopping, started down the Camas Creek trail. His plan was to make the Tappen Ranch before dark, and he was sticking to it. Now the three miles an hour didn't even include piss stops; the last time Buck just pulled in his horse for a minute, stood up tall in the stirrups, and let her fly. Alex had to will his frozen legs to stand up to do the same

Camas Creek was more of a small river than a creek. It dropped in shadowy cataracts over gray boulders, sometimes right next to the trail. The stream was so steep that Alex could look down off Major and see the rounded rocks under the water making alternating patterns of dark and light. Sometimes the trail was cut into an arch of solid rock, with rock for a tread and rock looming overhead. High above Camas Creek on an open talus hillside, Alex could see far downstream the river shining silver where it formed a bowknot bend against the last ridge on the trail. The white clouds were all around like in a dream.

Three more miles to the Tappen Ranch and Alex was done in. His back, his shoulders, his rear end, and especially his right arm from holding the lead rope were all begging him to get off his horse and lie down in the sagebrush like a dog. He was so tired that he couldn't remember not being tired and didn't know if he could make it the rest of the way. He rolled in the saddle with every step Major took, hand clamped tight on the lead rope.

Buck stopped the string and got off his horse to open a wire gate strung across the trail.

Alex slid off of Major's back with an effort, unsure if he had the energy to climb back on. He looked ahead, around a wide bend in the river and saw a short line of cottonwoods emerging from a side canyon, already green with leaf. There sat a small cabin, only about a half a mile distant. "That must be Grouse Creek," he said, almost like a prayer.

"This is the place," said Kloyd in his best Brigham Young tone.

"Thank God," and Alex meant it.

"Looks like you're goin' to make it after all," Kloyd said.

Buck, out front, overheard the conversation and laughed, "A little tuckered, are we? Clum Dummit, but it's been a good day. Not everyday you take a string all the way from Cobalt to the Middle Fork."

"I hope the hell not," said Alex.

"You know what, Kynwulf?" Buck said. "You might just make it after all. Remind me to tell you exactly how one of these days."

"Jeez-O-Friday," Kloyd said, as he swung into the saddle with a grin.

Buck was serious when he said, "We'll see how you do tomorrow working on the trail. You won't have it so easy. Have to get off your horse and do some real work, not just sit on your ass all day."

"I hear we got a lot of blow-down up ahead," Kloyd said. "Must of had a wind storm in that bug-kill this winter. Last year we must of cut sixty or eighty trees in the stretch before Loon Creek, and from what I hear, we've got a worse situation now. Probably two or three days of sawin'. I also got some blastin' to do on that rock face that always gives us trouble."

Buck looked down the trail as if he could almost see the downed trees, then turned to Alex. "We'll see how you do on the end of a crosscut saw. They don't call them misery whips for nothin'. Ha!"

Alex clenched his teeth and decided that, no matter what happened tomorrow, he would die on one end of that crosscut saw rather than quit before Buck did.

13

The stars were almost gone. Venus shone bright as it sank behind the dark cliff across from Tappen Island. Alex's face was cold and his hair was damp. There was a dusting of frost on the canvas manta that covered his sleeping bag. Kloyd was already wrangling the horses, and Alex could hear the bell mare ting-a-linging on and off way up on the bluff behind camp. Alex had just drifted off into that place partway between sleep and wakefulness, the pleasant place of womb-like warmth where thoughts of women and glasses of beer peacefully dwell, when he shot bolt awake from a stout kick to his feet.

"Burning daylight," was all the dark shadow of Buck said.

Even though it seemed like the middle of the night, it was evidently time to get up. Alex searched under the manta for his pants, cold but dry, and pulled them on as he stood on his sleeping bag, goose pimples and all. The rest of his outfit went on double quick: boots, down vest and his all-purpose packer hat. He lifted his arms high over his head and stretched, still sore from the long ride down Camas Creek. Alex took stock and decided he had no collateral damage.

Smoke rose straight up from the stovepipe. Kloyd had already started a fire in the old cook stove. It was dark inside the little cabin, and Alex heard mice scurry away from his footsteps. He hated mice with a farmer's passion and couldn't understand how Buck and Kloyd could sleep in the old cabin, hearing those mice and all. Kloyd had just thrown down a thick roll of upholstery foam on the bare box springs that were rusted in place on the home-made bed and just nodded off, with Buck right next to him. Soon Alex had the lantern going and the makings for breakfast on the stove top. Bacon sizzled in the big cast-iron pan, and the pancake mix was ready, waiting for the crew to drift in. Outside it was racing to daylight, as colors came into view like in time-lapse photography. Alex carried two collapsible buckets to the stream behind the cabin. Grouse Creek was cold. Kloyd said it was the best, coldest water on the entire Middle Fork, even in August. The creek rose from a series of springs not far from camp, where the rocks split, biblical like, and a gush of water rushed from beneath. Alex found a white enamel cup hanging on a cut alder branch and dipped it under a bubble of clear water that gushed over a small red stone. The water was so cold it hurt his temples when he drank. He hung the cup back on the alder branch next to a slick overhanging rock, where the spray from the waterfall collected and little green ferns grew in the shade.

Kloyd and the Gold Dust Twins were back with the stock and tied them up to the log hitch rack. Charley and Darrel stomped their muddy boots just outside the too-short door and then sat down at the home-made table with their coffee. The Gold Dust Twins were in a talkative mood that morning and began an argument concerning Christmas decorations. Alex had some trouble following the flow of the conversation, as Charley, the elder twin, had a bit of a speech impediment. Charley was talking about his plans for a "Tibbity Zibbit". The plans involved wood, department store mannequins, and some construction, of that part, Alex was fairly sure. All the while, Darrel didn't say much other than "yup" or "nope," and once in a while, "won't work."

When Charley started talking about his plans for lighting the "Tibbity Zibbit," Alex couldn't contain himself any longer. He put down his coffee cup and asked, "Charley, what kind of display are you talking about, anyway?"

"Well, there ain't but one kind of Tibbity Zibbet, now is there?"

Alex was flummoxed but managed, "You never know, do you? I mean there might be more than one kind."

Now both Charley and Darrel looked at him like there was something wrong with him. Charley said, "They's all the same. A Tibbity Zibbit is a Tibbity Zibbit. You got your Mary, and your Joseph, and your baby Jesus, and the wise men. They's all the same."

Alex now understood the need for mannequins. "Oh sure, I just forgot about the wise men."

"Forgot about the wise men? What kind of Tibbity Zibbit would it be without wise men? One thing for sure," Charley said, "unless we run out of mannequins, we're gonna have wise men."

71

Alex shrugged his shoulders and began to get ready to fry pancakes on the griddle, feeling right at home at the old stove as he remembered events from a past that never really occurred but seemed as if they should have. He felt he would have been a great cook at some Adirondack camp, like up at Saranac Inn or Paul Smiths. "What's for breakfast?" the old timers would ask him. "Pancakes and whiskey," Alex would reply. "Whiskey to wake you up and pancakes to stick to your ribs."

On this morning, Alex watched the pancakes bubble on a thin layer of bacon grease, flipping them expertly. "How would you like your eggs, guys?"

Charley said, "Over easy is fine."

"Works for me too," seldom-heard Darrel said.

Alex had a plate of pancakes with two eggs and bacon for each of the Gold Dust Twins in no time.

"Hey, these pancakes are good," Charley said in a somewhat surprised tone.

"Yeah, better than usual," chimed in Darrel.

Alex puffed up a bit. "Special family recipe."

The Gold Dust Twins had seconds and thirds on pancakes and cleaned up their dishes so well it looked like a dog had licked them clean.

Kloyd rolled in and the Twins made room at the table.

"How do you want your eggs, Kloyd?"

"Any way you want to cook them is fine with me."

Another order of pancakes, bacon, and eggs over easy hit the table, and Kloyd dug in hungrily. "Jeez-O-Friday, but I like these pancakes."

"Secret family recipe," Darrel said knowingly.

"Fry me up a few more there, Ace," Kloyd said.

Alex was feeling pretty good about this trip by now. He was reluctant to say that pancakes and eggs were about the only thing he knew how to cook. But, what the hell, he thought. Better this than a poke in the eye.

Buck, all business as usual, stomped into the cabin and reached for the coffee pot, sitting down with a sigh.

"How you want your eggs?" Alex asked.

Buck gave specific directions. "Sunny side up, splash the tops with grease, I like the yolk runny, but make sure it's done. I hate raw eggs."

Alex worked the stove, keeping the griddle not too hot, checked the firebox, and produced two perfect sunny-side-up eggs on a stack of three pancakes, two strips of bacon not too crisp and not too soggy on each side.

Buck lathered on butter, syrup, and cut into the pancakes, stashing a fork full into this mouth with his left hand. Alex watched as the oddest look came over Buck's face.

Buck swallowed hard and said, "What the fuck, these ain't Happy Jacks!"

"What?" Alex said.

"Clum Dummit, these ain't Happy Jacks. What the fuck kind of pancakes are these? We always have Happy Jacks for breakfast!"

"What the hell is Happy Jacks?" Alex shot back, his face reddening.

"Only the best fuckin' pancake mix in America."

Alex's blood was up now, and he had to struggle to control himself, saying through clenched teeth, "These pancakes are homemade."

"Homemade?" Buck boomed. "What, you probably used eggs and everything."

Alex tried to defend his rash decision. "We got ten dozen eggs."

"It doesn't matter. With Happy Jacks, all you have to do is add water," Buck said, like he was part of a television commercial, waving his hands for emphasis.

Kloyd piped in. "You know, sometimes it's sort of nice to have somethin' a little different for breakfast. These pancakes ain't bad at all. And look, Alex got you canned grapefruit for dessert, your favorite."

"Clum Dummit," Buck sighed as he picked up his fork and knife and began again to trim his three pancakes. "The kid just gets off the train from back east, and right away he wants to change everything."

After breakfast they saddled up and moved up the trail towards Loon Creek. The blow-down stretch was even worse than Kloyd had expected. The downed trees were stacked like matchsticks, one on top of the other. Kloyd unpacked the two crosscut saws. Alex purposefully teamed up with Buck on one saw. Buck smiled as the two started in on an immense spruce that had dropped lengthways right down the trail. Alex was a bull on his end of the saw, his arms, shoulders and back working like a machine. Buck sawed so hard that the sweat rolled off his face and made little puddles in the dirt.

14

"Horse sense is a good judgment which keeps horses from betting on people."
W. C. Fields

The days on the trail slipped into a comfortable pattern of packing and unpacking, riding and working on the trail, long hours and long days in May. Alex was enthralled with the newness of it all, and few thoughts other than the exact present occurred to him. Like in a kind of meditative trance, he viewed events from a distance, the movement of Major his mantra. At three miles an hour, the landscape moved by at a perfect speed, Alex thought, an evolutionary perfect speed for human eyes and ears, one where animals appeared and you saw them first. Three miles an hour was a human scale, like the inch, the foot, the yard.

It was yet another morning of sunshine, the clouds like pillows, the sky clear from canyon wall to canyon wall. The end of the trail was almost in sight, only eighteen miles to Little Creek Guard Station. Buck's plan was to move the pack train up to Little Creek. There the Forest kept a large, fenced-in pasture at the old Hood Ranch where the stock would graze for the summer. The State of Idaho maintained a dirt airstrip across the river from the guard station, and the Forest used Little Creek as its main back-country portal for administrative use.

Since the first part of the trail had already been cleared, the going was good all morning; no downed trees, no slides, no brush, three miles an hour. The sun was already high and the day warm by the time they reached Mahoney Creek. The last three days had been unseasonably warm, with temperatures in the high seventies, almost eighty, which was record warmth. It hadn't frozen the last three nights and the Middle Fork was up, rapidly rising from snow melt. Gone was the green, clear water of early in the trip. The river was brown now, coffee brown, its texture turbid. Alex could hear rocks rolling in the rapids, a fearsome noise, a noise of bad dreams.

Alex was just thinking of taking off his shirt when he heard a buzz like a bad radio. Major had been crossing a rocky talus slope of broken basalt, carefully picking his way, and Alex was moving his string slowly around a rock, looking down. Then he saw the rattlesnake in the middle of the trail, coiled tight, right in front of Major's nose. The horse didn't stop, but he did hesitate, looking right at the snake as he carefully lifted his foot high and placed it up and over the still buzzing snake. Alex looked down and saw the snake right there under Major's belly, between front and hind feet. Then it was the back feet, up and over easy, not stepping on the snake. Alex tightened up and froze, ready to jettison the lead rope as big Dun laid back his ears and high stepped over the snake. Mules two, three, and four did the same. Mule number five, the wide-eyed sorrel, had a different idea. He stopped in his tracks, as did the others and Major, as if it was some kind of group think. The mule hunched his back, so Alex was sure it was wreck city coming up and tightened the reins. From a standing start, that mule jumped up, leaping over the snake with three feet to spare and landed square flat on the trail, packs still on his back. The snake, tired now of watching these circus maneuvers, slipped off the trail and into the rocks.

"Whoo-Wee," Kloyd sang out. "That was a close one."

Alex let out the air held captive in his lungs and drew breath.

By the time they got to Little Loon Creek it was high and muddy, cold with runoff and threatening just to look at. Buck circled the pack train in on itself in a spiral and waited until all the stock had settled down.

"Clum Dummit." Buck leaned into the curse for all he was worth. "I knew we should of put a bridge in here after the fire. Fuckin' high water already. The fuckin' crick just doesn't hold snow anymore with all the trees burnt up."

Kloyd leaned forward in the saddle. "What's the ford look like?"

"Not too Clum Dum good. Can't see bottom." Buck seemed to decide. "Tell Kynwulf back there to take it real slow, and let the mules feel the bottom." And with that, Buck moved his small horse into the water. The Appaloosa never hesitated. The water was almost up to the horse's belly, trying to push the horse downstream. Picking their way, the mules followed the lead horse without hesitation, tentative but firm. One after another, heavy packs and all, the mules entered the water and dug in. Buck had his string across and waved Kloyd to follow.

Alex watched as Kloyd put his horse in exactly the same position that Buck had chosen, and like an instant replay, entered the raging creek in copied movements of slow motions. One of Kloyd's mules, the third one in the string, almost stumbled. Kloyd stopped immediately, and the mule lurched forward to good footing and was across.

Now it was Alex's turn. He looked at the water, dark and muddy, and headed Major toward the rushing water of Little Loon Creek. Major never faltered; and, tight reined, he stepped into the murky stream. Alex, watching the flooded creek, failed to take his feet out of the stirrups and felt the cold water rushing in. Major felt his nervous reaction and stopped mid-stream. Alex, not knowing what to do, began to freeze up, his arms out stiff, holding the reins and lead rope high. A long branch bobbed up out of the muddy current right under Major's belly. The horse shied to the side, lost his purchase on the rocks, slip-footed and went down on his hindquarters. He started to roll. The only thing that kept the horse upright were his hocks jammed against a big rock and his knees wrapped around another. Alex lost his stirrups, piled up right on Major's withers, and almost slid off into the water.

"Hold on!" Buck yelled from the other side.

Alex hung on with both arms wrapped around Major's neck, as the water pushed up against the horse's side. The current began to turn the animal.

Buck pushed his horse into the water, piled his little mare right into Major's side, frantically reaching out for Major's bridle before the horse rolled. "Clum Dummit, man, move!"

Alex tried to move, but he couldn't make his arms let go of the horse's neck. Wild-eyed, the big bay lurched to his feet, made a lunge for the shore, and Alex half rolled out of the saddle, face almost touching the water. He still had the lead rope locked in his right hand.

Gasping, Alex urgently pulled himself back in the saddle. He looked back and saw Dun, the longest-legged animal in the entire string, firmly planted in place, the brown current boiling past his legs. Alex kicked Major ahead and Dun stuck out his neck and followed. Mules two, three and four did the same. And then it was the sorrel mule's turn; and like Alex, the mule froze in its tracks, front feet just short of the water. The pack string stopped. Dun and the following mule were out of the water, but the next two mules were stuck right in the big part of the current, which was almost up to the packs, beginning to turn the last mule's rump downstream. Again not knowing what to do, Alex began to panic, the lead rope slipping in his hand. Then he saw Charley ride right next to the sorrel mule and kick it with his heavy boot, right in the gut.

"Get in there you worthless piece of shit!" Charley said.

Surprisingly, the mule obeyed and stepped in the water without jumping and started across. The other mules stepped forward and placed their collective feet well, and soon Alex had his string across. Sitting high on Major, Alex was

76

shaking like a leaf, couldn't believe he had stayed on his horse. A feeling akin to giddiness grabbed him, and he had to force himself not to laugh out loud.

By late afternoon, they had made Little Creek Guard Station and tied up the stock to the post-and-pole hitch rack in front of the old CCC barn. Alex helped unload the packs as Buck rode across the long suspension bridge over the Middle Fork. By the time Buck was riding back on the swinging bridge, the unpacking was about done.

"I got the gates closed at the Hood Ranch," said Buck. "Other than the saddle horses, might as well turn em' loose."

There was visible excitement among all the high-pricked ears when Kloyd flipped the halter over Dun's head. No sooner was the halter off than Dun was down in the dirt, rolling back and forth like a dog on a carcass.

"One dollar!" said Kloyd as Dun made his first roll, all four feet in the air. "Two dollars!" he added when Dun repeated the roll, and a high-pitched, "three dollars!" as Dun once more kicked all four feet in the air, rolling back in one motion. The mule stood up with a heave of his front legs, shook the dust from his coat like a dog shakes off water. He looked around at Alex as if to say, "about time," and lifting his head, trotted down the trail next to the little irrigation ditch, across that four-hundred-foot-long suspension bridge and down toward the Hood Ranch.

The other mules followed Dun's example, a few quick rolls in the dirt and over the bridge to the Hood Ranch. One mule, a dark bay, got up to seven dollars before she made the trip over the bridge. The last mule, the skittish sorrel from Alex's string, didn't roll at all, but walked stiff-legged over to the edge of the fence and stood looking at the bridge for a long while before eventually starting across, at first with careful steps, and then a quick trot as the bridge began to sway side-to-side.

Kloyd turned to Alex and said, "First trip."

Alex nodded his head.

By the time all the horses were brushed down and let loose in the corral, a gentle drizzle began to fall, the first precipitation in almost nine days. Alex dragged into the guard station, dog-dirty and smelling of horse. A hot fire burned in the old cook stove, warming the kitchen. A stack of Reader's Digest condensed novels lined the wall. Buck broke out a deck of cards and was playing "Spit in the Ocean," with the Gold Dust Twins, soon amassing a pile of wooden matches on his side of the table.

Alex turned to Kloyd and said, "You're not playing?"

"No way, I don't gamble."

"Not even for matches?"

"Jeez-o-Friday, especially not for matches."

"Kynwulf, get your ass over here," commanded Buck. "We need a fourth."

"Yes sir." Alex slid his chair around, stepping high over the top, plopped down and said, "So how do you play the game?"

"Just get your matches and watch and learn."

The early morning rain had turned to a cold mist and the fog lay low on the mountainsides, obscuring the peaks and saddles, and painting the landscape in shades of gray, like a Wyeth winter scene. The gray sameness leveled out the canyons to a temporal life below the cloud deck. The temperature had dropped drastically, at least twenty degrees.

Alex and the rest of the crew had been scheduled to fly out today, but there wasn't a chance that any aircraft would be flying through the ten thousand foot saddle between Twin Peaks and into the Middle Fork this day. Buck kept everyone busy with little odd jobs around the guard station, but by noontime they had pretty well worked themselves out of necessary things to do. Alex had finished splitting over a rick of wood to add to the at least five cords already in the lean-to woodshed. He even took the time to hand split half of the rick for the old wood stove in the kitchen in case the propane went out and someone needed it.

After a thin lunch of peanut butter and jelly sandwiches on ten day old bread, they broke apart to while away the afternoon. The Gold Dust Twins worked on the tack. Buck, without reserve, lay down and took a nap. Kloyd caught up his buckskin and took a ride over to the Hood Ranch to see if he could find some early rhubarb growing around the old homestead.

After Kloyd rode off, clippity clopping across the suspension bridge, Alex copied his actions. He took the grain bucket over to the corral and caught Major with a halter rope, and tied up the horse to the hitch rack. He thought he might take a ride by himself for a change, not leading a string of mules and not riding the unending "three miles an hour".

Still feeling clean from yesterday's shower, Alex had decided to wear his new uniform clothes, the only clean clothes he had left in his pack. He fretted with his badge, remembering finally to put it on his left shirt pocket, "over the heart". Alex was also overly conscious of the Forest Service emblem on the left arm of his long sleeved shirt. Looking in the little mirror in the bathroom, he felt the proper dandy, as if he were a model in the Forest Service uniform catalog. He then slipped on the Forest Service straw Stetson that he had so carefully packed away for the entire trip.

Alex confidently climbed up into the saddle and, without thinking about it, urged Major forward with his legs and rein hand. Major walked across the long suspension bridge. Alex felt the sways starting to catch up to them by mid-bridge. It didn't seem to bother the horse, and Alex and Major stepped off the bridge and turned upriver on the Middle Fork Trail.

Alex rode the length of the airstrip and then another mile or more to a second suspension bridge that led to the Middle Fork Lodge, built and operated by a Reno casino magnate. It was rumored to be the home of wild week-long parties, with showgirls to entertain the whales, the big losers from the Nevada casinos.

Alex had seen photographs of the lodge in the permit files at the office, but he was more impressed when he saw the structure as part of the landscape. The story goes that the builder of the lodge wore out a British Dehaviland Otter carrying in all the milled logs and construction supplies for the lodge and outbuildings. The resultant Middle Fork Lodge was more like one of the great Adirondack lodges, like the Rockefeller Lodge at Bay Pond, transplanted from the hills of the Saint Regis to the mountains of the Middle Fork.

On this gray day, Alex didn't see much sign of life, looking across the river at the lodge. He guessed that it must be a slow week for showgirls. He could see the famous hot springs swimming pool from his vantage point high on a sagebrush knoll. He turned Major back onto the path where the trail cutoff to Norton Ridge ran like a line of Zs as it switch-backed again and again, all the way up the open slope to timber. Major, charging less than normal with no horse or mule ahead or behind, still managed his customary three miles an hour, and Alex gave him his head as he listened to the rolling boulders booming on the river bottom and watched the spring birds moving along the riverbank trees.

The trail swung south with the river and laced its way across a sagebrush bar, now green and full with spring, and early blue lupine and yellow balsamroot dotted the dry meadow grass. Alex was lost in thought, his brain resting in neutral between hemispheres, neither right nor left side, just being. Suddenly he spotted two people in the distance sitting beside the trail. As he rode closer, the people transformed into women; and closer still, they metamorphosed into beautiful women, like the ones in the Victoria's Secret catalog, dark haired and sultry. In ten days, they hadn't seen a another soul. Now there were two ladies, and he was the only man.

And it got even easier. The two women saw him approaching and waved, their arms held high. "Holy smokes," he said just under his breath. Alex primped himself the best he could, slicking down his hair with his hand, adjusting the new uniform hat. Sitting tall and straight in the saddle, he gently urged Major off the trail and over to the small hillock where the two women sat on a quilt. When he rode closer, he saw the women were young and they were attractive; and it was not just because he had been in the wilderness for ten days with packers and mules. These women looked like pinups from the big war, only wearing new tight cowgirl outfits.

Alex willed that he would not hesitate; would not freeze-up; would not blow the opportunity; would not act like an idiot savant. "Howdy," he affected his best cowboy greeting. It sounded strange coming from his lips. He even tipped his hat. Then he leaned forward in the saddle, tilting his hat back, trying to strike that cowboy romantic pose he had seen in the movies.

"Hi," the first girl smiled. The second giggled.

The second girl, the one with black hair in a ponytail, her dark eyes shining, said, "Where on earth did you come from?"

Alex coughed and tried to form words. Nothing. Nervous now, he bit his bottom lip until it hurt. That seemed to work somewhat. He silently vowed not to make an embarrassment of himself yet again. His voice sounded far away, quiet, the words coming out slowly. "Well, yesterday I brought a pack string down from Loon Creek to the Forest Service guard station here at Little Creek." He neglected to mention Buck, Kloyd, or the Gold Dust Twins.

Now the first girl sat up straight and looked him over. Her hair was short, one of those modern haircuts almost like a man's, dark, nut-brown curly locks. Her face had long features. Alex felt the word "Aquiline" come into his head. He wasn't sure it was the right descriptor, but when she looked him square in the eyes, she almost knocked him out of the saddle.

"Are you a real forest ranger?" she asked.

Alex straightened up in the saddle, somehow got his courage up, looked out over the river valley like he was searching for something, turned and said, "Well, yes I am."

The second girl said, "See, I told you when he was riding up. An honest to goodness forest ranger, just like on television." She turned back to Alex. "Are you like on patrol or something?"

Alex tried to look thoughtful. "Yeah, I am."

The ponytail girl said, "You don't have a gun."

Alex sensed the right answer. "I don't really need one."

The taller of the two, the one with the short hair, said, "You don't say much, do you?"

Nervous now, he felt the familiar feeling of failure close at hand and tried to rally. He noticed the smiles, the long legs, the too-tight jeans, clenched his teeth and said in almost a whisper, "Sometimes I do."

The shorthaired girl sort of turned onto her side like she was posing, turning to show her thin waist, large breasts, and an almost wasp-like profile. "Well Jennifer, we have a bold cowboy here," she said and gave Alex a smile that made his neck sweat.

Alex was thinking that maybe, just maybe, things were going the way they were supposed to and that he was not going to screw up. He might just have a nice conversation with these beautiful girls and talk like a normal person. Who knows what might happen next? Maybe they might invite him to their picnic. Maybe one of them might think he was not altogether weird or ugly or otherwise out of his league. He was just on the verge of grasping at a minuscule feeling of self-confidence when he felt Major begin to tense. Alex's eyes shifted side to side three times quickly. "Oh, God, no, not now!" he said right out loud.

Alex pulled back on the reins hard, and gave Major a quick kick in the ribs. The two girls were frozen, sensing the situation wasn't quite right, but without a clue as to what to do. Alex kicked again and again. Major stood his ground and began to arch his back. Panic flooding his senses, Alex dug his heels into Major's side for all he was worth and pulled back so hard on the reins that the horse's neck bowed in a C shape, his nose on his chest.

Major let out a moan, more of a sustained grunt, and unleashed a hose stream of urine. In a strange accident of fate, the two women were boxed in by several strategically placed boulders, and Alex and Major were blocking the only way they could move quickly. On top of that, Alex had brought the horse sort of above the two girls and Major was straddling a flat rock, slightly tilted down toward the now doomed picnic.

In agonizing slow motion, Alex watched horrified, as a stream of urine like a waterfall fell off the flat rock directly onto the two stunned showgirls. Frozen from fear the two girls compounded their mistake tenfold by covering their eyes with their hands and screaming, as the golden shower sprayed upon them. Somewhat gathering control, the two girls bolted upright but right into each other. They both fell down, one face first into a still bubbly puddle of urine, the other backwards into the sagebrush with her shapely showgirl legs pointing straight up in the air.

Alex gave up totally. "I'm sorry. I'm sorry," he blurted.

"Sorry? You dipshit! I got horse piss all over me," the wet pony-tailed one said, looking as if she was about to cry.

"I didn't know he was going to go. I'm really sorry."

The shorthaired girl wiped her face with a now wet shirt. Alex couldn't help but notice he could see her nipples now, right through the fabric, erect and pointing. "Fuck you, jerkoff," was all she said.

15

"Not all who wander are lost."

J.R.R. Tolkien

"It's another lazy day in heaven." Kloyd motioned with his arm at the blue Idaho sky.

Alex looked up from his lunch spot on the loading dock of the fire warehouse. He took in the horizon to horizon view, from Twin Peaks in the northwest to Lone Pine Peak to the southeast.

"Where is Big Stan?" Alex asked. "I haven't seen him for a few days."

"Well, between riding old Stain and fighting the skunk wars, he's been pretty busy."

"What's this about skunk wars?"

"The way Big Stan tells it, he's got a family of skunks living under his house. It's to the point now that they're about half tame. The other night he opened the cabinet under the sink and one popped his head out, lookin' at him."

"Come on now, I don't believe that."

"God's truth, Buck told me he saw two of those skunks sittin' on Big Stan's porch, just like a couple of dogs."

"Why hasn't he got rid of them?"

"Well, Jeez-oh-Friday, that's the point, he don't know how. He's afraid to rile em up, as they might shoot off. Some biologist told him that skunks don't stink up their own dens, and Big Stan told me his plan is to win their confidence, and then sort of lead them away one day real soon, he hopes."

"Winning the confidence of a family of skunks?"

"Big Stan says he got some experience in the matter in dealing with his ex-wife's family."

"Like the Pied Piper of Hamelin Town, only it's Goldburg, and it's skunks."

"Big Stanley was in the office the other day, and I overhead him telling Sandy that he feeds a couple of them bread right out of his hand. Trouble is, he don't know how many skunks he's dealing with. Sort of hard to tell them apart, as they look pretty much alike."

"I can't believe Sandy will put up with this."

"She told him she's never coming over to his place until he gets rid of those skunks."

"Could be another reason why Big Stanley's taking his time."

"You know, Big Stan, he doesn't rush right into something. He's a big man for process. I wouldn't be surprised if we had a staff meeting on this situation, just to help him sort out some alternatives."

"I sort of like that idea. We could do an economic analysis and an environmental assessment; give Big Stan some real alternatives to choose from, with budget timelines and potential partnership opportunities."

"Now don't you be giving Big Stanley any ideas. He's got enough problems as it is. You never know, he might take you seriously. You are jokin', aren't you?"

"Jeez-oh-Friday."

It had been a busy week for Alex, dealing with the District budget, a job he had inherited the moment he walked in the door with that college degree. He also had a new seasonal employee to deal with, a retired Brigham Young University professor who had been summering in Goldburg the last couple of years and was the new recreation guard at Boundary Creek. Professor Robert Nehpi already had acquired a most curious town name.

Alex was at his desk. "Kloyd, did you remember the grocery list for Boundary Creek?"

"You mean for Yellow-Glasses Bob?"

"Yeah, for Bob. I have noticed he wears those big yellow-tinted shooting glasses."

"Yeah, almost all the time, but I've seen him without em."

"But you still call him Yellow-Glasses Bob?"

"Well, it's a town name and it just seems easier."

"We don't have any other Bobs on the District. I'm just wondering is all."

"Yellow-Glasses Bob, that's what everyone calls him."

"But not to his face, right?"

"Sure, of course not."

Alex sighed. "Okay, and the groceries are all taken care of?"

"You bet, everything bought and paid for. It's going out today on a Two-O-Six flight with old Rolly."

84

"Is there a young Rolly I need to know about?"

"There ain't but one Rolly."

"Good, good. I'm just trying to learn the territory."

Buck passed Kloyd in the hall and ambled into Alex's office. He seemed in an uncharacteristically affable mood; for Buck, that is. "So Kynwulf, are you still runnin' with that Kowalski girl?"

Alex pondered the verb "runnin" for moment before he said, "Yeah, I guess I am."

"Well Kynwulf, you know what they say, the coyote never sees the bullet comin'."

"What's that supposed to mean?"

"Don't mean nothin', I suspect, unless you're the coyote." Buck laughed again and headed back down the hall.

Like searching for a long lost secret, Alex was exploring his way around Angelica Kowalski. There was a lot of her under the surface, and so far Alex hadn't discovered much to help his understanding. The two had been keeping company, on and off, during these last few weeks, and everyone on the District seemed to know about that and wondered where it was headed, including Alex.

This Saturday they had a different kind of date. Alex had been searching for something to do that was lighter fare and had heard about the ghost town of Bayhorse, about fifteen miles up the road from Goldburg. Angie told him she hadn't been there since she was a kid and thought it might be fun. Alex's confidence level in the expedition rose to a high level.

Angie was working the breakfast shift that Saturday, six a.m. to two, so Alex had plenty of time to "dink around," the new local term that began showing up in his vocabulary. Alex was quickly adapting to the local vernacular. "Dinking around" on a Saturday morning in Goldburg was a six-mile trip to the Wise Buy, the only grocery in town. Alex had forgotten his checkbook and took advantage of the counter checks at the checkout register. These were blank checks, and you just wrote in your name at the space at the top and then signed them; no twelve digit account number or anything like it. It was legal tender everywhere in the county, courtesy of Elkhorn County Bank, one of the last privately owned banks in the old west tradition. Since everybody knew who everyone else was in Goldburg, there was no need for identification, just in case you forgot your wallet. Alex wondered at the sustainability of such a system as he wrote in his name and address and signed the check.

On to the Post Office he went to check his mail; not much, no letters from home, no mass mailings, not even a credit card application. Alex wondered if the zip code for Goldburg didn't have enough residents for the junk mail companies to bother with. The Post Office was also the best place in town to meet people and to catch up on local happenings. The relatively large foyer was a common greeting ground. As Alex was leaving, he ran into Argo, who had been busy contemplating a New-age catalog.

"How's it going, Argo."

"Alex, oh, wow, just fine." Argo fidgeted with a new growth of downy beard on his chin. "What are you up to?"

"Just taking in the sights. Doing my Saturday-morning shopping."

"Cool. Hey, did you hear there was a major solar flare?"

Alex looked up toward the sun.

Argo continued, "The solar wind at this time is unusually strong, and it could produce magnificent auroras, even this far south. But it stays light so late this time of year it might be hard to see. I plan on being up most of the night. Thought I'd head out to Antelope Flat. Should be plenty dark out there. You want to join me?"

"Sorry, Argo, but I've got a date."

"Oh yes, I've heard something about that. Going any place special?"

"We thought we might check out Bayhorse this afternoon."

"Bayhorse? Way cool, you'll like it." Argo became more animated, his arms and hands moving without respect to the conversation. "On the way, check out and see if Dugout Dick is home."

"Dugout Dick?"

"Yeah, Dugout Dick and his ice caves. He's this hermit that lives up by Bayhorse on the river. You'll see a sign on the Bayhorse road. He's way cool, lives in a cave," Argo said as he sort of danced out the Post Office door to some inner music that only he seemed able to hear.

Two o'clock came quietly, and Alex was waiting at his pickup at the Y café for Angie to get off work. He leaned against the hood of his truck, his arms folded across his chest. Through the café window, he could see her moving among the tables. He was overcome with the idea of Angie as design and studied her color, form, line and texture. He watched her move past the cowboys waiting at the cash register as they all turned their heads. Her long red hair was down her back, straight and flowing. The black jeans wrapped tight like in a magazine ad, and the hard edge of cheekbone and long nose, a form of beauty that held secrets.

When Angie saw him standing at the doorway, Alex had the strong feeling that he had done this before as he watched the girl through the glass door. The hair on Alex's arms stood on end with goose bumps as the scene unfolded as if in a movie, and Angie pushed open the door.

"Hi kiddo," Angie beamed. Her black Stetson bent low over her eyes and swooped high on the sides.

"I see you've got the picnic basket."

"Yeah, I'm hungry; let's high-tail on out of here."

Alex drove across the rickety steel bridge at Bayhorse Creek, a one-lane, rusted trellis-type bridge that had seen better days. He felt the bridge move a little bit each time he hit a bump in the wooden deck. Then it was up the canyon on the two-track gravel road, bouncing across BLM land, scarred and almost devoid of grass already. The few Hereford cows he saw were thin and had that look of being used to traveling between mouthfuls.

Bayhorse lay in a small basin, enclosed by fir and rimmed by rock. Above the zone of mountain mahogany, granite and quartzite spires marched up to the timberline, where the ridge rolled in piles of talus. Even from a distance, Alex could see the one large building left, the old stamp mill with its red-painted tin siding, built in levels on the hillside to get gravity assist in moving the crushed ore. A variety of small wood buildings lay spread out on non-existent streets below the stamp mill. There were at least twenty-five structures, Alex thought, some tar-papered, most sun scalded; red and brown, almost black in places. They fronted a grassy strip of rolled-down rocks and assorted mining debris that covered what once was Main Street.

Angie looked around. "My dad brought me up here with my cousins one day to run around and play cowboys and Indians. It still looks the same."

Alex was impressed. There wasn't an interpretive sign in sight, not one living history stage, and no roped off, refashioned, rebuilt, rewritten or sanitized historical exhibits. There were no dioramas or anybody dressed in period costumes telling you how great it was and speaking to you as if you were an uninformed idiot. There wasn't even a gift shop where you could buy a t-shirt or a commemorative mug. Just lots of junk, old furniture, tin cans and pots right where someone threw them aside. There were parts of cars and trucks from ancient to 1930's vintage, with tires rotted away, grass growing up through rusted steel frame and motor. Inside the buildings it was much the same, with moldy newspapers serving as wallpaper to keep out the cold. You could still read some of it. Broken windows, broken dreams, and faded promises; with plaster falling from the ceiling and light bulbs hanging on cords, a safe without a door, a wood stove lacking a top, the refuse piles of pack rats, and seven shades of rust on metal.

Alex picked up a wide-mouthed canning jar, one of the few unbroken. "What do you know about this place?"

"Not much really. I don't know if it was gold or silver or both. But it played out long ago, like in the 1920's or before. Our next-door neighbor, Nellie - she's dead now - was a cook up here for some mine farther up the canyon. This was like right after she was first married. I remember her telling us that Bayhorse was a ghost town even then, and that was probably just after the Second World War."

"Looks like people hung on a while after that, even after the moment was gone."

"It seems they always do."

"It's surprising that this place isn't overrun with tourists."

"I think it's only because it's privately owned, probably by a bunch of people who own separate mining claims."

"I don't see any No Trespassing signs."

"Probably don't need them. Anything worth anything is long gone by now, and this far off the main road, the tourists never get up this far."

Alex and Angie explored the massive stamp mill, probably the best preserved structure. Compared to most of the others, it was well built at the time and had a metal roof and metal siding over large-dimension post-and-beam construction. The timber beams were still straight and the roof was level. It appeared the building was set on solid bedrock, held together by huge anchor bolts driven and grouted into the rock. The stamp mill had the look that, with a little spit and polish, you could start crushing ore tomorrow.

They found a grassy hammock on a mound next to Bayhorse Creek and had their picnic lunch; leftovers from the Y Café - fried chicken, some jo-jo's, potato salad, and even two slices of chocolate cream pie that somehow had survived the ride in the cooler. Alex's surroundings encouraged his appetite, and he ate like a miner at Christmas dinner.

"This is great food."

"God, I would think you would know. You ate enough of it."

"The pie is great too."

"We get those from Pocatello."

It took a while, but Alex finally ate everything in the cooler, and then leaned back on the grass, lazily full, trying to stay awake. Angie sat up beside him, playing with the petals of some blue lupine still blooming along the stream. "So, what are you thinking right now?" she asked.

Almost asleep, Alex snapped his eyes open. "Oh, gosh, nothing much."

"There's no such thing. You're always thinkin'. I'll bet right now you're thinkin' you ate too much and you want to go to sleep, instead of bein' stuck here talkin' with me."

"No, no," Alex lied. "I love talking with you, and I'm not that sleepy."

"Oh, I don't know. I'm startin' to figure out this Kynwulf character pretty good, so you'd better pay attention."

"Okay." Alex forced himself to sit up straight and leaned against a cottonwood tree. "I'm cool with that. You're right. We should talk more, about the important things." Alex thought a moment but couldn't come up with any important things. "So, what are you thinking about right now?"

"Oh me, gosh, not much," and Angie laughed like a schoolgirl.

"Okay, all right, you made your point. You win. I give up."

"Seriously now," Angelica sat up straight. "We've been going out for a month or so, and I don't know much about you. We don't seem to talk much. We're always going somewhere or doing something, almost like you plan all this stuff out ahead of time."

"Well no, yes . . . well," Alex's face was getting red. "That's what guys do I guess, at least I always thought so."

"So is this the Bayhorse day of the tour?"

"No, no, of course not. It's just something to do, you know? I mean, you need something to do on a date."

"Not necessarily. We can just sit around and talk. You mentioned you could play a little guitar, maybe we could play some music together."

"I'd like that, I really would like that, it's just . . . "

It's just what?"

"I don't know. I sort of get stage fright sometimes. I really can't sing in front of people. I just do it by myself, you know?"

"Alex, it's only me."

"I know, I know."

"Then why do you hesitate?"

Alex let out a deep breath. "It's just really hard for me when I get embarrassed. Like I screw up every time."

"Everybody screws up now and then."

"Not like me they don't"

89

"That's just how it feels."

Alex was fairly certain that few people froze up like he did. It was as if he turned into one of the Gold Dust Twin's mannequins. He could feel it coming on as he looked into Angie's blue eyes.

"Alex?" Angie playfully knocked on the side of his head. "You still in there?"

"Yeah, yeah, just thinking is all."

"Sometimes you seem to think pretty darn deep."

Alex was ashamed and excited at the same time, and the opposite impulses were kicking in, flowing through his veins like a drug, animating all his words and actions. "Hey, this is supposed to be a date. Argo told me about this old hermit, Dugout Dick, lives in some kind of a cave, supposed to live around here somewhere. You want to go check it out?"

Angie didn't say anything right away, puzzled at Alex's sudden emotional shift. "Dugout Dick? I think he's like further up the canyon, beyond Bayhorse. I've never been to his place. I've heard he's sort of weird."

Alex continued in his strange mood, watching the clouds hanging on invisible strings. "Weird, eh? You want to give it a try? We're only here for a short while, might not get the chance again. Well, I heard he does give tours of some kind. Might be kind of different. Ah, seeking the different, the unexplained, walking the razor's edge, that's what we're about. Our brains crave newness, that combination of excitement, nervous tension, and simple risk. Let's see if we can find Dugout Dick. Meet the wise man and learn his enlightened secrets."

"You talk like a nut sometimes, you know that?" The freckles on Angie's face made a pattern in the sun. "Just like a nut."

Alex laughed, jumped up from his grassy seat and shouted, "You're a better man than I am, Dugout Dick, wherever you are!"

Back in the truck, Alex was winding down. He rolled the town name over in his head. Bayhorse. Who had the bay horse? Funny they would name a town after a horse. Must have been a memorable animal. They hadn't bounced more than two miles up the rock-rutted road when Alex saw a faded sign, hand-painted on a piece of plywood: "See the Ice Caves. Dead Ahead. Tours Daily." The lettering was neat and well done, white letters on a background of green. Alex parked the truck near a clump of cottonwoods where a track led up to a series of dark holes cut right into a nearly vertical clay-colored cliff, a fan of talus spread out in all directions from arched, man-sized holes.

Alex and Angie had only a few minutes of looking around before a white-haired, white-bearded scarecrow of a man, neatly dressed in overalls, long-sleeved undershirt, and black-and-white Chuck Taylor sneakers, came bounding out of the nearest and largest cave.

"You're here for the tour? Only two bits apiece," he cawed happily, still moving steadily down the trail. "Best tour in Elkhorn County."

Two bits apiece, Alex thought. Not much you can do for a quarter.

"I knew somebody was coming today. She told me so," the man said in a sing-song sort of way. He stopped in front of Alex and held out his hand. "I'm Dick, Dick Zimmerman. Some folks call me Dugout Dick because of the caves, you see." He motioned behind him with a wild swinging of his arms. "You want to take the tour?"

Alex fished in his pockets for change. "Sure, sure. Is this a good time?"

"Son, it's always a good time at Dick's ice caves." He motioned for them to follow.

Alex was looking down, watching his footing on the rocky trail, and noticed Dick's shoes. There was an odd sort of black sole that seemed to be glued to the bottom of Dick's sneakers.

"Ah, you seen my shoes, have you? Here, look'ee, I made them myself." Dick shucked off a sneaker and held it lovingly in his hand. There appeared to be a slab of tire rubber, complete with snow tread, neatly cut in the shape of a shoe and glued on. "Made them out of an old tire, and they're just as good as new, better even."

"Pretty nice," Alex said warily.

"Oh yes, oh yes, they're pretty shoes, and for winter, I even got a pair with studs on em."

When they walked into the first ice cave, Alex was surprised that the interior was walled off with wood and various auto parts. Most of the exposed front wall was made of windshield, carefully matched to mining timber. There was even a storm door made from a windshield turned on end, with a door handle from an old Chevrolet serving as the doorknob. Alex had never seen the like of this organic architecture from the auto wrecking yard.

"You made all this out of car parts," Angie said.

"Yup, plenty to choose from at the junkyard down below Bayhorse. That junkyard is a regular treasure house." Dugout Dick was searching his pockets and produced a car key tied to his coveralls with a long string. "I can even lock my front door if I decide to go on holiday."

Alex surveyed the work. "This is real craftsmanship," he muttered.

"Thank you, thank you," Dugout Dick said, stroking his beard with his long fingers.

Inside it was cool and cave-like. A series of steel truck frames formed a lattice work of ceiling beams, creating a great room with at least a nine-foot-high ceiling, roughly fourteen feet across and twenty feet deep. The green-brown rock had been carefully trimmed to vertical walls, smooth and dry to the touch. The rock floor, with only a slight incline, was swept and tidy. Light bounced off the walls in varying angles from the wall of windshields. A pair of horsehide seats from a 30s era Plymouth served as sofa and love seat. A handmade table had been created from a series of antique wooden dashboards. The speedometer and other gauge cut-outs held pots and pans and odd steel glasses. There was a mammoth four-poster bed in the rear of the cave, with a bedpost made from a single length of whitebark pine log with a top cunningly carved into a dragon head.

Alex was agog. "This place could be in 'Architectural Digest'."

"That's what I always say," Dick beamed.

Alex noted how the cliff overhead shaded the windshield wall from the high-summer sun angle. "In the winter, I would think this place would heat right up, just from solar gain."

"You bet." Dick started his herky-jerky movements again. "When the sun pours in that south wall in the winter, I can't hardly keep a fire in the stove if the day is clear. I got the idea from a Arizona Highways magazine I picked up at the library. These Anasazi Indians lived in caves years ago, before white men got there. They had these cliff houses, and they knew how to use the sun. The thing is, I improved on them. They didn't have no cars around, of course."

"How many of these caves do you have fitted out?"

"I've got five, but only two are available. This one here is mine, and the other two are rented."

"Rented?"

"Sure, it's tough to find affordable housing. Read all about it in the paper. I can rent you a furnished ice cave for four bits a night, five bucks a week, or ten dollars a month. Where you gonna find a deal like that?"

Alex, always on the lookout, thought about this bargain. He pictured himself and some of his old friends from Pennsylvania with their very own ice cave, warm behind their wall of windshields, having a winter hot toddy. "I'll have to keep that in mind."

Dugout Dick kept on the move. He produced a well-worn stick with a slab of car tire attached. "See this fly swatter? I made it myself."

Alex had no doubts.

Dick swished the swatter, as if daring a fly to venture near him. "Works good too. Kills flies deader n' hell."

The scene was repeated with various and sundry objects purloined from the automobile graveyard. Dugout Dick seemed to be running out of Objets d'Art, and was fumbling around some when Angie asked, "So, where are the ice caves?"

"Oh, the ice caves. Well, to tell the truth, there really ain't any ice caves. There is one cave that gets great big icicles in the winter, great big icicles that go all the way to the ground, sorta brown colored, but of course, it's all melted now." Dugout Dick was searching as he spoke, "But that's why the tour is only two bits."

Dick reached behind his massive bed and drew out a guitar, a poor, abused-looking thing of scratched spruce and man-handled mahogany. It had only five strings. "Care to hear a song? It's all part of the tour, no extra charge." Dick swung the twine string guitar strap over his shoulder and began a pitiful wailing rendition of an old Jimmy Rodgers classic.

A much too long yodel happened, more like a death scream, freezing the hairs on Alex's arms. Dick could not keep the tuneless guitar in time with the strange syncopation of dirty chords and straining voice.

Dugout Dick sensed a problem and stopped playing. "I've got other tunes, lots of them. I've even got a tape for sale, only two bucks."

Angie spoke first. "That's all right. It's just sort of loud here in this cave."

"Oh sure," said Dick. "I play even better outside," and he started moving toward the door.

The afternoon sun seemed unusually bright after spending time in the cave. Dick was desperately digging through a shoe box and brought forth a handful of tapes. "I've also got a tape of ghost stories, narrated by me. Only two dollars."

Alex felt he needed to buy something, and was trying to decide which would be less painful, ghost stories or cave music; wondering who he knew that even had a tape player, figuring it might make a nice gift, in a sick sort of way. Under Dick's watchful eye, he retrieved two dollars from his wallet. "I think I'll take a music tape."

93

"You won't regret it, no sir." Dugout Dick caressed the dollar bills, smoothing them carefully before he stuffed them into his overalls pocket. "A real collector's item. You sure you ain't interested in the ghost stories? The events took place right here, in these caves, as real as me talkin' to you here and now."

Two dollars was two dollars, and Alex was not about to make a further donation. "That's okay, I'm not fond of ghost stories."

"I can't say I blame you, young fella, but this here ghost is friendly. She's my old girlfriend, Romana, who died tragically at too early an age."

Angie seemed to get interested in the romance angle of the story. "She was your girlfriend?"

"Yup, we was gonna be married, but she drown-ded."

"Drowned?"Angie said. "Here?"

"No, it was way down in California, long ago. I don't know how she found me here." Dick hung his head. After all these years, he still seemed to grieve. "I just couldn't say."

Alex watched Angie's interest and figured he was out two more dollars.

Angie said, "Can you see her?"

Dick looked straight ahead and spoke softly as if reciting a poem. "Sometimes, sorta in the pale moonlight, she shines, all in a white robe. Mostly she speaks to me about things to come." Dugout Dick jumped and slapped the side of his head. "Cuss me for a dang fool. I almost forgot. She sent me a message to give to you two."

"For us?" Alex asked warily.

Dugout Dick looked up at the sky, his eyes staring without blinking. "She came to me last night. I woke up and she was with me, standin' by my bed, and she says, 'Tomorrow you will meet two and you must give them a message'."

"A message?" Angie said.

"That's what I just said, girl, a message."

Alex wasn't one to believe in this type of thing, but he found himself saying, "What was the message?"

Dick didn't say anything for a moment, seemingly somewhere far away, and just continued to stare at the sky. Then he said in a higher-pitched voice, talking slowly, "You must tell them, in their hour of need, to look for the heart-shaped rock."

"The heart-shaped rock?" Angelica said.

94

"In their hour of need, look for the heart-shaped rock," Dick repeated.

"The heart-shaped rock." Angie said the words like a mantra.

Alex said, "This sounds like something out the Hobbit, for Christ's sake."

Dugout Dick rolled his head in a slow circle, returning from wherever he had been. "Now I don't know nothin' about no Hobbit, but I've never known Romana to give bad advice, especially if it's a warnin' like." Dick scratched his neck under his beard, flicking his fingers forward. He looked right at Alex and said, "If you two get in a real tight fix, I'd be lookin' for that heart-shaped rock."

16

"So this is the guitar you were telling me about." Alex balanced the maple guitar on his knee, admired the ornate pick guard and the glossy finish.

"Yeah, it's an old Japanese model from the seventies, a Lawsuit guitar."

"A Lawsuit guitar?"

"It's a copy of a Gibson J-200, an exact copy, I understand. It has a pretty good sound, probably not as good as a real Gibson, but pretty good." Angie looked lovingly at her guitar. "I saved and saved and bought it used in Missoula. It's really a great guitar. Go ahead, give it a try."

"I'm no good at this. I can play like three chords."

"Well, that's all you need for some songs. Go ahead."

Alex stiffly held the guitar, and painfully strummed a D chord, an A, a G, and an E minor chord. "That's about all I can do. Everything else is too hard. I can't play barre chords at all."

"Barre chords are hard for everybody."

Alex looked at his big hands; he didn't look convinced. "Here, you play something."

Angie cradled the big guitar on her left leg and moved expertly up and down the fingerboard, cleanly picking out a blues scale in E. "What would you like to hear?"

"I don't know, anything you'd like to play. Hey, how about some blues. I really like the blues. You know any good blues tunes?"

"I know a few. But I have to warn you, I don't sing very well."

"You're being modest now. I bet you sing really well."

"Well, I sure don't think so, but here goes," Angie said, as she walked down the neck in a flourish of seventh chords, hitting the blues notes hard.

She sang on key, but so quietly that Alex could barely understand the words over the sound of the loud guitar. He was transfixed watching her make the quick chord changes and hearing the flat pick move across the strings. Alex recognized the song and started humming it at first, then sang along just under his breath. He was so into the music that he started singing in his full voice.

> "Looked down from the mountain, as far as I could see.
> My best friend had my girl, and the blues had me.
> Tell me, how long do I have to wait.
> Can I get you now, or must I hesitate."

Angie had stopped playing and was just watching him sing. She had a look of amazement.

"You've got a wonderful voice; you know that, don't you?"

"Oh, no, no, I don't." Alex was both shy and pleased at the same time. "It's loud enough, I guess. Sorry to butt in on your song. I didn't even realize it. You play so good; I just got caught up in the music."

Angie still had the look. "Believe me; you've got a really nice voice. It's sort of gravelly, like one of those old blues singers, but it's right on key. And you got a good range too. I could hear it when you changed octaves, real natural like, and you didn't have to strain at all. I know who you sound like. You sound like that English guy, Joe Cocker. How do you know the 'Hesitatin' Blues?' Did you learn it from your uncle's records?"

"I don't think so. It's an old song; some guy I knew at Penn State played the guitar and sang it once in a while. Funny that I should remember it."

"How about, 'She came in through the bathroom window?' That would be cool. Cocker did a great job on that old Beatle's tune."

"I think I've heard it."

"You'll have to learn it." Angie started back in the blues, was making her guitar sing. "Well, keep going. Let's finish it up."

"I think I remember a couple other verses."

"Then come in on the break."

Alex tried to sing the words right to Angie, directing them to her eyes.

> "Ashes to ashes, dust to dust,
> Got a red-haired girl that rain can't rust.
> Tell me, how long do I have to wait?

Can I get you now, or must I hesitate?

I rode the Hesitation Railroad,
read the Hesitation News,
Oh my Lord, I got the Hesitation Blues.
Tell me, how long do I have to wait?
Can I get you now, or must I hesitate?
Can I get you now, or must I hesitate?"

Angie seemed to be wearing a permanent smile as she played a flurry of blues notes, hammering the last one hard. She looked at Alex just as he looked at her, square in the eyes.

Alex held her stare. He started to turn red and wanted to say something more but couldn't find the words to match the feeling of the music. The song lyric "Got a red-haired girl that rain can't rust," overcame his thoughts, and he so wanted it to come true.

Angie pulled her eyes down toward her guitar and said in a half-whisper said, "You'll have to learn the rest of 'Hesitatin' Blues'."

Alex nodded happily. It shouldn't be too hard. It was only the story of his life.

17

*"There is nothing, nothing so absolutely worth doing,
As simply messing about in boats."*
                                        Kenneth Graham

Big Stanley was embroiled in the skunk wars as Goldburg turned toward high summer. The skunks had become such a part of the local culture that it became an acceptable form of greeting: "Hi Stan, how's the skunks getting along?" Big Stan would stop whatever he was doing and proudly tell the latest tale. "Funny you should ask. Why, just last night I had three of 'em in my kitchen cabinet, right there under the sink. I fed 'em some leftover lasagna, right off my plate." Big Stanley emphasized the "three of 'em." From this beginning, all other news, problems, or complaints were forgotten as Big Stan would be offered unending advice on how to rid his home of the skunk plague. The conversation would end on a positive skunk note, and seldom did any unsettling news - such as work, for instance - ever intrude into the conversation. It was such a wonderful defense mechanism against bad news and work that Big Stanley began to think of his skunks as good luck charms. Alex noticed that Big Stan was in no particular hurry to become skunk-free but rather seemed content to get his truck and horse trailer, load up old Stain, and leave the work to the rest of the District. No matter how early Alex seemed to get to work, the horse trailer was already gone, and it seldom returned before quitting time.

Alex was busy trying to get papers off of his desk and get out the door himself. Since he was the nominal head of the recreation department, the Wild and Scenic River program was his staff responsibility. Alex was anxious to get started on his first actual float trip on the Middle Fork. It was an early Monday morning, and Alex was trying to get more personal gear into his river bag, tense about running a raft for the first time.

All the office saw his nervousness, as Alex was never one to hide his emotions.

Buck chided him. "Clum Dummit, Kynwulf, river runnin' ain't like packin'. Only two things you need to be a Middle Fork boatman, that's a size five hat and a size fifty-two coat. I would say you're in good stead on both accounts."

Alex nodded and didn't say a word, pondering the hat-to-coat size equation as he dragged his overloaded river bag out the office door and over to the lime-green crew-cab pickup where the rest of the boat crew waited for him. Since this was a shakedown cruise for the season, the whole crew was there: Fast Eddie, Harmon, Argo, and Howie. In contrast to Alex's butterflies, the rest of the bunch couldn't have appeared more relaxed. It's old hat to all of them, Alex thought, and here I am, nervous as a cat. Middle Fork boatman, one of the rugged breed, my ass, he almost said out loud.

Alex worried about everything he could think of related to rivers. His mind ran through an anxious litany of water safety, high water, rapids, rocks, sweepers, and cold-water drowning. When they stopped for gas at Sunbeam, Alex thought the main Salmon still looked kind of high. The river was running clear now, but Alex didn't like the look of the white water.

The rest of the crew was laughing, joking, reverting to high school behaviors like punching each other in the arm and bear hugs.

"What's up, Alex?" Howie said. "You've been as quiet as a mouse all morning."

"Oh, nothing, really."

Fast Eddie said, "Ah, don't let him kid you. Alex is a river virgin, don't you know. He's worried it's going to hurt when he gets his cherry popped."

"Let's put two life jackets on him," joked Harmon. "He'll be fine. You're at work, Alex, you can't get hurt. Everybody knows you only get hurt when you do crazy things like this on your own."

"The way I see it," Eddie said, "There's no reason, with all of our combined experience, we can't teach a totally clueless person like Alex here to navigate one of the most technical white-water rivers in North America. With a little on-the-job training and hands-on experience, he'll be a regular river-runnin' son of a gun by the time we get to Cache Bar."

"God," Alex beseeched.

Fast Eddie laughed. "God can't help you much on this one. But with the talent of your teaching staff, it'll be a piece of cake. Look at it this way, you don't have any bad habits we need to break you of. You're a clean sheet of paper. But just in case, we got the kayak crew here, if things get tough."

"Don't let him scare you," Argo said. "It's a wonderful river. The color of the water, the sound over the rocks, the way the eddy lines sit crystal clear. . ."

Eddie interrupted, "Not the Zen of the river again. If I hear about the juxtaposition of positive and negative space again, I swear I'll go nuts."

"You laugh, Eddie," said Argo, "but you understand exactly what I mean. The river has life, and as we enjoy that life and become part of it, we inherently get in touch and in time with the river's rhythms and we find the path open and waiting for us."

"Yeah," Harmon joked, "Argo is so one with the river, he doesn't even get wet when he paddles. The spray just bounces off his aura."

"Alex," Argo looked directly at him, "moving through the landscape on a river is one of the most profound joys in life a man can experience. When everything is right, the light, the water, the reflections, the smell of water on a hot, dry day - it's as close to heaven as we can get on this earth."

Howie, who was driving, glanced back and entered the conversation. "Hey Argo, what was that you were telling me about seeing God? Was that on the river, too?"

"Oh, that was at orgasm. It was a common thread in many ancient cultures that at the time of orgasm, when a man's mind is totally clear with no thoughts of past or future, at that instant, he is able to glimpse God."

"Man, that's my kind of religion," said Harmon. "Where do I sign up?"

Eddie said, "You don't sign up, you moron, you have to experience it."

"Why, back home in Kentucky, I was high priest of experience."

"Harmon, your hands and farm animals don't count," Howie added from the front seat.

"Damn right they don't. Why there are more pretty girls in Kentucky, per capita, than in any other state. And that's a known fact!"

"Whatever happened to last girl you had, the one with the buck teeth?" Howie asked.

"That was Rebecca Lee. She got lonesome for her momma and poppa, and went back to Kentucky."

"Rebecca Lee, another hillbilly name," said Fast Eddie. "How come all these hillbillies give their kids these goofy names?"

"There does seem be an unusually high number of such names in the rural lexicon," said Argo.

Fast Eddie talked right over him. "It seems the hillbillies like these names with a lot of Rs and Ls in them. Harmon, how many brothers you got?"

"I've got three brothers," Harmon said slowly, like he was counting

101

them.

"What's their names?"

"Leonard is the oldest, then Larry, then Russell, and then me."

"See, I told you, Rs and Ls. It's like a cult or something, a group think of Rs and Ls. Maybe it's so the hillbillies can identify each other."

Harmon smiled. It was more like a grimace. "Just play around till you lay around."

"That's my plan," Fast Eddie said. "Play around and lay around until I see God's face."

"Enough already!" Howie said. "How do you expect me to drive with all this bullshit?"

Just as the road turned to go down Bear Creek they surprised a herd of elk, about twenty animals, with several bulls, their velvet antlers long and arching over their backs as they ran stiff-legged for cover in the subalpine fir.

Howie shifted the truck into a lower gear as he began the slow descent to Boundary Creek. As Howie slowed to allow the long boat trailer to negotiate the switchbacks, Alex got a glimpse of the river far down the canyon, running like a silver thread in a sea of dark-green fir.

The Boundary Creek boat launch was a whirlwind of activity, with rafts, kayaks, and dozens of people spread out around the long, wooden boat ramp and the brown administrative building. Argo explained that there were seven launches a day allowed on the Middle Fork, including both outfitters and private parties. Everyone wanted to get on the river at the same time. As a result, every morning there were over a hundred people in this small space, milling about, carrying gear, wrestling boats, and slapping on sun screen.

Alex looked down at the river past the boat ramp to the first bend in the river. A large rapids split by a small island forced the river hard right and out of sight. The sound and the fury of the water unnerved Alex, made his mouth dry and his head ache, right between the temples.

His crew knew what to do, quickly unloading the small oar boat by hand. Then they maneuvered ahead and positioned the boat trailer to slide the big sweep boat right onto the boat ramp without having to lift or carry it. Eddie and Harmon led the crew in walking the black sweep boat down the steep ramp and into the water to tie up and join the other rafts in the big eddy below the ramp. Alex wasn't given any time to ponder his anxieties but was kept busy ferrying loads of supplies, camping gear, and coolers of food down the walking trail to the boats. Virtually all the food, gear, and supplies went into the sweep boat, which

102

Harmon would guide down the river. Alex and Fast Eddie would follow in the oar boat, a small, twelve-foot Avon self-bailing raft that was very forgiving and, being virtually empty, quick and easy to position on the river. Howie and Argo were to follow the procession in their kayaks.

Howie tried to assure Alex. "It really is a piece of cake. You're going to follow Harmon down the river. I just checked the water level. It's about four point three feet, which is a good level, fast with plenty of water over the rocks, especially in this upper section."

Alex didn't say anything back. He was still thinking about the phrase "plenty of water over the rocks" and trying to decide if this was a good or bad thing.

Howie went on. "We've got some great camps. Fire Island, just above Powerhouse, which is really cool. Then Marble Creek, Aparejo Flat, and Elk Bar."

Eddie sidled up beside Alex. "We're about rigged up and ready to go. Let's go visit Yellow-Glasses Bob, and we'll get our required wilderness ethic, leave-no-trace camping talk done. Then we'll hit the river." Alex hoped the river wouldn't hit back.

He saw the Yellow-Glasses shine in the sunlight before he actually saw Bob. Yellow-Glasses Bob had taught in the Engineering Department at Brigham Young University and was a very logical and precise individual. Small in stature but not in intellect, Bob adapted well, and soon had the Boundary Creek boat launch running with Germanic efficiency, with a strong tilt towards law enforcement. Though he had only been on the job for a few weeks, Yellow-Glasses Bob took the responsibility most seriously. His greatest fear was that someone would try to sneak onto the river without a permit under his watch. Consequently, his greatest passion was an eagle-eyed vigilance to prevent that from happening. Late into the evening until well after dark, Yellow-Glasses Bob would sit on the hill overlooking the boat ramp with his trusty Leica binoculars, watching and waiting for a rogue kayaker or rafter to try to circumvent the process by putting in at Dagger Falls, or even at Marsh Creek, and try to sneak past him. Early in the morning, Bob would be on the radio to inquire about parked cars in suspicious places and listen for reports from the District office. And all the while he waited, he savored the inevitable confrontation when he would apprehend the lawbreakers and they would feel the full wrath of federal law.

He was also most serious about all the other river rules and regulations

103

and was never tempted to cut any corners in identifying the rules. He never tired of giving the same presentation seven times a day, day in and day out. All of which made him a perfect mouthpiece to lecture heathen river-runner groups on campsite cleanliness and litter pickup.

"It's the micro-trash that is our most pressing problem, the cigarette butts, the gum wrappers, fishing line, dental floss, items like these." Bob gave the presentation with a fundamentalist zeal, walking slowly one way and then the other, head down as if remembering some ancient code, documenting disdainful examples of human excess with letter specific instructions on how to do it right. If asked a question or clarification, Bob would explain the rules from the beginning. His conversion rate among unbelievers was very high, indeed. The wages of sin was a visit from a federal law-enforcement officer. There were few listeners who did not fear the wrath of Bob.

Alex was happy to have Bob. It was one less thing to worry about. Alone among his group, he enjoyed Bob's apostolic zeal and iron grip on the audience.

Yellow-Glasses Bob said to Alex and the boat crew, "Now I know you fellows know the rules, but you're going to hear them again, just like everybody else who goes down the Middle Fork. No exceptions."

"You bet, Bob," Eddie said.

Bob started with his favorite subject. "Soap! Soap is not allowed in the river or within fifteen feet of its banks. Let me repeat. Soap is not allowed in the river or within fifteen feet of its banks. This includes all tributary streams, large and small. This especially includes all hot springs. There will be no soap in any hot spring on the Middle Fork of the Salmon River. There have been questions concerning so-called biodegradable soap. Let me repeat myself again. Soap is not allowed in the river or its tributaries or its hot springs, and this includes biodegradable soap." Bob said "biodegradable" with the same feeling as others might say "pedophile" or "necrophilia". "The water quality of the Middle Fork is pristine, and the USDA Forest Service intends on keeping it that way."

Bob covered soap and trash pickup most exhaustively and then launched into the proper use of portable toilets and explained the government's requirement to pack out all human waste. After thirty long minutes from start to finish, timed almost to the second, Bob was finished with his diatribe.

"Good talk, Bob," Alex said, looking at his watch. "You really laid out the rules and regulations well."

Yellow-Glasses Bob puffed out with pride. He followed Alex right down to the boat, keeping up a constant chatter concerning the latent conspiracy to illegally float the river. "I heard a rumor yesterday that a group of kayakers were going to try to sneak on the river from Marsh Creek."

"There weren't any cars parked at the pullout," Alex said, as he tried to disengage himself. "But then you never know, someone could of dropped off a couple of boaters."

This idea froze Bob in place. He hadn't thought about the obvious possibility that someone could sneak on the river without leaving a vehicle parked somewhere. "That's right," he said slowly, "you just don't know, do you?"

Alex couldn't delay any longer. Howie, Harmon, Eddie, and Argo were down at the boats waiting for him. He left Yellow-Glasses Bob still pondering the problem of illegal visitor use, and, dry mouthed and jumpy, he put on his life jacket and got into the oar boat.

"Okay," Fast Eddie said. "Are you ready?"

Alex tried to sound nonchalant. "As ready as I'm going to get."

"Remember, just follow right behind Harmon. I'll be calling out directions, river right or left. Now, Harmon is carrying all the gear. We've got virtually an empty boat. You should be able to spin this raft on a dime and move it anywhere you want. There's nothing to it, just hit the correct oar at the correct time, and the raft runs itself."

Alex played with the oars, whiffing them through the air as he faced the imaginary class-five rapids.

"Easy now, big boy. Wait until we get moving down the river."

Harmon climbed onto the big sweep boat like he was climbing up onto a yacht, head held high. All he was lacking was the debutante on his arm.

Alex felt somewhat small, crouched in the twelve-foot Avon raft, sitting at river level, looking up at Harmon pacing the deck of the sweep boat.

Argo and Howie played in their kayaks, seemingly without a care in the world, holding in the big eddy behind a white boulder. Their joint assignment would be to inspect and clean up camps on the way down the river as well as to provide backup for Alex and Eddie, just in case Alex's training program didn't go as planned.

Harmon tilted his Forest Service cap back at a jaunty angle and adjusted his wrap-around sunglasses. With two sweeps of the oars, the big boat was in the current, surprising Alex with its speed.

Alex took a gulp of air and dug into the oars, catapulting the light raft

105

forward and almost dumping Fast Eddie into the drink.

Immediately below the big eddy the river turned hard right, and Alex only made half of it. He whiffed a key-oar stroke trying to turn the raft. The boat quickly turned sideways and hit the first rock in a series of shallow boulders barely above the water surface. Bouncing and dragging from one rock to another, Alex shamefacedly imagined the laughter and redoubled his efforts, which only made it that much worse. He missed the next slot and dragged along a series of rocks on the opposite bank.

"For Christ's sake, slow down already!" Eddie said, finally getting a firm grip on the boat. "You missed at least two rocks back there."

"Sorry." Alex was still rowing frantically, trying to keep the boat straight as he zig-zagged down the river. He hit the last rock dead center, knocking Eddie into the bottom of the raft.

Eddie picked himself up off the rubber floor. "There, you feel better now? It looks like it might take you awhile longer to understand the river."

"Understand the river? I can't understand what I'm doing, let alone the river."

"Just calm down and look at the river. See how Harmon is doing it? Nice and easy. Look at Argo back behind us, feeling that river Zen." Eddie seemed about out of his run of sunny sayings. "Remember that bumper sticker, 'Rafters take deeper strokes.' Just think about that, will you?"

Alex did think about the deeper strokes. His thoughts ran quickly to Angelica Kowalski, and strangely enough, he did calm down somewhat, managing to spin the raft around and cleanly make a class two drop in a narrow boulder slot without hitting anything.

"There you go," Fast Eddie said. "Left and right, Yin and Yang."

"Now you're beginning to sound like Argo."

"Hey, Argo has his shit together on the river. His problem is off the river. Just keep thinking like Argo for a while."

"That's asking a lot."

"Hey, you can do this. The right oar at the right time . . ."

"I know, I know, and the raft runs itself. Nothing to it."

"Well, try like hell to get it together in three miles, because we'll be down to Sulphur Slide."

At the mention of the rapids name another blast of adrenaline mainlined in Alex's bloodstream, sending the raft smacking into and off of a rock wall.

The next three miles, in river terms, was pretty bony. Alex consistently

106

overcorrected and hit many rocks, though none seriously, as the raft rebounded from one boulder to another. Fast Eddie shouted advice and directions constantly the first mile but then, like a wind-up doll, slowly lost energy and seemed to realize that Alex would have to work it out for himself somehow. Alex's batting average began to improve in mile two, as he avoided the more dramatic head-on collisions in favor of more glancing blows with a dazzling array of gray and black boulders in the continual class-two water below Boundary Creek.

Up ahead, Alex heard some serious river music.

"Okay, Alex, let's eddy out here on this gravel bar. It's time to get out and take a look at Sulphur Slide."

Harmon had also eddied out in the sweep boat and was waiting on shore. Howie and Argo followed Alex in. Everyone seemed relaxed except Alex, who was on high alert.

"Good job, Alex," Argo said. "For your first time, at least you're still upright."

"I feel a little battered."

"Not to worry. A raft can handle a few mistakes."

They followed an informal user trail along the shoreline that paralleled the quarter-mile-long rapid. Sulphur Slide was just a pile of boulders, a veritable rock garden, with a white-water dressing on top. Alex wondered how on earth he would get the raft through.

"You see, Alex," Fast Eddie was back in his instructional mode, "you have to enter center right, move back to the left bank, and then after you pass the big hole, move back center into the standing wave train. See the line?"

Looking hard at the rapids, Alex almost believed he saw the line that Eddie was talking about. "What about all those rocks on the left?"

"Don't worry about them. There's plenty of water covering them at this water level. It just looks like you're going to hit them, but you'll float right over. Just make sure you miss that big hole in the center of the run. Are you ready?"

"I guess so."

"Let's just sit here a minute and watch Harmon take the sweep boat through."

True to form, Harmon worked the big sweeps easily, entered the rapids as planned, and brought the boat back to the left bank, past the big hole, and then into the standing waves in the center, hardly making a fuss.

"You see, you got to be thinking ahead, where you want the boat to be and watching for the key points to avoid."

107

"The trouble is, it all looks so different when you get on the river."

Argo lent some advice. "Try to focus on one or two reference rocks, like that obvious big one in the center left that marks the hole. Make yourself a spatial map in your head, and then place the boat upon it as you move down the river."

Eddie smiled. "Yeah, Argo, you're the one that should be talking about spatial maps in the head."

"Try to approach the problem logically," Argo said. "Think of the river as a spatial net, similar to the representation of gravity in the relativity theory, and the rocks as deformations in the net, like the planets forming after the Big Bang. The rocks have gravity and mass. Both create disturbances in the space-time continuum."

"Huh?" Eddie said.

"It works for me."

Actually, it began to work for Alex. He tried to imagine the river as a three-dimensional net, remembering his physics. Alex hopped in the raft and without a word immediately pulled into the current. Three strong pulls on the oars, and they were in the V-slick of Sulphur Slide, the water a fast curl of silky smooth clarity all the way to the first wave.

"Hey, remember the entry rock." Eddie shaded his eyes.

"I got it, on the right."

Alex hugged the entry rock, passed it smoothly, repositioned and pulled hard to the left and ferried across the river. Then it was a quick dip of the oars to straighten out the raft before the big drop, a clean run so far; another ferry to the right, moving through the rock garden, seeing the linear string, moving across the spatial map in his head. Alex watched for the big hole, passing just a foot to the right and then quickly straightening out, dancing down the standing waves to the long pool.

"Wow, you never touched a rock! Don't tell me it was Argo and that space-time deal."

'Okay, I won't tell you." Alex's confidence soared as he followed the sweep boat down river.

The two miles above Velvet Falls were a continuous band of whitewater, class two and class three. There was little room for error or experimentation. Alex rowed feverishly, avoiding rocks and most of the boulders, spinning the small raft around in circles, sometimes going backwards over a drop. He was still hitting rocks, but only glancing blows. His spatial-map system was working, but it was developing slowly. Sometimes Alex saw the line to follow only at the last possible second. He was trying to plan ahead, but the immediate present required most of his energy. A blip in the spatial net appeared when Alex looked down river and there was a line from bank to bank. The line wasn't moving but the river was, which seemed to crimp the netscape in his head somewhat. How could there be a line?

"Velvet Falls," said Eddie. "Right there by Spike Creek."

And then Alex saw the sweep boat. Impossibly so, it appeared that he was higher than Harmon was. He hadn't seen the sweep boat take the drop at the Falls, but there it was, and it must have taken a big drop.

"Left, left!" Eddie cried.

Alex saw the mist rising from the line and froze at the oars, just froze solid, the oar blades held up waiting for that next saving stroke that just wasn't coming. He saw it all happening in slow motion but couldn't seem to make his arms move. The river picked up speed as the raft entered a V-slick, and Alex was on the wrong side.

"Left, left!" This time Eddie was screaming.

Alex bit his lip so hard it bled, and this seemed to snap him out of his self-induced spell. He hit the oars hard, turned the raft and pulled left as hard as he could, as the line across the river turned into a shelf. Sitting in the oar boat he couldn't see the bottom of the falls, but he could hear the rumble and the roar. And then he saw it, six feet or more, straight across the river, water, frothing white, rushing over the shelf and into a hole. This was the hole, the grandmother of all holes, and the raft was heading for it dead center.

"Straighten it up!"

And then the spatial map in Alex's brain just seemed to go out. The gravity net he had imagined, a smooth-flowing ribbon, twisted in upon itself like a double helix and broke apart. He was two strokes too late as his left oar pulled through empty air and the raft hung suspended for the shortest of seconds on the brink of Velvet Falls.

Before he had time to think, Alex was underwater, holding his breath, his eyes wide open. He was in a green room, slowly turning revolutions under the water. He looked up and saw white and struggled, with strong swimming strokes, to try to break free of this green place. Slowly, too slowly, Alex pulled upward, following the streams of bubbles in the green water. He could see the undulating sun shining clearly and he pushed himself toward the light in frantic frog kicks. His movements were barely enough. Alex broke free of the reversal and the buoyancy in his life jacket shot him to the surface, bobbing like a cork.

109

He gasped air, and then gasped air again. Downstream, there was the raft, upside down, and Fast Eddie was holding onto the side.

Alex remembered Yellow-Glasses Bob's directions on how to swim in white water and rolled over on his back, kept his feet high in front of him, and started a strong backstroke to shore. Alex clawed at the riverbank, standing up just as Argo appeared in his kayak.

"You okay?"

"Yeah, fine," Alex coughed up some water and shivered as the cold water ran down off his head and hair. "How about Eddie?"

"Looks like he and Harmon got the boat on shore. Good thing you didn't have any gear."

Alex stroked his hair back with his hand. "Man, that happened fast."

"Bummer, I should have told you about the effect of a black hole on the net."

"That was a black hole, all right."

They all successfully regrouped about a half mile down river. Howie had chased down the two oars in his kayak, and other than being wet and cold, Alex and Eddie were uninjured; a few bumps and bruises, but nothing that required mending.

Eddie was visibly shaking and swaying side-to-side. "Did you guys see Alex? He was in the Green Room!"

This brought a hushed response from Argo, Harmon, and Howie. Alex vividly remembered the Green Room, and it was not a good memory. The water had been like a luminescent green box, and he was looking out at the light and the world beyond from the wrong side, all clearly defined through a wall of falling water.

"I wasn't there for long."

Howie broke the spell. "It's a good thing. From what I've heard, most don't make it out of the Green Room."

Alex found it a sobering thought. He felt somehow both changed and blessed, and if anything, had less fear because of it. He had survived his Middle Fork baptism, and now as a penitent on its shores, was ready to face it again.

Eddie took some time to approach him. "Alex, you've had quite a morning. Do you want me to take over the oars for a while?"

"No, I don't think so. I can do this."

Harmon slapped him between the shoulder blades. "Good man, right back on the horse."

110

Eddie said, "It's a nice day, we'll dry out in no time."
"Another lazy day in heaven," Alex said.
Back in the boats, they moved down river like ghosts.

18

"She was an Amazon.
Her whole life was spent riding at breakneck speed
Along the wilder shores of love."

Lesley Blanch

In Central Idaho, like much of rural, small-town America, the Fourth of July is still the biggest holiday of the year - a hold-over from the old days, a vestige of pioneer times, a summer holiday for gold miners, lumberjacks, and cowboys. In Elkhorn County, the place to be on the Fourth of July, bar none, was at the Mackay rodeo, on the banks of the Big Lost River.

Alex was looking forward to his first rodeo and was high strung and excited about nearly everything. Something seemed to have happened to him during his week on the river that heightened his sense of awareness. Everything he saw had a harder edge to it. The light was more intense and the shadow lines sharper drawn. Maybe it was the weather, he thought, as he readied for the rodeo. Strange thoughts had been zipping through his head all morning. As he looked over at the sun high above Grouse Point, it wasn't just the ordinary, everyday sun. It was fifteen million degrees of Celsius mass, with twelve times the density of lead, with four and a half trillion tons of hydrogen gas converted to helium every second, a regular thermonuclear miracle, that sun up there, and with only five billion more years left to shine. "I must be going nuts," he said right out loud, smiling.

As he drove the Chevy down Garden Creek, he passed the big rock ledge at the bridge and wondered how many eruptions of the Goldburg Volcanics it took to create the Idaho Batholith, how many basalt and lava flows from the Twin Peaks caldera it took to bury the landscape, how many eons of pressure and burial it took to metamorphose into the twisted, layered structure of rock, and finally, how many years upon years it took for glaciers and creeks and rivers to erode away the cap rock and expose that same big rock ledge next to Garden Creek that he drove past every day. He laughed at the mind-boggling time spans and said, "What the hell?" to no one in particular.

Alex pulled into the long-axis driveway at the Kowalski ranch, still mired in a space-time mood. When Angelica opened the door, he had that dreamy feeling again, that rare one when time seems to slow down and all the colors are clean and hard-edged, the light and shadows like looking at a painting. He looked at the girl like the first time again, admiring the tight black jeans, the oversized black hat tilted back, the red-blonde hairs at the base of her neck, the downy, almost invisible sideburns, wondering how many hairs per square inch, and was it the same texture as on her arms?

"What are you staring at?"

"You," was all Alex said.

"Well, quit it." She laughed. "You're making me nervous. You got that psycho-killer look."

"Sorry." Alex smiled a formal smile and tilted his head to the side like the models in the clothes catalogs. "How's this? More like the boy next door?"

Angie sighed. "More like the nut-case boy next door. That pencil-thin mustache just seals the deal."

Alex involuntarily covered his downy upper lip with his hand and tried to change the subject. "That's a pretty outfit you're wearing. Black shirt, pants, how come you always dress in black?"

"I don't always dress in black,"

"If you wear other colors, I've never seen you."

"I like black," she said, somewhat defensively. "It shows off my coloring well."

"Now that I can agree to. I can see that black is definitely your color."

Angie made a little "whiff" noise and said, "Brother, now I got real trouble. I got a whole closet full of clothes that you approve of."

"Well, you could trade them in for some long white dresses with flower patterns on them. Sort of corner the homespun pioneer look. You know, start baking biscuits and such."

"In your dreams, in your dreams."

"That's what I'm always working on, dreams of you."

"Ah, that's sweet, but I don't know how to bake biscuits. So don't plan on it." Angie seemed to turn serious. "Let's just take it like this for a while, all right?

Alex let the daydream go as Angie went back to looking out the window, and thoughts of geology again intruded. The Horse Heaven Hills, the White

Cloud Peaks, Basin and Range, again the odd facts and thoughts of geologic time flitted through Alex's brain. How many thrust-block fault earthquakes does it take to push a mountain range five thousand feet into the sky? How much glacial outwash and flash flooding does it take to fill a mountain valley with three thousand feet of sediment? And how, against all odds, was he here, in this truck, at this time, with this unusual specimen of a girl named Angie Kowalski? He wished Einstein was still around so he could ask him to calculate it out in an all-reaching mathematical equation and figure out how a date to the Mackay rodeo would fit into the fourth dimension of a curved and folded universe. "Relativity, my ass," Alex said out loud.

"What's up with you," Angie said. "You act like you're going to have a vision or something."

"A vision, yeah, that's what I need. I'm ready Lord, slap me with a vision. Right here on Double Spring Pass, hit me with your best shot."

"Alex, you're crazy. Ever since you got back from the river, it's like you're going sixty miles an hour all the time."

"Yeah, isn't it great? I like to think of it as one hundred kilometers per hour, sounds faster and more European." He reached over and grabbed her knee.

"Ahhhh! Stop that. You know I'm ticklish. Now watch the road."

"You bet I'll watch the road, clear down through the crustal plate, the miles of mantle, all the way to the iron-nickel Earth's core."

"Again with the geology. What, did you read a book again? What kind of kick are you on?"

"I don't know, but I like it. Care to join me?"

"I don't know, you sound a little dangerous, or maybe even a little high. You been smokin' that evil weed?"

"Just high on life, that's all. You know Kloyd says he can always tell if someone is smokin' dope. All you have to do is look at the 'peoples' in their eyes."

She looked him square in the eyes, and her gaze lingered. "I think your 'peoples' look just fine. The trouble must be somewhere behind those eyes a few inches."

Alex smiled back. "It doesn't matter, it's nothing but quantum mechanics anyhow."

"Okay, okay, I get that one. But what's with your preoccupation with physics and geology all the time? After all, it's only rocks."

"But it's not just rocks. It's about history happening right in front of us.

114

I mean the Lost River Range here is mostly limestone, sediments from an ancient sea, and now they're ten thousand feet above sea level."

"Well, I guess it's interesting if you don't have anything else to think about, but a process that takes like a hundred million years to get going isn't going to play too well on the big screen. Like really, what's the point? Mud gets washed down from the mountains to the sea, slowly gets turned into stone, and then even more slowly, rises up again to make mountains. There's surely a nice metaphor there if you look hard enough, but all this faith and fervor about something you can't see happening seems too much like religion to me."

"No, no, not at all. Just think about all the giant earthquakes, the massive landslides, the floods. It's great drama."

"Maybe if you like waiting ten thousand years between episodes."

"That's just the point. Thousands of years to raise up this mountain range a few inches. What do you think of that?"

Angie acted out an exaggerated sense of surprise, held her hands to the side of her face and opened her mouth wide. "And to think, I just missed it by a few thousand years."

"You never know. It could happen tomorrow, some huge natural catastrophe or something."

"It's just that there's a lot of boredom associated with rocks. And now you're starting to sound like your buddy Argo."

"Okay, okay, point taken. No more rock talk," Alex laughed. "So what do you want to talk about?"

"You, tell me all about yourself. Like, how come you always wear that funny flattie hat?"

"My driving hat?"

"Yeah, and those goofy round sunglasses that you hang around your neck. Fair is fair now. You started it you know."

"My glacier glasses? What's funny about them?"

"Just about everything."

"Ah, come on now, just because of that crack I made about you wearing black?"

"Now don't try to change the subject. We're talking about you now."

"Me?"

"Yeah, you never talk much about yourself. Which is different from the other guys I've known. You're like this big mystery man or something."

"Mystery man, me? You must be kidding?"

"You're just dripping with mystery, almost shrouded in it."

"No, no. Maybe there's just not much 'me' to talk about."

"I don't believe that."

"Like what would you like to know?"

"Okay, like what's your plan? What are you really doing here?"

"My plan?" Alex clenched his teeth together in his best Mexican bandit impression. "I don't need no stinkin' plan."

"Come on, you're making this hard."

"Hard on who? I'm the one under the magnifying glass here."

"I just want know more about you is all."

"Okay, okay, like what?"

"Will you really answer?"

"Sure, why not?"

Angie slid around on the truck seat, coming back to the same exact position. "Why are you so concerned about your job at the Forest Service? You seem really nervous about it."

"Well, yeah, I am. I just don't want to screw up. I'm on this probationary period, you know. I can be let go for any old reason."

"And why do you think you might screw up? This probation thing looks like an easy ride. It's a government job after all."

"I don't know, I guess. I seem to be able to do the hard stuff fine. It's the easy things that come hard for me."

"What kind of things?"

Alex almost told her about how many times he screwed things up by not acting in time, not moving when he should, not saying the right thing in time, even though the words were on his lips. "I, I don't know, all kinds of stuff. I guess I'm just a work in progress."

Angie looked away for a moment, out the truck window at the fence posts flying by in vertigo, a flock of birds all wheeling and whirling in time like one organism, turned and said, "But aren't we all?"

But not like me. Not like me, Alex was thinking. But he didn't say it.

The little town of Mackay was packed with rodeo revelers. Straw hats, pointed boots, overlarge belt buckles and boot-cut jeans were the uniform of the day. Except for Alex, of course, who was still running on Eastern Standard time. His deck moccasins, flattie hat, baggy short pants, glacier sunglasses, the kind with the side eyecups and string, sealed his reputation as someone from far away and without a clue.

116

Alex held Angelica's hand and like a lightning rod, little electric shocks ran up his arm and down his right leg, completing the circuit. The stands were already crowded, but Alex and Angie found a spot right up near the top of the grandstand. Alex had a good overview of both the rodeo and of Mount McCaleb and several more peaks to the south all the way to the Pass Creek Canyon.

Angie and Alex got settled just in time for the grand entry and the flying of the colors in the rodeo parade. There was a roar from the crowd as the rodeo queen and her court carried the American flag, the Idaho flag, and a series of colored banners in a slow canter around the arena and then carefully lined up in the center. Introductions were made in a tinny voice over the loudspeaker: the rodeo queen, a local girl decked out all in pink, her entourage, the rodeo committee. There was applause for all. Then the national anthem, everyone standing, all hats off and held over the heart, all eyes on the flag.

After some whoops and yells, there were introductions by the rodeo announcer, a one-way banter with the rodeo clowns in which the announcer replayed the clowns' lines. The audience enjoyed this tomfoolery, aided by the many trips to the beer tent.

The first event was steer wrestling and a local boy from Arco brought down the first scrawny steer in six seconds flat, a good time for a small-venue rodeo. Most of the steer wrestlers took longer or were penalized ten seconds when their horses broke the string at the start before the steer cleared the chute. Some even missed the steer's horns and slid over the animal and rolled into the dirt. A few never even left the saddle, unable to line up on the animal before they ran out of arena. In the end, nobody came close to the six seconds and the big kid from Arco was top hand at bull dogging for the day.

Alex liked the layout of the rodeo grounds and its setting in the willows and cottonwoods at the edge of town. Whenever there was a break in the action, he found his gaze going back to Mount McCaleb, stovepipe-topped, towering over town. A big glut of snow sat in the basin, the fringe of whitebark pine at timberline looking like a haircut, the bare rock spine curving into Lower Cedar Creek like a snake. He decided then and there to start climbing some of these mountains.

Most of all, he liked sitting next to Angie. He found he couldn't seem to get close enough. He draped his arms over the top rail of the grandstand and snuggled into her side.

Alex was also busy people-watching. There were some interesting types sprinkled in the grandstand, the kind you sort of turn your head and wonder

117

about. Some were obviously serious rodeo fans and were getting pretty liquored up on beer and whatever they brought in with them in hidden flasks and bottles. It was definitely high-test, whatever it was. There seemed to be a direct correlation between the excitement of the crowd and the number of paper and plastic cups that were being passed around.

After the calf roping it was time for team roping, an old skill from the real cowboy era. One man on horseback ropes the head, preferably the horns, of a steer, and the trailer cowboy ropes the hind legs, rendering the animal immovable. This was probably a great skill back in the open-range days, but it was not used much any more in an age of squeeze chutes and portable corrals. Half the printed program was filled with the names of team ropers. It seems that every local kid and his buddy wanted to give it a try and get into the rodeo.

Alex started to get thirsty. Others shared his opinion, as evidenced by an outpouring of spectators from the stands to the beer tent as soon as the black Dodge truck drove into the arena with the yellow racing barrels.

Girls in cowboy hats and plaster-tight jeans sat on muscular quarter horses and raced around the three barrels set in a triangle, cutting so close as to almost touch each barrel in an explosion of dirt and dust. From the far barrel at the edge of the arena it was a full-ass gallop back across to the timekeeper. Each girl had slightly different flair as she slapped the quirt or leaned up in the stirrups and almost hugged the neck of her horse on the last run to the finish. Plenty of racers were penalized for knocking over one of the barrels. Except for the penalty times, no more than two seconds separated the current leader, a small cowgirl from the Pahsimeroi, and the far end of the pack.

The last barrel racer was a friend of Angie's, a slight, brown-haired girl named Arlis. She was riding a short-legged buckskin named Peaches.

Angie nudged Alex in the ribs with her elbow. "You watch this girl ride."

Off the mark, Arlis and Peaches flew at the first barrel. Peaches dug a circle around the barrel and the horse lunged toward the second. The horse broke cleanly around the second barrel, digging in for the third, almost laying on top of it but not touching. Arlis turned Peaches and hightailed it home, breaking the radar beam at seventeen point five seven seconds and winning the event by one quarter of a second.

Angie was hooting and hollering and waving her hat in the air. "I knew Arlis could do it. That horse of hers is so quick around the barrels. Did you see the way they cut that last barrel?"

118

"Yeah. I thought they were going to go over."

"No, that was just from Peaches diggin' in. What a horse!"

The two clowns started a show during the intermission driving around in a miniature jeep that kept shooting firecrackers out of the exhaust. Every time one of the clowns bent over to inspect the jeep, it backfired loudly and a firecracker rocket would come out at him, usually hitting him in the pants. Timeless humor, Alex thought, man getting hit in the ass when he bends over. The spectators that weren't either getting beer or getting rid of it loved the clown show and laughed like they'd just gotten off the farm.

Alex joined the beer brigade and got in line at the entrance to the beer tent. Even surrounded by a sea of cowboy hats, Alex was tall enough to see Angie sitting up in the grandstand. God, she's beautiful, he thought once again. How did he find this girl? Alex returned to his spot in the stands just in time for the clown grand finale, where the little firecracker-shooting jeep, in a cloud of red, white, and blue smoke, chased the rodeo clowns all around and eventually, right out of the arena.

"Oh, Alex, you'll like this. They've got a wild horse roundup this year."

"Are they real wild horses?"

"You bet. Right from Spar Canyon, part of the BLM roundup."

"I didn't think they did this kind of thing anymore."

"This is the real deal, just like in the old days, only now they do the wild-horse roundup with a helicopter. The rodeo string must have bought them."

"I thought you had to adopt them?"

"I think these are the ones nobody wanted."

This was an old time rodeo event, one not seen much nowadays. Probably due to the dearth of wild horses, Alex thought. The object of the event was for each team to rope, saddle, and have someone on the team ride the pony around the ring, all without getting killed. Ten teams of four assembled in the center of the arena. Each team had a roper, a rider, and a couple of beefy helpers.

"Hey," Alex said, surprised. "That's Big Stanley and the Gold Dust Twins out there."

"Yeah, it is."

"Who's the little guy with them?"

"I think that's Charley and Darrel's cousin, Leroy, lives out by Patterson in the Pahsimeroi."

"More Rs and Ls."

"What's that?"

119

Alex thought that this wasn't a good time to explain the theory and said, "Nothing."

With a grand introduction by the announcer and a cheer from the crowd, the green gate was thrown open and a dozen small, wild-eyed horses were chased into the arena. The horses certainly looked wild, Alex thought, with their long manes and tails reaching to the ground. Most of them kept their Roman noses up, searching for scent or perhaps a way out of this place. The group of horses stuck tightly together as the ropers converged with gentle talk and a stealthy stalk, ropes twirling and ready to fly.

The action began, hot and heavy, with several horses roped and fighting. Three men hung on the rope, the fourth quartering closer with a saddle in hand. One horse stood on his hind legs, pawing the air with its hooves. Another was held tight but kicked out each time the fellow with the saddle crept closer. It was bedlam out there. People were getting kicked, bitten, and hit with hooves; falling down, rolling out of the way, and getting right back up again. The horses ran and they fought when they were roped. Some broke free and ran around the arena trailing a rope or two. One team managed to get a saddle on, but their rider was thrown in the dirt almost before he sat in the saddle.

Alex turned and saw Big Stanley in the corner of the arena. Charley and Darrel were on the rope, and Big Stan had his hand on the horse's neck and seemed to be talking to the animal. The horse, a small pinto, was frozen with fear, his ears back, leaning back on the rope so hard he was almost sitting on his haunches. While Big Stanley continued his one-way conversation, the horse appeared to be letting young Leroy slip on the saddle and tighten the cinch. Quick like a bunny, Leroy jumped up on the horse, still held on the rope by the Gold Dust Twins and Big Stanley's hand and his power of persuasion. Big Stan slipped the lariat over the horse's head and Leroy clamped down both hands on the saddle horn. The horse stood for a second as Big Stan quickly sidestepped out of the way, and then the little animal launched into a bucking, running race around the arena. The crowd cheered as Leroy stuck tight in the saddle, the horse running and kicking and everyone else scattering for the fences. Leroy got the flag, held on for a few more seconds, and then sort of jumped off just as the horse bucked, sailing clear of the saddle, and landed like a gymnast, feet together and arms raised.

"Bloody hell, they won!" Alex was cheering.

Angie put her little fingers in the corners of her mouth and let out a piercing whistle that froze Alex in place.

120

"How do you do that so loud?"

"It's easy. You just put your fingers to your lips and blow."

Alex lost himself to thoughts and possibilities and had to shake his head to get himself out of the self-induced daze. "Christ, what could top this?"

"There's still the bull riding."

But first there were the bucking horses. The arena was cleared and the first string of bucking horses was lined up in the chutes for the bareback-riding competition. Angie told Alex that a few of these broncs started out as wild horses, but most of them were actually spoiled and ignored pets that developed a talent that kept them from being broke to saddle. All of the horses were truck and pasture tame. Looking at them in the corral, Alex thought one would never suspect they were rodeo stock. Rodeo was their life now, and all the horses were trained from chute to gate, knowing what they had to do. These horses came out of the chute bucking hard, getting some air, not frenzied with fear and running like their wild cousins.

"Everyone loves the buckin' horses and the bull riding," Angie said.

Alex noticed that almost all of the bronc riders were small, wiry guys. Probably easier to keep their balance, he thought

Each of the six bucking chutes had an advertisement on the front: Carnation Feeds, Lost River Ranch Supply, Wrangler Jeans, Dodge trucks, Lenore's Town and Country and Lost River Trail Riders, hung proudly in print.

The bucking stock was pretty good, and not many cowboys made the eight-second ride without getting bucked off. There were some elegant spirals and somersaults as the local boys flew off into the dirt.

Between the bareback and the saddle-bronc competition, there was a bit of a sideshow going on several rows in front of Angie and Alex. A little old man had dropped his broken-down black hat under the grandstand. For some reason, probably related to alcohol, the old boy seemed to think he could reach down and pick it up. The hat was about a good four and a half feet down on the ground. Accompanied by the loud taunts of his wife, the man managed to roll over and then fall down, flat on his back, under the grandstand.

"Oh that Otto, did you see him? The best show at the rodeo!" The old lady roared when the old man fell.

Old Otto was reunited with his beloved hat, but for a second strange reason felt that he could climb back up into the stands instead of simply walking around.

"Look at that crazy Otto. Thinkin' he can climb back up here!"

121

Possibly because of his wife's tormenting laughter, no one moved a muscle to try to help the old cowboy back up into the stands. It was as if it was really part of the rodeo pageant, and somehow Otto would have to figure this one out for himself. Otto tried valiantly, and with a steady and slow progression, had managed to get one leg up in the grandstand and one leg down; and now he was looking confused.

"That Otto, he's killing me!" the old gal went on, "Best part of the rodeo."

Now, each time Otto tried and failed and fell back down under the grandstand, a few more people joined the old lady in laughter. About the third time old Otto rolled over, hat in hand, even Alex started to laugh. Angie hit him in the arm, and he immediately stopped, looking most serious but all the while, watching Otto's progress. By about the fifth time Otto rolled onto his side on the grass under the stands, even Angie was laughing.

"Otto, Otto, stop, you're killing me! Best show in the whole damned rodeo."

With a grunt of cowboy pride, Otto gave a mighty heave and got both feet and both cowboy boots hooked on the grandstand plank, and rolled up and over and into history. Stoically standing up, black hat back on his head, Otto seemed somewhat pleased at the rousing ovation of "Ot-to, Ot-to, Ot-to," coming from the whole southwest side of the grandstand He raised his arms above his head as if he had just won the main event.

His wife still laughed, "Best show in the rodeo, by God."

The saddle-bronc riders were ready by the time Otto sat back down. Once again there were spectacular throws and falls, but not as many as in the bareback bronc competition. Quite a few riders made the time. A local boy from Mackay stuck the required eight seconds and almost won the competition, but he was upstaged by the last rider, a kid from Mountain Home.

Alex was marveling at the skill of the pickup riders, able to maneuver on either side of a bucking, kicking horse and quickly get that rider to safety, holding steady in the saddle when the bronc rider jumped for it and grabbed the pickup rider, as the bucking horse pulled away, still kicking. When done well, it was art, he thought. The riders made it look effortless.

The crowd was tuned to the maximum by the time the bulls were pushed into the bucking chutes. They were big, ugly brutes with overdeveloped necks and shoulders, sawed off horns and svelte hindquarters with enormous scrotums and balls. These bulls had little in common with the average beef bull you see on the range or in pasture. Selectively bred, some with Brahma bloodlines mixed with the common Hereford and Angus beef breeds, some with Santa Gertudis and Limousin and Charolais mixes, the bulls were a Technicolor bunch. They were built to spin, leap, and otherwise throw themselves around as violently as possible, and with a poor attitude to go with it. As soon as that chute opened, they were going to get busy.

Alex watched the spectacle unfold. "These guys are nuts," he said, and he believed it. "This is how it must have been at the Roman coliseums."

By the mid-way point in the bull-riding competition, every rider had been thrown before the eight-second time requirement. The two rodeo clowns had been very busy, right there every time a cowboy hit the dirt, avoiding disaster by distracting the bull while the cowboy rolled clear, got to his feet and sprinted for the chutes and safety on the steel rail pipes.

One of the rodeo clowns was superbly athletic, taunting the bull and getting it to charge right at him. Often the clown turned and leaped high into the air just as the bull reached to hook him with his horns.

It all seemed to work out with no blood in the sand and no ambulance runs. The crowd loved it when the clowns did the barrel trick with one of the bulls, a massive horned beast. One of the clowns sat in the barrel, the other taunted the animal. The bull finally went for the guy in the barrel, who popped down inside like a squirrel while the bull sent clown and barrel spinning across the arena.

Then it was down to the last bull rider, a young, pimply-faced cowboy from the Little Lost River Valley. He responded to the challenge and rode High Pockets, a whitish, Charolais-looking animal, through spin after spin to stick for the whole eight seconds.

With the last bull rider, the last cheer and the parting, "God bless America," from the announcer, the Mackay rodeo was over for this year.

Fireworks zipped into the early evening sky as Alex and Angie and the rest of the crowd headed for their trucks.

"Angie, do you want to stay for the fireworks?" he asked. "There's supposed to be a street dance after the rodeo."

"All right, but let's get something to eat first."

Angelica and Alex had a long wait for their Idaho beef cheeseburgers. It was already dark by the time they finished, and the stars were out. A large crowd mingled on Main Street. Two cowboys were down on the asphalt scuffling and wrestling.

"Looks like there's trouble, right here in River City," Alex said.

"Alex, you're not going to do the Music Man routine again, are you?"

"No, of course not, at least not out loud."

The main street of Mackay was closed down for a whole block in front of the two bars. There was a band from Sun Valley. They seemed to do quite a bit of rock and roll mixed in with the cowboy swing music. Sticking to his two-drink driving rule, Alex was probably the most sober male adult in town, he thought. Asphalt was a poor surface for serious dancing, but no one seemed to mind and the street was crammed with dancers.

Even under the dim streetlights, Alex could see the stars, the Big Dipper hanging on a string above the Lost River Range, pointing to the North Star.

The band was playing an old song called "Sister Golden Hair." Alex was quietly singing along, except he kept changing the words to "Sister Copper Hair." If Angie heard it, she didn't show it.

"God, you're beautiful," Alex said it right out loud, without even thinking.

Angie matter-of-fact said, "Thank you. You're not bad looking yourself, for an easterner of course."

Alex was thunderstruck by the comment. Other than his mother, no girl or woman had ever given him a compliment on his appearance. He felt so thankful to Angie that he couldn't suppress a silly giggle. He felt he had to say something and finally came up with, "Just think how much more handsome I would of been if I would have been born right here in Elkhorn County."

Angie snorted a laugh. "Yeah, you'd of known how to rope and ride, just like a real cowboy."

"Lucky me, then." He grabbed Angie around the waist, pulling her toward him, and she didn't resist. "I get the chance to learn it all new like."

"We'll see how far you get." She was acting coy now. "Come on. Let's go show these Mackay cowboys how to dance."

Angie and Alex swung into a two-step in time with the music. The half moon was just beginning to rise over the White Knob Mountains to the south, and Alex was intoxicated holding Angie in his arms. He could feel her small breasts against his chest when she moved with him side to side. He was close enough to taste her breath, sweet and food-like. The strange mood that had accompanied him all day suddenly crystallized into a vision. He was thinking about the Music Man again, the old movie version, the part where the barbershop quartet had just learned to sing together, or as Professor Harold Hill had taught

124

them, sustained talking. They were doing some song that he could never seem to remember the right words to but it was about falling in love, and kept repeating something about sin and sincere. It was more of a postcard memory, hard and clear, of these four guys in old-time striped suits and flat-rimmed straw hats, posed like in a picture, all lined up and looking out at the camera. The bottle rockets go off, the sky behind them is blazing, and arms outstretched, they sing, "Fall-ing-in-Love," in perfect four-part harmony.

And it was just like that, except in Mackay, Idaho, in the middle of the street dance, everyone stopped to stare at the firework rockets streaming off the hill above town, the band still playing "Sister Golden Hair." Alex looked up and saw the star clusters exploding in red, white, and blue, looked down and saw the smile on Angelica Kowalski's face, her eyes, almost blue-black in the gloaming, framed by straight-cut bangs of auburn hair; the small bump on the bridge of her nose in shadow; her lips quivering with the sound of the exploding fireworks.

In that brief nanosecond of time, another singularity exploded, another universe was born. White-hot basic elements, helium and hydrogen, evolved into heavy metals in the early seconds of this parallel universe, expanding beyond comprehension. Stars and galaxies were born from a swirling mass of cosmic gasses. From that stardust, a red-haired girl emerged on magic wings made of hopes and dreams. And Alex Kynwulf fell in love, so fast and so hard that he almost passed out.

19

*"There may be great fire in our soul,
yet no one ever comes to warm himself at it,
and the passers-by see only a wisp of smoke."*
Vincent Van Gogh

The summer high-pressure system that is characteristic of the intermountain west set up residence right over central Idaho. The color green began to leech out of the landscape. Bunch grasses turned brown, and the sagebrush took on a tone of dusty olive brown that seemed to flow from the bedrock. Soon the only green color in the valley came from either irrigated hay fields or from the cottonwoods and willows along the river and stream bottoms. All else slowly turned to brown. And as the land browned, it began to dry out. This was the deep drying of cracked soil, falling water tables, rock-hard earth, and dusty dirt roads, where in the morning the dust from a lone pickup moving across Antelope Flats created a plume of brown that hung in the air like a jet contrail come to earth. It was the lizard-like, snake shade, bleached cow-bone dryness of high-altitude desert land. It hadn't rained for a month and it felt like it wasn't going to rain for another.

Buck Twiddle sensed the season and the dryness that came with it like a human hydrograph. Intuitively he felt the lowering of the streams, the drying of the heavy fuels. The ingrained memory of twenty summers of drought and fire worked within him without conscious thought. Tasting smoke where there was none, watching fire storms rise in cumulus clouds of darkness and lightning in his mind's eye, anticipating the inevitable and wondering if this was the year it would come to pass. Buck became immersed in his fire-planning duties, going over all the details. He was a slave to his pager, cell phone, and the daily fire weather forecast. He walked over to the dispatch office to check the fire status reports at least three times a day.

"Hi, B-B-B-Buck," Augie Tug, the long-time forest dispatcher said. "W-w-w-w-what's the good word?"

126

"Don't have a clue. Just thought I'd look over the situation report. See what's happening in the rest of the Great Basin."

"They b-b-broke a b-big fire over on the Targhee."

"Man-caused?"

"Dry lightning."

"They callin' for forest crews yet?"

"N-n-n-not yet. They got three h-hotshot crews on it and a b-b-b-big airshow."

"What's the fire weather look like?"

"M-m-m-more of the same. Hot and dry. Talking about a r-r-r-r-red flag warning for the weekend. Might get some d-dry lightning."

"Clum Dummit, I think it's time to pre-position some firefighters at Indian Creek for initial attack, at least for the weekend, see if this red flag warning pans out."

"How many you want B-B-Buck?"

"Right now, probably two squads. If it gets nasty we'll push the helicopter over to Indian Creek, just to get it over the divide."

"I'll work on the flight orders."

"Thanks, Augie. I'll line up some District folks for you." Buck suppressed a sly smile as he left dispatch and headed back to the office.

Halfway in the door, "Kynwulf, I need you and every swingin' dick on the District." Buck stopped in mid-stride, noticing Teffonie standing in the hall. "Sorry Teffonie, no offense."

Teffonie just smiled at him. "None taken."

Buck continued on. "As I was sayin', Kynwulf, I need every swingin' dick on the District this weekend, so get your fuckin' fire pack ready."

Alex thought, there goes my date with Angie.

As if reading Alex's mind, Buck said, "Sorry if you had plans. Life is just a bitch and then you die." He laughed; and even Buck's laugh was authoritative.

"Well, I did have plans."

"You know, I can only think of four words of consolation." Buck smiled. "And that's just: Too Bad For You." Buck then spelled it out, "That just T - O - O bad for Y - O - U." Buck laughed that happy laugh he had whenever he was busy busting balls. "Actually, I need you and you need the fire experience. I'm going to pre-position some forces to go into Indian Creek in case we get a fire bust back in the Middle Fork." Buck took the small notebook

127

he always carried, the one with Smokey Bear on the cover, out of his shirt pocket. "What do you weigh??"

"About one ninety five."

"With fire pack, boots, probably two fifty. I'll need to pair you with a little fellow." Buck bent over the notebook, pencil in hand. "You'll be going in on a flight with Argo."

"That's fine. When?"

"Planning for mid-day Friday, earlier if we start getting any build up. Bring you back probably Monday or Tuesday, depending on fire weather; could be longer." Buck could tell that Alex felt the fire excitement, saw it in his eyes. The kid hadn't been on a fire yet.

"Now don't get too excited. With a little luck, you'll get to initial attack a fire or two. If not, I'm going to have a list of projects for you and the crew at Indian Creek to keep you busy."

"I imagine you will."

"Damn straight I will," Buck said as he stopped standing still and resumed his normal pacing, walking out of the office and onto the compound.

On Friday morning Alex came to work wearing his fire clothes: yellow Nomex shirt and green Nomex pants, the kind with all the pockets; hard hat; leather gloves that hung on a carabineer on his belt; radio and web gear. He was scheduled for a helicopter flight to Indian Creek at ten hundred hours.

As with any helicopter show, this one was running late; and at noon, Alex, Argo, Howie and Teffonie, were eating lunch on the fire warehouse's loading dock, watching the cumulus clouds building up into young thunder heads. The red-flag warning had been extended through Sunday. Dry lightning and potential high winds were likely.

The fire situation in eastern Idaho had become more serious with a second big fire on the Targhee National Forest near the southwestern corner of Yellowstone National Park. It was a high priority fire for the Forest Service and all efforts were being made to keep the fire from spreading into the park. It was going to become more difficult to get fire resources if the Sleeping Deer District had a fire bust. Virtually everybody that was red-carded for firefighting on the District was on stand-by. Alex was with a group of six - Harmon and Yellow-Glasses Bob had been added - all to be sent to Indian Creek Guard Station. Each person on the squad was paired with another to match weights for the helicopter. Because they were working near the maximum working altitude, helicopter weight was always an issue, and Buck was constantly working on the manifests to balance it out. Each person was also matched with someone with fire experience. For this exercise Alex had been matched with Argo, Teffonie with Harmon, and Howie with Yellow-Glasses Bob. It was almost thirteen hundred when finally the sound of the helicopter was heard. Alex watched the ship hover and land on the helispot in the middle of the compound. Alex and Argo went out with the first load and met the contract helicopter pilot, Henry Skaggs, still alive and flying after innumerable fire seasons in central Idaho. Henry talked incessantly, whether on the ground or in the air. As they prepared to lift off, Henry was talking to dispatch on the radio about how he had found a ram's skull embedded in an old whitebark pine and was planning on going back to cut it down, and put it in his house.

"I tell you, Augie. This sheep skull is a totem, a magic thing, full of power."

Over the earphones, Alex could hear dispatch repeating, "Helicopter four-three-zero, bound for Indian Creek, with four souls on board."

Alex wondered why Augie never seemed to stutter on the radio. He also began to worry about the "four souls" on board part. The plan to cut down the totem tree was sort of unnerving, kind of bad karma, he thought, and hoped that his soul would stay firmly attached to his body.

The jet ranger came to life and lifted off easily. Henry put the ship on its side and Alex had a good view of the compound as they flew over. He even caught a glimpse of Buck at the fire warehouse. Round Valley and Goldburg faded away, awash in rotor noise, and in a few minutes at one hundred and forty miles per hour the ship approached the Twin Peaks saddle and the gateway to the Middle Fork.

Henry's voice crackled on the radio, "There's a cool place, right down there, in the creek bottom, Shower Bath hot springs. The hot water comes right out of the hill and over a rock ledge, just like a natural shower."

"Yeah, I've heard about it," Alex said softly into the radio mike on his helmet. "Sort of like Sunflower Flat, I guess."

"But this one is all natural, nobody built it. Captain Bernard found the Shower Bath when he was chasing the Sheepeater Indians back in the Sheepeater War of the 1870s."

"Yeah, I've heard that."

Henry talked right over him. "Never caught the Sheepeaters but had a good bath, ha!"

Alex was beginning to learn the landscape. He enjoyed studying the

129

topographic maps of the wilderness and was able to follow the route they were flying pretty much from memory. Henry took a slightly different route. From Warm Creek, he crossed over Loon Creek, well above Falconberry, and flew over the ridge to Little Loon Creek and down the drainage. Alex could see a small cabin at the bottom of Little Loon, next to a grove of cottonwoods and determined it must be the Fur Farm, a depression-era fox-raising operation that didn't pan out. Henry flew right down Little Loon, all the way to the Middle Fork, then followed the river south past Little Creek. It wasn't long before they were on the ground on the helispot at Indian Creek, just off the runway and right in front of the log cabin guard station. Henry kept the helicopter going as the helitack foreman escorted Alex and Argo, heads bowed down low, out of the range of the spinning blades and then returned for their tools and fire packs. Alex watched Henry through the clear bubble of the jet ranger, still talking to someone on the radio, and a minute later watched the helicopter, with two souls on board, pull up and away for another shuttle trip. The thwack! thwack! thwack! of the rotor blades faded quickly as the ship pulled up and flew down river.

"Hey Alex," Argo said. "I'll introduce you to Eli."

Eli had been at the Indian Creek Guard Station for over thirty years. A small man, barely five feet tall and one hundred pounds, Eli was a loner. Alex had heard his voice occasionally on the radio but had not yet met the man.

Argo and Alex stashed their fire packs and lined up their tools next to the post and rail fence, ready to go out if called. Argo led Alex over to a small log house set amidst a grove of towering ponderosa pines.

Eli hobbled out on the porch to meet them. Alex saw, even at a distance, the lines of age in Eli's face, lines creased deeply into forehead and around his eyes, disappearing into a shock of snow white hair.

"Good to see you, Argo. Who's your buddy?" Eli said in a surprisingly strong voice.

"Eli, this is Alex Kynwulf, the new recreation forester."

"Kynwulf? Yeah, I heard about you. From back east somewhere."

"Pennsylvania. Good to meet you, Eli." Alex shook his hand and noticed the coolness.

"So how have you been?" Argo asked Eli.

"Not too good, not too good," Eli repeated in a downward tone of his voice. "I got pneumonia last winter. Never thought I'd see green grass again."

"Man, I never even heard that you were sick. Are you okay now?"

130

"I don't know. I don't know." There was the same slipping tone in his voice. "That pneumonia chilled me clean down to the bone. I just can't seem to get warm any more. It's got a hold of me, I fear."

"Well, Buck gave us a list of things to do for you while we're on fire standby, including cutting and splitting firewood for you. That'll help keep you warm."

"That's fine." Eli had a far-away look in his eye, like he was looking over a vast divide, unsure of where he was. "Never thought I'd see green grass again."

Two more helicopter flights and all were safely offloaded at Indian Creek. They kept their fire packs ready at the helispot and, except for Teffonie, took off their yellow Nomex shirts and went to work for the afternoon cutting and splitting wood. By supper they had at least two cords of pine in Eli's woodshed, with at least a rick split small for the wood cook stove.

After supper the crew moved outside and sat on the edge of the airstrip watching Harmon and Yellow-Glasses Bob pitch horseshoes in the quiet evening light. Bob was inordinately skilled at throwing horseshoes, so much so that after he quickly dispatched Harmon and Howie no one else wanted to play him. Finally Alex agreed to give it a try and was soundly embarrassed by the ruthless efficiency of Bob's horseshoe skills.

A peal of far-away thunder rolled across the canyon. "That's the sound of the cash register," Harmon said. "Come on baby, it's all overtime now."

Alex stood, arms akimbo, a horseshoe in each hand, watching Bob adjust his Yellow-Glasses and throw a second ringer over his first throw. Disgusted with the game, Alex looked down river and saw a dark cloud rearing over Pungo Creek, mammary-like on the bottom with a white anvil head of cold air. Thunder, still far away, sounded a low, continuous peal.

"Looks like Norton Ridge is getting hammered," Harmon said. "I've been on initial attack on a couple of fires up there. It's almost like that mountain attracts electricity."

"Were they big fires?" Teffonie asked anxiously.

"Not really, there isn't much up there but rocks and snags. Actually, just thinking about it, they were really pretty good fires, just an acre or two; made some good hazard pay and didn't have to work too hard."

"Harmon, that doesn't sound like you," Argo said. "Where is the hyperbole? Where are the slim facts stretched so thin that they're almost unrecognizable?"

131

"Fuck hyperbole," Harmon shot back. "If I said it wasn't much of a fire, it wasn't much of a fire."

"This is definitely out of character for you, Harmon." Argo said. "Are you sure you're feeling all right?"

Just as the discussion was getting interesting, Eli came out on his porch waving his handkerchief like a flag. "Argo, Argo, get your crew ready. We just got a fire called in on Greyhound. The ship will be here in ten minutes."

Almost as soon as Eli had told them, dispatch came on the radio and Argo took the information on the fire. "It sounds like it's just a small fire right now, but it's low on the ridge and Buck wants us to put it out."

There was a flurry of activity. A bolt of excitement shot through Alex, and he struggled not to show it outwardly. Nomex shirts went back on, along with hard hats and gloves. Canteens were filled, at least four per person. The plan was to move the firefighters to the lightning-strike fire below timberline, just off a side ridge of Greyhound Mountain. A helispot had already been determined; one that had been used on previous fires in the area; and it was less than a mile to the fire. With luck, the crew would walk the ridge and get to the fire before dark.

Chasing the sunset, the sound of the jet ranger came over the ridge and soon Henry was on the ground. It was a quick reverse order of events from landing. The helitack foreman ferried tools into the helicopter, then came back, leading Alex and Argo, heads down, across the front of the ship in full view of the pilot, helping them into the ship and securing their seatbelts. Alex felt a momentary thrill as the aircraft left the helispot then banked and reared toward blue sky, gaining altitude.

Henry was less talkative and more businesslike on this flight, circling the helispot twice to better assess the site, a flat notch above timberline on a fir-covered ridge. Hovering above the helispot, Alex could see the fire now. It was far down the ridge, a thin white column trying to gain that foothold that would enable it to live and run. The fire wanted to back down into the canyon bottom so it could run up the other side.

In less than thirty minutes, all six firefighters had been delivered. The helitack foreman unloaded three plastic cubitainers of water and an extra case of MREs (meals, ready to eat). With a quick look at the darkening sky, Henry lifted off, flashing Alex a peace sign as he powered the helicopter off the ridge.

Alex watched the helicopter disappear, the noise growing fainter and fainter, and then it was gone into the quiet dusk. He turned to Argo. "Okay,

132

you're crew boss, what's the word?"

Argo seemed somewhat stunned for a moment, and clearing his throat, said, "First we'll hike to where we can see the fire better and we'll do a size-up before it gets dark."

They picked up and shouldered their heavy fire packs and, tools in hand, started picking their way down the ridge. There were a few small whitebark pine among larger dead snags from previous fires. They reached a position where the fire was directly beneath them. The fire appeared to cover several acres in strips of flame and black earth. Some of the subalpine fir was actively burning, and several individual trees were starting to torch. It was almost dark. There would be no retardant planes or water drops until morning.

"Okay everyone, drop your packs and let's talk about this one," Argo said without emotion. "It looks fairly straightforward. Harmon, Bob, it looks like we can sling a line right underneath this fire from this big rock on the ridge, all the way to that rock outcrop on the next drop of the ridge."

"Yeah, we can catch this baby," Harmon said.

To Alex is looked like a lot of fire, moving in all directions.

Argo seemed to notice his concern. "Alex, this flame length isn't much, just a foot or so. We can build hot line right next to the black in this rocky ground."

"Direct attack." Yellow-Glasses Bob sounded willing.

Argo continued, "We sling a good roll trench under this fire, work all night, we can have this thing contained by morning."

Alex nodded his head without conviction.

"Harmon, you take the lead with your Pulaski, just cut a scratch line. Teffonie, you follow and improve the line. Alex, you and Howie finish it up with your shovels. I want a good trench, down to mineral soil. We need to watch for and catch any rolling debris in the trench, so let's get it right up to the black. Bob, you bring the saw and I'll be your swamper and scout out a line." Argo looked for acceptance of his plan. "Okay, folks, what's the final word?"

Teffonie and Howie, in unison, verbalized the Forest Service firefighting mantra. "Fight fire aggressively, but plan for safety first."

"You got it, boys and girls. Safety is always first. Remember, nobody gets hurt. We've got several safety zones of rock and lots of black we can move into. The rock outcrops are obvious, but I will mark them with pink-and-white tape." Argo began to dig into his fire vest. "There isn't any wind, nor is there supposed to be. It's going to stay clear tonight and it will cool off, so this fire should really lay down. The way I see it, the key safety message for tonight is snags. Watch yourself, watch your buddy, and keep an eye on these trees. Some of the roots on these dead snags have probably been burned near clear through. They look solid, but they could come down any time, without any warning and without any wind. So keep a sharp eye out. Bob and I will be dropping a few trees. I'll be the lookout, but stay back from us. Everybody have a head lamp? Let's keep them on." Argo pulled his belt weather kit out of his fire pack. "Does everybody understand their assignment? Where the safety zones are? Alex, Teffonie, this is your first fire assignment, so don't be afraid to ask questions."

Teffonie said, "Don't worry, Argo, we won't be in awe of your leadership. If I don't know, I'll ask."

"Looks like a good plan," Alex said picking up his shovel.

As the first quarter moon rose over Shellrock Ridge, the crew began work in a macabre landscape of fire and smoke. The steady pace of Pulaski and shovel, of metal clanging on rock, somehow reminded Alex of the seven dwarves going to work in the mine, pounding rock in a musical union. Tonight there were only six, and all of them happy dwarves, even Yellow-Glasses Bob, as they formed a chain gang. Harmon went first, cutting the crusty dry sod with his Pulaski, creating a rudimentary fire line. Teffonie, her wide shoulders planted with each stroke of the Pulaski, struck deep into the rocky soil, turning a dark furrow. Alex followed with his shovel, building the trench, and Howie, right behind, scooped out the last of the organic material and dressed the roll trench down to mineral soil. The ground was rocky and their progress was slow, but the resultant fire line was clean and right on the black. There was the occasional roar of the chain saw as Bob dropped a small snag or cut some roots and limbs for the fire line. Alex could see the reflections of small fires dancing in Teffonie's eyes.

The work developed a symmetry of motion, contained in a conservation of energy and matching strength and finesse. They worked without breaks, following the edge of the fire along the small basin below the ridge. The moon cast a glowing light through the perspective-flattening smoke. Alex, head down, eyes on the fire line, was surprised that it suddenly was four o'clock in the morning. He hadn't really been tired until he looked at his watch. Argo and Bob were back with the others. "Okay, let's take a break," Argo suggested, and the sound of work stopped immediately.

Alex looked about and thought, what a strange and wonderful scene. Here we are, high on a nameless ridge, the moonlight on the river below, the trees too dark to see; six grimy firefighters, their faces and shirts black with soot matching the night, the smell of wood smoke, the fire itself, a living thing of orange-yellow coals and short flame that was described in arcs across the hillside.

They had enclosed the entire lower section of the fire, closing off the direction of spread that led to the heavy fuels below, the legions of dead and dying fir down in the basin. The fire was now approximately five acres in size, and they had traveled a good distance to contain that acreage, following the burned area of the fire along each of its many-fingered lobes, always working the hot line. Now they had a continuous fire line from rock outcrop to rock outcrop. Alex was trying to estimate how many chains of line they had built and only realized that he was sound asleep sitting up when Howie nudged him awake.

"Alex, wake up."

"Yeah, yeah, I'm awake." Alex was now cold and shivering in his sweat stained shirt, his mouth pasty with too-short sleep, a bit of a buzz in his head. He checked his watch. It was four thirty.

Howie told him, "It's always the worst just before dawn, that's when you're the sleepiest. When it comes daylight, you'll pop up."

Argo said, "Okay, let's complete the line around the top. It shouldn't take as long since it's a cleaner shot to the ridge, not much fuel. Maybe by late morning we can call it contained."

Alex was tired, bone tired. His excitement had waned with the fire, as it died down to red embers and smoke during the night. Alex saw that the sky to the northeast was getting bright and the stars were almost gone. He hadn't pulled an all-nighter for at least a year, and it took him awhile to shake off the tunnel-like feeling of sleep lost and not found.

His strength returned with the sunrise. The first rays of sunlight hitting Shellrock Mountain to the west made Alex audibly gasp with surprise. The fire line construction was progressively easier and the pace continually slowed. The smooth cadence that the crew possessed during the night had dissolved to a hackneyed staccato of chop and shovel, with many a long pause in between.

At eight o'clock Argo was on the radio to dispatch, reporting to Augie that the fire was ninety percent contained. Alex looked around at the completed fire line and thought it was one hundred percent contained, but evidently Argo knew better.

Argo saw and understood Alex's look, and said, "You never want to call a fire contained until you sit on it a while and you're certain that you've got it surrounded."

135

They spent the rest of the morning improving the line, mopping up some hot spots on the edge, then took a long lunch break before they began mopping up inside the line. The fire had quickly cooled as it ran out of fuel. Much of the afternoon was taken up with dropping two large whitebark pine snags that had fire in their tops. Argo and Bob were careful not to drop the trees over the line, or more importantly, put anyone in a dangerous position; so it took a long time to drop the snags successfully. Yellow-Glasses Bob took his time and laid both trees up slope and into the fire. The crew chopped the fire out of them.

The mop up went slowly, since they didn't have any water to cool down the hot spots until Henry flew in some bladder bags and water on an afternoon flight. They found a small spring down slope and took turns carrying water up slope. Alex liked the feel of the cool rubber bladder bag on this back and enjoyed the pistol grip spray nozzle. He worked with Howie all afternoon cooling down and chopping out hot spots inside the fire line. Buck had told Argo that he wanted the fire mopped up one hundred percent, since it was early in the season and there was just too much at risk, and too much fuel nearby, to take any chances. Just before dark, Argo called in to state the "Dirty Dog Fire" controlled. The fire was surreptitiously named after Greyhound Ridge. Alex liked the name "Dirty Dog." After a cold supper of MREs, Alex lay his sleeping bag on a plastic sheet in a lumpy swale of bear grass and fell asleep in moments, still thinking about the "Dirty Dog."

Six hours later, Alex shook, shivered, and dressed. The night had been cool and the fire cold by morning. After more MREs for breakfast, the crew cold-trailed the entire fire, palms to the ground, looking for and finding a few hot spots but not many. They worked the fire with water from end to end.

Henry flew in with a hot lunch at mid-day, right from the Y café: two large sandwiches, cookies, candy, a red delicious apple, and two tin containers of apple juice.

The plan now was to de-mobilize the fire and get the crew started back to Goldburg with the first helicopter flight at six o'clock. Alex was not surprised when he waited almost until dark for his flight out.

Alex went on six more fires in July and the first half of August. He was away from the office for one stretch of twenty-one straight days. All of the fires were lightning-caused and all were in the Middle Fork. One fire, the Little Elk Fire, high in some subalpine fir above Camas Creek, went on extended attack. Alex and the crew lost the fire in a wind event after it had been contained. The fire escaped into some thick subalpine fir and really started to run. Buck himself came in as Incident Commander. For two days it looked like they would have a project fire, but two 20-person crews and one medium helicopter with a bucket were finally able to control it.

Alex was beginning to feel he was earning his stripes in firefighting. Twice now he had gone out as squad boss trainee, and seemed to have a talent for it. When Alex did return to the office for one day, it was a changed place. All talk and thought was about fire. Big Stanley was stuck in the office all day, every day. His poor horse, Stain, stood in the corral, looking forlorn waiting for Big Stan to walk out of the office and load up.

Resources in Idaho were stretched thin. The drought indexes were looking bad and the big one, the Haines Index, was on high. Idaho was getting ready to burn in a big way.

Alex was on another fire, up on a high ridge above Sulphur Creek. He was squad boss now and was thinking that this one might be difficult to control, when he noticed the sky was full of mare's tails. He hadn't seen that many since spring and had gotten so used to a clear blue sky that any clouds at all seemed unusual. But these mare's tails, they were just streaming out of the north, and Alex thought it most odd. Late that night Alex felt the breeze shift to the north and noticed that the stars were gone and it seemed very dark, lamp-black dark, and the fire was laying down fast. An hour later he felt the first drops of drizzle. By morning he and the rest of the crew were huddled together trying to keep a fire going in an old root wad in an effort to stay warm, as the rain came down in sheets. In two days, central Idaho received over an inch and a half of precipitation, an unheard of amount for August, effectively ending the fire season on the Sleeping Deer Ranger District.

20

"Life is just one damned thing after another."
Frank Ward O'Malley

It was a double date of sorts. Howie was busy explaining to Alex how the British-made Land Rover four wheel drive was superior to any domestic model, and Nedra, ensconced in the back seat with Angie, was telling of the dog sitter they had found for their golden retriever, Lazlo. Angie bobbed her head like one of those bobble-head toys they give away at the ballpark. According to the dog therapist, it seems that Lazlo was using destructive activities such as chewing up the furniture as a defense mechanism against boredom. Both she and Howie thought it best that the dog have a regular full-time sitter when they both were out of the house. So far, Nedra was happy to report, it seemed that Lazlo and the dog sitter were getting along famously. After thirty minutes of this discussion, Angie decided that they would have to resort to Nazi torture before she would ever baby-sit and read stories to a dog.

Howie shifted into four wheel drive at the Bureau of Land Management access road next to the Wiley Jones ranch, just past the turnoff to Doublesprings Pass. They were on their way to climb Borah Peak, at 12,622 feet elevation the highest mountain in Idaho. Alex noticed a flock of Sandhill Cranes feeding in the flood irrigated alfalfa. The birds, alert on long spindly legs, croaked a hoarse call of danger when the Land Rover stopped and Alex leaned out the open window. After a nervous minute, the group of nine cranes lifted off at the same instant, as if it was a group consensus.

"Nothing flies like a crane, does it?" Alex noted.

"Cranes, is that what they are?" Howie said. "I thought they were like herons."

"No, they're cranes. You can always tell cranes, even at a distance. They fly with their necks and legs straight out, and they're almost always in a flock. Cranes make that unusual croaking sound that nothing else makes."

When they got out of the Land Rover, Angie was staring at the mountain. "Are you sure you want to do this, Alex? The climb looks sort of nasty."

"Sure," he said. "You've lived in Idaho all your life, within view of the peak, and you've never climbed Borah."

"Actually, I haven't climbed any mountain. Growing up on the ranch, I never had time to develop hobbies." She said the word "hobbies" as if it was a sin or something.

Alex laughed. "Now, don't start with the preppy deal again."

"Okay, I won't accuse anyone I know of being an elite, intellectual snob, if that certain someone will stop doing parts of old comedy routines I've never heard of."

"You mean like Monty Python climbing both peaks of Kilimanjaro?" Alex put a hand over his eye, simulating the double-vision joke. "Our plan was to build a bridge between the two peaks."

Now Angie laughed. "Yeah, just like that one."

Alex hoisted his arm over his head, striking a pose. "'When my love swears that she is made of truth, I do believe her, though I know she lies'."

"And definitely, no Shakespeare!" Angie cried. "All you know is little snippets anyhow. It drives me nuts." She laughed and pulled her Goldburg Vikings sweatshirt up over her head, exposing her flat stomach as her t-shirt rode up all the way to her sports bra.

"Tempt not a desperate man!" Alex yelled and grabbed her around the side, just above the belt.

Angie squealed and pulled free, faceing off against him like a wrestler. "'Lord, what fools these mortals be'."

Howie sighed. "Not the Shakespeare kids again."

Alex ignored him, reached for Angie again and said, "Aha, I always knew you were a debutante."

"I'm nobody's debutante."

"Not even if I say please?"

Angie folded her arms and looked sideways. "Especially not if you say please."

The group of four assembled their climbing gear and prepared for the climb. Nedra and Howie looked like two models that just stepped out of the REI catalog: Patagonia shorts, Swiss knee socks, canvas shirts in festive new colors, and brown-red leather Italian hiking boots, custom made. Howie wore a hat that had a flap in the back and a logo in the front. Nedra had a pair of sunglasses that cost more than Angie made in a week as a waitress, and both held matching ice axes.

Alex felt a little shabby in a white T-shirt without a logo and his faded jeans. Even his government issued green day pack seemed to him a bit tattered compared to Howie and Nedra's racing backpacks made of the newest ultra-light fabric.

"This is supposed to be a pretty straightforward climb," Howie said. "A long one, almost six thousand feet of elevation gain."

"Hey, does everybody have enough water?" Alex said. "I'm carrying a gallon."

"I've got three canteens," Angie said.

"Howie, how many canteens are you carrying?" asked Alex.

"Actually, Nedra and I have hydration reservoirs built right in our backpacks, four liters apiece."

"Oh, okay," Alex had never heard of a hydration reservoir. "Well, bring a sweater or a coat. It might get cool up there."

As he smeared zinc oxide on his nose, Howie said, "From the looks of the weather, heat may be our problem today. Anybody else want some sun screen?"

It was the end of August and probably the end of the summer heat, clear, warm already in the morning. Just a few mare's tails lay far, far on the southeast horizon. Their backpacks fairly light, they started up the track, not really a trail, just a sheep track that wound across the face of Borah in zigs and zags until it broke out of the whitebark pine on the first high ridge. Howie led the way followed by Nedra, Alex, and then Angie.

Their pace was steady and they gained elevation quickly on the steep ascent, leaving behind the mountain mahogany zone and bitterbrush. They entered a small stand of stunted Doug fir, ancient, short and squat, water starved, like full-scale bonsai trees. They climbed higher into the whitebark pine, rocky dry limestone cobble and talus mingled with an occasional streak of quartz showing in the shallow bedrock. Straining muscles and sweating profusely, they stopped for a short rest right at timberline. The last pines grew in small hummocks of tight entwined branches that looked like skeletons, four hundred years old and four feet high.

The group had gained elevation and the view of the landscape started to take on that aerial-perspective look that Alex liked so much, like a view from a small plane, only without the plane. To the south Alex could see Mackay reservoir and the White Knob Mountains, and maybe even where the rodeo grounds sat on the Big Lost River. Across the Valley of the Big Lost, he clearly made out the Burma Road snaking its way over the top and into Copper Basin.

All by itself to the northwest, Lone Pine Peak sat, Tolkien-like, smack in the middle of Antelope Flats. Alex felt the strong pull of folded strata and thrust-block faulting. It was a textbook example of Basin and Range structural geology.

"Man, you can see Goldburg," Howie said, pointing to the little smudge of geometry forty miles away, imposed like a pimple on fair skin.

"It's like the capital of the rock country," Alex said.

"It's, it's just like incredible." Nedra was shaking her head. "I have never been this stimulated by being outdoors."

"She needs to get out more," Angie whispered to Alex.

Howie was adjusting his titanium watch, a combination chronometer, altimeter, and barometer. "Actually, we are at nine thousand five hundred and forty feet in elevation, almost a three-thousand foot gain. I set it at the Rover. About thirty-one hundred feet to the top; close to the halfway point."

Snaking their way along the long ridge, all traces of trail long gone, they picked their way among angular boulders of gray limestone. Sometimes the rock took on sharp, strange, almost sexual forms as they followed the dinosaur backbone of the spine of Borah Peak.

The hike became a rock climb when the ridge rolled to the north and west, the rock strata now fully exposed and breaking over into a cirque basin of snow and ice. They came to a thin place on the ridge overlooking the only glacier in Idaho, a pitiful poor thing of dirty ice almost covered in talus. The drop neared vertical. An illusion formed that it was more than vertical, giving the impression that one false step would launch one cartwheeling into space, a thousand-foot plunge to the first bounce. The climbers carefully crawled along the serrated ridge, hands on rocks.

"They call this Chicken-Out Ridge," Howie said.

Alex tried not to look down. "I can see why."

"If I'd known how thin it was up here, I'd of brought my climbing rope," Howie stated, matter- of-factly.

Angelica sucked air and puffed, "That might have been nice."

Howie looked up at Angie and said, "Ah, but we don't need it. Just take your time."

Angie mumbled something under her breath and Alex grinned.

The serrated ridge ran for a long way and it didn't get any easier, even when it flattened out some. Anticipating the end of this bony ridge, Alex could see where the rock spine dipped down to a basin of snow just below the summit. He kept looking at this point, thinking that if he could just get to the end of the

141

ridge, he would make the peak.

Alex had two surprises in store before he met the end of Chicken-Out Ridge. The first was a vertical knife of yellow rock that thrust like a finger, straight up, on the only possible climbing route. The only way around the finger was a nasty bit of derring-do that had Alex wondering just how badly he wanted to get to the top of this mountain.

"This must be the Yellow Streak I heard about," Howie said, laughing. "This is a bit of a sticky wicket."

"A sticky wicket, he says." Angie was muttering again.

Howie grasped the ledge with both hands, and in less than a minute he was safely on the other side. "Hey, it's not as bad as it looks. Nedra, you ready?"

"Yeah, it looks like a piece of cake."

Alex didn't think it looked like a piece of cake.

"More like a piece of crap," Angie said.

Nedra scooted along the yellow band like she was on skates. Angie followed, slowly, her hands and sneakers stuck to the rock like flies' feet.

Alex never thought he had a problem with heights, since he was always comfortable on ladder or roof, but this was different. This was exposure, on a grand scale, and he didn't like the feeling. Just like it isn't the heat, it's the humidity, Alex thought, it isn't the climb, it's the exposure. And there was just a little too much of it at the Yellow Streak. It was a sheer drop between rock formations. Alex looked down; a mistake. He felt a little like Jimmy Stewart in that Hitchcock movie about the church steeple.

"Alex, are you coming?" Nedra asked.

"Yeah, just working into it."

"Take your time," Nedra said slowly, like she was talking to a third grader. "It's . . ."

"I know, I know, it's a piece of cake."

Alex hugged the Yellow Streak so hard his fingers hurt. His small backpack felt like it weighed a hundred pounds or more and was trying to peel him backward off the rock. There was too much empty space, especially under his feet. Halfway across, he froze. He didn't say anything or make any noise at all. He just stopped.

Finally Angie said, "Alex, are you okay?"

"Sort of."

"Sort of what?"

142

"Sort of not."

"Alex, Alex, just stay cool," Howie said as he scrambled around the yellow rock, quickly climbing over to Alex. "Nothing to be afraid of."

They were talking quietly now. Alex whispered, "Man, I don't know, I just can't move."

"Hey, no problem," Howie whispered back. "It happens all the time. The little computer in your head just said, like, 'this is no place for Roy' and just sort of shut down."

"Howie, we're not talking about getting it up, I'm, like, worried about dying."

Howie ignored the statement. "Hey, here's what we're going to do. Watch my feet. I'm going to move them from rock to rock. See, no big deal? Now watch my hands, right and left." Howie moved with fearless grace. "No big deal. Here, I'll do it again, right and left. Now, how about you take a breath and try it?"

Alex took a good, deep breath, but his right foot didn't move.

"Okay, Alex, time out," Howie said quietly. "How about this line of thinking? Think about it, like what's the worst thing that could happen?"

Alex cast him a worried look, started to get angry. "If I fuck up, I fall into space and plummet in unimaginable fear to a certain, painful death."

"Yeah, so what?"

"So what? Don't bust my balls here."

"Well, you've got to go sometime. So you really think this is your day?"

Alex thought about it a bit and said, "No, not really."

"That doesn't sound too confident there." Howie leaned right over Alex's shoulder and whispered in his ear. "If you check out today, you won't get the chance to bang that pretty cowgirl."

Alex thought some more and decided that his day was far away, so far beyond the curvature of the earth that he couldn't see it from up here on Chicken-Out ridge. His right foot moved. Then his left followed. A quick skitter step, and he was across.

Howie gave a forced laugh. "Good job, good job, you can breathe now."

Alex took a deep, deep breath, and let out a long, long sigh. He had to rest to get the rubber out of his legs. Then the group continued to the lip of the ridge, where it met the main massif of the peak. Alex had been looking forward to this spot, the end of the ridge. Unfortunately it ended in a twenty-foot vertical drop of rock.

"Always one last surprise, eh, Alex?" Howie kidded as he looked over the edge. "There's good handholds here. It just a little difficult because you have to climb down." Howie demonstrated by working his way down a little chimney like an overgrown monkey. He was down in moments. Nedra followed almost as quickly, her boney girl arms splayed out, rock to rock.

"You okay, Alex?" Angie looked a bit worried.

"I think so. You go first."

Angie did and Alex watched. Her sports bra was well defined under the sweaty T-shirt.

Alex started down the moment Angie's feet hit the flat rock. He watched his hands and feet go from rock to rock and step to step, kept his back braced against the chimney side, and had no fear.

"Atta boy," Howie said.

"Hey, no exposure," Alex said. "It's the exposure that got to me."

Nedra said, "It'll be easier going back. It's always easier when you're climbing up."

They rested in the small saddle where the south face of Borah Peak sloped down into the cliffs of the upper cirque basin of Cedar Creek. There was still a bit of a climb left to go, but Alex could see a trail again, zig-zagging up around a perennial snowfield all the way to the top.

"We've got it made. Eleven thousand eight hundred feet, only eight hundred more vertical feet to go." Howie seemed satisfied. "Looks like a cakewalk."

"More cake talk," whispered Angie.

They sat and drank some water, quite a bit of water. Alex was surprised at how hot it was at this elevation and how still the air was. He thought he could light a candle, it was so still. "There's no wind," he finally said.

"Yeah, it's a real Idaho bluebird day," Howie said as he started to take off his clothes. Alex thought that he was just taking off his shirt, but then Howie took off his blue Pantagonia shorts, and he wasn't wearing any underwear. Nedra was doing the same, her small breasts well tanned and happy looking.

"What a great day to climb naked," Howie said.

"Is this great or what?" Nedra added as she stepped out of her shorts, no tan line visible on her bare rear end. It looked like two letter Cs, Alex thought, his eyes drawn like magnets to the small patch of fur in front.

Alex was sort of lost in the moment, so lost that he didn't notice right away that Angie was staring at him in a rather peculiar way, like he was starting

144

to spontaneously combust or something.

"What do you say, Alex, Angie?" Howie said.

For a moment, just a moment, it sounded to Alex like something free and fun and dare-devilish; but then he caught Angie's stare, and her meaning was clear. Deflated, he said, "Naw, Howie, too California for me, I guess."

"No problem," Howie said. "We climb naked in the Sierras all the time."

Angie was nonplused about it all. "I'll bet you do, but I think I'll keep my pants on just the same."

Alex looked over at Angie and those jeans of hers, and now he really was disappointed. But his disappointment was short lived as he fell in line behind Nedra. Alex didn't even remember the last half mile of the climb. He was glued to the sight of Nedra's well-turned buttocks pumping him up the mountain. Each time he caught a sight of that pubis of hers it was hard to suppress a guttural noise in his throat.

"Alex, would you please take your nose out of that girl's ass?" Angie finally whispered to him.

Alex was more than a little flummoxed. "Yeah, but what's a guy to do?" he whispered back.

Louder this time, Angie said, "Well, for one thing, you can act like you're not living in a beer commercial."

"Fine, fine," he said, but his eyes continued to wander in a more discreet fashion.

"Honestly Alex, you remind me of one of the bulls on the ranch," Angie said with a tone of disgust.

Alex turned around. "Yeah, which one?"

Angie immediately punched him in the arm and grinned. "The stupidest one!"

Alex sort of got used to a naked Howie, watching him swing from side to side, but he couldn't seem to do much about ignoring Nedra waltzing around in the all-together. It was just a little too incongruent, a little too unusual. Hell, he admitted to himself, it's just too damn nice not to look.

It had taken almost six hours of climbing to reach the summit and was close to mid-afternoon by the time they made it. The summit area was really quite small for such a massive mountain, not much bigger than a standard kitchen and living room combined, except all made out in rock with lots of window space.

Alex was fairly worn out but not dangerously, still interested in the eye

145

candy sitting on the space blanket next to Howie. There wasn't any wind and the naked climb looked like it was going to turn into a naked lunch, sort of like that famous impressionist painting, the Manet one, with the guys sitting next to the naked woman at the picnic. This is just sort of an updated, western version of the scene, Alex decided, noticing that Nedra's nipples were rock hard, like little brown cookies.

Once again, Angie caught him looking and jabbed him in the side. Alex almost - but didn't - mention that she seemed to have more than a passing interest in Howie's pilot stick.

Cooling down, Howie and Nedra almost reluctantly put their clothes back on; at least most of them. Howie spread out a picnic lunch that would have been impressive at a football game tailgate party. Howie unloaded little tins of kippers and European crackers and chocolate-covered shortbread cookies from France.

"Angie, Alex, have some lunch?" Howie drew a thermos out of his pack. "How about some green iced tea?" Alex looked down at his half-eaten peanut butter and jelly sandwich. It was an easy decision.

Alex said, "God, I can't believe you lugged all this stuff up here. I mean like, like . . ."

"You mean like Jeez-O-Friday?" Howie finished the phrase.

"Yeah," laughed Alex. "Like, Jeez-O-Friday, this is a lot of shit to pack way up here."

"But it's worth it," Howie said. "I mean, like, does this stuff taste great way up here or what?"

Satiated on European yuppie snacks, Alex stood up and did a slow three-hundred-sixty-degree scan from the summit of Mount Borah. He could see the whole Lost River Range, from the little town of Howe on the southern end where the range died out in the great desert, to where the Pahsimeroi mountains stepped down to the Salmon River in the north. The north face of Leatherman Peak, the second highest in the state, stared back at him, the Three Sisters standing just beyond. To the north, Dickey Peak and September Mountain looked like they had grown out of the valley floor. The mountains marched in parallel lines from northwest to southeast, following an invisible line of structure that started far beneath the surface. Alex found it easy, up here on the top of Borah, to imagine the concept of geological time and of epochs, the countless earthquakes, the mountain building of thrust-block faults, the history of the country open like a textbook, the mountains like figures drawn in schematics, the landscape like a

146

dream.

Alex pondered his own personal, geologic time scale. He wondered about where he was on the scale and what epochs lay ahead of him. He picked up a shiny rock. It had a fossil of a fern on one side, gray on black. Struck by the obvious questions, Alex had no answers and he put the rock in his pocket, rolling it over with fingers and mind.

"Great view, eh?" Howie seemed to be practicing a Canadian accent.

Alex looked down at the north face of Borah Peak, the rock falling away in slabs. Far, far, below, a rock glacier of talus rolled in lobes down into the cirque basin, the rock suggesting movement even at rest, the snow in frozen drifts in the deep, dark shade, never melting.

"It's like looking off the back of God's head."

Angelica walked up next to the two, shading her eyes from the sun, looking west.

"Hey Angie," Alex said, pointing. "Look at that mountain over there, the lumpy one. It's sort of heart-shaped. Do you think that's the one Dugout Dick warned us about?"

She looked where Alex was pointing, saw a lumpish pile of rock against the skyline that somewhat resembled a jagged heart, felt the chill in the new-found breeze and didn't say anything.

21

The old Chevy pickup was straining in second gear as it climbed up the switchbacks of the Burma Road, spinning and spitting rocks on every hairpin turn. Alex had found that whenever he got the truck to high elevation he could pick up Boise radio and was singing along with the song "Pancho and Lefty."

The dirt and the dust were seeping in the floorboards of the truck and Alex felt the engine heat from the steep climb. His windshield framed a view of the quartzite peaks of the White Knob Mountains, the rock so white it looked like snow. Harmon joined in on the chorus.

"Man, what a great song," Harmon said. "How does a guy write a song like that? Does he channel it or something?"

Alex said, between bounces, "Careful now, you're starting to sound like Argo."

"Shee-it!" Harmon said, his arms braced against the doorframe. "That'll be the day. Anyway, it's just perfect, like how could a guy create that story? It's perfect, like Mr. Bojangles."

Alex was steering the truck like one of the big rigs, all exaggerated arm motions and hand-over-hand steering. "I read somewhere that there really was a Mr. Bojangles."

"No shit?"

"Yeah, in a jail in New Orleans and everything. Just like the song."

"So it's like a true story?"

Alex bounced the truck onto a little turnout right at the summit of the Burma Road, leaned out his window and looked back the way they had come. "Yeah, I guess it's a true story. There really was this character, Bojangles Robinson."

"In worn out shoes?"

"Probably."

"Son-of-a-bitch," Harmon said, in his best Kentucky accent. "Hey, hold on here a second. I got to piss so bad my back teeth are floatin'."

They both popped open their doors and got out of the truck at the same time, facing away from each other, unzipping and urinating out their own marked territories on either side of the Chevy. Alex looked across the Big Lost River valley, across the Chilly Flats, at fresh snow on the Lost Rivers, the first snowfall of the season. The snow ran like a line at nearly ten thousand feet, the landscape like tapestry. The mountains were ghostly images, unfolding from north to south in shades of brown and gold.

It was mid-September. Alex and Harmon were going fishing in the high country before the weather came in and closed it out for the year. The rumor was that the trout in the alpine lakes were really on the bite, racing to fatten up before winter and the nine months of ice cover.

When Harmon wasn't floating the river, he spent all his time fishing. He was a semi-pro fly fisherman, one of those zealots in their Orvis waders and multi-pocketed fishing vests, spending more money on his Loomis and Sage fishing rods than he did on food. Harmon even tried to make a living at fly fishing as a fishing guide, but he said he couldn't stand watching other people catch fish while he stood alongside and coached. Harmon said he also had the same problem with pornography; he didn't want to watch other people do it, he wanted to do it himself. Harmon was so into fishing that he really didn't care to take others with him - unless, of course, they were driving and buying the gas, which Alex had offered and Harmon quickly accepted. As Harmon's thoughts went, a tank of gas saved was a tank of gas earned. It was, after all, a goodly drive down to Copper Basin on some pretty poor roads, and even the thought of the cost of fixing a flat tire, or worse yet, buying a new tire, sent Harmon into fits of hand-wrenching anxiety.

Alex felt that Copper Basin was one of those special places, only slightly marred by two political realities: first, the chewing, stomping presence of thousands of Angus and Black Bally cattle and their untold millions of piles of cow manure in the main river and every tributary stream; and second, the strange incongruity of the Forest Service guard station, an unsightly single-wide white trailer with a shiny steel snow shed roof built over the aluminum box, prominently located so that everyone can see it, even if they don't want to. The visual intrusion of the reflection of the metal roof, just by itself, thought Alex, was enough to damn this building to hell. It was as if the trailer had been designed and sited for the maximum effect to diminish the scenic integrity of the

149

landscape.

Alex fumed as he passed the heinous building. "God, that's got to be the ugliest guard station in Idaho. I mean, compare this to the elegant design, the craftsman architecture of the CCC guard stations at Wildhorse Creek or Iron Bog. It's like they tried to make it as ugly as they could. Where was their sense of design, their sense of place?"

"You're in the Forest Service now. Architecture doesn't count, landscape doesn't either. It's trees and cows now. You want elegance in design, stick to music, stick to Mr. Bojangles, stick to Pancho and Lefty, and you'll be okay."

Alex was worked up on the subject and wouldn't let it go. "Now, von Goethe said that architecture is frozen music."

"Frozen music? Well, I'll bet your buddy von whatever-his-name-was never made it out to Copper Basin guard station. If he would of, he'd of sung a different tune."

"That I do not doubt one bit."

He steered the pickup fast down the narrow gravel road with a rooster tail of dust his constant companion. The Pioneer Range circled Copper Basin in a ring of granitic mountains with yellow and black volcanic intrusions, with local names like descriptive terms of endearment: Big Black Dome, Broad Canyon, Lake Creek, Castle Creek, Falls Creek. If you were imaginative, you could envision a complete landscape in a name. Alex's favorite was Surprise Valley. What a name, he thought, and wondered what the surprise could be, as he pulled into a copse of Douglas fir and the small trail head at Broad Canyon.

The trail crossed an avalanche path and a series of waterfalls as it wound through a graveyard of whitebark pine, skeletons of trees brought down by snow slides. A few mountain columbine were still blooming yellow and red along the stream. After a two thousand foot elevation gain, the last of the whitebark pine gave out and they were in the alpine, a rock-filled expanse of tundra and grass. Miniature herbaceous plants and flowers, some only inches high, carpeted the cirque basin. Ancient ice scratches striated the smooth bedrock. Betty Lake, twenty acres of ultramarine blue, reflected only sky.

There was no wind on the water and the only disturbances on the sheen were the dimples made by rising trout. Harmon was rabid at the sight of fish, assembling his Sage four-piece number four fly rod like it was a surgical instrument.

"The hatch is on. See those little mayflies? Would you believe it? Here

150

we are up at over ten thousand feet, in September. The sun's on the water, but the hatch won't last long."

From the constant stream of fishing stories that Harmon had been telling him all the way up the trail, Alex would have been surprised if there had not been trout rising, hungry for the fly.

"So what kind of fly are you going to use?"

"I'm going to start out with a number sixteen Adams. I don't suspect that these rainbows will be very sophisticated. We'll see how it goes." Harmon had opened his aluminum flybox and was trying to decide which of his creations he could give away to Alex. All the flies were meticulously constructed, small works of art of feather and yarn arranged by pattern, size, and color. "Here, try this one. Remember to put on a light tippet and use a little fly floatant. You want the fly to float high with as little disturbance from the line as possible." Harmon put on his fishing vest, a modern design miracle of pockets and do-dads, and his polarized fishing glasses, completing the Scientific Angler look.

Alex was still fumbling with his fly rod. Harmon was already false casting along the shoreline, shooting the line with a quick roll of his wrist. The fly line circled out in a precise, exaggerated hoop, presenting the fly with barely a ripple on the surface of Betty Lake. The size sixteen Adams barely had the opportunity to form a ring on the water surface before it was sucked under by a hungry fish.

"Hoo-wee! Got a nice one," Harmon whooped. The trout jumped twice, sun shining on the orange-red stripe on its side, and then took the fight deep underwater. The ultra-light rod bent gracefully. The fish tired quickly and with pressure, came to shore on its side. Harmon grasped the trout firmly behind the gills and lifted it from the water, its eyes still full of life. "I think it will go fifteen inches."

"Nice fish," Alex said, still trying to tie the fly to his line. "Are you going to keep it?"

"Yeah, I think we can eat four this size. I know I'm hungry. How about you?"

Alex was anxious to fish, and his fingers were not helping him tie the knots. "I can eat two, but give me a chance to fish, okay?"

Harmon laughed his cackling Kentucky laugh. "No problem. I'll keep one more, and then I'll catch and release. Let you catch a couple."

The fish were not reluctant to bite, almost as if they knew that the ice was coming and had an instinctual drive to put on fat before the lake surface went to darkness in the long, long winter. After many errors and tangles, Alex was finally able to make several successful casts and caught two trout, neither as big as the first one that Harmon had pulled from the lake. Harmon was in a transcendent state of bliss as he caught and released fish after fish on his barbless hooks. When the sun dipped below the serrated ridge that separated Broad Canyon and Surprise Valley, the trout stopped rising and the surface of the lake went smooth. The hatch was over.

Alex and Harmon had Broad Canyon all to themselves. They made a simple camp, planning to sleep under the stars. They cooked the trout on a small butane stove and gobbled them down like wild dogs.

After the meal, Harmon cracked a seal on a plastic pint bottle of Old Packer, the cheapest bourbon in the Goldburg liquor store. Alex worked at starting a fire. Both had gathered a small bit of firewood at the avalanche chute and tied it on the exterior of their backpacks to haul it up the trail. Soon there was a small, crackling fire, just back from the shoreline. Making backrests from their packs, they both leaned back to sip a little whiskey and water and watched the stars come out to reflect over Betty Lake.

Alex grimaced a bit with his first swallow of Old Packer. "Man, I don't know how you handle this stuff. Too much bite for me."

"Oh, you need to develop a taste for it, which doesn't take long, and you really come to appreciate a good glass of bourbon," Harmon said, conveniently forgetting the rank of Old Packer among the fine whiskies in the world. "What is that saying? Candy is dandy, but liquor is quicker?"

Alex looked inward for a moment. "Ogden Nash."

"Yeah, that sounds right. And it does, gives you a nice buzz, especially at ten thousand feet. Doesn't take much hooch with this oxygen content to get you tuned up quick." Harmon poured himself another. "Sort of naturally makes you want to wax poetic, or else get sentimental."

"So, you're the sentimental type?"

"Aren't all guys?"

Alex carefully added two more small sticks of wood to the fire. "Yeah, basically, I think that guys are more sentimental than women."

"You got that right, ace." Harmon held his Sierra cup up to the stars in a toast. "God damn to the third level of hell all ex-wives and their boyfriends, too."

"You were married?"

"Fuckin' A right I was, little boy and everything." Harmon smiled in the

152

firelight, teeth flashing. "This here is the part where I'm supposed to say it was both our faults, we drifted apart, or there were irreconcilable differences, or even that she needed more than I could give her. But that's not what happened. The fuckin' bitch ran out on me and hung me out to dry."

Alex never knew how to handle these types of situations. He would have preferred to cheerfully change the subject but sensed correctly that with the whiskey tiger out of the bottle, he was going to hear the whole bloody divorce deal. So he just asked, "What happened?"

"What happened? Shit, I'll tell you what happened. I'll give you the whole dirty story." Harmon seemed to be enjoying the opportunity, and settled back against his pack like an actor on stage. Alex was his audience. "Feodora was a first-rate bitch. Met her right here on the Middle Fork. She was a kayak queen. Things went pretty well, and next thing you know, we're a couple, living in Missoula in the off-season." Harmon locked his hands behind his head. "And hey, things were going pretty good for us. We had a little apartment off Reserve, some cool friends, and she was pulling in a paycheck at the university. I was helping a friend of mine build kayaks in his garage."

"So it started out all right?"

"Sure. Hell, it always starts out right, just doesn't seem to end up there. The first black clouds showed up on the horizon when these friends of hers, Erin and Sergei - God, that Sergei, I hate that fucker - announced that they were expecting a baby. Hell, at the time, it was no skin off my nose, but I remember the old radar hitting on a little something right then. If I would have been smart, I should have ran from that apartment that day, ran all the way over Lost Trail Pass back to Idaho. I saw the look in her eye. Man, I tell you, I should of bolted right then and there."

"What, she wanted to have a baby?"

"Yeah, she did. I tried to talk her out of it, get a dog or something, but it had to be a baby. I'll tell you, she got her hooks in me good. Comes in one day wearing a little halter top, nothing else, no pants or anything, holding a thermometer in her hand. She gives me this look, and we're off makin' babies. Hell, I was a slave. She was a good lookin' woman, and I loved the work." Harmon started moving his hands around for emphasis like a TV weatherman, waving at invisible weather maps and fronts that only he could see. "And Christ, how she planned by this thermometer. When she was in heat, she'd just about drag me off to bed. Anyway, unfortunately, we weren't one of those couples with fertility problems, and she conceived by her next period. Next thing you know,

153

there's me, never even been in a furniture store, picking out a baby crib and bumpers."

"Did you get married right away?"

"No, no, it wasn't right away. What clinched it was when Erin and Sergei decided to get married. I was doomed. There was all this pressure. It was never said, but I could feel it, to do the right thing, you know, before the kid was born." Harmon sat up straight and looked over at Alex in the pale firelight. "You know when you've had it? When you're lost?"

Alex scratched his head. "No, not really."

"Well, I'll tell you. The moment that first thought comes into your head, that maybe getting married isn't too bad of a deal. You start thinking magic thoughts and all. You're dead meat. It's too late to run then. Take it from me."

Alex thought that maybe since Harmon had answered his own question, that now might be a good opportunity to change the subject and had just inhaled a breath to speak.

"But I digress," Harmon slurred after a quick sip of bourbon. "You wanted to know what happened. Hell, the first thing I know is I'm getting fitted for a tuxedo, picking out rings. We got married in that little white church in Darby, right down from the ranger station. It rained that day, I remember."

Alex inhaled in one last vain attempt, but he was too slow.

"And that's how it went. We set up housekeeping in our little apartment, happy enough, I guess. No more kayak crew for me. I got a job laying asphalt for the JDC out of Deerlodge. God, did I get sick of laying asphalt. Got a hell of a tan, though. Anyway, little Tobben arrives with only eight hours of labor and a caesarean section. Feodora had those narrow little hips, you know, and the kid couldn't make it past her tail bone." Harmon looked up at the stars and then at Alex. "So, we're like this little nuclear family now, Harmon, Feodora and Tobben. All we needed was a dog named Queenie, and we could of been a poster family for the wonderful world of mediocrity. But it was okay, I liked it. The kid was a blast. The trouble was that Feodora didn't think so. She was hell bent for leather to get back to work. She was bored out of her skull taking care of the kid. I mean, her six weeks of maternity leave was over, and she was out of that apartment like a shot."

"So who took care of Tobben? Did you put him in daycare?"

"Well, that was the good part. I was on unemployment all winter, so I took care of him, liked it too. I was a damn good daddy. Took the kid everywhere with me. That damn Feodora, the fuckin' bitch, could of cared less.

154

I didn't want to put Tobben in daycare, so come spring I said sayonara to the asphalt business. I just stayed home and Feodora went to work." Harmon lay back again in the dark. "It was the best two years of my life."

Alex inhaled, thought about it, and decided to ask the question that Harmon needed. "So what happened then?"

"The bitch was two timing me." Harmon sat up like a shot. "I find out she's fuckin' this asshole at work, the assistant manager. She just waltzes in one day and announces she's movin' out, or rather movin' in with Bernard. Bernard, what kind of name is that for a man? Fuckin' Bernard, what a dickhead."

"Did she try to take Tobben?"

"Holy shit, no. She couldn't of cared less, at least, not then. I had to get a part-time job. Man, I was broke. I put Toby in daycare three days a week. It was pretty rough, but we did okay, just Toby and me in Missoula."

There was a long pause. A little too long. Alex was concerned about what to say next, since Toby obviously wasn't with Harmon any more.

"Ahhh, shit. Then came the divorce. Man, was I set up, like a bowling pin. God, was I stupid. I still didn't want to get divorced, had these foolish ideas that maybe we could work it all out somehow, go the counseling route, you know? Christ, listen to me. I sound like I'm on one of those afternoon talk shows or something. So, her lawyer serves me the papers, and guess what? Now she wants Toby! The bitch didn't give a fuck about him for two years, and now she wants custody."

Alex tossed some dry tundra scrub into the fire, watching it crackle and fizz and rise in red embers into the darkness. "Did you get a lawyer?"

"That's where I really fucked up. Yeah, I got one, but not until it was too late. There I was reading self-help books on divorce law in the library, and all the time she was sharpening the knife." Harmon rolled over on his side, facing Alex in the dark. "This is what really happened. She had it all figured out, and I walked right into the trap."

"Jesus, what did she do?"

Harmon's eyes glinted in the dark each time they caught the firelight. "Like I said, I had Toby in daycare, three days a week. I come back from work one Wednesday, and no Toby. The gal at the daycare said he went with some friends of Toby's mother. Had a note from Feodora and everything. Man, I just went ballistic. The gal described them. It was my pals, Sergei and Erin, for sure. So I call the cops, they check it out, then visit me and tell me there's nothing they can do. That Toby is there with the permission of the mother, and the law can't get involved with this type of domestic affair. That's what the asshole called it, a domestic affair."

"So did you go to court then?"

"No, that's where I really, really fucked up." Harmon sighed in the dark, with an almost Jesus-like sorrow. "See, Sergei and Erin had this cat, Mr. Rollo, and they set great store on this cat. Anyway, I was out there in my old Subaru, circling the block around Sergei's house, and out comes Mr. Rollo to the curb. So, I looks at him, and thinks a bit, and I snatch Mr. Rollo and throw him in the back seat of the Subaru."

"You took the cat?"

"Yeah, I took the cat. I took the cat," Harmon said, pronouncing each work slowly and deliberately. "It was me. I took him. I confess. I get back to my apartment, call Sergei. Erin answers the phone and I tell her to put Sergei on. She almost hangs up on me, but I tell her, I've got Mr. Rollo. Sergei gets on the phone, yelling and screaming at me. I just take it and then say to him, if you ever want to see Mr. Rollo again, I want Toby back in ten minutes."

"Holy Christ, you took the cat and held it for ransom? That's a real balls move."

"It was a real stupid move, but let me finish. I get Tobben back, Sergei stands there without a word. I damn near decked him, but instead, I hand over the cat, and Mr. Rollo goes home with Sergei. I figure it's all over. God, was I wrong. Anyway, about a half an hour later, the same two cops are back at my door, all big and huffy now. They asked me about the cat. I said, yeah, I took him, but I gave him back. That was it. They slapped the cuffs on me and put me in the squad car. I kept saying, this is a mistake. I gave the cat back! All the neighbors saw me and everything. It was terrible."

"Did they take you to jail?"

"Shit yeah, they threw me in jail. Put Toby in child services and threw me in the tank. It was Saturday night, I couldn't get a lawyer and spent all weekend there. Alex, I was in jail with some very undesirable people! You talk about time passing slowly. Christ, it was like being trapped at the Ice Capades, and you couldn't get out."

"So did your lawyer get the charges dropped?"

"Fuck no. It seems Mr. Rollo had suffered psychological damage, and Sergei and Erin wanted the book thrown at me. Anyway, I made bail, and after I was out, I figured this had to be one big joke, and that it would blow over. God, was I stupid."

156

"Did you go on trial?"

"We had a hearing. My lawyer freaked me out. Seems like both the District Attorney and the Judge are like big animal rights people in Missoula. My lawyer tells me I could end up doing time in the big house."

"Doing time? Going to prison? For a cat?"

"Yeah, I couldn't believe it. Like, I gave the cat back. Anyway, this dirtbag lawyer of mine talks me into plea bargaining and pleading guilty to a class three felony of cat abuse."

"So that kept you out of jail, right? Did you have to pay a fine?"

Harmon smiled in the dark. "Yeah, I paid the one thousand dollar fine. But that was nothing. The real shit dump came at the divorce hearing. I'm now a felon, a criminal, and Feodora's lawyer pins me against the wall with this crap about being an undesirable parent for Toby, a poor choice for custody. I kept trying to tell the judge I gave the cat back, but he looks at me like I'm some kind of serial killer or something and gives Feodora primary custody." Harmon seemed to deflate like a balloon. "Toby lives with her now. I get to see him twice a year, and I can't take him out of the state."

"God, Harmon, that's a tough deal. I don't know what to say."

Harmon took a long pull of bourbon right out of the bottle. "It's okay man, I'm hanging in there," he said softly.

Harmon didn't say much more after that and Alex didn't ask any more questions.

The air cooled off rapidly and the afternoon warmth quickly dispersed into the thin night sky, the long-wave radiation all going out into space. There would be a hard frost before morning, Alex thought as he snuggled deeper into his sleeping bag.

In the night, sometime near morning, Alex awoke to a stifled cry out in the basin, like the cry of a woman sobbing. The hair stood up on his neck. In the dark, he could make out the form of Harmon, still asleep. And there it was again, the "huh, huh, huh, huh" of a woman crying out in the darkness, behind him and Harmon in the rocks. Alex searched every synapse and every neural connection he had as his mind raced to avoid panic. Then he remembered reading that a cougar can make a sound like a person crying. He lay stiff in his bag listening, cognizant of each breath, listening for the cougar to cough or growl or something. Alex lay awake for a long time, until the stars began to fade toward morning, but he did not hear again that sound of sorrow.

157

22

"Best of all, he loved the fall.
The leaves yellow on the cottonwoods,
Floating on the trout streams,
And above, the high, blue, windless skies."
                                   Ernest Hemingway

Standing at the foot of Ernest Hemingway's grave in the Ketchum cemetery, Alex looked dispassionately at the flat, unimposing monument. For some reason, Alex thought visiting the gravesite would be an uplifting experience, that he might feel something special. Instead, there were no omens or portents to read in the sky, no sense of place, and no deeper understanding of anything, let alone life's mysteries. There was just a steady stream of traffic on nearby Highway 75. A dried up bunch of flowers in a soup can that someone had left as a tribute sat near the rather nondescript gravestone stuck next to two large arborvitae.

Angelica was even less impressed. "This sure isn't much. I think the sculpture of Hemingway's head down at the irrigation ditch is a lot better."

"I think so too. It's a much nicer setting up on Trail Creek road."

"Blew his brains out, right?"

"Yeah, makes you wonder, doesn't it?"

"Hey, why the long face? It's not us laying there. We got plenty of time left."

Alex recycled his thoughts and looked again at Angie all dressed up in black. "I guess it's more how you spend your time."

"Boy, aren't you the blue boy today. A nice, sunny day, and all you can think are dark thoughts. You know, you can make too much out of this stuff. He's only another dead guy. He had his run, and it was a good one. You gonna just stand here in this cemetery, mopin' around and feelin' sorry for yourself, or are we gonna do Sun Valley?"

Alex was yet again surprised by this girl. "Right, Sun Valley it is. Let's do her."

Saturday in Sun Valley in the off-season felt more like how traveling should be, Alex thought. The moms and pops of summer had gone back to jobs and school board meetings. The jet set wasn't there yet, just waiting for winter snow while taking advantage of the opportunity to strengthen portfolios; or like Uncle Scrooge, taking a well-deserved swim in their money bins. Most of the big homes in Elkhorn Village sat empty, like loyal dogs waiting for their masters. Nine-thousand-square-foot structures of select redwood and western red cedar with triple-glazed windows that ran from floor to ceiling, the finest of appointments and fixtures, commercial grade kitchens, and of course with actual wine cellars. All this, and no school bus ever stopped in front.

Angie and Alex roamed the sidewalks of Ketchum with room to spare. Alex was uncharacteristically window shopping, going through the high priced art galleries and antique stores, admiring the fine paintings and sculptures but rolling his eyes at the price tags. Most of the pictures and representations were of a west that never was, or at best was long gone. There were rows and rows of expensive paintings, all much the same: pretty Indian maidens carrying water or combing their jet-black hair; war-painted warriors on spotted horses, searching woodland, prairie, and desert for something mysterious; and cowboys, lots of them, nineteenth-century grizzled denizens of the frontier, displayed in all sorts of honest work and toil. The sculptures followed the same theme, lots of floppy-hatted cowboys on bucking horses of bronze; and Indians, heads down, riding the lonely trail. A few galleries did a spin-off of wildlife paintings and bronzes, and the thematic content was even more constrained to a specific formula of bugling bull elk and enormous grizzly bears.

Alex did find one watercolor that he really liked. It was a simple original, a picture of a small group of antelope running, the background a series of wet washes done in a loose, impressionistic style. The painter had captured the movement and grace of the animals without resorting to exaggeration. Alex thought about his checkbook and considered buying the watercolor but decided to hold off for what he had really come shopping for.

Alex was looking for a wood cook stove. He had it in his mind that he wanted to try to cook on a wood stove like the ones in old photographs of farm houses and hunting camps, big black things with chrome all around, cast-iron tops, and round burners. At least four cords, neatly split and covered with a blue tarp, sat waiting for his new cook stove. For some reason, Alex had deduced that Sun Valley might be the place to find one. So far, the tour of the antique shops

159

had been disappointing, with not one cook stove to look at.

Alex ambled into another store and started a conversation with the proprietor, a small, round Frenchman with a strong accent. Alex was not having much luck describing the kind of stove that he was looking for, and the Frenchman was quickly losing interest in him.

Finally Angie interrupted. "He's looking for like an old Monarch cook stove with the bread warming trivets on top."

"I know what you speak of," said the shopkeeper, "but I am afraid I cannot help you."

Alex was not giving up. "Any place else in town that might have one?"

The Frenchman gave Alex a look. "I seriously doubt it. Perhaps you can find such things in Montana." He said the word "Montana" with a tone of undisguised disdain.

As soon as they were back out on the sidewalk, Angie parroted, "Perhaps you can find such things in Mon-tan-a," stretching out the syllables.

"I seriously doubt that," Alex answered back in a fake French accent.

Angie was laughing. "God, that guy made me feel like I was a peasant or serf, trying my best to sneak into the nobleman's party."

"That reminds me of the old antique store joke," said Alex. "This kangaroo comes into the antique store and is looking around. The shopkeeper looks at him and says, you know, we don't get too many kangaroos in here. The kangaroo turns around and says, at these prices, I can see why."

"Oh, ho-ho, big funny." Angie pushed Alex across the sidewalk. "Perhaps you should think about going to Mon-tan-a."

The rest of the afternoon moved on in cheerful colors and musical notes, and like a Bach concerto, it was all upbeat, up and down the scale.

Dinner was at Louie's, the remodeled white church that was now stuffed with tables and chairs back to back and turned into an Italian restaurant. In an unusual display of affluence, Alex splurged on a bottle of imported wine.

"This is pretty good wine," Angie said, smiling with an alcohol glint in her eye. "I like it. What was that thing you ordered? Started with a C."

"The calzone?."

"Yeah, that's it. What was that green stuff in there?"

"I think it's artichoke heart."

"Really? Looks sort of funny."

"Here, try some." Alex held out his fork and Angie leaned over. Alex concentrated on how Angie took the offering with her tongue.

"It's good, sort of creamy."

They finished the bottle of wine and Alex ordered two more glasses as they sat, not saying much, just sort of smiling at one another. Almost two hours sped by before Alex and Angie, arm in arm, headed for the door.

Alex took the summer shortcut back to Goldburg, driving the Trail Creek road out of Sun Valley past the old Sun Valley Lodge and past the end of the pavement six miles north. From there the gravel road deteriorated to one lane with turnouts, a gravel berm on the outside, no guardrails, and a two-thousand foot climb to the pass. The last rays of sunset hit Alex in the eye as he turned for a glancing look at the Trail River far below. Avalanche chutes and slick-rock waterfalls appeared across the canyon, so close you could almost touch them.

Sometimes the sunset on the mountains made Alex feel like Peter Pan, as if by blinking and using his eyes like magic thoughts he could fly across the mountains and valleys at the speed of thought.

Angie pointed. "Look at the light on the mountain."

Looking past Angie, he saw the alpenglow on the Devil's Bedstead, a prominent dihedral peak sitting high above Kane Creek. The glow had lit just the tip of the peak. The result was almost religious, a yellow-gold beacon that seemed to pull you towards it. Without thinking, Alex steered the truck onto a little two-track that wound through the sagebrush, downshifted, and crawled up onto a small knoll above the road with an unimpeded view of the mountain. "God, that's something. Let's watch awhile."

Angie undid her seatbelt and slowly slid across the vinyl bench seat to lean against Alex.

He slid his arm around her shoulder and immediately noticed some pleasant physiological responses within himself. As her scent filled his nostrils, his breathing became more rapid. The touch of her cotton blouse aroused him. He became conscious of the sweat under his arms and alongside his temples. Angie slid closer, and he could taste her breath.

It didn't take long before Angie and Alex were intertwined like those illustrations in the Kama Sutra. It was kisses upon kisses, hands moving all the time. When his tongue met hers, Angie gave out a little moan which spiked up Alex's blood pressure even higher. All by themselves, as if preplanned, Alex's hands began to search. His left hand found Angie's right breast, the nipple hard beneath his fingers, while the right hand explored between her opening thighs. Angie fiercely inhaled, the belt on her jeans became loose, and Alex's big hand slipped in easily where the panties met her smooth stomach to rest awhile where

161

hairline met her mound. Angie, in turn, fumbled with and opened his zipper and felt inside, finding him ready.

Soon, clothes were being discarded as if they were on fire. Angie spread herself across the seat, heels in the air, her long legs filling the cab. It was still light enough for Alex to see the donut of muscle around her navel and the swatch of red-brown hair between her legs. Angie massaged him as he desperately tried to get the condom out of the plastic wrapper, the little Trojan man not totally cooperating until Alex finally got the correct side lined up and rolled it on.

Alex was cinched up tight, ready in the chute, and Angie guided him into the winner's circle. It was all rope and ride, and Alex let her buck. Angie was trying to stay on the somewhat slippery vinyl seat of the old Chevy, Alex was trying to stay in, and both of them were trying to avoid the cunningly placed gear shift lever of the four-speed transmission. The truck sat in the sagebrush, and as if possessed, began to shake from side to side. There began a series of alternating low and then high-pitched moans, at first without structure, and then beginning an unusual alternate staccato, one moan immediately followed by another, like a strange code. First a high ahhhhh!, followed by a low ohhhh! It was almost a musical score, with the rocking of the truck keeping time.

Alex's eyes were open, and he liked what he was seeing. Angie's eyes were closed, as if she couldn't even think about seeing. Everything went the way it was supposed to be for a while. Then Angie made her move and almost unseated the rider, three quick bucks with her hips, her back arched off the seat; and Alex, perfectly in time in the saddle, gave three quick lunges, as they locked for the final eight seconds. As Angie bucked, Alex held on as if life itself depended on him finishing the ride. Angie let out a long, long moan. Alex responded with all the instinctual programming of a million years of evolution, leading him right to the precipice and over the top, his own moan in perfect time and harmony. Alex's eyes rolled back, his nostrils flaring, his nipples hard, and he emptied both barrels, his six gun blazing. All the ammo he was carrying went up in one flurry of fireworks, and Alex's mind was totally, unequivocally blank and devoid of even a grain or semblance of thought.

They lay like two dead persons on the seat of the Chevy, Alex's arms hanging useless at his sides, his head buried in her hair, Angie's one heel on the dashboard, the other on the seatback. Alex had traveled so hard and so far that he had a difficult time coming back. He did not seem to have the will or the strength to disengage, or even to move in the saddle. Angie was the same but different; her first movement was her right hand and fingers playing in the curls

162

at the back of his head.

At this point in time, Alex's I.Q. was down about a hundred points. His reptilian brain stem kept him alive, his autonomic functions working perfectly. His mammalian brain was satiated, and it was still there, willing and able. The wonderful trouble seemed to be in the pre-frontal cortex. The mind's interpreter had just shut off for a while, it seemed, and Alex was still far away but heading in the right direction.

Angie made the first attempt at conversation, a slow giggle that began down at her navel, a series of sniffs, and then more giggles.

Alex began to come to life also, and managed to giggle back. His lips moved, formed a circle, and he said one quiet word. "Angie."

Angie giggled some more and wrapped her legs and arms tight around his limp body, so relaxed that he would have rolled off the seat if Angie hadn't held him.

"That was great." Alex said, inhaling deeply and sighing out a long, happy breath.

"Did you see God?" Angie whispered.

Alex smiled like a child. "He told me to say hi."

23

"You may not be an angel
'Cause angels are so few,
But until the day that one comes along
I'll string along with you."
                                    Al Dubin

Angie was in a black mood that Sunday morning. She was uncommonly disappointed with herself. Try as she did, she couldn't rationalize why she made love to Alex. He was supposed to be a safe boyfriend, an in-between boyfriend, she reminded herself, not a lover. She told herself over and over again, almost out loud, that she not going to get serious about him. And in his truck for God's sake, in the front seat of his pickup truck, about as unromantic as . . . as unromantic as just about anything! It wasn't just the wine. She knew she shouldn't drink much, but she had, and she did, and she liked it, at the time anyhow.

Now what was she going to do about Alex? He probably was going to go all sloppy lovey-dovey on her. She expected as much. It didn't sound like he'd been with many women, which was good, but then it wasn't either. She liked him, too, she admitted, but Angie sternly told herself that she wasn't going to get into a long-term situation with a short-term guy. After several attempts at deciding that Alex wasn't the right guy for her, she hadn't quite talked herself into it. Instead, she kept thinking about how shy and gentle he was afterwards, and how he held her for so long, and how nice that felt.

She couldn't seem to calm down, and kept fidgeting, so she decided to go outside she started walking. Angie walked past the corrals and the tool shed and found herself aimlessly wandering toward the hill slope beyond the ranch. Walking along and kicking stones, she spied a strange one. She stooped over and picked it up. Flat on one side, about the size of her hand, red-brown, the stone looked like a heart, shaped just like one except for a small chunk broken off on the left side. She thought about her trip to Bayhorse with Alex, and how much fun it was, and then meeting that crazy old guy, Dugout Dick. She remembered what Dick had said, the warning. She looked closely at the rock, got angry at herself all over again and threw the rock as hard and as far as she could. The flat stone sailed over the sagebrush, curved slightly in flight, hit a brown boulder, and broke in two.

24

"Clum Dummit, come on you deadbeat, get going," Buck Twiddle admonished. "Let's get moving or we won't even get there by opening morning. Your elk ain't gonna wait for you to show up, you know."

It was a bright Sunday morning. Alex had just stumbled out of bed twenty minutes before, the day after the big date, and his mind was still on Angelica Kowalski. As he hurried to get dressed, Alex thought that he wouldn't care if he ever went hunting. All he wanted to do was see that girl again.

Alex had a bit of luck back in July, drawing an early season elk tag to hunt in the high country of the Lost Rivers when the bulls were in rut and still bugling. Everyone in the office chided him on his beginner's luck in drawing the permit, as they were highly sought after and the odds in the annual lottery were low. Since it was obvious that Alex didn't know much about elk hunting and even less about the logistics of butchering and transporting such a big game animal, Kloyd and Buck had offered to help him out.

The conviction that "plans made are a debt unpaid" prompted Alex into action. In a stumbling daze, he packed his duffle, borrowed rifle and cartridges and headed for Buck's open truck door.

"Alex, you okay?" Kloyd asked.

"Oh, I'm fine, fine."

"Looks to me like he's love struck," Buck said, steering the truck in roundabout motions of the wheel. "That Kowalski girl has stunned him good. Looks like he's down for the count."

Alex smiled, sitting between the two smaller men on the bench seat of the truck.

"I do believe you're right. He's got that sort of hangdog look about him. Reminds me of a young bull we had down at the ranch." Kloyd rolled down the window to spit. "Lucifer was his name. Mean little cuss, even after we had him dehorned and put a ring in his nose. You always had to watch yourself around that bull. I remember we turned him out to pasture with about twenty heifers."

"That should of kept him busy," Buck said, still steering violently, as if he were at war and under fire. "Cows come into heat every twenty-one days."

"You bet, and a bull will follow a cow for two days before and one day after she's ready to go."

"So Lucifer shoulda been a busy boy."

"Right you are. Anyway, after about a month and a half, I got to looking at young Lucifer there. He'd dropped like two hundred pounds and was as tame as a puppy. Took a piece of twine and made me a halter and then led that bull back to a box stall in the barn, and he slept for three days, even ate his feed lying down. What made me remember was the look on that bull's face." Kloyd went to spit again. "Lucifer looked just like Alex does now."

Alex didn't say a thing, just rolled from side to side with the motion of the truck, but he couldn't stop smiling.

"Yeah, love struck," Buck said. "And from the looks of it, struck pretty well."

By the time they came to Doublespring Pass, Alex was functioning at a minimal level and was able to keep up the idle banter with Buck and Kloyd about elk and horses, and weather and horses, and horses and horses. All the horse talk seemed to make Buck steer even more passionately, the gooseneck horse trailer bouncing along behind. Buck turned off the Doublespring road just down on the Pahsimeroi side of the summit where two rutted tracks led off into the sage, then slipped the truck into four-wheel low range. After six or seven miles of bouncing through the sagebrush, Buck stopped the rig on a ridge above Mahogany Creek that overlooked the valley of the Upper Pahsimeroi River. Buck and Kloyd unloaded the six horses, three saddle horses and three to pack, two of which were Buck's and four of which were from Kloyd's extended Mormon family. They didn't have much of a camp to pack in. They were only planning on three or four days, as Alex was the only one with an elk tag. It didn't take long to pack up and get on the trail. The washed-out road was rocky and hard on the horse's hooves, and Buck led them through the sagebrush on a straight line to the forks of the river.

167

Yesterday's warm weather had gone and today it had just not warmed up much at all. There was a distinct solar halo, a pale arc of ice crystals encircling the sun.

Kloyd searched the sky as if he had lost something up there. "Got a weather change comin'. You feel it?"

"I feel it's colder, that's about it," said Buck. "You having one of your visions or something?"

"No, no, it's just that we never got our equinox storm, and we always get an equinox storm. Sort of a late summer this year." Kloyd paused to look over the gray limestone peaks, still mostly barren of snow. "By now we should of had one good storm, at least."

Buck turned in the saddle. "Clum Dummit, now don't be jinxing us. I ain't too excited about packin' out of here in belly-deep snow."

Alex didn't have a packhorse to lead, so he was free to rubberneck as he rode easy in the saddle. When they came over a small rise he could see all the way to the Donkey Hills, purple and brown in the distance. One more hill and Alex saw Standing on Edge Mountain, perfectly named, guarding the East Fork country.

Alex put his wool jacket on, thinking about Sun Valley. "It sure is getting colder."

"Yup, it's a-comin'."

This time Buck didn't say anything as he glanced at the mares' tails, grouped phalanx-like in the southeast.

They set up camp on a small flat where the East Fork of the Upper Pahsimeroi splits and a long deep valley flows from the north face of Mount Brietenbach. By the time the horses were unpacked and taken care of, the wall tent up and a fire made in the sheepherder stove, it was almost dark.

A scud of stratus clouds obscured the sky. There was no wind. High up in the valley, beyond the curve of the ridge, a bull elk bugled, the piercing whistle starting low, slowing rising in pitch, lasting for a full five heartbeats.

Alex jumped at the sound. "We've got at least one bull up there."

Kloyd didn't say anything for a full minute, still listening. "We'll give it a go come mornin'."

There was a new moon and, combined with the growing cloud cover, it made for a dark night. Alex slept fitfully as an up-canyon wind whipped the canvas walls of the tent. Inside, it cooled off quickly as the fire died in the sheepherder stove. Alex burrowed further into his sleeping bag as he tried to

168

keep the wind out of his dreams.

Alex struggled awake in a gray-black pre-dawn as Kloyd started the lantern puffing into life, bathing the white walls of the tent in a yellow glow. Buck was already outside with the horses. Alex could hear them nickering at the hitch line. When Buck opened the tent flap to come in, flurries of snow swirled in an aura.

"Looks like tough sledding this morning," Buck said as he dusted snow from his green wool coat.

Kloyd was busy building up a fire in the stove. "What ya think, we should hang tight?"

"Probably at least until mid-morning, see if it stops snowing."

Alex sat up, still wrapped in his sleeping bag, his breath clouding the air. "How much snow is there, Buck?"

"Well, whataya know. Young Alex is revived." Buck scratched the stubble on his chin. "Just a few inches, but you can't see ten feet in front of ya. Best to probably hunker down, drink more coffee."

Kloyd, always the Mormon, said, "I got hot chocolate, Alex, if you don't want coffee."

Daylight came late with the snow. Sometimes the wet flakes were as big as quarters. Alex, Buck, and Kloyd ate breakfast, brunch, and lunch before the snow started to back off and Alex could see the base of the mountains again.

Buck pulled back the tent flap and peered outside. Putting his enamel coffee cup down, he said, "What say we go for a ride, boys?"

Alex piled on his clothes, wearing just about everything he had brought with him from his silk underwear, wool pants and shirt to a down vest, wool coat, bomber hat and wool gloves. He carefully placed his rifle in the saddle scabbard, three bullets in the magazine, none in the chamber.

"Let's ride over towards the West Fork," Buck said. "Maybe we can catch that herd of elk movin' down."

Alex could see halfway up the mountain and, at times, through breaks in the cloud deck, all the way to timberline.

The three packhorses were anxious about being left behind tied to a line between two fir, and they carried on a bit, snorting and nickering as Buck, Kloyd, and Alex pushed their saddle horses into the timber. Alex could see the breath of the horses in the cold air.

Buck led the group under the trees where the snow lay smooth like a carpet, eight inches of powder, places of pine grass still sticking through under

169

the dark fir. Alex watched how Buck moved through the woods and tried to imitate him. They traveled slowly, stopping at each clearing or opening in the timber, Buck scanning the timber edge with his binoculars. Less than a mile from camp they found fresh elk tracks in the snow. Kloyd figured it was a small bunch, maybe seven or eight animals, the tracks deliberately following the edge of the timber, the elk reluctant to show themselves in the open.

Buck stopped and took a small, coiled tube from his coat pocket. Putting it in his mouth and taking a deep breath, he let loose an elk bugle. The notes of the whistle, the timing, seemed identical to what Alex had heard the evening before. They listened quietly. Alex's buckskin stamped his foot in the snow. Far, far off on the mountain, so soft you scarce could hear, came an answering call.

"Clum Dummit, but they're headed up," Buck said. "I was hoping this snow would push em down to us."

Kloyd stood up in the stirrups and stretched. "Might be headed over Leatherman pass, over to Sawmill Gulch and the south side of the range."

Buck clicked up his horse. "If that's the case, we won't catch em'."

They followed the elk tracks up a middle ridge of Douglas fir and whitebark pine that rolled toward Leatherman Peak, riding slowly and quietly. Buck was constantly looking ahead with his binoculars. By late afternoon the group had crested a bald hill near timberline and they had an unobstructed view of the basin ahead.

"There they are," Kloyd whispered, pointing. "They're making for the pass."

Buck framed the herd of elk in his binoculars. "Bloody hell. We can't get down to them."

Alex swung his binoculars around and saw the elk almost a mile away, seven cows and a bull, antlers easily visible, the last elk in the bunch. The rack of antlers stretched tall over his head, seemingly as long as the animal itself. The elk were far above timberline and in the open snow, pushing hard and making tracks.

"God, he's a beauty," Alex said.

Kloyd had his binoculars steadied on the elk. "A right hum-dinger of a bull. You don't see too many big ones like that on public lands anymore."

Buck put down his binoculars in disgust. "That about tears it. That old lead cow has spotted us, and it don't really matter anyhow cause they're gone already. Once they make the pass, it's steeper'n hell on the other side, and they ain't about to stop. Clum Dummit!"

"Probably bed down in the canyon, in Sawmill or Upper Cedar Creek. Almost impossible to get on them from here," Kloyd said.

"You can kiss them goodbye," and Buck turned his horse, officially ending the pursuit.

Alex lagged behind. His horse was nervous to follow the others. Alex watched the elk push through the deep snow, one after another, slipping from sight as they moved over the top of Leatherman Pass. The large bull stopped and turned broadside right on the summit, looking back at Alex, and then began a slow process of disappearing from view, first the body and then the disembodied antlers sinking below the snow horizon.

The ride back to camp was accomplished more quickly. The snow had stopped completely now, replaced by pockets of blue sky as the clouds just appeared to tear apart on the sharp peaks of the Lost Rivers. Alex heard the nickers and snorts of the pack horses in camp just as it was approaching dusk.

Kloyd stepped off his horse and gave a grunt when his boot slipped in the snow. "I think that's all the snow we're gonna get."

"Tomorrow we'll try the East Fork," Buck said.

Darkness came in slow stages of starlight on crystalline snow. The Milky Way was out in full force, with star clusters that no one could ever count. Alex could still see forms outside with only the light from the reflected stars. The crescent moon that tottered over Standing on Edge Mountain looked like it was going to roll over and down the mountainside.

Buck cracked the seal on a plastic pint of whiskey, offering Alex a cup. "Kloyd, what do you say?" Buck offered the bottle.

Kloyd looked at Buck and thought a bit. "Well, what the heck, the wife and the bishop are far off."

Buck poured him three fingers of Jim Beam. "I'll never tell."

Alex felt more than fine after his glass of bourbon and water. As he went outside for his last piss before he turned in, he was startled to see the northern lights, a scarlet streak tinged in green racing over Standing on Edge Mountain, pulsing like something alive. He called to Buck and Kloyd and soon all three gazed at a green curtain hanging, dancing, over the Donkey Hills, alive with light, translucent like a jellyfish, moving like a snake.

"Jeez-O-Friday," Kloyd said. "One drink of whiskey and this is what happens. I'm about half tempted to have another."

The lights came from the north-east, the green curtain now suffused with

171

pink, burning, trailing a whisper-thin tail of white that pulsated in the solar wind.

Buck tilted back his hat. "Go ahead, Kloyd. It's on me."

"Lookee there, it's roundup time in heaven." Kloyd pointed directly overhead, almost straight up.

A strange, green-white image seemed to coalesce just above the Pole Star. Swirls of light, feather light and free, moved in an inward spiral, a slow circle, the glowing light more than suggesting a pair of wings facing each other in an endless sky.

"It looks like an angel," Alex said softly, without thinking.

"Easy now. It's not magic, only the northern lights," said Buck. "But I'll be damned if I ever saw an aurora like this." He paused a moment and then methodically added. "You can't trust this country, you know? No matter how much you love the land, it just doesn't love you back."

The three of them stood rooted to the spot, shivering in the cold, watching the sky angel of the northern lights slowly recede from their view as the lights moved back to the north and beyond the Donkey Hills.

Later, Alex lay restless, trying to sleep; he listened to both Buck and Kloyd quietly snoring, their snores like the windshield wipers on the old school bus, slightly out of tempo with each other. As the snore tempo changed, the timing became closer and closer, and then the snores harmonized for one full exhalation. Alex had to resist the urge to count snores and predict the next harmonic. As he slipped toward sleep, his thoughts, like the northern lights, moved effortlessly about the night sky.

They were three more days in the saddle, the new snow sparkling. At dusk, the alpenglow on the Three Sisters shone like the diamond.

There seemed to be fresh elk tracks and sign in every drainage, but they couldn't find any elk, no matter how far they rode or how hard they hunted.

Buck swore more than once, "Tracks make mighty thin soup."

25

"I'd like to get you
On a slow boat to China. "
                    Frank Loesser

"So what's the big deal about this boat?" Angie said. "It looks like just a regular canoe to me, except it's red."

Alex stood to his full height, arms akimbo, and recited the canoe salesman's pitch. "This is a Rock-flex canoe, specifically designed for white water. The material has memory."

"It doesn't look all that memorable to me."

Alex explained the creed to the unbeliever, reciting the product literature by memory. "Rock-flex is a foam-core construction, and can be repeatedly formed back into shape if damaged by rocks or other sources of contact. The hull has a strong rocker for white-water conditions and a tumble-home design for quick turning, good initial stability and excellent final stability."

Angelica seemed unconvinced. "Is this what the salesman told you before he soaked you for fourteen hundred dollars?"

"Well, yeah."

"And what's the deal with the paddles? Why are they black?"

"They're made of graphite, weigh only sixteen ounces each, perfectly balanced," Alex said proudly.

"Is this more salesman banter?"

"No, really, check it out."

Angie took a paddle and did seem to enjoy moving it through the air. "Yeah, it is pretty light."

"Ah, you'll love it. And I bought the best life jackets too, Super-High Float, and all at season-end savings."

"Enough of the sales pitch." Angie picked up one of the powder-blue high-tech life jackets. "I don't know if I like this name, Super-High Float. Sort of seems to imply we're gonna be floating around in it, and super-high all the time."

Alex laughed and grabbed Angie around the waist, easily swinging her around as he step-walked in a circle.

"Stop, stop, I give up. You win. It's a great canoe." She was laughing in shrieks. "I love it, I really do!"

"I guess cowgirls really can sing the blues if they want to."

Angie dusted herself off. "Just remember this pal, I'm not a cowgirl."

Alex looked askance. "But, you are my pal, right?"

"Sure," Angie smiled. "Why wouldn't I be?"

She walked around the canoe and stopped, stretching her arms high above her head. "So, I know there's some rapids on this stretch of the river. What do you know about white-water paddling?"

"Well, I bought this book at the canoe shop and almost finished reading it."

Angie didn't like the joke. "That's scarcely a replacement for actual experience, now, is it?"

"Supposedly, there's not much above a class two rapids, maybe a short class three. It's fall, and the water's way down."

"I don't know. I seem to remember a few rocks in this part of the river."

"No problem. Remember, we've got Rock-flex on our side."

"I swear that if you start that discussion about memory and foam sandwich stuff, I'll scream."

"Anyway, the water's not that cold, and it is a blue bird day. Must be sixty degrees out."

"I don't know about this canoeing bit. I've always gone down the river in a raft, and they don't roll over like canoes do. I've always heard that canoes are tippy and meant for farm ponds, not the Salmon River."

"Oh, gosh no. These new white-water canoes can go anywhere a kayak can go, as long as they have enough floatation. These new designs are great."

"So this inner tube here in the middle is the floatation?"

"Hey, after I wrote the check, I was broke. We won't need floatation on this easy river stretch."

"Okay, okay, I'll give it a try. But you remember now, I do not want to fall in the river. Whatever else happens today, I do not want to fall in the river."

"Hey, consider it done. No falling in the river. You about ready?"

"I guess."

Alex picked up the canoe in the center, one hand on either side of the gunnels, and hoisted it up and over his head in one sweeping motion, resting the middle thwart, at the center of balance, square on his shoulders. The canoe was perfectly balanced fore and aft.

"Well, that was impressive."

Alex grunted, "Read about it in the book."

He carried the canoe down to the riverside and lowered it gently, all fourteen hundred dollars worth, on the polished rocks and pebbles at river's edge. Alex tied on an extra paddle, clipped on the water bag that contained a spare set of dry clothes, and then added a small lunch cooler. He admired the canoe and liked the new red color, thinking he should take a photograph of the boat with the yellow-brown cliffs in the background.

"You gonna keep looking at that boat, or are we going to go canoeing?" Angie jabbed Alex with a paddle.

Alex slid the canoe into a small eddy, holding it from shore as Angie stepped in and sat down on the varnished ash wood and cane seat. "You ready?"

"You bet, let er' roll."

Alex glided the canoe forward, stepped in neatly, and knelt down, all without unnecessarily rocking the boat. They began to move with the current.

"Hey, so far so good," Angie laughed. "I'm not swimming yet."

Alex mentally ran through the repertoire of paddling strokes he had memorized from the book and made a selection. He reached out and attempted a draw stroke. The canoe responded, the aft end moving toward the stroke just as the book had promised.

"Angie, let's try this together." He explained the physics of canoe paddling as a team effort. Their first practice exercise had Angie drawing left as Alex swept right, with the result that the boat neatly pirouetted in place. They reversed their strokes, and the boat went back to its previous position in the river. "See, it's working."

"I hope so. Because I see some rocks."

Alex looked downstream, saw two rocks splitting the river, a wide V slick of water flowing between them. "Okay, draw left."

The boat responded as planned. Angie knelt down in the front seat as Alex turned and lined up the canoe straight on the slick. The boat had a burst of speed in the flat fast water above the small rapids. Alex looked down and saw cobble-rock bottom going by and whitefish hanging in the current, spooked by the canoe, darting out of sight.

The boat ran the slick and over the standing wave easily.

"Yee-ahh!" yelled Angie, holding the paddle high above her head.

"This is all right," Alex said, more cautiously.

175

The winding river continued in a pattern of riffles, small class two rapids, and deep rock-filled pools. Only once, when a downed cottonwood almost blocked the river channel on the high bank, did Alex and Angie have to do any serious paddling.

"Now I know there's rapids in Cronk's Canyon," said Angie. "You can see them from the road. You're not planning on taking this canoe down there, are you?"

"Well, I did have Argo shuttle my truck and park down just below the canyon."

"Let's think about this now. We can pull out right here along the highway and you can walk down to get the pickup."

"Aw, come on, it'll be fun. The boat's been handling pretty well, the water's low. We can do this."

"Yeah, but this is the first time you've had the boat out."

Alex didn't say anything, waiting for Angie to decide.

"Okay, okay," she said. "Just don't dump me in the river, life jacket or no life jacket."

"I brought some extra clothes in my dry bag."

"Why, are you planning on falling in?"

"No, no, just in case."

"So did you bring any clothes for me?"

"Not really. I've got an extra T-shirt in there you can have."

"You'd like that, wouldn't you?"

Alex smiled deliberately. "Yeah, yeah I would."

"Just for that, if I do fall in, I won't wear your stinky T-shirt."

"Damn, there goes another dream." Alex adjusted his sunglasses. "So, what do you say, ready to give it a try?"

"Just don't put me in the river."

Alex had more than a few butterflies as he directed the canoe into the long riffle that led to the entrance of Cronk's Canyon. He had a passing thought, wondering who Cronk was and why the canyon was named for him. Alex was thinking of who he might ask, when he heard the sound of water moving swiftly over rocks.

"That sounds like sort of a big rapids."

"Don't worry," he said, though he was holding the same thought.

They didn't have long to wait, as the river turned hard right; and Alex slumped forward when he saw the riverbed narrowing into a V-slick, with a

176

series of white-topped standing waves extending all the way to the next turn of the canyon.

Angie turned back toward Alex. "Is there still time to get off the river?"

"It's too late. Just stay low and keep paddling. If we get turned, keep your paddle on the downstream side."

"This doesn't look like one of those class two rapids to me."

"Hard to say, you can't see this one from the highway. Just keep paddling."

Angie was paddling like a person possessed.

The canoe picked up speed and ran on the V-slick of clear water. The big drop came in a hurry. The canoe plunged straight over and only by accident avoided the two holes on either side of the chute. Alex was paddling furiously, trying to keep the boat straight as it rode up and down and over the series of standing waves. Angie screamed with delight.

"Keep paddling!" Alex panted.

Up and over each standing wave, the canoe shipped a little more water. Alex fought to keep the now sluggish boat straight and upright until the waves finally ended at a long, deep pool.

Angie beamed a smile, kneeling in two inches of water. "I can't believe we did it! I'm just about as wet as if I did fall in the river."

"Yeah, that was bigger water than I thought there was on this stretch of river."

"But we made it! When I saw that big hole on the right, I figured that was it. I was sure we would go over."

"No, we slid right past it."

Alex guided the canoe onto a small sandy beach right between two massive boulders. "Here, let's turn over the canoe and get the rest of the water out."

Angie stood up dripping, her jeans and shirt plastered to her body. "That was so cool."

"Yeah," he said, and stepped close, pulling her to him, as close as two life jackets would allow. "Are you cold?"

"No, it's just my legs. I'll be okay," she said quietly. Their eyes met and then their lips.

"Come on back to my place. I'll get you some dry clothes," he whispered.

Angie tensed and then pulled slightly away. "I don't think I should."

177

"Don't think you should? Why not?"

"I don't know, you know?"

"No, I don't know."

"Well, what happened a couple of weeks ago, well, it just sort of happened. I'm not sure I want it to happen again."

Alex looked at her chest moving strongly under the blue life jacket. "Why not? I thought we had a good thing going."

Angie broke free from the embrace. "Well, sure, but that's not the point. I think we need to be realistic about this. You and I are both just here for a while. I don't expect you to stay long in Goldburg, and I don't plan on it, either. I just don't think we're ready for this kind of thing yet."

Alex blinked rapidly, a nervous tick that appeared at the most inopportune times. "So what's all this? Who said anything about leaving? This is the first I've heard that you've got plans."

"Hey, we're just sort of here right now, and it's fun and all, but I don't want it to get too serious. I don't want to get tied down yet, especially in Goldburg."

"What's the problem with Goldburg, anyhow? And what makes you think I'm not going to stay?"

"Come on, you don't fit in here. I've heard you talk about graduate school. We'll have our fling, have some fun, and you'll end up back east somewhere. That's okay. I'm not gonna spend my life here either."

"So, what's this plan you're working on?"

"Oh, I don't know, maybe California, maybe not. I'd like to go somewhere where there aren't any cows, sagebrush, or dumb cowboys. I've about had it here."

"Hey, I'm not a dumb cowboy. I barely know how to ride a horse."

Angie smiled that sweet smile. "I know you're not. That's what I like about you."

"Then why don't we give it a chance?"

"I'm not making any promises."

"So, what are you trying to say, are we done or something?"

"God, men are so dense. No, I don't mean that at all. I'm just not ready for this yet. You know? Maybe in a while, but not just yet. I want to keep seeing you. I just want it all to go slower, you know?"

"Just go slower."

"Yeah, slower."

"Like a lot slower?"

"Alex!"

"But you don't have someone else?"

"No, I don't. Nobody else."

Alex was feeling guilty and didn't know why. He tried to make a joke. "You're not pining for the fjords?"

"Pining for the fjords? What is that? More friggin' Monty Python? Alex, this is not the time."

"Sorry."

"In that case, no, I am not pining for the fjords, Alex. I'm only pining for you."

The way she said it made him sort of jump inside, like being thirteen again and dancing his first slow dance at the freshman mixer. "You know, don't you, that I'm always pining for you."

Angie leaned forward and kissed him lightly on the lips. "Friends?"

"Friends? Sure." Alex rubbed his hand through his wet hair. "You know, we better get moving, or we'll get cold when the sun goes behind that ridge."

"Okay."

Alex emptied the water from the canoe. The last half mile down to the truck was a series of simple, straightforward rapids, so they handled the boat well and were never in jeopardy. They paddled through the long pool and the last bend of the river canyon. The October sun cast acute angles of shadows on rust-colored basalt, the mountain mahogany hanging on the cliff face, the reflections in the water disturbed only by their paddles.

"Look," said Alex. "There's the truck."

26

"No matter how thin you slice it, it's still baloney."
Alfred E. Smith

It was a decent kind of day for November, sort of cold, Alex thought, as he swept the first snow of the season off the small deck at the back of his cabin on Chipmunk Hill. Just a dusting of snow, but a harbinger of things to come, he thought. A harbinger, he noted, where did I come up with that? Sounds like the weatherman on TV, talking about the robin as the harbinger of spring. Well, if they can have harbingers of spring, it should work for winter, too.

"Harbinger or not," he said aloud. "Looks like more snow's on the way."

Maybe I should get a dog, he thought. Then I could talk out loud all I wanted, and it would be okay. It would be like I was talking to the dog. Anybody start to look at me funny, I could just point to the dog.

His neighbor's cougar dogs started to howl, great, long, mournful Bluetick-and-Redbone yowls.

Alex looked down the canyon and thought, Mrs. Onslow must be giving yodeling lessons again. That always seems to set the dogs off. Usually she waits till evening. Maybe yodeling is like day-length dependent or something, an instinctual timed event caused by a low sun angle, like birds migrating or bears hibernating. Having heard Mrs. Onslow yodel, Alex couldn't believe that yodeling was a conscious, deliberate act. There had to be something more to it, something uncontrollable, a conditioned response like Pavlov's dogs; or in this case, Moody's cougar dogs, which just had to join in whenever Mrs. Onslow started hitting the high notes in the "Blue Moon Yodel."

Once when he was driving down Garden Creek on his way to work, Alex caught himself just at the beginning of a quiet yodel. It was just a baby-step kind of yodel, nothing serious, but it made Alex worry. He pictured himself wearing canvas pants, the ones with the hammer loop on the side, and leaning his head back in a long yodeling frenzy. It was a slippery slope, he thought.

Images of Mrs. Onslow in full yodel began to fade by the time Alex drove into the Forest Service compound. The District had just about made the transition from field season and summer work to winter quarters at the office. All the back-country guard stations had been winterized and shut down. All the stock was back out of the Middle Fork country and positioned on winter pasture on the edge of town. The last of the summer seasonal employees had been laid off, some happily collecting unemployment in Boise, Missoula, and other college towns around the intermountain west; others, like most of the Sleeping Deer District employees, were hanging around Goldburg for a while, waiting for ski season.

Most of the work of a Forest Service District, especially a wilderness District like the Sleeping Deer, is outside work: things like clearing trails, building trail bridges, taking care of trailheads and transfer camps, and dealing with outfitters and guides and all the people hiking, climbing, rafting, kayaking, riding, hunting, and fishing. In the winter, there just isn't that much work to do out there. Sure, there are some cross-country skiers and snowmachiners, but they mostly take care of themselves. With everyone stuck in the office for the winter, work needed to be created to justify their collective positions as full-time employees. The Forest Service had responded years ago to this problem by creating the budget process.

Alex was amazed how all-consuming the budget process was on the Sleeping Deer Ranger District. He couldn't help but notice that it seemed to take much more time to plan a project budget than it took to actually complete the project on the ground. After seventeen years of schooling, counting kindergarten, and always a scholar, Alex was dismayed to find out that he couldn't make heads or tails of the Forest Service budget process. It seemed to him as if everyone was talking in a secret language, most of it in acronyms that were never written down or defined. It was as if this arcane knowledge had been passed down to everyone but him, and he was forced to fumble about as if he had landed in Bulgaria with the wrong phrase book. Alex found that he could follow the sing-song language of budget terminology. It was somewhat calming in a way, but rarely could he comprehend what people were actually talking about.

Big Stanley sauntered into his office and came right up to Alex's desk. "Big budget meeting coming up. Do you have the latest PWPs that show our projected MYPs?"

Alex rustled papers and wondered, what in the hell is a MYP? "I'm working on it, Stan."

181

"Well," Big Stan gave him a fatherly look and put his big paw on Alex's shoulder. "Let's get together tomorrow afternoon and go over it."

"Sure, Stan. After lunch okay?"

"Why don't we just plan on one o'clock."

"Um, Stan, would that be our time or correct time?"

"Well, probably a budget meeting should be on correct time. Wouldn't want to jinx it or something." Big Stan's words trailed off as his eyes followed Sandy Spotts and her tight green uniform skirt as she waltzed down the wood-paneled hallway.

As soon as Big Stanley left to follow his eyes down the hall, Alex walked over to the next office where Kloyd and Buck sometimes fumbled with pencils and paper. "Hey Kloyd, what's an MYP?"

"Jeez-O-Friday, I'm surprised at what they teach in college these days. Everyone knows that MYP stands for man year potential."

"Oh, yeah, right."

Buck looked up from the Filson catalog. "MYP? Big Stan must be getting budget fever again. I swear, it seems to happen earlier every year. Seems we spend half the winter doin' budget. But hey, Kloyd, we got it made now. We got a college boy to do budget for us."

"Buck, but you're right again. Can't expect a couple broke down cowboys to do the budget. Just wouldn't be right."

"Right, right, enough play acting the simple cowboy stuff," Alex said sarcastically. "I get the drift. You just better be nice to me or I'll budget your rear ends right out of here."

"Well, have fun doin' it," said Buck. "Cause she's your baby now. Big Stanley couldn't budget his way out of a Glad Bag, and he knows it. So it looks like it's up to you."

Alex had that sinking feeling in his gut again. "By God, if it is up to me, then I'll do the damn thing in plain English."

Buck started to laugh so hard that the last swig of coffee he had just taken blew out his nose. He coughed three times and sputtered, "Plain English? It can't be done."

Kloyd was kinder when he said, "It's just not the nature of the beast. It requires names and terms that aren't in the dictionary to feed itself. I know what you're up against, but you'll just have to learn the language."

Buck leaned back in his oak chair. "Instead of plain English, it'd be easier to invent your own terms and slip them in. Everybody's so confused, no

182

one would ever notice."

"Well, bloody hell," said Alex. "Maybe I will."

Alex went back to his office, closed the door, and started trying to make sense of one point three million dollars spread among thirty or more acronyms that seemed to have no basis in English, or an English equivalent. By lunchtime, he was rubbing his eyes and peering longingly out the window at early winter. After lunch, he spent two hours staring at a blank sheet of paper, willing himself to think about work but wandering with persistent thoughts of being with Angelica Kowalski. Just before the end of the day, Alex had a budget epiphany. Some major neurons in his brain had arced and come to his rescue, and he began to furiously scribble with a magic marker on a flip chart tablet. As any good federal employee should, Alex used different colored magic markers for different budget codes. By the time he went home for the night, long after November dark, Alex had his chart, his write-ups, and a somewhat dangerous plan well in hand.

The next day after lunch, Alex set up his flip chart as Big Stanley sat behind his desk, using two blunt fingers to type on the computer. "Damn Email," Stan said. "About as worthless as tits on a boar hog."

Alex cringed, remembering all too well last month's sensitivity training, and hoping he'd never have to sit through it again. He cleared his throat, getting a reminder taste of the Trail Boss burger he had just wolfed down at the Y café, and started in with his prepared presentation.

"Stan, I've displayed the District budget by fund code for the last three years and shown the percentage of growth or rescission in each program."

"Yeah, yeah." Big Stanley held his big fingers to his mouth like he was holding an imaginary cigar. "Looks about right."

"And here I've displayed the overall forest budget for the last three years. You'll notice that there's a rough parity among Districts of sorts, with only a couple of minor variations."

"Ye-ah, that's about how I remember it. The District gets about eighteen percent of the Forest budget across the board in historical funding."

Alex stopped in mid breath, suddenly flustered, and said, "You mean the District gets eighteen per cent, automatically?"

Big Stanley rocked back in his swivel chair. "More or less, more or less, depending on specific conditions. The management team looks at the historical budget, mainly, but we do watch out for emerging issues. The trouble is, after we pay all our bills, we never have any money for emerging issues."

183

Alex was sort of overcome by nervous energy, quietly bouncing from side to side, and blurted out, "So if we get eighteen per cent, why do we waste all this time and effort doing make-believe budget work?"

"Ah, my boy, you're catching on. If we didn't do make-believe work, tackle all these fluffy new initiatives, upward report all these flimsy memos, those fine folks in the organization way up ahead of us wouldn't have any jobs."

Alex felt flummoxed on hearing this. "Is that why we use all this made up terminology?"

"Why sure. It's an unwritten law of large organizations, especially in government, that if you invent a term or two and use it long enough, pretty soon they have to kick you upstairs to explain it to all the people that aren't as smart as you are." Big Stanley clasped his hands behind his head. "Ah, but we wander far afield. The game's afoot; so enough of this idle banter. Show me your budget figures."

Alex stood perfectly still and wondered at the odd twist of events, and a strange idea came into his head: that his real federal employee role was as a modern-day Civilian Conservation Corps or Works Progress Administration worker. Instead of a mule and a Fresno shovel, moving earth to build a Bureau of Reclamation Dam, he had a computer and a flip chart and was given the task to build a phantom budget. He took a deep breath before he continued with his plan. What the hell, he thought, it's nothing but dreaming anyhow.

"So how many man-years do we have in the budget? I hear that Riddles is really tracking hard this year on workforce numbers and man-years."

"Ummm, Stan, we can't say man-years any more."

"What? We can't say man-years any more?" Big Stan leaned aggressively forward in his oak chair, no longer feigning interest. "Why the hell not?"

"Ummm, it's a sexist term. We just went over that in sensitivity training a couple of weeks ago."

"Jesus H. Christ, I'll be damned and go to hell. Can't say man-years." Big Stan waved his arms like he was shooing away flies. "Son of a bitch, who woulda known. Well, then, how many person-years on the District?"

"Uh, we can't say person-years either."

"Holy mother of mercy! Can't say person-years! I would think that person-years would be sensitive enough for a National Public Radio lawyer?"

"Well, the trouble is, Stan, it's a masculine term, per-son, get it? All our phraseology has to be gender neutral these days."

"Gender neutral? Well I'll eat hotcakes in hell." And as if pondering that possibility, Big Stanley let out a long, dispirited sigh. "Ahhh, fuck it. What's the new term? I wouldn't want to be insensitive to the proper phraseology." He said the word "insensitive" like it was composed of four letters.

Alex knew then that he had him. "It's, umm, humanoid-unit years."

"Humanoid-unit years! Jesus jumping Christ! Who in the hell makes up this stuff?" Big Stan just sat there a moment, his eyes fixed on a point high on the wall where the wood grain formed spirals. Then he shook his head slowly from side to side, as if feigning surrender. "Okay, All right, how many humanoid-unit years do we have on the District?"

"Twelve-point-five. And that includes all the seasonal employees at one half humanoid-unit year each."

Big Stanley pondered the figures. "Looks about right to me, I guess."

"I have it all broken out by fund code; recreation, trails, wilderness, fire, minerals, lands, all the way down to one tenth of a humanoid-unit year."

"Well, looks good there. Leave me the flip chart so I can make notes. I have to present the budget to the forest supervisor next week."

"Do you want me to go, too?"

"Why hell, all the humanoid-units have to go to the budget meeting."

The big budget meeting was a major event on the Forest, an annual get-together that was one part catharsis, one part tent revival, another part town meeting, and all passion play. It was a meeting not to be missed, a mandatory meeting of the shepherd and his flock. Chester M. Riddles, supervisor of the White Cloud National Forest, a small, bespeckled survivor of two heart attacks and bypass surgery, was noted as a stern disciplinarian. Riddles was a thirty-five-year veteran of the Forest Service, totally devoid of humor in even its most rudimentary form. He was all business all the time and universally feared by all beneath him in the Forest Service family.

This was Alex's first face-to-face meeting with Riddles, and as Big Stanley did the introductions, Alex heard a deference in the pitch in Stan's voice - and could sense Stan's fear of the little man, a thing that Alex had not thought possible. A twinge of remorse gripped Alex as he shook hands with Chester M. Riddles, and a premonitory fear curled his stomach into a ball. It was too late to change anything now. The humanoid-unit flip charts were up on the wall, joining the other District flip charts in a strange stations-of-the-cross that circled the antiseptically clean conference room.

185

The Sleeping Deer Range District was scheduled to present its budget first. No one on the rest of the Forest called the District by its given name but rather by the shortened version, D-one. The other Districts followed suit, with D-two, D-three, and D-four. Because of this incessant desire for order in all aspects of the Forest Service, Big Stanley was the first presenter.

Chester M. Riddles sat right up front in a brown suit and tie, puffing his pipe, confident that no one would dare mention that there was a rule prohibiting all smoking in government offices. The rest of the conference room was standing room only. Alex, Kloyd, and Buck had seats near the back. Big Stanley loomed large in his green uniform, laser-light pointer in hand. The gathered crowd quieted quickly as the forest supervisor cleared his throat and began to speak. Alex almost expected Riddles to lead them all in prayer.

Soon it was Big Stan's turn on stage. He was really good at this type of thing, thought Alex, watching Big Stan work the crowd like a politician at a bake sale. Big Stanley just seemed to have the right mix of statistic and colloquialism, hard data and a soft-touch story.

Alex tensed up when Big Stan explained how many humanoid-units the District needed next budget year and watched him carefully position himself in requesting an additional two humanoid-unit years, or HUYs, for an expanded program in wilderness trail work. There was a general murmur moving about the room, even a bit of quiet laughter, each time Big Stanley repeated "humanoid-unit years."

At the end of Big Stan's budget presentation, Chester M. Riddles slowly took the pipe from his mouth and drawled, "Stan, what's all this hubbub about humanoid-unit years?"

Alex held his breath as he saw Big Stanley freeze, a blush of red on neck and cheek, his eyes darting around the room.

Stan cleared his throat, his voice sort of breaking as he spoke in a unusually quiet tone. "Umm, Chester, humanoid-unit years are a new requirement this year in all of the budget formulations. It's part of the new non-gender specific, non-sexist budget terminology."

Chester M. Riddles's little head jerked upright when he heard the word "non-sexist."

"Right, right, of course I knew that. My question to you really was, and I probably should have directed this to Moe here, is what is our humanoid-unit-year target on the Forest this coming year?"

Moe Rose, Forest Budget Officer and Mormon Bishop of the first ward of Goldburg stood up, budget book in hand, and with military precision said, "Chester, we're dealing with a forest budget target of one hundred and ten humanoid-unit years."

Alex thought he saw a bead of sweat run down Big Stanley's cheek and neck.

"So do we have the budget flexibility to give D-one an additional two humanoid-unit years?" asked Chester M. Riddles.

Moe Rose went on. "At this point, I think we need to see the other District presentations before we change the HUY mix on the forest. As I understand, the Washington Office is determined to follow the national budget advice in freezing total humanoid-unit years at last year's level."

Chester M. Riddles tapped his pipe into his hand. "Well, Stan, good job on your budget. I will try to see if we can get you those two additional HUYs for your trails work."

Big Stanley snapped to attention. "Thanks, Chester. Those two humanoid-unit years will make a real difference on the District." And Alex caught a glare from Big Stanley that just fixed him to his chair.

Alex listened to the other three rangers all make strong points on why they also needed additional humanoid-unit years, as their program of work had outgrown the humanoid-unit year budget limitation on their Districts.

By the end of the day, after all the dust had settled, it was decided that D-two, D-three, and D-four, would each receive one additional humanoid-unit year. The Sleeping Deer Ranger District, primarily due to the strength of its budget presentation, would receive two.

Just before the meeting ended, Kloyd leaned over to Alex and whispered, "There ain't no such thing as a humanoid-unit year, is there?"

Alex looked around at all the anxious faces, caught a quick glance and a smile from Big Stanley, and said, "There is now, Kloyd, there is now."

27

"In heaven an angel is nobody in particular."
George Bernard Shaw

The draft beer tasted good. All during the day dark-blue clouds had been coming over the mountains from the west, and now heavy snow warnings had been posted for the mountain passes. Alex had not noticed until now that The Wild Bunch sign reflected in the long mirror above the bar.

"Do you realize that we've known each other since we've been five years old?" said Rodney. "I still remember your dad, saying he had a boy the same age as me."

Everything felt good as Alex slipped into the pattern. Rodney was an old buddy from back east, Pennsylvania, and staying the weekend. He was Alex's first company in his little cabin on Chipmunk Hill.

Rodney's eyes turned toward the snow swirling when the bar door swung open. "Man, I don't know how I'm ever going to get back to Boise tomorrow. I think this actually is the middle of nowhere, said so right on the Idaho state map. This is like so far from Penn State it's not even on the same planet. How did you ever find this place?"

"You know, it sort of found me. It seemed all the roads I went down led me to Goldburg."

"Pretty damn philosophical, but Christ, it's such a dump. Next thing you'll be telling me is that it grows on you."

Alex had been thinking of saying just that. "Well, as a town, it is sort of rough sided. But the country, it just fits me --"

"Like a fine shoe? A fine glove? Like a condom?" Rodney interrupted. "Now don't go getting New Age on me, talking about past lives and such. From what I've seen of Goldburg, the whole place looks like a past life."

"You know, I think that's why I like it. Every time I come to town, it's like a time machine of sorts. Cheap thrills, I guess."

188

"More like sloppy seconds. I just don't see how you can live all by yourself way back in the woods. It's the end of the road, man."

"Just in the winter. That's where the snowplow turns around."

"Yeah, but it's like the last house in the world. The last electric light, which, I guess, is kind of cool in a way. You need to find a better name, though. Chipmunk Hill sounds like something from a Dr. Suess book."

"Hey, Chipmunk Hill is a great name. Beats the hell out of Cow Creek or Bear Creek, must be a dozen of those just on the forest. Somebody says, 'Cow Creek,' and you answer, which one, the one up Morgan Creek or the one in Pahsimeroi? Then it's, what fork? And pretty soon you're down to the north fork of the east fork."

"Alex, you're babbling again. I don't have the foggiest idea what you're talking about. Is this one of those rural Idaho things again?"

Alex grabbed Rodney by the shoulders, playfully shaking him, as only a close friend could. "Oh man, I should just bust you one right here. An Idaho thing? I'll show you an Idaho thing."

The Wild Bunch was beginning to fill, starting another timeless Saturday night. It was all sort of like a scene from one of those new movies, filled with now people, filmed in a then place, Alex thought.

Rodney swirled the beer in his glass. "So how's this Forest Service gig working out for you?"

"So far, it's going pretty good. It's sort of weird sometimes, like we don't get much done and just go to meetings. We like to plan everything to death all the time. I guess maybe I'll fit in better after I learn more of the corporate culture bullshit."

"How long you plan on staying? Or are you planning on going to graduate school? I remember you saying it was just for a year. Oh yeah, this was supposed to be a life experience."

"That's the fuckin A big question. You know, I do kind of like it here. This outdoor life is kind of cool."

"Yes, that's the life for a man. A Forest Service man, in the wilds of Idaho, with his best gal by his side," and he began to sing, "I'm in the Forest Service and I'm okay, I sleep all night and I work all day."

A few cowboy hats at the pool table lifted up and looked Rodney over a few times.

"Take it easy, Rod. This isn't Penn State. I don't want to have to fight my way out of here."

Rod composed himself quickly, his blood alcohol content too low a match for his behavior.

"Hold on now, this might be interesting." Alex swung his chair around to face the bar and the barking of a furious small dog.

"What's going on?"

"Somebody's going to try to put the collar on Teddy."

"Teddy?"

"He's Shugg's dog, the guy who owns the bar. That's him right there." Alex pointed to a forty-something-guy with a crew cut and muttonchops sideburns, an always-smiling type with the stereotypical look of a cowboy movie sidekick. "If you get the collar on Teddy, you win fifty dollars."

The barking had turned into a spitting chorus of snarls and growls as Teddy backed into view, all thirteen-beagle inches of him.

Rod crowded over next to Alex. "Anybody ever get the collar on him?"

"Not that I ever heard. Shugg told me that these cowboys will get a few too many drinks under their belts and think they can put a collar on a grizzly bear."

It was a heavy-set cowhand about Alex's age, with a thick, black handlebar mustache, that cautiously circled old Teddy around the now-empty dance floor. He kept repeating, "Nice dog, that's a good dog," as he held the red collar hidden behind his back.

Now, Teddy was an old beagle that never did like strangers and had played this game before. His teeth showed white behind quivering black lips, spitting snarls. Ears up, he was totally focused on the hand the cowboy held behind his back. He had no more room to give, backed up into a corner, frozen hard on his haunches, waiting. The mustached cowboy seemed to hesitate, his plan for an easy collar stymied by a reluctant Teddy. The whoops and yells of his friends urged him towards a poorly thought out, desperate, quick-loop move, a sort of a dog shock-and-awe effort, to try to get the red collar over Teddy's small head. Not even halfway through, Teddy had bitten three times, twice on the right hand and once on the left.

A yowl of drunken pain and a dropped collar ended the barroom drama. Teddy streaked back behind the bar. The cowboy rocked back on his heels and then forward on his toes, his right hand bundled up in a red neckerchief. "Sumbitch dog bit me good!" The Wild Bunch crowd burst into equal parts laughter and applause, and Shugg drew out two pitchers of beer on the house for the loser.

"This is what they do for fun in Goldburg? We need to get you back to

190

State College, where the drunks just sort of laugh and fall down.

"So you're not going to give Teddy a try? Fifty bucks; easy money."

"No way, man, you're tying to corrupt me again. I see I'm going to have to keep a close eye on you. This Idaho thing is starting to show in your behavior." Rodney seemed spellbound, shaking his head. "So how about this girl you keep talking about? When are you going to show her off?"

"Man, she is like wonderful."

"I can't picture you as a cowboy. How are the two of you hitting it off?"

"You know, strangely enough, even though we have almost nothing in common, it seems to be going okay. I don't know where it's headed, though. I'm confused all the time."

"Be careful, it sounds a lot like love."

"All I can say is, give me some more of it."

"Well, hell, just remember, the sun doesn't shine on the same dog's ass all the time."

"Christ, the way you talk about my life, I would think there should be a soundtrack playing in the background."

"Hey, I tried that, but the cowboys at the pool table didn't appreciate it."

By the time Alex and Rodney left The Wild Bunch, it had stopped snowing. About two new inches covered the sidewalk. A few lonely stars shone through ragged openings in the clouds.

Back at the cabin on Chipmunk Hill, Alex turned on the last electric light and made up a spare bed. Rodney turned in and was asleep within minutes. Alex succumbed to a strange restlessness and put on his boots and walked outside onto his little deck. The sky had almost cleared. With a new moon, the stars went all the way down to the horizon, the Milky Way bright and beckoning. Maybe it was just the alcohol, but Alex couldn't ever remember seeing so many stars. He saw the familiar constellations, but there seemed to be thousands of new stars glittering in between. He had a strange magic feeling of seeing the winter sky for the first time. The Big Dipper really seemed to dip low, pointing to Polaris. Cassiopeia, the big W, stared back at him in bold letter form. He could count all six Pleiades, it was so clear. Alex dusted the snow off his chaise longue, lying down on the cold plastic, shivering under his wool cruiser coat, just watching the stars move in that big circle around the pole.

He sat up suddenly to a flash of light in the northwest. Now it was directly above him, a shooting star that blazed across the night sky, so close Alex swore he could hear it burning. It turned yellow, then blue, then a pulsating white. He expected it to burn out, but instead it just got brighter. Almost to where the east ridge meets the horizon, it broke in two pieces. The smaller piece shooting behind the ridge. The larger flashed white toward Goldburg, looking like it would crash into the canyon. Alex held his breath, listening, but didn't hear an impact.

"Jeez-O-Friday!"

Questions of omens and meaning crowded Alex's thoughts as he leaned back in the lounge chair. Historical records of shooting stars presaging the king's death came first to mind, and then the Battle of Hastings and Halley's comet stuck in his brain. Alex knew his mind naturally searched for patterns in life and wasn't satisfied until it found some. As he watched and waited, no hidden meanings became clear, no visions or premonitions rose to the top of his consciousness. Try as he might, he couldn't establish a shred of connectivity so far in his life patterns in Idaho, except when he thought about Angelica Kowalski.

Alex felt himself falling asleep, staring at one group of stars that twinkled on and off. As he closed his eyes, he thought to himself that he had never been happier.

28

It was after midnight, the day after Thanksgiving. Alex pressed Angelica deep into the cushions of her parent's flower patterned couch, trying to establish that beachhead that would allow his landing party to come ashore.

"Alex," Angie panted. "Time to stop."

More panting, this time from Alex. "Oh God, Angie, just a little longer." His hands stayed rooted up her short skirt, now halfway up her thighs and getting closer.

Angie wriggled underneath him. "But we have to stop."

Defeated but still determined, Alex pleaded on, "But it's so nice."

"Sorry." That one word ended it for the evening.

Alex rolled to the side, hands now covering his eyes, still dreaming of an alternate twenty minute reality.

Angie sat him up and wrapped her arms around his shoulders. "It's probably about time for you to go home."

Alex's thoughts came in micro-bursts of strange logic. "Angie, you know the Amish have a tradition where the suitor stays overnight with the girl. Just lays there. They don't do anything, they just lay there next to each other, spend the night. Seems like a wonderful tradition."

Angie snuffled a series of giggles underneath a throw pillow, coming up for air to say, "But Alex, we're not Amish!"

"Hey, it's just a quaint folk tradition that I thought you might enjoy."

More snuffles and a quick, "We're not even in Pennsylvania!" before she plunged under the pillow again.

Alex was giggling right along with her. "I've got a black hat, and you've got the horses."

Angie took a deep breath. "Alex, I don't think the litmus test of being Amish is having the right hat."

"You never know." More giggles before he finally was able to say, "It's a really nice hat!"

He collapsed on top of her in reckless laughter.

"Alex, keep it down, you'll wake up my parents!"

Alex was laughing so hard that he had tears in his eyes. "I would think they would be happily surprised if they did."

She punched him in the arm. "You're terrible, you know that?"

A big sigh, "Yes, that I most certainly do." Alex sat up straight, folded his hands in his lap, and held his head down, eyes closed. "Angie?"

"Yeah?"

"I love you."

Angie placed her hand on the side of his head and held it there, looking into Alex's eyes. She started to say something, her lips began to form words, but then, she took a deep breath and stopped.

Alex was frozen with embarrassment, and mumbled, "I guess I better get going."

29

The much-anticipated office Christmas party at Big Stanley's house was fast approaching. Plans had been ballyhooed about the office all the previous week with ideas for skits and the type and amount of liquor, what type of decorations and what kind of beer, and what kind of music and what kind of chasers.

Big Stanley owned a big, rambling house at the edge of town, right on Garden Creek. It was one of the oldest homes in Goldburg, with a steep-pitched roof and long, upright windows that curved at the top. Big Stan lived alone in the house with his guns, his dogs, and his taxidermy. Big Stanley, for his part, didn't do much preparation for the party other than hand Sandy Spotts four new Ben Franklins and cheerily tell her to "Go to it."

Sandy made certain that everyone in the office had an assignment. Alex's job was to coordinate the entertainment. Buck found his work a somewhat easier task, as Sandy recognized a natural talent when she saw it and put Buck in charge of the liquor. Kloyd had the food patrol, which was really pretty easy, as most everyone brought a dish. Stan's one and only task was to make certain, doubly so, that his now well-trained skunk family would be fed and safely secured in his chicken coop come Saturday night. Sandy, inherently knowing the seriousness of the event, could not trust anyone else with the responsibility and coordinated the decorations herself.

The big event began as soon as it got dark, which was barely four-thirty in the afternoon, with an early raid on the liquor supply. By the time Alex and Angie arrived around an hour later, they could hear happy sounds at Big Stan's place from clear across the street.

Alex had never been inside Big Stanley's house and was held speechless when he came into the long living room with its ten-foot ceilings. Animal heads were everywhere; horns and antlers, fur and feathers were plastered on every possible wall space. It was a cowboy safari room with a camouflage-patterned sofa and love seat offset by a life-size mount of a black bear standing on two legs, claws outstretched in greeting. There was a small herd of elk heads lining the north wall and a corresponding one of mule deer on the south. On the two side walls, set among the windows, were four antelope, two mountain goats, and a full-curl bighorn sheep. There were bear and cougar hides on every flat surface of furniture. You couldn't put down a glass without placing it on fur.

Sandy Spotts had a natural feeling for interior design and had arranged rows of Christmas lights that wound through all the elk antlers, across onto the antelope and mountain goats, following the spiral of the bighorn sheep horns, and linked across into the many antlers and the watching eyes of the mule deer bunch. The effect of the twinkling, colored lights somehow softened this aura of death and transformed it into an expression of Christmas appreciation for the miracle of quality taxidermy.

Big Stan's two dogs, his German Shorthair, Wanda, and his black Lab, Zeke, worked the crowd for handouts and snacks. They smelled crotches, man and woman alike, as it didn't seem to make much difference. It was a cowboy kind of Christmas at Big Stanley's place. The women were all pretty, and the beer was all free.

The food was as varied as the assortment of liquor and was going just as fast. Kids ran around, climbing on the furniture. Alex suspected most of them were Kloyd's. But no one seemed to mind, least of all Big Stan.

Around seven o'clock there was a bit of a tumult around the scraggly Douglas fir Christmas tree when Santa made an early appearance. A head taller than anyone else in the room, his red suit several inches short at cuff and ankle, he was the most physically imposing Santa that Alex had ever seen. Some of the smaller children screamed in fright when they saw him and had to be dragged over to sit on his knee. But Big Stanley played the part well, and every child left happy with their own special present, while Santa took sustenance from a long-necked bottle.

As Alex looked around, he decided that virtually everyone at the party would have to walk home. He knew how much booze Buck had bought and calculated the liquor quotient and averaged that among the party revelers. No one, not even Kloyd, could pass a breath test in this crowd. Alex was still stuck on his fourth bottle of beer, holding the empty bottle religiously as a way to keep someone from placing another drink in his hand. Alex was in charge of the entertainment, and he was determined to be clear headed in the faithful discharge

196

of his duties.

The satirical skits were a cut above most that Alex had seen, with plenty of sexual innuendo, easily enough to get fired if expressed at the office. The best skit had to go to Sandy Spotts and Buck. Sandy, in an extremely tight, short mini-dress, two sizes too small when she bought it from the Victoria's Secret catalog, played the part of the big-city bird-watcher environmentalist, asking her faithful Forest Service friend, played by Buck in full uniform, where she could see some rare birds. Buck, acting the ranger, dutifully pointed out a "prairie-green falcon" far to one side; and Sandy, right on cue, binoculars to her face, bent far over and exposed her Forest Service green polka dot panties. Buck and Sandy pulled the gag twice more, and all the crowd loved it.

Alex was next, his big debut. He had practiced the song with Angie over and over. She had played twelve bar blues on her guitar again and again, getting Alex used to the beat. He still didn't believe Angie's high opinion of his singing skills. He didn't feel like a blues man, just a guy with a deep, husky voice pretending he could sing. He knew the only reason he was doing this was to please her, and he was scared.

With Charley on the mandolin and Darrel on the dobro, and Angie with her guitar and amp, the Christmas party music program began, featuring the "Caring for the Land Four." Angie and the Gold Dust Twins played two instrumentals and seemed to keep in time, even though Charley and Darrel were so drunk the only thing keeping them upright were their instruments.

Alex nervously cleared his throat. "Folks, I want to sing a little blues tune that I wrote, called the Forest Service Blues." He turned and whispered "Blues in E, guys." Angelica walked it down the scale, running through a twelve-bar blues riff. Alex followed the beat and took a deep breath. When Angie hit the downbeat where he was supposed to come in, nothing happened. He just stood there with his mouth open. Angie looked at him and kept the beat going. She caught Alex's eye, smiled and nodded her head, and his fears just faded away. Right on time on the next riff, Alex began to sing in his gravelly baritone.

"Went to the office, walked by the fax machine.
Went to the office, walked by the fax machine.
I got that hardware and software, arguing over me."

There was a couple of hoots and laughter in the crowd. Alex's face

197

involuntarily reddened as Darrel went up and down the blues scale on his dobro.

"I just stand here wondering, will a flash drive hold my soul.
I just stand here wondering, will a flash drive hold my soul.
I ain't got that much hard drive, but Lord, I got so far to go."

More hoots, some clapping. Alex was getting into the song now. Charley seemed to sense a window of sobriety and played a mean blues mandolin, hitting some anxious blues notes.

"I got Email, sugar babe, I get more every day.
I got Email, get more every day.
Baby the more you Email, the further you drive me away."

Angie walked down the neck of her guitar with her favorite blues riff, hammering the last blues note. The Gold Dust Twins finished right on time. The whole room erupted in applause, and Alex was grinning, red faced and happy.

A towering Santa Claus, slightly weaving from one side to the other, came over to Alex and asked, "Did you really write that song?"

"Sure enough, Santa."

Santa Claus stood up straight and said, "Well, I'll eat hotcakes in hell."

30

"At Christmas play and make good cheer,
For Christmas comes but once a year."
                              Thomas Tusser

   The snowflakes were falling straight down like in an old black-and-white movie, stark white pinpoints on a gray background. It was Christmas Eve, and the President had closed all federal offices two hours early. Alex had stayed after, enjoying the last of the Christmas cookies and fudge with Big Stan, Buck, Kloyd, and Sandy. Big Stanley locked the front door and reached deep into his bottom desk drawer to retrieve a bottle of Jack Daniels, the official whiskey of the "good old boy" Forest Service. Sandy wrangled up some glasses and ice and Big Stan offered a Christmas toast, glasses raised all around; "May ye be a half an hour in heaven before the devil knows you're dead." Alex laughed, sensing a bond had been set in the almost nine months he had worked on the Sleeping Deer Ranger District. If he was not yet family, Alex thought, he was at least a shirt-tail relative.
   Alex was wearing his new Pendleton shirt, a green-and black-plaid right off the rack from McDougal's and his best pants and shoes. He had been invited to the Kowalski home for Christmas Eve. It was supposed to be some kind of Polish deal, a Christmas Eve celebration called "Wigilia". All the Kowalskis, from Pocatello all the way to Boise, were supposed to be there. It was going to be a housefull. Angie had explained that Christmas Eve is the most important day of the year, even more so than Christmas itself, and everything about the day is special. And the "Wieczerza Wigilijna" or Christmas Eve supper, is the highlight of the day. Angie had told him, "How you are on Christmas Eve is how you will be all the next year."
   The snow was beginning to taper off as Alex stepped from his truck and saw Angie waiting for him in the yellow glow of the porch light. She kissed him quickly. "Alex, if any of my relatives start to get on your nerves, you can leave anytime you want."

199

"Why would they get on my nerves?"

"We'll see what you think in an hour or two."

Inside it was a bustle of large bodies and plates of food. Other than Angie's dad, it seemed that the rest of the Kowalski clan was quite wide. A particularly wide body with an Elvis-style mop of black hair came up to Alex.

"So, you're the new boyfriend?"

"Alex, this is my Wujek, my Uncle Joker." Angie did the introductions.

Uncle Joker shook Alex's hand like it would be his last chance, and he didn't seem to want to let go. "Angie is my godchild, and I just think the world of her."

"Well, ah, ah, Uncle, ah, Joker, so do I." Alex noticed a definite lifting of both Angie's and Uncle Joker's heads when he made this statement and was a bit embarrassed at his uncharacteristic temerity, but when he caught a glint in Angie's eye he decided it was a good thing to have said.

"Here," Uncle Joker said, still clasping Alex's hand and dragging him into the living room, "This is my wife, Alice."

Whether because of a hearing problem or just because she liked to, Alice spoke loudly, to everyone, all the time. No doubt when she was talking in the house you could hear her from out in the barn. "So, this is the new fella?" she said. "Hey, Angie he looks a little bit like that guy in the movies, you know, what's his name. The fella that shoots all the people, you know, the spy guy."

And not for the last time that evening, Alex blushed scarlet red from neck to cheek.

"So, I hear you work for the government," Uncle Joker asked.

"Yeah, the Forest Service, here in town."

"Well, just keep that federal job, those benefits, don't ever give it up." Uncle Joker finally dropped Alex's hand, and Alex gently shook it to restore the feeling.

Angie grabbed Alex by the arm. "And, Alex, this is my Ciotka Gina, my aunt Jenny.

Ciotka Gina looked Alex up and down. "Oh, he doesn't look like that spy guy." Aunt Jenny grabbed him by his cheek. "He looks more like my cousin Bernie from Chicago only bigger, and with blonde hair." She pronounced the city name as "Chee-ca-go" in three long, musical syllables.

Angie kept moving. "And this is my Ciotka Sophie." Aunt Sophie also seemed to like Alex's looks, as she grabbed his arm and said in another loud voice, "Hey, Popsy, take a look at this boy over here."

Uncle Popsy came over obediently, clasping Alex in a hug with both arms. "So this is Alex," and Uncle Popsy's voice pealed like thunder. "I heard all about you. Hear you like to eat."

Alex just didn't know what to say to something like that as he slowly emerged from the bear hug. "Yeah, sure."

""Well, we've got plenty of food," Uncle Popsy boomed. "I brought some special sausage up from Potacki's meat market down in Pocatello. You know Potacki's, don't you?"

"I haven't been down to Pocatello yet," Alex apologized.

"Haven't been down to Pocatello? Angie, what, you keeping Alex up here all for yourself? You bring Alex down to Pocatello and we'll feed him up real good."

Angie didn't respond but kept moving down the line. "And Alex, this is Dziakek Kowalski, my grandpa."

Grandpa Kowalksi was a big man, with large ears, coal-black hair, white at the temples, a look of strength about him. He moved easily and formally shook hands with Alex. His voice was surprisingly soft, the only such voice in the house. He had one question. "So, Alex, I hear you're Roman Catholic."

"Yes sir," Alex said, trying to remember the last time he had been to Mass.

"That's good, that's good. Angie should have a Catholic boy."

"Now, Dziakek, don't be giving Alex the third degree."

"You look big and strong," the old man said. "Are you a wrestler?"

"Well, I did wrestle a little bit in high school."

"No, I mean like on television, you know, professional wrestling. I watch it every Saturday on TV, comes all the way from Buffalo."

"No sir, I'm not a wrestler."

"That's too bad. You look like you could wrestle. Angie, don't Alex here look like he could wrestle?"

"Sure Dziakek, whatever you say. He'd be a great wrestler. And Alex, this is my Babcia Kowalski."

Short and heavy, Grandma Kowalski had a wonderful smile that just radiated everything that was grandmotherly. She was wrapped in a white apron with a big spoon in hand. Her voice was high and loud. "Oh, Alex," she said. "Angie has told me all about you." And one look told Alex that, indeed, Angie had. Grandma Kowalski knew the score, he thought, and behind that apron, she was one sharp lady. "So, how do you like Idaho? I imagine it's quite different from Pennsylvania."

"I like it just fine."

"Good, I would think you might be homesick sometimes."

"Sometimes."

"But Angie here helps, I hope?

"Babcia!"

"She helps me a lot."

"Babcia, don't you have to finish the cooking?"

"Oh, I've gone and embarrassed my little girl. I suppose I better get back to the kitchen. Lovely to meet you, Alex."

"Sure, Grandma, wonderful to meet you too."

Alex met at least five more sets of uncles and aunts. Leo Kowalski had seven brothers and sisters, and all of them were here for Wigilia. Alex was having trouble remembering names, as everyone was anxious to hug him, shake his hand, carrying on like Angie had just found him wandering alone in the wilderness. Alex had been raised in a somewhat reserved family setting and was having difficulty adapting to this wholesale expression of emotion from people he was meeting for the first time.

"Angie?"

"Yeah?"

"Why do they call him Uncle Joker?"

"Oh, I don't know. I guess maybe cause he tells a lot of jokes. Uncle Joker, that's what all the kids call him."

And there were cousins, lots of them. Alex was amazed that all these cousins, aunts, and uncles had traveled all this way for Christmas Eve. The big rambling farm house was stuffed with people and packages.

Alex noticed that the house was decorated differently. He asked Angie about the swatches of hay in the corners of the dining room.

"That's to chase away misery," she explained. "And see the mistletoe over the door? That's to ward off evil."

There was another thing that Alex noticed about the Kowalski family that was different. Everyone was talking, all the time. The conversation formed a constant din, a background hum almost like a giant hive of bees. If it wasn't for the laughter, there wouldn't have been any breaks at all. Especially the women; they talked like machine guns, all going at the same time. Somehow it all worked out, and everyone seemed to understand everyone else.

Alex couldn't help but be entranced by the mixture of Polish and English among the older generation. Ciotka Tresa and Babcia Kowalski were in some kind of hot discussion, possibly about rock music or rock musicians. All Alex heard was "bla, bla, bla bla, bla, Elvis Presley. Bla, bla, bla, Rolling Stones." It went on like this for long minutes, drawing Ciotka Sofie into the discussion with a, "I don't believe it, not a Polish boy. A Polish boy would never do that." Alex wondered what the Polish boy might have done but was too embarrassed to ask.

He did ask Angie, "Do you speak Polish?"

"Oh, just the odd word or phrase."

Alex noticed her listening to some of these mixed conversations, saw her lift her eyes on the continuing Polish-boy conversation, and thought she might have been modest about her linguistic abilities.

The smell of the cooking started to draw Alex in, moving him closer and closer to the kitchen. Angie had told him to come hungry, and he certainly was, having fasted all day as was the tradition that had been explained to him. When the women started to set the table, he began to drool like a St. Bernard.

The food, literally tables full, and all of it stuffed with fat and sugar, looked like something from a medieval feast. There were simply wondrous things; and Alex, in his true element, began to lust for this food, waiting for the meal to begin.

They waited for the first star to appear before they started the dinner, to commemorate the star of Bethlehem. Alex was so hungry that he thought it was more than dark enough, and maybe he would just go outside and find that star. But Uncle Joker came through with the first star in the sky, and everybody gathered around the Christmas tree. Just before dinner, Grandpa Kowalski took the honor to turn on the Christmas-tree lights.

The dinner was a formal affair. All the men were seated, while the women and children brought out the food on trays and placed them in the center of an enormous dining room table set with a white tablecloth. An extra plate and table setting was placed for an absent Kowalski or an unexpected visitor.

Before the meal began, Grandma Kowalski offered a prayer and then passed the blessed Oplatek wafers around the table. Everyone stood up and offered the Oplatek to the one next to them and then exchanged kisses on the cheek. Angie offered the Oplatek to Alex, and he took the initiative, which was not unnoticed, of kissing her right on the lips. Angie screwed up her face for a second but let it pass. Ciotka Gina, on Alex's left, grabbed him by the shoulders and pulled him down in a hug and kissed him on each cheek. And then kisses and hugs went around the room as uncles and aunts and grandma and grandpa and cousins gave each other the Christmas Blessing. It took some time to get some of them back to the table, and Alex was even hungrier by now.

The first course of twelve meatless dishes was fried mushrooms, breaded in cracker crumbs and fried in vegetable oil. This was followed by a thick vegetable salad with potatoes and red beans. Then came the sledzie, pickled herring, one of Alex's favorite treats. The way that Uncle Joker made it was much better than what you found in the small jars in the supermarket. The bigos, or hunter's stew, was prepared without meat, as was the Christmas custom. It didn't even have lard in it, just vegetable oil, with lots of cabbage and sauerkraut. Then it was Grandma's deep-fried fish, fresh fish from the coast deep fried in olive oil, not lard, and so wonderfully tasty that Alex could of eaten a bucketfull.

Alex was implementing his special talent, to the delight of all the women.

Ciotka Wanda came out of the kitchen carrying yet more dessert cookies. "Look how he eats."

"And so skinny, too." Ciotka Tresa said.

Clear borscht with dumplings was next, followed by krokiety, little crepes filled with kaska (barley, and onions). The beets from the borscht were shredded and sliced, salted and peppered, and served with bread and butter. The ninth dish was pierogis and Alex tried every kind there was, deciding that he liked the cottage cheese ones the best. This was followed by two dishes of eggs: stuffed eggs fried in oil and hard boiled eggs with mustard dressing. The twelfth and last dish was more herring, this time in oil, and just sprinkled with onion and lots of pepper.

Alex was finally full. He had eaten more than anyone else at the table, even Uncle Popsy. And for some reason, all the women, even Angie, seemed to appreciate it. More comments came from all the aunts about how well Alex had eaten and how thin he was.

And then the special glasses came out of the sideboard for the wine.

"It's a mead made from honey, imported right from Poland," Uncle Joker told Alex. "It's a Polish specialty, this wine. I get it from my cousin in Detroit, Hamtramck. Have to order it almost six months in advance."

After the wine, Grandpa Kowalski, as the patriarch of the clan, made a special effort to heap up an enormous pile of leftovers on a metal tray. Then putting on his wool coat, he struggled to pick up the tray and headed to the door, explaining to Alex, "On Christmas Eve we feed the animals in the barn from our own table, for the legend is that only on Christmas Eve can the animals talk to us."

Uncle Joker and Uncle Popsy joined in and helped him take the food to the barn. Alex fantasized a bit about talking dogs and cats and cows, wondering what they would say.

Everyone gathered into the living room. Angie sat down at the piano and started to play a selection of Christmas carols. And everyone began to sing, just like that. Nobody held back or mouthed the words, they all started to sing like it was their last day on earth and, by God, they were going to go out singing. Even Grandma and Grandpa lifted their voices up high. Somewhat surprisingly, almost all of them could carry a tune. Few of the voices were special but all were loud. Alex found himself singing with tears in his eyes, and he didn't know why.

When they got to "Silent Night" there was a hush, for it was Grandma Kowalski's special song and everyone waited for her to begin singing before they added their voices. Alex felt himself begin to choke up as the old woman, eyes upraised to the ceiling, sang without reserve or false feeling, making the words of the carol shine with a religious fervor.

After "Silent Night," everyone began to exchange hugs and kisses. Alex was welcomed without reserve, with tearful kisses and heartfelt hugs from these almost complete strangers. It was like he had been part of the family for years.

Just before the gift exchange was about to start, Alex found himself mired in a fierce debate between Uncle Popsy and Uncle Joker about the best caliber of firearm for elk hunting when Angie came and rescued him, dragging him off to the relative solitude of her parents' bedroom. They sat on the bed, amid an imposing mound of down, sheepskin, and wool coats.

"I got you a gift," she said excitedly, reaching under the bed. "I hope you like it."

"I got you one, too," rummaging on the bed and finding his coat, reaching in the pocket and extracting a long narrow box, about the size of a legal envelope. Alex noticed a definite lift of Angie's shoulders and a widening of her eyes when she saw the box. Alex had wrestled with his best intentions as to a suitable gift for Angie and finally, in desperation, drove down the river to Salmon to the only jewelry store and brought back a necklace of gold with a ruby in the center. "You go first."

"Okay." Angie smiled as she inspected the box, obviously store-wrapped, taking her time with the red ribbon and bow. She opened the box with that special look of anticipation, slow and easy, like an archaeologist opening a sarcophagus. "Oh, Alex, it's perfect! Here, help me put it on." She pulled up her long red hair and held it in a bun while Alex fumbled with his big fingers and tried to work the clasp. There was an oversized oak mirror in the room, an old antique with claw legs and a beveled-glass plate, and Angie strutted before the glass, turning first one way and then the other. "It's perfect."

Angie dove down under the bed and pulled out a large box, lifting it easily. Something light, Alex thought, and he didn't have a clue as to what it could be.

"Go ahead," she nudged him. "Open it."

"I don't know," he teased. I was raised not to open my presents until Christmas morning."

"You nut, you're in my house now."

"All-right." Alex exaggerated his response into a hillbilly drawl. "I reckon I just might."

He had a little trouble with the wrapping, and couldn't seem to get the tape loose with his fingernails. Exasperated, Alex just tore the gift wrapping to pieces.

It was a hat. Not just any hat, but a tan-brown 4X beaver Resistol, size seven and a quarter, with a three-and-half-inch brim, in long oval, just one shade darker than his hair; the top of the line.

"Try it on."

It fit well. Alex took his turn in front of the mirror, turning and posing, pulling the brim low over his eyes, then backing it off some in his adjustments. "Man, this is a nice hat."

"Do you really like it?

"Oh man, it's like perfect."

"I knew it was something you would never buy yourself."

Alex sat down next to Angie on the big bed and in an exaggerated pose, firmly kissed her on the lips. Her response seemed somewhat muted, Alex thought, almost like it was measured, a commodity to be traded. He opened his eyes to see Angie looking sadly into his.

"Thanks again for the hat. Is something the matter? Don't you like the necklace?"

"Oh, I love the necklace. I really do. Maybe it's all this Christmas stuff. It's such a big deal with my family. Makes me think about things too much, I guess."

Alex didn't know what to do or say. Strange thoughts interfered. He wondered if Angie had been conceived on this bed and tried to force the thought out of his head. They sat there side by side with nothing to say as the Christmas Eve party swirled outside the bedroom door.

"Alex, do you ever get scared?"

"Scared? About what?"

"You know, scared about stuff in the future that might happen."

"Like what, like dying or something?"

"Yeah, I guess. Maybe."

"Well, sure, I try not to think about it."

"It's not dying exactly, more like, how it's gonna happen."

"Angie, are you sick or something?"

"No, no, I feel fine. Everything is fine. It's just that sometimes I get scared."

"What's scaring you? You can tell me, you know."

Angie didn't say anything for a while. She looked down at the floor and said, "Sometimes I have dreams."

"What kind of dreams?"

"That's what's scary. It's always the same one."

"Hey, everybody has scary dreams."

"I know, I know, but this is different. It's like it's something intruding into my regular, everyday dreams. I had the first one a couple of months ago. Didn't think much about it, but now the dream comes on every couple three nights or so. This is not like a regular dream. It's too real for a dream. Sometimes I even know I'm dreaming, and I can change stuff if I want to, but this is different. I'll be dreaming away on something, I mean, all sorts of stuff goes on, you know, the usual crazy dream stuff. I'll be riding my horse or drivin' around, and then I can tell it's happening again. All of a sudden, I'm in the woods, all by myself, and I'm scared."

"What's scaring you?"

"That's just it. I can't see it. It's like all foggy or smoky or something. I can see it through the smoke. This great big blocky thing, it's got like two lumps." Angie traced a big M in the air with her finger. "I know it sounds crazy, but the thing's sort of heart-shaped. I'm not scared of this big thing as much as what's behind it. I'm hiding behind this big thing and it just scares me almost to death. Then it's like I can't breathe right. I'm in this tight bag thing, and I can't breathe. I can't get out and I can't breathe and I know I'm gonna die."

Alex could see she was struggling to hold back tears. "Did you have this dream last night?"

"Yeah, it was the worst one yet. I was in this bag thing and I'm trying to see out. And then, real weird like, everything starts getting smaller, like I'm looking at a circle closing. You know, in the old Popeye cartoon, the circle gets real little and then closes? It's just like that. The circle gets littler and littler, until there's just a speck of light."

"What happens next?"

"I don't know, that's when I wake up gasping for air."

Alex became conscious of his own rapid breathing. He reached over and pulled Angie close. "It's okay. It'll all be okay, you know. It's only a dream."

31

"My heart is a lonely hunter that hunts on a lonely hill"
Fiona Macleod

Alex smoothed the green wax on his skis with a rounded piece of cork and wondered how it would feel if things had gone differently. He knew it was a tenuous thing to delve too deep on a Christmas Day, but he felt as if his reflective mood had been thrust upon him by both current events and those set in motion with only a little of his own help. It was a strange feeling to be alone on Christmas, and this was his first one away from his family. He had enjoyed Wigilia and stayed until late, one of the last to leave, but Angie's dream kept bothering him.

After an early morning call to his parents, two time zones to the east, Alex began to feel the first pangs of loneliness come creeping in the door.

The country was empty. Alex hadn't seen a vehicle or even a fresh track all the way up Morgan Creek. All he saw were cows, standing waiting for hay, hunched over in the cold, steam rising from their backs. The sagebrush hills that looked so dry and lifeless in the fall now resembled smooth white blankets, with snow drifts in pillows, and blue shadows where the low sun angle followed the ravine and canyon edges. Alex stuffed his white wool sweater in his rucksack, clipped down his bindings, and skied in a circle around his truck to test out the ski wax.

There was a hill at the end of the road, just past the last ranch where the snowplow turned around. A ranch access road ran all the way down to Van Horn Creek, where red osier dogwood stood defiantly bright in the snow. Alex dipped into a crouch, went fast, felt the wind on his face, and then made a good step turn at the bottom. He pushed his pace on the unmarked snow. A flock of cedar waxwings materialized and began to pick the last few wrinkled rose hips of the season.

As Alex came over the first hill on the trail, he looked back and saw the Angus cattle milling about the fenced-in haystack. A lone figure of a man stacked bales of hay on a horse-drawn bobsled. Alex listened to the faint tinkle of bells on the harnesses of the black draft horses. Christmas bells, he thought, as he looked at the rolling hills imitating the big snowy mountains on the divide, his ski tips pointing right at Van Horn Peak.

He skied easily. The green wax and his strong kick pushed a long glide, and he began to count map miles in his head. Alex was very particular about distance, and while tolerant of exaggeration in most instances, could not bear it when it came to matters of measurement, especially concerning miles walked, run, boated, or skied. Often when mileage was mentioned by his buddies, Alex took the number and divided it by two. Alex had to make a special dispensation for Harmon, so that divisor was four and sometimes even five. In one of his few instances of compulsive behavior, Alex carefully studied topographic maps and laid out accurate trail distances, usually with the aid of a planimeter, to the nearest half mile. To avoid even the appearance of exaggeration, Alex always rounded down.

There was a willow spring at the base of a hill where the rock was brown and broken and rabbit tracks covered the snow in a spiral maze. Alex undid his bindings, stepping carefully around a mounded ice flow, created when the warmer spring water froze solid, one layer upon the other. Alex got down on his knees and was able to get to moving water. It was cold, tasteless, and Alex drank too much, making his temples throb.

Alex stood up and stretched, hands high above his head, looking at the sky, thinking about Angie and that hat. So now he had a cowboy hat and was wondering about symbolism when he noticed a movement deep in the willow brush. He turned his head, and the movement was attached to a black spot and a short tail. It was an ermine, snow white except for the tail tip, and it moved fast. It ran across the snow in little leaps, diving under a black sagebrush right at Alex's feet. The ermine popped up an instant later with a deer mouse clenched firmly in its jaws. The ermine stood still, staring at Alex, only the tip of its tail quivering, its black eyes like holes in the snow. The standoff lasted several seconds, the ermine only a ski-pole length away, until the ermine turned quickly in weasel movements and bounded into the brush and aspens in the creek bottom with the mouse still in its jaws.

Back on his skis, Alex bent forward, climbing hard as the trail turned steeper, following the drainage that flows from the northeast side of Van Horn. High on a sagebrush divide, Alex could see from Round Valley to high on the headwaters of Corral Creek. His attention was fixed on the apparent symmetry

210

of Van Horn Peak. It appeared to be a perfect triangle of snow, an accident in landscape geometry. There's no such thing, Alex thought. Symmetry at mountain scale just doesn't exist, yet his eyes kept telling him different. There were too many agents at work, too many variables, the nature of structural geology itself. This had to be a trick of light, sun angle, or a distortion of perspective or something, he thought, looking at a mountain like a big white triangle, the kind little kids draw in their first art classes. Alex even skied all the way up to the edge of the timber, where he began to lose view of the peak, just to see if he could create a distortion in the two perfect sides of Van Horn.

As Alex stood on his skis, the wind at his back, a curl of snow breezing from the summit, his thoughts continued to line up in perfect symmetry with the lonely mountain.

32

"I'll love you dear, I'll love you
Till China and Africa meet,
And the river jumps over the mountain,
And the salmon sing in the street."

W. H. Auden

"So, why do they call him Bang Bang?" Alex looked quizzically at Kloyd. "Has he ever shot anybody?"

"Naw, Bang Bang never shot anybody. But I guess I should take that back, never really hit anybody that I've heard of. He's a nervous sort, especially for a county cop type. It don't take much for Bang Bang to pull his gun out, and he's quick to fire a warning shot or two. Why I even heard he drew down on old Doc Dime once."

Alex grinned. "Maybe he figured that Doc was going to do him in, so he had to act first. Or maybe Doc had more sinister plans, like spiking Bang Bang's Prozac."

"You been readin' too many mystery books. Now Doc Dime may not be the best doctor in the world, but he's all we got in Goldburg. If he wears down and leaves, it's a fifty-eight mile long trip down river to Memorial Hospital, the casket-maker's friend. So don't run down Doc, 'cause we sure don't want to discourage him."

Alex was immediately penitent. "No, No, I'd never do that."

"And steer clear of Bang Bang. He don't know you yet, and we sure don't want to have any accidents. Might hurt the District safety record, even."

"Believe me, Kloyd, I would never want to do that, mar our perfect safety record," Alex said, as he remembered all the broken fingers, cuts, horse-stepped-on feet injuries, falls, and bent bumpers that never seemed to get reported. "Let's keep that record perfect."

Kloyd understood the sarcasm but let it pass.

"There's a big New Year's Eve party at The Wild Bunch. Are you thinking of going?" Alex asked aimlessly, already knowing the answer.

"I don't think so. Me and the little woman sort of made plans for our own private party, shipping the kids over to grandma's."

"Well, Angie and I and most of the seasonal crew left in town are headed to The Wild Bunch around seven thirty, make sure we get a seat."

"Jeez-O-Friday, by midnight they'll be tearing the place down. Goldburg tends to get rowdy on New Year's Eve, so watch yourself."

"I can't imagine Goldburg getting rowdy. Why, the place seems more like Mayberry every day."

"Even so, watch your backside."

Alex picked up Angie and headed to town, Kloyd's veiled warning still in his head. They arrived at The Wild Bunch before eight o'clock and the place was already packed. Fast Eddie and Harmon had been there most of the afternoon and had saved a big table in the back. Howie and Nedra, Argo and Teffonie had already arrived and joined them.

Fast Eddie waved them over. "Hey Alex, get over here. I've got two chairs left that I've been guarding with my life."

Alex took Angie's sheepskin coat and draped it over the railing. "Guess we should of got here earlier," he said.

"Yeah," Fast Eddie said, a delirious smile on his thin lips, "Harmon and I have been here for a while and are pretty well tuned up already. You'll have to go some to catch up to us."

Alex reached for the pitcher of beer. "Well, seeing you guys in your current condition sure doesn't encourage me to start."

"Hey, Alex," Harmon said, his eyes ablaze with alcohol, "tune in, turn on, drop out, just like in the Sixties; or is that supposed to be the Seventies?"

Argo, as always, jumped on any of Harmon's inconsistencies. "Harmon, you weren't even born yet by the Nineteen Sixties."

"Hey man, that doesn't mean I don't want to turn on."

"How do we turn this guy off?" Eddie asked. "I can't even hear the cowboys swearing at each other."

Alex looked around at far too many overly excited people for this early in the evening. "So when do they give out the funny hats? I don't think this crowd will make it till midnight."

"Hell," Harmon said. "I won't make it till midnight!"

A band from Mackay called the Lost River Primates was setting up. They were rumored to be pretty good but no match for the Letgo brothers, who were chasing bigger game in Sun Valley on New Year's Eve. When the Primates started to play, and play loudly, the small dance floor was immediately packed. The amount of alcohol already consumed was more than enough to preclude any grace period of listening to the music for a few songs and then working up to it. The scene was almost tribal, a cowboy mosh pit of big hats and belt buckles, all trying to dance at once. Watching the crowd, shoulder to shoulder, bobbing drunkenly up and down, Alex and the rest at his table hesitated to go out on that dance floor just yet.

And it turned out to be a pretty good decision. Before the end of the first dance number, punches were thrown. Nobody seemed to know who hit who, but the affair seemed to take on a life of its own, with cowboy punching cowboy and cowgirl doing the same. For the first minute or two nobody left for the exits, either eagerly watching the melee or excitedly joining in. The Lost River Primates tried their best to quell the crowd, immediately switching to a waltz number; but it was just a hair too late, as a few too many punches had landed to put the thing back in the box. Alex watched the fight expand in concentric circles from the center of the dance floor. There were almost as many women fighting as there were men, handfuls of hair and small fists flying. In a wave, the battle surged into the bar and out the door and into the street.

"Let's get the hell out of here!" Eddie yelled.

With only some minor pushing and shoving except for Teffonie, who decked a drunk cowboy that was grabbing her at the door, they all made it out onto the sidewalk unscathed.

Alex saw the black-and-white county sheriff's rig braking hard and skidding to a stop right in front of The Wild Bunch. It was Bang Bang, all by himself. When he exited the car, his hand was on his holster and his eyes had a peculiar glaze.

Teffonie and Argo, still sober, and Howie and Nedra, always in control, had seen the situation developing and were safely out of the way.

Bang Bang seemed to settle his sights on Alex, the tallest person in the crowd mingling outside the bar, and demanded, "Hey, you, what you doing?"

"Yes, sir, we're just leaving."

"Well, leave now!"

Alex watched Bang Bang's right hand all the while. "Yes sir, we are on our way; right, guys?"

"Hit the road. Now!" Bang Bang said, as he waited outside The Wild Bunch for reinforcements before attempting to go inside.

214

By the time Alex and Angie got to his truck the rest of the county deputy's patrol had arrived and, with batons held high, charged into the bar. Alex listened for gunshots but heard none. The sound volume inside The Wild Bunch kept getting lower and lower, like the end of a record.

Howie finally said, "Looks like they got it under control. I don't hear any more screaming and yelling."

Nedra was shaking. "I can't believe it. I was actually involved in a bar-room brawl. It was so exciting. Just wait until our friends in Marin County hear about this."

Argo said, somewhat sarcastically. "Actually, except for Teffonie here, I didn't see anybody who knew how to fight very well."

Teffonie took that as a compliment and smiled.

"Well, hell," Harmon said. "In Kentucky, I seen better fightin' than that at a church social."

Angie shot back, "Harmon, you're just lucky that Bang Bang didn't brain you."

Adrenaline was still racing through Alex's system. He felt like running in circles, he had so much energy. Trying to calm down, he said, "Man, that was something. What do we do now?"

Howie said, "I'm not in any hurry to head back to The Wild Bunch. Anyplace else we could all go?"

"I agree," said Angie. "Too crowded anyway."

Fast Eddie was beginning to sober up. "Yeah, let's blow this pop stand."

And then Argo suggested. "How about we all go to the Goldburg Hot Springs?"

"Argo, it must be ten below zero. You can't be serious," Alex said.

"The water temperature is one hundred and three in the hot pool and approximately one hundred in the big outside pool," Argo told them all.

"Do they have swimming suits?" Teffonie asked.

Eddy grinned, "Sure, if you need them. I'm up for it, what do you say?"

Alex, stone-cold sober, tried to resist the peer pressure; but even Angie seemed intrigued with the idea, and soon he was in his truck with Angie, following Howie in his Range Rover, driving south out of town under the stars.

The Goldburg Hot Springs was one of the few original pioneer buildings left in Elkhorn County. Located on a natural ford of the Salmon River, the antiquated Hot Springs Hotel was originally a stagecoach stop and roadhouse in the old days. There was a bit of a boom back when it became fashionable to take the waters as a cure, but the railroad expansion stopped at Mackay and the tourists never came in sufficient numbers. Now the wooden buildings were in a state of arrested decay, the trickle of visitors just enough to keep the place going.

Alex had only had a taste of beer and his head was clear. Other than Angie and Howie, the rest of the crowd was fairly loose around the hips and shoulders, even Nedra, who could never handle any amount of liquor. Harmon had once said that, "Nedra's a girl who could get drunk on a bad apple and dance at a car wreck." Eddy had spirited a bottle of hard stuff in his jacket and was passing it around the Range Rover. When Alex met up with the rest of them at the hot springs, they were even further gone than when he left them on the sidewalk in front of The Wild Bunch. Harmon and Eddie were just stinking drunk, and Teffonie was slipping and sliding in the snow and ice, laughing at the stars. Nedra was like Jello. All of them, except Alex, were anxious to swim in hot water.

The grizzled proprietor of the establishment, Herman - or Herman the German, as was his town name - had seen this scene many times before, and drunken revelers didn't faze him a bit. He acted like it happened every day. He happily took their money and provided swim suits and towels that were old and faded, but clean. Then he directed them to the changing rooms. "If you get cold, come back to the hotel," he told them more than once.

The only heat in the changing rooms came from the covered-over hot pool. It was below freezing in a fog so thick you could barely see. The concrete floor was unbearably cold, and it didn't take long for both sexes to doff their clothes, put on their suits, and get into the hot water. Sobriety seemed to make the transition the most difficult for Alex. He almost ripped his shirt off and tossed his wad of clothes in a locker in his desperate race to reach the hot water before his toes froze off. He skittered across the wet concrete, muttering a series of oaths, including "Clum Dummit!" at least three times in a row.

But when he stumbled down the stone steps and the hot water hit his legs and thighs, stomach and chest, all struggles were forgotten. An involuntary "Ahhh!" escaped Alex's lips as he sank to his neck in the wonderful water. The others, somewhat limited by an alcoholic haze, took a little longer to get in the water, but soon wild laugher echoed off the wood walls of the hot pool.

Harmon was singing in the steam: "I loves to go swimmin' with women, and women love swimmin' with me."

It was so steamy Alex couldn't see Angie until she was right next to him, red hair plastered down wet, eyes dreamy looking. He made a grab for her, but she pulled away, laughing in the mist.

One hundred and three degrees of water is just too hot to stay in very long, and Alex was feeling the effects, lightheaded and happy. He climbed back up the stone steps, his pink body radiating steam. Alex called out to the rest to join him in the outdoor pool, swung open the door, and walked outside. Immediately his wet hair and eyebrows froze solid with ice. He calmly walked the few feet of frozen flagstone over to the only slightly cooler outside hot pool. He felt the wonderful rush of warm water again as he rolled in the pool like a seal, laughing and calling for Angie to join him.

Angie and the other two women came out huddled together, screeching and squealing like schoolgirls. Nedra and Teffonie held hands to try to keep from falling over, fighting the combination of hot water and alcohol. All three women were identically dressed in blue one-piece swimsuits and all filled them well, Alex thought. Even big Teffonie, all muscular and athletic, flat breasted, and narrow hipped, was still feminine. Nedra was a beauty, but Alex's eyes were fixed on Angelica. Her silhouette in the moonlight as she stopped still for just a moment, looking back over her shoulder, was statuesque. Lusty images raced through Alex's mind as he looked through the steam at the women scrambling down the steps and into the water.

More noise came from the hot pool as Howie herded Argo, Eddie, and Harmon out of the hot water before they passed out. Then they followed the girls outside.

The outdoor hot pool was nearly seventy-five feet in length, with the hottest water near the entrance step. It had been built directly over the natural hot spring, the hot water bubbling constantly up from the gravel bottom. Alex noticed that the water temperature at the far end of the pool was almost too cool on this well-below-zero night.

A swirl appeared on the surface of the dark water. Angie popped up right in front of Alex, her red hair steaming and quickly turning to dreadlocks of ice.

"Hi," she said, her eyes flashing on reflected moonlight.

"Hi, yourself. Nice night for a swim." Alex studied the position of Angie's head framed by the stars.

Whether accidental or not, her hand brushed against Alex's thigh. It was like an electric shock.

Alex wrapped his arms around her waist and pulled her underwater with

217

him, the hot water like a blanket. He opened his eyes and saw Angie looking at him like Ophelia, her hair floating in coiled patterns all on its own. When he surfaced with a gush of water, still holding Angie tight, Alex could hear the ice forming on his head, tinkling like small hidden bells.

"Happy New Year," Angie said quietly, her mouth only slightly open. Alex saw, perfectly framed around her head like a halo, the flash of light from the first of the fireworks on the hill above Goldburg. By the time the speed of sound had crossed the valley to the hot spring, Alex and Angie were deep in a kiss, their tongues touching.

Alex, seeing her eyes glow as the fireworks flashed, started getting that familiar feeling again. He smiled, stating simply, "Angie, you're driving me nuts."

Angie snuggled up close to him, only a thin film of water separating their two bodies, their ice covered heads touching and rubbing together slowly; she whispered, "I know."

Alex wrapped her in his arms like a shroud. "I love you, you know that?"

Angie stiffened and said, "Please, don't say it."

"It's true."

"I believe you think it's true."

"What does that mean?"

"I think you're in love with the idea of being in love. It's more like the chemicals talking."

"Are you saying that I'm addicted?"

"Not that. It's more like an infatuation, you know?" Angie rolled her ice-sculptured head from side to side. "Really, we hardly even know each other."

The fireworks show ended with three rockets going off at once from the hill above town, bursting in different colors. The star clusters drifted down like snowflakes.

Alex and Angie were interrupted by Fast Eddie. "Happy New Year, A-squared!" Eddie was swimming in circles and laughing like a lunatic.

Teffonie and Nedra swam up beside them, and Alex reluctantly broke off the embrace. Teffonie said, "Herman, the old boy that runs the hotel, has invited us in for a drink. What do you all say?"

Eddie instantly said, "I'm in." Harmon, realizing an opportunity for free alcohol, echoed Eddie's remark. Howie, who had been swimming laps, was the last to join in affirmation.

It took a while for the group to exit the pool successfully. Howie made the first attempt, quickly realizing his mistake when he tried to put on his frozen pants, stiff as a board from the condensed steam in the changing room. He howled when he tried to force his way into them, hopping on one leg and then the other. Finally he gave up, clattering his jeans into the corner, shivering and cold-footing his way back to the outdoor pool.

"Jesus, our clothes are frozen stiff," Howie said. "How do we get out of here?"

The whole bunch was cloistered at the step, neck deep in hot water, slowly sobering up with the true realization of their position.

"It's like twenty below and our clothes are frozen," Alex repeated the obvious.

"Why don't you go for help, Alex? We'll stay here in the warm water," Fast Eddie said.

"Seriously, now," Alex said. "We need to make a break for the house."

"But it's so cold out!" Nedra was no longer happy.

Argo chimed in, the hot water lapping at his chin, "It's only about thirty yards. I say we put on our shoes and run for it."

Eddie said, "No problem. The trick is to get real, real hot. You won't even feel the cold, and you won't have to run. Your hair will freeze up, but that's it."

"Sounds like a plan," Harmon said. "I'm with Eddie, and heading for the hot pool."

All agreed and shuttled over into the hot pool, hovering near the hottest part.

Harmon was the first to complain. "Eddie, man, I can't take much more of this hot water. I'm too hot."

"You candy ass."

Alex took the lead. "What do you say? Ready?" And with Angie in hand, he was the first to woozily climb from the hot pool. True to Eddie's prediction, his bare skin steamed but he wasn't cold yet. He and the rest gathered their frozen clothes, put on their shoes, and stepped outside.

When Alex hit the below-zero air, his hair froze to ice crystals in seconds. He looked over at Angie, an ice queen, he thought, long hair frozen in reggae braids of ice. As he hurried to the porch light, Alex took one glance at the cold sky, the stars bright, the moon shining. He felt the cold hit him just as he reached for the door.

Herman was waiting for them. "Come in, come in, hurry, get in and close the door. How you like that hot water, ya? It really feels good on a night like this."

Alex obediently followed Herman into the kitchen, so totally relaxed he didn't care if he came or went.

The old German and his wife, Florence, were racing around, gathering up the frozen clothes. Florence placed them on a wooden drying rack near the big woodstove. "Herman," said Florence, "you fix our guests some drinks while I get these clothes straight. It won't take long to dry them out."

"That's right, it's not "Zember" any more, it's a new year," Herman said, finding a full bottle of peppermint schnapps that he had been saving for just such an occasion. "And such lovely young women," he said, sidling up close to Teffonie. "I am so lucky,' he laughed.

"Just watch your step, Mr. Herman," Florence said.

"Pay her no mind, girls, she's always been a little jealous."

Florence took the good glasses out of the china cabinet and placed them straight in a line on the kitchen hutch. Herman broke the seal on the bottle and poured the schnapps like a sacrament. He proposed toasts to his adopted country, his adopted state, another to Elkhorn County, draining the bottle with a toast to the Republican Party of Idaho. By the time the drinks were finished, the clothes were dry enough to put on and the now happier crowd moved into the main living room of the hotel.

Herman proudly showed off his prize possession, a music machine complete with actual instruments, taking up the entire west wall. He explained how he found it in Wisconsin after the war, had it shipped out to Idaho in pieces, and how he had adapted it and converted it to run on compressed air. There was a player piano, a trumpet, saxophone, clarinet, bells, even a bass viol; and of course, an accordion. All it played was polka music. "It's a bastard to keep it all in time and in tune, but it's worth it," Herman said.

The living room became a dance floor and everyone began to polka, with Herman and Florence showing off the German style. Argo grabbed Teffonie, swinging her around in wondrous circles. Howie and Nedra, always hungry for new life experiences, tried their best. Fast Eddie and Harmon had to sit and watch until Florence noticed them and taking turns with each, taught them the polka. The music machine rattled on. Old Herman, in a Germanic, gravelly voice, sang along to the "Pennsylvania Polka."

The dancing expanded to encompass all thoughts and actions. Alex lost himself in waking dream time, swinging Angie around and around, watching her hair swirl out in wet curls. The bouncing polka music filled the night with magic.

33

"In the bleak midwinter
Frosty wind made moan,
Earth stood hard as iron,
Water like a stone;
Snow had fallen, snow on snow,
In the bleak midwinter,
Long ago."
                Christina Georgina Rossetti

Winter set in with a vengeance that January. There was no January thaw, no warming Chinook wind to strip the snow off the south slopes, there was just continued cold and it kept getting colder. The cold snap started the day after Christmas. It seemed to get a degree or two colder every morning, and the temperatures in the afternoon didn't rebound. By the first week of January, the high temperatures for the day were still below zero. With only a few inches of snow on the ground, the frost started to go deep into the soil. Duration, not intensity, drove the cold down. By the second week of January, the frost was down five feet on Main Street. By the third week it was down seven feet, and people all over town were burning tires in the street to try to melt frozen water and sewer lines. The temperature inversion locked the cold air at the surface, with no wind, not even a breeze. The wood smoke lay over town in a pall. Goldburg began to look like a third world country, enveloped in an gritty ice fog of burning rubber, as more homes went off the water grid with frozen pipes. There were excavators all over town, backhoes ineffectively scraping the few inches of thawed ground from the overnight tire fires in a desperate attempt to reach the frozen water lines. The sub-zero weather did not break; and Goldburg settled into survival mode. Every day was clear. It couldn't seem to snow, and during the night the moon and stars shone through the sooty tire haze in a strange, distorted perspective. The air was too dry for a heavy frost to form, and in the mornings just a veneer of angel wing frost tinted the windshields.

Alex had it easier up on Chipmunk Hill. Over a thousand feet higher in elevation than town, his cabin was above the inversion and almost ten degrees warmer both at night and during the day. There were two feet of snow on Chipmunk Hill, and Alex's water pipes were well insulated. Each morning as he drove into the ice fog about a mile from Goldburg, he could feel the cold come right at him through the truck windows.

The cold weather put an edge on things, and once again office life was getting a little murky. There wasn't enough inside work to do, but it was too uncomfortable to spend much time outdoors. Kloyd had organized the tack shed, and Buck had cleaned the fire warehouse until the fir floors shined. Buck organized and reorganized the fire cache until even the smallest item was located, documented or reordered. Other than feeding the horses and mules, there wasn't much real work left to do, so Big Stan made certain that there were meetings to attend. Alex was learning from Buck and Kloyd on how to duck a meeting and always volunteered to help feed the horses.

The Sleeping Deer Ranger District had over forty head of horses and mules kept on winter pasture just north of town. It was good pasture, right on the river, with some cottonwood thickets to get out of the wind and, most importantly, there was warm water for the horses to drink from a hot spring that ran through the property in the High Line irrigation ditch. Kloyd had explained that horses can live on eating snow but winter much better on water. The warm water was a decided advantage in keeping healthy stock through the winter. The wild hay pasture grass was gone by the first of November and since then, either Buck and Kloyd or Alex, or sometimes all three of them, loaded the stock truck with twenty four bales of hay every day for the stock. If they worked it right, and there was a particular boring meeting scheduled, they could stretch the task to take all morning. On the weekends, they took turns. Big Stanley knew exactly what was going on and never uttered a word about it. Alex felt certain that, if he had the chance, Big Stan would also be out there with the hay truck.

More often than not, Alex was in the back of the stock truck, cutting bales, throwing out the thick flakes of hay to the group of horses and mules following the truck, as Kloyd or Buck completed a slow loop of the dry part of the pasture. The idea was to spread out the hay so that the stock didn't congregate and stomp it down, wasting some.

The mules always made Alex kind of wonder. They seemed to have an inferiority complex compared to the horses, and this complex seemed to be universal. Whenever he spread hay, the horses always pushed to the front, the mules hanging back until the horses had staked out a claim. There was a pecking order among both the mules and horses. Dun seemed to be the boss mule, and Major ruled the horses. But that was as far as it went. Even the lowest horse on the social order ladder could move Dun away with just a nod of his head. In the icy cold, Alex thought about the causes of this mule complex. Was it being not enough horse or too much burro?

Alex liked watching the animals eat hay and always tried to linger a bit. Just to see the horses eat, somehow made him feel better connected to this winter landscape of pale morning light, thin snow, bare cottonwood branches, and slush ice thick on the river. It was a good feeling to come back to the warm office in mid-to-late morning and get that cup of hot tea and just sit around for a minute, thinking about the horses. More than other animals, horses stay with you a while, and the smell of horse on your hands and clothes often brings good thoughts. Horses are just like that.

Angie was sick of the snow, the ice, the darkness, and the cold, cold nights. The cows wouldn't start calving until the first of February; but even so, the cold forced Angie's dad to feed a lot more hay than he had planned. Angie didn't have to buck bales any more. Her dad had gone to round bales years ago, and now all the hay was handled with a front-end loader on his John Deere tractor. But even wearing insulated coveralls, she was cold on that tractor seat, and thoughts of warmer geography often intruded on her daydreams.

Covered in clothes, Angie walked the quarter-mile-long driveway to the mailbox on the county road. The letter surprised her, even though she had been thinking of it for several weeks. Not wanting to wait, she took off her mittens and opened the letter while she stood unmoving, her breath forming a halo around her face.

She read the letter three times, just to be certain. She smiled wide and then read it again. It was an acceptance letter from Western Oregon University. She had been accepted as a transfer student into the Education Department, and the University agreed to transfer all of her credits from her two years at Idaho State. In addition, Angie was pre-qualified for the advantageous tuition rate of the Western University Exchange, and she was awarded a sizeable tuition waiver grant in financial aid. She quickly did the math in her head, realized that she could afford it, that she could do it, and smiled again.

Angie held the letter close against her chest as she slowly walked back down the long driveway, looked at the winter sun casting blue shadows on the wind-blown snow, and wondered about Alex. He was in love with her; at least

224

that was what he kept saying. She really liked him, Angie had already decided that; but the chances of them staying together seemed so slim. She couldn't envision a probable future with both of them in Goldburg and wasn't going to take any more long-shot chances at love.

By the time she got to the farmhouse, the frost in her hair had formed a circle around her face, and she still didn't know what she was going to do. The letter said she had until June to decide. Maybe something would happen before then to help her make up her mind about Alex.

34

"She gave me a smile I could feel in my hip pocket."
Raymond Chandler

January had turned to February, and still the cold spell held firm. The old boys in town were comparing it to the winter of 48-49, when the cows froze solid standing up, and the valley snow didn't melt until June. The cold air mass over central Idaho had been stagnant for so long that a large inversion had set up, trapping the below-zero air in the valleys as the growing strength of the sun warmed the slopes up to near freezing during the day. It was thirty-three degrees below zero in Sunbeam that Saturday morning, with an ice fog hanging in crystals over the town. The heater in Fast Eddie's decrepit Jeep barely kept the interior above freezing. Alex scraped off frost on the inside glass in an attempt to see out.

"Jesus jumping Christ, it's cold," Eddie complained.

Argo and Harmon in the back seat were either asleep or not bothering to comment. Alex felt it was up to him to keep the conversation going. "Eddie, you sure about this temperature deal on Galena Summit?"

"Hey, I got it first hand from the guys on the Ketchum District. It's been up into the teens every afternoon, with champagne powder up to your knees. If it gets any deeper, we'll need snorkels to ski."

"The teens sound positively tropical."

"Yeah, but the temperature drops off fast after sunset."

Alex was a little worried. "But how steep is it? I've only been telemarking on Chipmunk Hill."

"Time you started to move up in the world. You'll love skiing the Cross. It's a great run, a classic. With powder like this, you'll float down, no problem."

They drove past Redfish Lake, the little hamlet of Obsidian, then Alturas Lake. Everything was trapped in cold air, ice fog and grim reality, and no one, absolutely no one, was moving around outside. They hadn't seen a vehicle since

Sunbeam. Through the hole in the windshield frost, Alex saw the highway winding its way toward Galena Summit, the sunlit peaks of the White Clouds to the north a golden pink. As the Jeep climbed up the steep grade towards the pass the frost crystals on the windshield began to break down, and Alex felt the rise in temperature, even inside the vehicle.

Fast Eddie caught Alex wiping the melting frost off the side window. "See, I told ya. It won't be spring skiing, but we'll be out of the cold." Eddie parked in the large pullout at the saddle next to the marker sign "Galena Summit, 8701 Feet Elevation."

Eddie stretched his arms up over his head, looking over the empty parking lot. "Look at this, we came all the way from Goldburg, and we beat the boys from Sun Valley, and we're right in their backyard."

Harmon said, "Yeah, but if you live in Sun Valley, and all that nightlife, it's a little hard to get up early in the morning."

Alex put on his sunglasses. "Looks like an exceptional day. Man, that sun feels good."

"Hey, that's why they call it Sun Valley," Harmon said.

The Cross was an unmarked, un-maintained, natural ski run that started high on the eastern ridge above Galena Summit on an unobtrusive peak. The preferred ski route dropped eighteen hundred feet through scattered whitebark pine on a stable slope that ended right at the curve in the highway on the Sun Valley side of the pass as it began to climb upwards to Galena Summit. The pattern of the bull pine on the open slope suggested a cross when the winter snows covered the landscape. It was a steep ski run but fairly bombproof and below the cutoff zone for low-angle avalanches. On the east side of the pass, facing away from the winter wind, the slope usually lay deep in powder. The Cross was a very unusual mountain, the perfect back-country ski hill.

Alex geared up with his friends, attached his climbing skins onto his telemark skis, and loaded his backpack with clothes, avalanche shovel, water, and lunch. Around his neck he wore a set of "peeps," an avalanche beacon. In case the worst happened, and if he was caught in a small snow slide, there was a chance he might be found under the snow before he suffocated.

Alex fell in at the rear of the group, following Eddie, Harmon, and Argo. It was a relatively short ski, less than two miles, but a fair climb up from the highway following the spine of the ridge. All Alex could see were mountains, the Sawtooths to the west and south, the White Clouds to the north, the Boulders and Pioneers to the east, all covered deep in a snow blanket. The sky was a cobalt blue, that dark blue of high elevation and clean air. The visibility was limited only by the curve of the Earth and the inherent limitations of the human eye. Alex blinked and thought he could make out the Teton Range on the Wyoming border, almost two hundred miles away.

There was one steep pitch to climb to the highest knob on the ridge and Fast Eddie led the way, switchbacking up as he broke trail on the face. Soon they all stood on the top of the Cross.

Alex was daunted by the drop, more slope than he had expected. "This is friggin' steep," he muttered anxiously.

Argo tried to settle him down. "It's not as steep as it looks. It skis well. Really."

Without much more discussion than that, Eddie, Harmon, and Argo stripped off their climbing skins, did a few stretches, and got ready to ski down the hill. Alex imitated them as best he could, but with more fear than anticipation

"So, what's the plan, Eddie?" Alex asked.

"Plan, what plan? We don't do planning. We climb up, we ski down, that's it. You need to forget about all this planning stuff. It just tires you out, you know."

Argo piped in, "We'll make a series of turns and wait for you, Alex. Just head straight down the mountain, toward that stand of trees, jog a little to the right and go around them, then it's straight down to the highway."

Alex rubbed his gloved hands together, more from nerves than the temperature. "Then we just try to hitchhike back?"

Argo clamped his bindings down tight. "Yes, and we probably won't all four get a ride together. But we'll wait on top and regroup before we do it again. I've never had to wait very long for a ride." And then Argo slipped on his goggles and pushed off the rounded top of the hill, dropping down expertly into a series of quick telemark turns, making a pattern of perfect S turns in the snow.

Fast Eddie and Harmon were right behind him, linking their turns, going faster and making slightly wider turns, but no less precise. Harmon followed Eddie down, his turns exactly opposite of Eddie's tracks, making a wondrous series of figure eights all the way down the mountain.

Alex stood alone at the top of the ridge, watching his friends floating effortlessly down in the deep snow. Hoping that all his practice at Chipmunk Hill would pay off, Alex pointed his skis downhill and pushed off the slope.

He surprised himself by linking, somewhat torturously, his first four

228

turns. The knee-deep powder helped him to control his speed as he consistently passed through the fall line. On his fifth attempt, Alex crossed his ski tips and was plowing face first in powder snow before he even knew he was going to fall. He popped up through the snow like a ground squirrel, so deep that only his head was showing. Blowing snow off his mustache, he looked downslope and realized that his companions had been watching.

The powder snow made for painless falls, but also made it difficult to get back up on your skis. Alex tried to plant his ski poles, but they went down in the snow all the way to the grips. He was forced to roll over on his side and, heaving with effort, finally struggled upright, plastered with snow from cap to gaiters. Alex got ready once more and forced his skis downhill. There was a quick rush, three more haggard turns, and another quick fall in deep powder. Three more times Alex got on top of his skis, and three more times he made a few turns and then fell hard before finally reaching the trio waiting for him at mid slope.

"God, Alex, I thought you'd never get here. I was starting to get cold," Fast Eddie said.

"I was wondering myself."

"Don't worry about it," Argo said. "I thought you did fine. A couple of times you linked five or six turns."

Alex looked behind him at his tracks. There were some nice turns between the divots of snow where he had fallen. He hadn't linked them very well, but he had gotten down the mountain. "Well, it's a bit more difficult than Chipmunk Hill."

"From here on down to the highway, it's a little easier," Argo said. "It's not as steep, but there are a few more trees. You'll do fine."

"Hey, don't wait for me, okay?" Alex hoped not to be observed falling so much. "Go ahead and try to get a ride, all right?"

Eddie said, "We'll wait long enough to make sure you get down. We'll meet you back on top of the Cross."

"Sure. Just wait for me at the top."

Harmon said, "We'll eat lunch and wait for you."

Alex tried to take his time and only fell four more times before he stood on the high bank above the highway. He had seen a van stop for Argo, Eddie and Harmon just prior to his last fall and knew he was just a short time behind them.

Alex stood alone with his skis, waiting for a ride. There wasn't much traffic, and only two cars passed him by in five minutes. Alex was wondering how long it was going to take him to get a ride when a red Audi slowed down, pulling off to the side of the road. Alex gathered his skis and poles and was walking toward the car when the door opened and he saw a dark-haired woman emerge and ask, "Need a ride to the top?"

Alex walked closer, nodding his head, and was just about to answer when she said. "Hey, you work for the Forest Service, don't you?"

Alex noticed she was wearing ski clothes and telemark boots. "Yeah, I'm Alex Kynwulf, work on the Sleeping Deer District."

"I thought so. I work for the brotherhood also, on the Ketchum District."

"Really? Glad to meet you."

"Oh, I'm sorry, my name is Shaulane. I've seen you around somewhere, maybe at some meeting or other."

Alex was certain he had not seen a woman like this in any Forest-Service-sponsored meeting. She was striking, with that thirty-year-old, head-cheerleader kind of look. Her short, black hair curled in at the neck. Her posture and her face were telling a story to Alex, and he was listening. "Yeah, maybe. I don't get down to Sun Valley much."

"Here, let's put your skis on top. You mind if I join you? I don't usually ski alone, but my friend didn't show up."

"Sure, but don't expect much, I'm sort of a beginner."

Shaulane looked him over up and down. "Somehow, I don't think so."

Alex installed his skis and poles on the ski rack on the Audi, and climbed in the car, his head brushing against the roof.

"My, you are a tall one," Shaulane said. "I didn't realize it when you were standing in the snow. Move the seat back if you can."

"Maybe I was standing in a hole or something. So what do you do on the Ketchum District?"

"I'm a wilderness ranger during the summers. In the off-season I do just about anything they want me to. This winter I'm working on a carrying capacity study for the Sawtooth Wilderness."

"No kidding? We're doing the same on the Middle Fork."

"Isn't that an interesting coincidence," she said slowly.

The way she said the word "coincidence" put a chill on Alex's spine for some reason. He tried to shake it off as due to the weather.

They soon arrived at the summit parking area and Alex began to undo the skis from the Audi. Shaulane, seemingly without any degree of self-consciousness, started a series of stretches that Alex couldn't help but notice. First, she bent over, placing her palms flat on the snow surface. Then, grasping the backs of her ankles, she pulled her face flat against her knees. Alex admired more than her suppleness. Then it was a series of lunges, aggressive lunges directed toward Alex, one knee to the snow, the other at a ninety degree angle. Shaulane let out a deep breath, each time with an interesting pursing of her lips into a tight O shape, and a loud "wheh!" that had Alex transfixed, not even pretending to be fiddling with the ski rack. She then closed her eyes, placed her palms together over her head, one foot on the other knee, and held the classic yoga pose for at least a minute. All this time, Alex didn't say a word.

Shaulane's eyes popped open and looked right into Alex's. "Alex Kynwulf, do you believe in kismet?"

Alex cleared his throat, still trying to recover from her use of his full name and the formal question. "Only if it's good. I'm still trying to make up for some past lives, probably."

Shaulane smiled and said, "Your past lives are what brought you here."

Alex didn't think she was joking.

Shaulane put on her skis and took the lead, following the ski tracks up to the Cross. Alex followed closely, her tight ski pants like an invisible tether. It seemed only moments to Alex before they were back on the top of the Cross. He was somewhat disappointed to see that Eddie, Argo, and Harmon were waiting there for him, eating their lunches.

At the sight of Shaulane, Fast Eddie and Harmon became highly animated, acting out their roles even more excessively than normal. Eddie stated the obvious. "Alex, I see you brought a friend with you."

"Yeah, Shaulane gave me a ride."

Fast Eddie and Harmon knew Shaulane by sight and quickly began a lunch-long discussion of wilderness and work. Shaulane was polite but reserved as she ate her sandwich in small bites, looking mostly at Alex. Eddie and Harmon grew discouraged and even Argo picked up on the clear message. Alex dug out a Swiss chocolate bar and passed it around. He couldn't help but stare at Shaulane as she closed her eyes and rolled the dark chocolate with her tongue, her mouth held open.

The mid day sun cast long blue shadows on the snow, and Alex and Shaulane stood side by side on their skis. "Eddie, Harmon, you and Argo go first, and Alex and I will follow," she said.

Argo, Eddie, and Harmon again cut perfect, symmetrical turns down the steep face of the Cross.

"God, I wish I could ski like that," Alex said, not really thinking.

231

Shaulane turned to him and gave him a look. "You already know how to ski like that. You just have to believe you can."

"I don't know about that. I like the idea of positive thinking as well as the next guy. I've read that stuff about forcing your mind to imagine your perfect performance and all that, but to ski like those guys, that takes years of practice."

Shaulane spoke formally, with a strong stilted style and an exaggerated diction, almost like she was channeling, Alex thought. "Not for you, Alex Kynwulf. You've been here before. You've skied this mountain."

"Yeah, but it was only one run, just an hour ago."

"No, you don't understand. You have descended this mountain many times, in many forms."

"So, like, how would you know that?"

"Because I have been with you. Don't you remember?"

The hair was standing up on the back of Alex's neck. "No, I can't say that I do. I just came to Idaho in April, last year."

"I am not speaking in metaphors, Alex," she said sternly. "You have skied this mountain before, with me. I have dreamt it, so I know it is true."

"Must have been some dream. I'd just like to get down this hill without falling down. That would be a dream for me."

"I'll show you. Ski next to me, and we'll go down together."

"Hey, I'll give it a try, but I'll probably fall after two or three turns. The last time down, I fell like sixteen times, so don't get your hopes up."

"You will not fall, Alex Kynwulf. Just trust yourself and ski with me."

Alex thought of two snappy comebacks, but the use of his full name again sort of unhinged him and gave him that grade-school feeling, and he didn't use either one. He looked at Shaulane. "I won't fall?"

"You won't even come close to falling. It was in the dream."

Alex decided on the "what the hell" approach and said, "Well, dreams have to end sometime, but let's give it a try," thinking that Shaulane might be a space cadet but, God, she was a good-looking one.

"Just empty your mind and watch the snow fly off the front of your skis as you go down the hill," Shaulane said. "Are you ready?"

"As ready as I'm going to get. Try not to go too fast."

Shaulane seemed to jump off the mountain, and Alex, still tethered on the invisible string, jumped the same. It was like a reflexive response, and then he had his knee down on the front ski, the powder snow flying up over his

232

shoulder as the ski carved a tight turn. Vaguely aware of Shaulane on his right, somehow Alex's next turn was exactly in time with hers. Again the front knee bent, the powder flew, the ski carved. He wasn't counting his turns, he wasn't looking at Shaulane, he just stared down the fall line at his ski tips rising out of the powder, a feeling of exhilaration overcoming all conscious thought, his mind resonating only speed and snow. The clarity of his thoughts and his purpose almost mirrored the sexual act, the mountain his desire. His quadriceps muscles began to burn and his breath came in hard gasps, but it was like he was watching someone else ski, and the effects did not touch him.

He cut his final turn at the bottom of the Cross, shaking from deep within himself, panting, his chest heaving, still exactly in time with Shaulane in a flurry of snow. The two of them ended up facing one another. Alex looked at her, and then he looked back at the Cross and saw two long, long series of tight S turns, matching in perfect symmetry, magic marks on the face of the hill that belied all logical thought. Alex leaned forward on his ski poles, trying to catch his breath, his astonishment beyond understanding.

Shaulane looked him right in the face, her own chest heaving, a strange smile on her lips. "Welcome back, Alex Kynwulf."

35

"O, my Luve's like a red red rose
That's newly sprung in June:
O my Luve's like the melodie
That's sweetly play'd in tune."

Robert Burns

The long month of the shortest days, February, settled in on Goldburg like an unwelcome relative. Everybody had to do their best to get along. The cold snap started to fizzle, but only in fits and spurts. The temperatures during the day approached freezing, but the thirty-two-degree mark remained an unattainable goal, and falling short, each night it was back into the deep freeze. More tires burned now night and day, and more backhoes and excavators plied the frozen ground. Water pipes froze up almost as quickly as they could be thawed out. The suffering of the populace seemed to take itself out in two forms: geography and alcohol. Those that could afford it mortgaged themselves and got out of town for a while, hoping it would all sort out by the time they returned. Most of the rest tried the numbing effects of excess alcohol consumption as a potion against bad times.

Two interesting developments at the office brightened the otherwise dreary month. The first began with a postcard with a San Diego postmark. This postcard was the first in a series addressed to Buck Twiddle, USDA Forest Service, Goldburg, Idaho. This first one was a photograph of a street scene in San Diego, showing a close-up view of a street tree and a cast-iron grating surrounded by an intricate design of granite pavers, New England Granite Pavers from Burlington, Vermont, to be exact. On the back, in a flowing feminine script, was a short note addressed to Buck:

> "Dear Buck, Do you remember this spot? This is the exact place we were when we first fell in love. I remember the day like it was yesterday. We were inseparable, like Siamese cats.
> Signed, A Woman from your Past"

234

Sandy Spotts made a big display of bringing the mail into the break room, walking her tight green skirt side-to-side down the hallway. Buck had just finished making one of his famous M & M sandwiches, two slices of Wonder Bread with a generous handfull of M & M's, carefully spaced and embedded in the soft white squares.

Alex was badgering Buck when Sandy came into the room. "Why do you even bother with the bread? Why not just eat the M & M's?"

Buck held the special sandwich up to his lips, as if savoring the smell of store-bought bread and chocolate. "Now, that wouldn't be a balanced meal. Haven't you ever heard of the food pyramid?"

"Food pyramid! For all you know, they built it somewhere in Egypt."

Sandy stood right next to Buck, holding the postcard straight upright and waving it around like a wand. "Buck, you've got a postcard here, just for you."

"For me?"

"Yes, for you." She placed the postcard up to the side of her face, closed her eyes and acted out an exaggerated swoon. "And it has a wonderful fragrance on it, too."

"From a woman?"

"Read for yourself." Sandy placed the postcard square in front of Buck, neatly lining it up with his Wonder Bread.

Buck stared down at the card.

Kloyd had joined the lunch crowd. "Ain't you gonna read it , Buck?"

Buck growled, "Give me a minute, will ya?" and picked up the postcard.

Buck sat still and read the card several times. He started to mouth a suitable expression of surprise, but it just wouldn't happen. His mouth held open, and no words came out.

"Who's it from, Buck?" Kloyd asked.

Buck read slowly, "It says, a woman from your past."

Sandy Spotts still stood there, looking at Buck. "You were in the Navy in San Diego, weren't you?"

"Yeah, but that was over fifteen years ago."

Kloyd slipped in closer. "Could I see the postcard?"

"Might as well. It appears everybody knows all about it already," Buck said, tossing Kloyd the card.

Kloyd took his time. "Jeez-O-Friday, Buck's got himself a secret admirer."

Buck sort of smiled. "Hell, I'm lucky I got any admirers at all, secret or not."

It was only four days later; the office excitement from the postcard had barely died down when a second card appeared from San Diego. The photograph on the postcard showed a park bench, again surrounded by granite pavers, this time in a sparkling spiral design.

Sandy Spotts broke into the break room on a run, saying, "Buck, Buck, you got another postcard!"

The coffee cup froze an inch in front of Buck's lips, as his eyes darted around the room. The whole office quickly surrounded Buck as he read the card to himself. Sandy leaned over his shoulder and read it out loud.

> "Dear Buck, Here is a picture of the bench where we first kissed, our feet firmly placed on Vermont granite. Our passion knew no bounds. You were like a starving wolf at the sight of his prey, and I, the little helpless fawn. Signed, A Woman from your Past"

Buck still held the card tight in his hand, his eyes fixed straight ahead, as he stood up and walked slowly out of the break room without saying a word.

That happened on a Friday, and on the following Thursday another postcard arrived, causing Sandy Spotts to burn rubber in the post-office parking lot in her effort to get back to the office. Again, it was lunchtime. Sandy actually ran into the break room so quickly that she skidded on her shiny leather bottomed pumps. Buck was in his office on the telephone, so Sandy carefully placed the postcard at his usual spot at the table. News of the postcard filled the lunchroom. Even Big Stanley was there. As Buck strode in, black lunch box in hand, he surveyed the smiling faces, saw the postcard on the table, and quietly said, "Bloody hell."

The postcard was similar to the first two in that there was a lot of granite, this time surrounding a fountain. It read:

> "My Dearest Buck, Do you remember when we swam naked in the moonlight in the fountain? You were like a Greek God, and I was the lonely Godess. The water was like wine. Our love was as solid as this formidable Vermont granite. Signed, A Woman from your Past"

Buck read the postcard carefully, then placed it his coat pocket, buttoning the flap down. He looked up at his expectant co-workers and said, "Hey, don't look at me like that. Everybody knows I can't swim."

The second unusual development during the month of February was even more bewildering, and again, Sandy Spotts was the first to see the pattern. It seems that Big Stanley had for the last two weeks, been receiving letters of proposal from desperate women in Eastern Europe and Russia, and the letters were coming to the office. Since Sandy opened all the mail, it was more than a moderate surprise when she read a personal letter from Sophia Ivanova, of St. Petersburg, addressed to Big Stan. His office walls may have been wood paneled, but they weren't thick enough to contain an obviously upset Sandy Spotts, and the whole office could hear the sound of Big Stanley backpedaling.

"What in the hell is going on here? You got another letter today."

"I swear I don't know these women from Adam, or Eve, rather."

"What, you expect me to believe that?"

"Hey, I don't know how they got my address."

"What, did you join some kind of Russian swingers club or something?"

"Of course not, I've never been to Russia."

"So, how do I know that?"

"Come on, be reasonable."

"Well, you better keep yourself at home here, or you can kiss my ass goodbye."

"Sandy, now . . ." But that was as far as Big Stanley got before the sound of his office door slamming put everybody back to work, innocent-faced, as if they hadn't heard a thing.

The rumor mill had it that Big Stanley was getting two or even three letters a week from women in Russia and the Baltic republics of Lithuania, Latvia, and Estonia. The office scuttlebutt was that most of the letters contained photographs of the women, some of which were supposed to be pretty racy, and all of the women were said to be quite attractive. The letters seemed to follow the same general format; the women would be more than happy to marry Big Stanley, sight unseen, if only they could come to America.

Some days, Sandy Spotts typed on her computer keyboard so hard you could hear the little buttons bouncing from way back in the break room.

36

"Would you like to sin
With Elinor Glyn
On a tiger skin?
Or would you prefer
To err with her
On some other fur?"
                                        Anonymous

Angelica pulled herself up and away from Alex's clinging arms. She stood up, pushing her hair back with her hands, then quickly zipped up her jeans and buttoned her black blouse and adjusted her breasts back underneath her bra.

A moan from the direction of the sleeper sofa in Alex's small front room, "Oh Angie, you're killing me, girl, just killing me." Alex rolled over on his back, breathing hard, tight against the couch cushions. "I don't know if I can live like this. I'm so horny, I could just die right here on this couch."

"I seriously doubt that."

"Yeah, but when they find me self-impaled on the cushions, dead from terminal horniness, how are you going to feel then?"

All serious now, "I'm sorry, Alex, but we agreed to slow it down."

"Well, as I remember, you agreed to slow it down, but I'm the one with a bad case of blue balls."

"Ah, I'm sorry. I really am. But we did agree we wouldn't push one another into something until we were both ready."

"You're right as usual, Queen Friday." Alex got up off the couch and tried one more time with a bear hug from behind, Angie's saddle-firm posterior tight against his jeans. "Have I told you lately that I love you?"

Angie easily rebuffed his advance by squirming back toward the shower stall. "Yes you have, many times."

Alex waited through a long moment. "This is the part where you tell me that you love me too."

"Alex, I do have feelings for you. Who knows? It may turn into love,

238

but I want to be sure this time." She sighed. "You know, you don't even know me. We're like so different, it's not even funny. I mean, Jesus, look at how we grew up. How different could it be?"

"Since when does that make a difference about anything? Love happens every day."

"Listen to yourself. You sound like one of those songs you're always singing. The question you need to answer is, is it love, or is it infatuation?"

"Now that's a title for a country western song."

"Make jokes if you want to, but a relationship should be built on similarities, not differences."

"If you really believe that, what are we even doing here?"

She tucked her shirt back in her pants. "That's the question I keep asking myself." She paused for a long breath, then said with a smile, "But I never seem to get an answer."

"Maybe you're not asking the right question?"

Angie bit down on her bottom lip. "That was a good come back. But what about you? What are you doing here?

"That's pretty obvious. I'm the desperate one, remember?"

"Yeah, yeah, that's it. You do seem desperate. Like someone or something is going to come up to you and take it all away. What makes you think like that? Are you afraid of something?"

"No, no, I'm not afraid. I'm really not. Maybe it's more like I'm getting prepared."

"Prepared? Prepared for what? I don't think the end of the world is scheduled anytime soon. Why do you have to be the one who is prepared?"

"That's the thing. I don't know. I don't know. I just have this feeling that I have to be ready for this one big thing. It's sort of nuts, I know, but it's real to me."

"Why does it have to be a big thing? Why can't it be a bunch of nice, little things?"

"I, I guess I'm not built that way. I always felt that I'm here to do something important. Sort of like one big thing. It's hard for me to describe. It's a feeling, but it's real. Sometimes I swear I could reach out and touch it. I don't know. I'm talking crazy now."

"No, you're not. You're not. I sort of understand." Her eyes turned sad. "It's seems like such a hard way to live is all."

"Well, it's never been easy. Just like me and you. I don't know why it has to be this hard. It's always the easy stuff that goes so hard. I really like you. I think you know it."

"It's not as simple as that. There's a lot for me to figure out too. You know? Some stuff happened before that I don't want to go through again."

"What kind of stuff?"

"I don't want to talk about it. At least not yet."

"Hey, that's okay. I can wait. How about we just keep it going half-way? I can be your regular guy, just half-way of course."

"Before I settle on someone, it's got to be all the way, not partway, halfway, or even sideways, but all the way and all the time. I'm not gonna be two-timed by some guy, and I'm not going to be neglected. If I decide on someone, brother, he better be ready."

"Hey that's me! You described me to a T. All-the-way Kynwulf, that's what they call me."

"Humph, maybe more like all the time Alex."

"That too."

"Well, to tell you straight, I haven't made up my mind yet. But I'm gonna be the one to do it. I'm not going to be pushed into anything any more."

"All this goal oriented talk has got me wondering how I'm doing on our measurement scale. Like what's the trend line look like? Positive or negative? Or like the eye doctor, better or worse?"

Angie slung her arm over Alex's neck and pulled close. "I'd say you're doing a little better all the time. Just keep up the good work." And then, just as quickly, she pushed away.

37

"For I have sworn thee fair,
And thought thee bright,
Who art as black as hell,
As dark as night."
Shakespeare

"I don't know, you can spend too much of your life reading. Who knows what kind of ideas you can end up with?" Buck said, as he drove into the state of Utah on Interstate 15 at a steady seventy-five miles an hour. "And then there's so many books, how the hell do you choose?"

Alex sat up straight in the front seat of the government truck. "But that's the beauty of it, that sense of discovery."

"And that's the part I don't like. I want to be sure what's in a book before I start to read. Like the last time I went to the library, I sees this book. I remember the title, 'A Confederate General at Big Sur,' and I thinks, hey this'll be a good one, a nice read about the Civil War."

"That's Brautigan, isn't it?"

"I don't remember, but it sure as hell wasn't about no Civil War, just a bunch of hippies in San Francisco, taking drugs and everything. Almost made me scared to check out another book. Who knows what could be in it?"

"Ah, there's lots of great books out there, all kind of things you'd like, westerns, war, even romance."

"Now, don't start in about those postcards! I think I'll just stick to westerns, and then I won't be surprised again. You can always tell a western book by the picture on the cover. Sort of like those romance novels, they put those pictures on the outside so you don't make a mistake."

"Heaven forbid that you get the wrong book again."

"That's just what I say."

Alex and Buck were on their way to Salt Lake City for a recreation management workshop sponsored by the Forest Service, and Alex was excited.

Not counting Salmon or Sun Valley, Alex hadn't been out of town since he moved to Goldburg. He was going to the big city and he was being paid for it. Such a deal, he thought to himself, more than one time.

Alex found himself staring at the tall buildings like some country rube as Buck nervously negotiated the downtown rush hour traffic.

"Clum Dummit," said Buck. "This is the third time I been around the block at North Temple, and I still can't find no Hotel Utah Motor Lodge."

One left turn and two "Clum Dummits" later, Alex and Buck were safely situated at their hotel. Buck lined the green Forest Service truck up next to several others, and then both of them muscled their luggage into the motor court. They were checked in with a Mormon efficiency. Alex was just opening the door to his room when Buck turned back and reminded him, "There's a party tonight on the third floor, room 308. You wouldn't want to miss it. You'll be able to meet most of the other recreation folks in the region."

"What time?"

"Supposed to start around six."

"I want to walk around town a little first. See you there in about an hour. Can we get dinner later?"

"This ain't like Goldburg. The big city never sleeps."

Alex was light on his feet, trying to take in as much of the Salt Lake skyline as he could before the party. He was intoxicated by the sight of new buildings and all the new construction. Seeing all the large construction cranes and big equipment gave him a jolt of excitement. Alex took a circuitous route starting at the Temple Square gardens and then up the hill towards the copper-plated capitol dome. From up on the hill, he scanned the downtown District, particularly noting several post-modernist buildings in the central business District that he planned on checking out later in the week.

He returned to the hotel around six thirty and wondered whether to stop by room 308 now or wait until later, when more people would be around. Alex didn't want to be the first one to show up. He decided on a quick walk by, just to check it out. As it turned out, he needn't have worried. The party was going full throttle, with at least twenty-five or more jammed into the small social room. Buck was already there, drink in hand, talking with another cowboy-looking character. From Alex's best estimate, there were at least twenty bottles of hard liquor on the table, most of it Jack Daniels. The only other party accessories were a big bucket of ice and three rows of plastic glasses. From the look of some of the revelers and the liquid levels in the bottles, the party seemed to be moving

242

right along.

A short man with a moon-like face and flattened nose jammed a drink into Alex's hand. He at first tried to refuse it, but the fellow was persistent, and Alex decided it wasn't worth the bother. Alex kept the drink, holding it in his right hand, pretending to take a sip now and then. A bad college experience with brandy had discouraged Alex from the hard-liquor life, and he rarely imbibed.

Alex caught up with Buck. He noticed the waxy look in Buck's happy eyes. "They have any pop or something for a chaser?"

"A chaser, what are you, some kind of candy ass? Now don't embarrass me in front of these guys."

"I just don't think I can drink this stuff straight."

"They got ice."

"Yeah, I see the ice. Why don't they have any beer?"

"You ever try carrying a case of beer in a suitcase?"

"Why don't we just go out and buy some?"

"This Salt Lake here is the buckle on the Mormon bible belt. You don't just walk out the door and buy some booze. They got these different liquor laws, you see, and you have to plan it out real careful like. Anyway, we can't use the government truck. That baby's parked until we leave."

Alex tried a little sip of his bourbon, grimacing as some trickled down his throat, noticing more bottles on the table as additional guests arrived. His own personal rule began to relax some and he had another sip, not grimacing as much this time. Feeling somewhat more gregarious, Alex began to mix in the crowd. It was a mostly male, older, conservative-looking kind of crowd. The more Alex sipped the better he felt, and after a while he sort of began to lose track of how many refills he had taken in his plastic cup. Soon all thoughts of supper began to fade. An alcoholic haze warmed and relaxed him. He was so relaxed that he didn't even feel the hand on his shoulder until another hand curled around his waist.

Alex turned around. It was Shaulane, dressed in pants so tight you could have cracked an egg on them. "Oh, Shaulane, it's you. Funny meeting you here in Salt Lake City."

"I could say the same to you, Alex Kynwulf." Again she used his full name, this time suggestively.

Alex leaned his head towards her, as the alcohol pushed him away from hesitation and towards an uncharacteristic temerity. "Of all the Mormon hotel parties in all the world, and you walk into mine."

Shaulane moved closer. "If you can stand it, I can. Play it, Alex."

"The lady knows her classics."

Shaulane moved in close, creating a margin of space so narrow between them that a sheet of paper would have trouble passing through. "So tell me, Alex Kynwulf, how did you get so tall." And she said it not like a question.

Alex held his ground, the heat from the top of his head like a stove. "Would you like a drink?"

Shaulane licked her lips and said, "Jack Daniels, three fingers."

Alex was acting like one of those bears that got shot by some wildlife biologist with a tranquilizer gun. He knew where he was and what was happening to him, but he couldn't seem to do much about it. Stumbling over to the drink table, Alex concentrated and poured the bourbon, almost forgetting to add the ice. Sweat formed on his downy mustache as he walked in slow motion back toward Shaulane watchfully waiting at the doorway.

She sipped her drink without expression and said, "Are you familiar with the ancient Greek view of time, the concept of Chronos and Kairos?"

Alex shook his head slowly from side to side, his eyes fixed on Shaulane's big brown eyes.

"We are in Kairos right now, an inward, spiritual, qualitative time, measuring reality in the depth and intensity of experience. Do you feel the depth and intensity of this experience?"

Alex nodded.

"Kairos transcends Chronos, Alex Kynwulf, and in this time of broken eternity, this time, now, Kairos, is our only eternal present. The past, present, and future have no meaning for us, and all that happens in this lower dimension is reflected in the higher. Do you understand?"

Alex desperately wanted to understand, especially that part about the depth and intensity of experience, and said, "Yeah."

One more sip of bourbon and Shaulane said, "It's getting too warm in here. Let's go outside."

Alex followed like a puppy.

Four doors down, Shaulane produced a room key and opened the door deftly, pulling Alex in by the hand. The door closed, and a moment later, she held Alex by his buttocks with both hands, her lips hot on his. Shaulane's tongue shot in, wrapping around his, as she unzipped his pants in a smooth, practiced motion and grabbed him in a slippery grip.

Alex experienced a wonderful hesitation. He was frozen in his tracks

244

and couldn't seem to move a muscle and was, for once, glad of his problem.

"Well, what have we here," Shaulane whispered, as she wriggled free of Alex's arms and sank down to her knees, undoing his belt on the way down.

Before Alex could muster a clear thought, she began to lick him like an all-day sucker.

"Ahhh," Alex said, his brain now unable to process even rudimentary information. Reflex seemed to take over the situation. He looked down. The low light level created a strange sheen on Shaulane's black hair moving up and down in a piston-like fashion. Shaulane seemed to know very well what she was doing, and Alex was only too content to let her continue. His own free will had shattered at the moment she pulled down his zipper.

A prickling sensation began in Alex's belly and rose through his heaving chest, past his rolled-back eyes. It seemed to exit through the top of this head in a moment of extreme experience, as heat lightning bounced around the corners of his mind.

When it was over, Alex, almost hyperventilating, his knees near to buckling, looked down at Shaulane and tried to speak. The look on her face held both form and substance as she smiled a cold smile.

She stood up and whispered in Alex's ear, "How did you like that, Alex Kynwulf?"

Alex tried to form rudimentary short words, and was finally able to say, "Nice."

"Was it better than the perception of a promise in the future?"

Alex took three deep breaths and said quietly, "Much better."

Much later that evening, Alex found Buck face down and all but passed out on the couch in room 308, the party over, as the wounded were being taken off the battlefield. Alex gently roused him and helped him back to his own room in fits and tries of stumbles and curses. Alex left Buck fully clothed on the bed, almost leaving before remembering the last part of the task, to remove the boots of the drunken one.

Out on the walkway balcony, Alex remembered why he didn't drink hard liquor. He bent hard over the railing, spreading his cookies all over the parking lot below. As he stumbled back to his own room, he wondered how much more of this Forest Service training he could take.

The next day at the recreation management meeting, he felt much worse than he looked, and he looked a lot better than most. Buck resembled a walk-on from the "Night of the Living Dead" and sat virtually statue-like all morning. By lunchtime, Alex had re-hydrated some and was feeling a little better. He spent most of the afternoon watching the dark-haired woman in the front row and wondering what he was going to do about her. He was torn with guilt about Angie but also consumed with interest in Shaulane's sexual preferences. The two hemispheres in his brain had a lively discussion that day, right and left, and then left and right. Alex's thoughts bounced around like tennis balls.

As the session ended for the day, Alex had worked up the nerve to talk to Shaulane, to explain his hopeful relationship with Angie. Then he saw a swarthy fellow come into the meeting room amd make some small talk with her. As if he were collecting the prize at the fair, he left with Shaulane, arm in arm.

"That Shaulane, she's quite a package," said a returning-to-life Buck. "Just watch where you're headed, 'cause it's dangerous country."

Alex turned to Buck. "What do you know about her?"

"Not much, a beautiful package, like I said." Buck moved his hand through his bristly short hair. "But from what I heard, the odds are good, but the goods are odd."

38

"Fate keeps on happening."
Anita Loos

    It was a National Public Radio kind of day: that kind of day when, no matter which direction you look, the threatening clouds always seem to be coming from the right. It was the last day of April, and tomorrow Alex would be packing into the Middle Fork with Buck and Kloyd. Since it was a Sunday, Angie was off work and she and Alex had planned to spend the day together before he left for ten long days.

    They went for a drive; just drove around, taking the long way, heading south to Arco, and then east to Howe, a speck of a town at the edge of the desert. Alex stopped for ice cream at the log-sided gas station that comprised the entire business district of Howe. The scene reminded him of that old photograph of the gas station on Route 66 in Arizona. The clouds looked the same: white, fluffy, dwindling to perspective.

    Up the Little Lost River they went, through the one house ghost town of Clyde, past Sawmill Canyon, the Donkey Hills, the old mining town of Patterson. They stopped at the old store in May just to look around, decided not to head back to Goldburg yet, and turned north at the post office in Ellis.

    Looking at the world through his windshield, Alex said, "Would you like to go for a short hike to watch the sunset? Eddie told me a great place to go."

    Angie smiled, "Sure, I've got no plans."

    "This trail leads up to a hot spring, right in the creek; supposedly has a knockout view of the river valley. If we stay for the sunset, we should be able to get back before it gets too dark. It's supposed to be a full moon tonight, but I'll bring a flashlight just in case."

    Angie nodded in agreement and they started walking through big sage and willow. It took less than an hour to hike the two miles or so and climb the seven hundred vertical feet to a flat rock bench of river birch and fir. At the lip of the rock outcrop, a waterfall cascaded from a dark fissure of moss-covered rock and formed a small pool, a natural tub of scoured bedrock. Alex knelt down and dipped in his hand. It felt like bath water..

"Look at this, I can't believe it," he said. "This creek, it's all hot water. Must be almost body temperature."

Angie turned to face a reddening sunset. The clouds looked like they had been painted with palette knives, with sharp edges and textures and a pink filigree that looked like it came right out of the paint tube. "Look at the sunset."

"God."

Angie nuzzled close, and Alex put his arm around her waist, very much aware of her breathing and body movements.

"Want to try out the hot spring?" Alex whispered in her ear.

"I don't know. It's still light out."

"I can see all the way to the highway. We're the only vehicle in the pull-off. There's nobody else around. Come on, it'll be fun."

"Okay."

Alex took off his shirt, his heart beating quickly now. He heard Angie giggling as he took off his pants. Alex stood there, naked, and looked at Angie, still half dressed, her shirt and bra off, her nipples erect and tuning-fork firm in the evening chill. Angie slid her pants down, facing away from Alex, showing her silky thong underwear.

"Hey, those aren't cowgirl panties."

"Don't look at me."

"Well, I won't look, much." Alex counted back seven long months since the trip to Sun Valley, remembering.

Angie slid off her panties. In the growing darkness Alex could make out the mound between her legs as she stepped into the water.

"Oh, it is nice."

"What did I tell you?"

The hot water bounced off Alex's chest like a spray fountain. "Oh, this is great. Come on, try this."

Angie crouched closer and let the waterspout pour over her head, plastering her with warm water. They stood hip to hip in the waist-deep water, slowly rubbing against each other. Alex placed his hands on Angie's hips and turned her around to face him.

"We better not."

"Angie, it's been almost seven months."

It went like this for several minutes, on and off, Alex rubbing against her, their sensitive body parts communicating without words.

248

"I do love you. You know that, don't you?" he said.

Angie pushed against him, backing into the warm waterfall. "You keep saying that." She folded her arms firmly over her breasts. "But you never say you like me."

"Like you? Of course I like you. I like you so much I love you."

"But do you really like me?"

"Is this some kind of trick question or something?"

"No, no it's not. I'm just asking if you really like me. Like me, not like this, but in an everyday way. You know?"

"Angie, I liked you the first time I saw you riding in Little Grand Canyon. Something just went "ping," and I knew I liked you. I didn't know if we'd ever get together. I just had a feeling, you know?"

`   "Yeah, I do, sorta."

Alex looked up and down Angelica's naked body in the fading light, "God, you're beautiful."

"Now, this is important to me. Try to keep your focus."

"What were we talking about?"

"Do you like me?"

"Oh yeah, I do. You're the best friend I've got. Angie, you're different from any other girl, and it's wonderful different. I wish I could be with you all the time. I just wish you knew how much I like you."

Angie was making little swirls in the water with her hands. "You wouldn't ever lie to me, would you?"

"No, never, I'd never lie to you, Angie."

"Promise.'

"I swear, I'll never lie to you."

Angie hesitated, and then said, "I like you too, a lot."

"Really?" Alex said it like a small child.

She gave up a nervous giggle. "You got yourself a girl."

Alex lunged at her, scooping her up in his arms, working his mouth closer to her lips in frenzied face kisses. Angie moved like a snake against him.

Finally, close together now, moving in well-established, synchronized patterns, Angie said, "Don't you think you better put on some protection?"

Trying not to show his excitement, Alex hopped out of the warm water, searched through his clothes, grabbed his wallet, quickly finding and installing his prophylactic friend.

Angie had stayed leaning against the sloped rock, the spray from the waterfall showering over her breasts. When Alex came to her, she threw her arms around his neck and lifted her legs high, wrapping them around Alex's moving hips.

It was swirls of warm water under a red sky, with willow leaves floating in the hot spring. There were intense moments in the hot springs pool, with soft cries and moans. The waterfall washed over their locked bodies. The intensity of the experience limited the duration and, like all great endeavors, it didn't last that long.

Angie seemed wrapped around Alex like a second skin. He had to fight to stay upright in the pool. His breathing started to return to normal. As the rest of Alex started to relax he discovered a problem, a problem that caused him to snap to attention, a problem that was more than just a little bit delicate.

Angie clearly sensed his anxiety. "What's the matter?"

He reached below the waterline and discovered that the tip of his manhood was protruding from his condom. "Hell, it broke."

Angie untangled herself from him and dropped down into the pool. "What?"

"The damn rubber broke."

Angie reached down into the water, grabbed Alex in a firm grip and felt the damage for herself, looking down on the dark water surface as if she could see what had happened.

"Oh my God. Couldn't you tell?"

"Well, you know, it's not something you think about. I meant it felt really good, but I didn't suspect that anything was wrong."

"Oh Christ." Angie's eyes darted up and down. "I think it's okay. I really do. It's okay."

"Are you sure?"

Angie pressed the heels of her hands against the side of her head. "I think it's okay," she repeated. "I think it's okay."

39

"I have spread my dreams under your feet;
Tread softly, for you tread on my dreams."
W. B. Yeats

As if in a dream, the sweep boat rode over the standing waves of Aparejo Rapids slow and easy. No matter how much time Alex Kynwulf spent at the sweeps, it always felt slow and strange compared to an oar boat. The long strokes at the oars moved the boat across the current and into the fast water. Alex liked rowing the sweep boat, especially on a summer day with the clouds in patches, dwindling in perspective like an Escher print. The blue Idaho sky showed wind up high.

Alex turned to look back at Aparejo Point, the rust-colored basalt standing on edge and plunging into the Middle Fork. He saw where the rockslide came down back in 1983 from the big Mt. Borah earthquake. Three boulders stuck up like shark's teeth. A previously easy run was now a difficult class four rapids. But that was behind him now. All he had ahead was Haystack Rapids. Then he would be sitting under the black locust trees at the Flying B Ranch, enjoying a cold beer in the shade, watching the afternoon sun move on the cliff face across the river. When the canyon was in shade and had cooled down, if he wanted to he might move the raft down river, maybe even ghost along all the way to Rattlesnake Cave if he felt like it. It was a nice thought to keep in reserve.

Too quickly it seemed, Alex was coming into the slot at the head of Haystack Rapids. The house-sized boulder, the big haystack, loomed like a sentinel at the end of the rapids, splitting the standing waves like a knife on the smooth surface of the rock.

The boat was moving too slowly, as was Alex. He felt lethargic and tired, and the sweeps wouldn't bite into the water. The oar blades sliced air as the black raft lumbered closer to the wrong side of the current. The hair on Alex's neck stood up straight as he remembered the story of Elton Biggs, the river guide in that lost it in Haystack in high water. They didn't find him until his body made the Salmon River, floating in circles, face down in the big eddy

251

where the Middle Fork meets the main Salmon. Alex didn't seem to know the water level today; and it troubled him, because he always knew the water level. The water seemed much higher than it should be for July, mud-brown and full of snow runoff, branches bobbing in the whirlpools. He was on the wrong side of the river and he knew it.

His arms moved like automatons, again and again, but he couldn't seem to get the raft over river left. Each time the main current hit him like a wall and pushed him back right, toward the haystack.

The raft was accelerating now, too quickly it seemed, as if it was on a downhill ski run. The perspective was skewed and the river looked like it was flowing downhill. Ahead, the Middle Fork was split in two by the Haystack rock. The white-brown foam rolled like a drum and pulsed up and across the rock face, and Alex knew he was going to hit it.

He didn't know why he looked back at Angie at this time; but he did, and his glance lingered. She sat unconcerned, just smiling, auburn hair long in the sun, blue eyes shining. She wasn't wearing a life jacket. Alex tried to yell back at her, but something caught in his throat and the words wouldn't come. When he forced himself, the words were like a whisper, the sound of the rolling white water drowning out all other sound.

Ahead was the Haystack. Neither right nor left could save the sweep boat, but Alex still tried vainly to row left. He pulled so hard he felt blood in his ears. He braced himself for the collision but knew he didn't stand a chance of staying in the boat if he hit the rock head on, standing at the sweeps. It was just too fast, he thought. Rivers don't move this quickly. Water just can't run this fast. Again the tunnel-like perspective and the downhill slide, too steep and too funneled, and he was right in the middle of the tongue that led up to the Haystack.

Then he saw the raven, flying right in front of him, so close he raised his arm to ward it off and almost lost his grip on the oar. There was sound where there shouldn't have been, coming from the rock, the water almost musical now as it rolled off the Haystack. For a moment in time, the sweep boat perched on the top of the standing wave, a moment too long it seemed. Alex caught his breath as the boat lurched forward off the face of the wave and plunged toward the rock, no longer smooth but hard with a knife-like edge.

Alex's yell echoed down the canyon as he found himself sitting upright in his sleeping bag, his hair slicked back wet with sweat, the stars still shining in the blue-black of early morning, not sure which was real and which was the

252

dream until the sound of the bell mare came ting-a-linging down the slope and across the gravel bar.

40

"You can't step into the same river twice."
Heraclitus

The differences from one year to another can be measured in miles and measured in moments. The first of May came and went, and Alex rode down the trail to the Middle Fork with Buck and Kloyd and the Gold Dust Twins. Though Alex had not strayed much in miles, he felt the past year could have been measured in light years.

This year, Alex brought some Happy Jack pancake mix but also brought the makings for his own recipe. There were no complaints about breakfast, not even from Buck. Taking turns with the mixes meant today was a Happy Jack morning.

Alex started frying the eggs and flipping the pancakes. He broke the over-easy eggs over his own pancakes to form one wonderful mess of bacon, egg yolk and Happy Jack. Alex dug two oranges out of the cook box for the trail.

After breakfast, Kloyd rolled up his sleeves and started washing the dishes. The water was scalding hot in the pail on the cook stove. Buck worked on his last cup of coffee, walked over to the doorway, and straightened out the pinup girl that hung on a nail above the door. Alex stole a glance at the cowgirl in the picture. She looked so happy, he thought. A lariat curled around her sizeable breasts and down around her mousey brown pubic hair. In the picture, the girl licked the barrel of a Colt revolver with a long tongue, a dreamy look in her eyes, her black hat tipped back; just like the real thing, the queen of the rodeo, riding around the rodeo grounds at the head of the parade, hand high in the cowgirl salute, an honest-to-goodness barrel racer, eighteen seconds flat.

The sun was high on the canyon walls, but the river bottom was still in morning shade. The frost turned to dew, the droplets bright on the short grass. The oily smell from the saddle followed him in his work, his hands smelling like horse. Alex put an extra saddle blanket on Major to keep the saddle from rubbing on the horse's high withers. He thought Major had aged a bit over the winter. He was thinner, and Alex could see it in the way the saddle fit him.

254

With his slicker tied behind the saddle, Alex was ready, anxious to start. Buck had planned some work on the trail bridge for the afternoon and wasn't interested in tagging along. Alex had asked the Gold Dust Twins if they wanted to come along, but they said they could probably see it from the canyon bottom just as well. Alex wanted to be certain not to miss it, and was concerned about the sun angle in the deep canyon, so he and Kloyd had decided to ride to the top of Red Bluff.

Across the stream they splashed, under alder and willow and up into the sagebrush, heading south, following the river. This year it was wild and muddy with early runoff in a race to get to the Snake. A double blaze on an old Doug fir showed where the trail split, the right fork climbing up to Red Bluff. Kloyd turned his little buckskin mare up the hill and pushed into the trees, Alex and Major right behind. The horses sweated, chests heaving, as the grade increased, a long climb between switchbacks. Up, up they rode along the narrow trail, cresting on a narrow ridge where the trail went down into an open basin of Doug fir and balsam root.

Kloyd stopped his horse and turned in the saddle. "How much time we got?"

Alex checked his watch and scanned the sky. "Oh, about a half an hour or so, that's until it starts."

Kloyd reached for the non-existent can of Copenhagen in his shirt pocket. Even though he had been married now for years and the wife wouldn't allow it, the habit died hard. "I sure hope these itty-bitty clouds burn off."

"Sort of looks like it," Alex said, scanning the sky. "They're moving to the south, and there's lots of blue to the northwest."

Alex got off Major, reins in hand, and yawned loud and long, stretching his arms high above his head. He tied the horse to a dense, forked tree where Major couldn't step on his halter rope or wrap himself around, then loosened the cinch strap and used his gloves to wipe the sweat off the horse's neck and withers.

Kloyd and Alex sat on flat brown slabs of basalt on the crest of the ridge. The bunch grass was green on the hills, and the early wild flowers were in blossom; balsam root was yellow on the dry slopes and lupine blue in the bottoms.

"Did you bring that stuff to protect your eyes?" Kloyd asked.

Alex was certain he had and rustled through his saddlebags until he found the box. "Yeah, I got it right here. I read you're only supposed to use

255

color negatives, but I don't know why. Must be something in the emulsion, I guess." Alex shuffled through the protective plastic sheets in the box. "Just to be on the safe side, we should probably use two or three. I've got plenty."

"Jeez-o-Friday, where did you get such big negatives? I never seen negatives that big. What kind of camera do you have?"

"I used to play around with a view camera when I was in college, a real nice camera, a five-by-seven Burke and James. It was on a full slide rail with tilt both front and back. It had absolutely great depth of field. I could focus from three feet to infinity with that baby, and I mean focus sharp as a tack. It was old, but a damn fine piece of equipment."

"Whatever you say, I guess. You still have that camera?"

"Yeah, but it's back in storage in Pennsylvania and I haven't used it for a couple of years now. It's just too much trouble, and besides, I don't have access to a darkroom and enlarger anymore."

"Is it all right to touch them?"

"Sure, they're extras. The film was old or something, and they're really not good enough to print from."

Kloyd screwed his eyes up and looked through the box of negatives. "Sort of hard to tell what's going on with all of the colors backwards. Did you ever print any of these?"

"I think so. Check in the bottom of the box. I remember making a series of contact prints."

Kloyd dug into the box and came up with a handful of prints that had been stuck to the bottom. "Yeah, there's a whole ding-dang bunch of them. Where did you take all these pictures?"

"Oh, back east, Pennsylvania mostly. I did a couple trips to Canada, probably some pictures of Nova Scotia in there."

"Looks like some pretty nice country." Kloyd flipped through his stack of prints one more time, took out one and handed it over to Alex. "Who's all these rough-looking characters in this picture?"

"That's my forest ecology class, junior year, back at Penn State. I got everybody together for an informal class picture. That's me over on the left, in the back."

"That's you, there, with all the long hair?"

"Everybody had long hair back then."

"Not in Idaho."

"No, I imagine not."

256

"You look like a genuine hippie type here in this picture."

"Like hell I do."

"Here's another picture of another bunch, not as many, but some of the same ones."

"Oh man, I remember this. This was our last night in the lab. We all went down to Zeno's to celebrate."

"Zeno's?"

"Yeah, it was a little bar, dance joint, right across from the Mall on College Avenue and Allen Street. It was the hot place to be." Alex remembered it often. He didn't know why. He could remember where everyone was seated and how they looked that night. He could even remember what the tall waitress with the big breasts jammed into her Zeno's T-shirt looked like. All his friends had gotten drunk that night. Alex had to carry Rodney out of the place. Back then, it was the thing to do, especially at the end of your college career. But then the next day came and all his friends began the process of drifting away. He wondered if any of his friends ever thought of that night in Zeno's cellar, when all problems seemed to be conveniently far in the future. Probably no one else ever remembered, Alex thought. It was, after all, an insignificant thing.

The last of the clouds moved over the mountains to the south. A breeze, one of those springtime breezes, blew the smell of fresh churned soil up the slope. A red-tailed hawk, high above, floated like a kite.

"How about this one?" Kloyd pushed another contact print towards Alex.

"You're really getting into this, aren't you? I didn't realize you were this interested in my life."

Kloyd smiled that cowboy grin of his. "I just like pictures is all. This one sure is weird, a bunch of people in costumes or something."

"Here, let me see. Man, this is a long time ago. I think I'd just gotten my camera. This is up in Quebec City, at winter carnival."

"Up in Canada?"

"That's the one."

Alex pointed. "That's me, right there."

"Holy smokes! I thought you had long hair in the other picture. Why, you look just like a girl here in this one. Your hair is all the way down to your shoulders!"

"Jeez." Alex caught himself before he finished the phrase. "Anyway, what's the big deal?, I was in college then."

257

"Well, now I know something about you. Just treat me good, and Buck'll never know."

"Well, Clum Dummit, that's it! I'm letting my hair grow starting right now!"

Both of them laughed like fools.

Kloyd was the first to recover. "Anyway, what are you bunch of hippies doing in this picture?"

"It's the Quebec Winter Carnival. I was a sophomore in college, and I went up there with I guy I knew who was an exchange student from France. I remember we were making an ice sculpture with some girls we met up there."

"You carved that out of a block of ice?"

"Actually, you carve it out of several blocks of ice and then put it together."

"So, what did you make? It sorta looks like a guy petting a pig."

"No, can't you see? It's Paul Bunyan and Babe the blue ox."

"Whatever you say."

"Haven't you ever been to winter carnival in McCall?"

"Gosh, no, I would never go to McCall. Full of hippie-types and mother earthers."

"Hell, we could ride over there in three or four days from here if we wanted to."

"Like I said, don't care to go. And your ox still looks like a pig."

"Damn cowboys got no appreciation for art."

"So, who's this girl here holding on to you?"

"Gimme that." Alex grabbed back the print and, looking at it, said, "Damn, I didn't think I had a picture of her."

Alex remembered her well, but he had to search to think of her name. Natalia, it was Natalia something, something different, short, but different sounding. He did remember how pretty she was and how he had developed an instant crush on the girl, and that she didn't seem afraid of him. Natalia Timkin, that was it; meant "little finger" in Russian. She was a Russian girl going to school at McGill in Montreal: dark hair, almost black, straight, cut right at the shoulders, strong features, really looked like a Russian, he thought. She was up for the carnival. He remembered walking with Natalia through the old part of Quebec City, the deep snow cut vertically on both sides of the walk. Snow was everywhere, sometimes higher than you could see over.

They went to the art museum; and, suitably, a French Impressionist show

258

was on display. It was the first time that Alex had seen famous paintings, the ones in art books and on the designer calendars. He walked with her through the museum, his hands in his pockets, talked with her at each painting and sat on the black foam benches, marveling at the colors that never seemed to be able to be reproduced on the gallery prints and postcards in the gift shops. Most of the famous Impressionists were represented in the show: Alfred Sisley's landscapes of towns and canals, Monet at Argentueil, Manet portraits and a Degas pastel, a Renoir of a red-haired man dancing with a pretty girl, on loan from London, and even a little painting of a peach tree by Van Gogh. Alex and Natalia seemed to have the same tastes in art; but then, so did almost everybody. Alex remembered that he walked back to the youth hostel with Natalia that night, happy and singing a Christmas song together as it began to snow, big wet flakes floating down without wind in the dark. They agreed to meet for breakfast, and Alex waited for her at the French café till late morning but the girl never showed.

Alex put the prints back in the box. "I read that the next total eclipse won't be for over a hundred years in North America."

"Sorta makes you think about how much time you got left."

"Not a hundred years."

Kloyd tore off some grass tufts and threw them up in the air. "That's fine; I don't think I'd like doing this kind of work at a hundred and thirty."

"You know, you just might be able to pull it off. You're not any great shakes at it right now, so I figure you'll be well rested," Alex joked.

"Well, if you feel that way, this is the last time I go see an eclipse with you."

"Speaking of eclipses, hand me back some of those negatives. It's starting already."

Kloyd held up a handful of negatives toward the sun. "Judas Priest, would you look at that!"

The light was changing. Even though the sun was shining, it was somehow getting darker. The difference between sunlight and shadow was lessening and everything took on a yellowish haze. It was as if the sun were dying out, the sunlight just draining out of the landscape.

Alex held a sandwich of negatives up to his face. He could see a picture of himself smiling back at him in the negative with a red face and white hair and all the color values reversed. Sort of funny, he thought. Over the picture of him, the moon covered three quarters of the face of the sun.

"How long will it be totally dark?" Kloyd asked.

"I'm not really sure. We're at the edge of totality at this latitude. I don't think it will be dark for more than a minute or two."

"It's really getting nice now." Kloyd squinted through his negatives. "You can see it real good."

The moon shadow moved across the sun more quickly than Alex would have thought. He looked away for an instant and saw that it was almost as dark in sunlight as in shadow. Alex glanced back at himself in the negative and how he looked four years ago. He was happy and smiling, like nothing at all could ever bother him. Everyone else seemed to be smiling too.

The moon covered all but a speck of the sun. The stars began to come out, first just a few; and then, as in a magic time lapse, all the stars were there. Orion the hunter hung low on the horizon. The Big Dipper suddenly swirled overhead, the pole star floating cold in space. Alex looked at himself again in the negative, smiling, smiling with a total eclipse over his shoulder.

The eclipse was complete. Blazing with white fire, the corona surrounded the black hole of the sun. Alex tried to hold it still, to mark it in his memory, if such a thing could be done, to try to slow it down, knowing that it would be over soon. It was as black as a new-moon midnight, the corona blazing, the sun shining elsewhere but not on the Middle Fork.

Four years ago smiling, and what was he smiling about? Alex thought, just for the picture? He always was a smiler.

He was thinking that, whatever it was, whatever really mattered, it always came down to the people in his past and the friendships. Alex felt that he must have an extra gene for loyalty or something, and the end of friendship bothered him the most. He could remember the places, the events that happened as well as anybody, probably better than most. But remembering the people never seemed to work, for they changed too fast. The memories seemed short and scattered, built on bits and pieces that never did fit right, the way it really happened. The tricks of memory were too many and too sophisticated to trust, he thought. The people in his past just went too soon. Just as he was getting closer, they were gone, waving goodbye with tears in their eyes, saying they would see him again soon, and all the while, the years ran by like spring high water.

Kloyd never said a word, remaining frozen with his mouth open, staring at the black sun through his negatives.

And just then, a shot of sunlight, a light beam, appeared at the lower left corner of the sun. The eclipse was ending. That small beam of light was enough to erode the stars, fading in reverse time lapse now, rolling away and fading to a blue-black sky. Alex looked down river to the far horizon, and a black shadow streaked toward him, a magic thing, something that could not be. It was the leading edge of totality coming right at him at incredible speed like something out of science fiction, the amorphous shadow leaping past him in an instant as the sun returned. Alex caught a last glimpse of the shadow as he turned his head and saw it streaking up and over Camas Creek.

The eclipse reversed order. Thin shadows appeared behind the trees, and a yellow haze of sunshine grew and became stronger. Soon the moon covered only one half of the sun, and the next time that Alex hazarded a glance through his negatives, the moon was gone, the sun blinding and permanent.

Alex looked around, blinking, the image of the sun still on the back of his eyes. Everything around him seemed different, new, somehow changed without his knowing. From high on the ridge, he looked at mountains fading away to blue on the far horizon. To the west a few clouds lingered, thin and in a line, the perspective intense and strongly defined. The foothold of fir trees were deep green, greener than he remembered, and the Middle Fork, far below, seemed to sparkle. It was a strange feeling, sort of like coming back home to the country from a long trip to a far away city, finding your old room just as you had left it as a kid, the baseball trophy still on the shelf, not a picture moved out of place; but you had been gone just the same.

Alex couldn't define the source, but happiness seemed to well up inside him like a spring. All the negatives didn't seem to matter anymore. He had a strong impression that something wonderful was going to happen just for him, and he didn't have to do anything to find it or make it happen. Unexplainable as it was, Alex was certain it was coming.

"Well, I hope I didn't hurt my eyes," Kloyd said, blinking.

"You didn't stare the whole time, did you?"

"No, just on and off. Except when it was full and then I watched all the while. Couldn't take my eyes off it."

"Neither could I."

Kloyd handed his negatives back to Alex. "I guess it's over."

"Yeah, I guess we better be going. Buck will be expecting us back at camp."

The total eclipse was over and done, and Alex was certain he would never see another. That didn't bother him any more, but thoughts of the future kept turning over and over in his head on the long ride down through the trees.

261

41

"Here's another fine mess you've gotten me into."
Oliver Hardy

Alex left the District office and saw Angelica standing next to his pickup, drawing little circles in the gravel with her left foot, and then smoothing them over with her right. Her head popped up like a wind-up toy when she saw him.

"I'm late," she said.

"Not at all. You're right on time. I just barely got out of the office." Alex was all smiles.

"No, you dolt. I mean I'm late. Remember? The hot spring?"

"Oh?" Alex's eyes became very round. His voice broke just a little. "Are you sure?"

"Yes, I'm sure. Of course I'm sure. You think I'd be telling you if I wasn't?"

"Ahhh, like how late?"

"A couple days."

"So you think?"

"Maybe."

"Christ!"

"Well?"

"Maybe, maybe there's another explanation. Sometimes it's just late, right? It's not like it's the moon or anything." Alex was lost in thought sequences of twenty-nine and half days, multiplying forward the months to a future he had never really thought much about. "I mean, like, it is the same amount of time as the moon phases, but it's not like physics or anything? It can vary a few days or so, can't it? Without meaning, necessarily, you know. Maybe it's just a funny period or something?"

"It doesn't seem too funny from this end."

"No, of course not. I didn't mean funny ha ha, but more like funny, you

262

know, unusual." Alex's head began to shake a little bit from side to side.

"You don't sound too enthusiastic."

Almost hyperventilating now, "Do you really think you are?"

"I don't know, maybe. I was thinking about getting one of those test kits they sell in the drugstore."

Alex seized on the idea. "That's right, a test kit! I've heard about those. A test kit. Supposed to be like really accurate."

"Pretty much so, I've heard."

"Like accurate, if it showed up negative, then you wouldn't be like . . ."

"Like pregnant?"

Alex closed both eyes and opened his mouth and winced with the invisible blow. "Ye–ah."

"I really don't know if I am, but I'm scared I am."

"Me too."

"What do we do now?"

Alex let out a dead man's breath. "I guess we go get one of those kits."

Angie crossed her arms and then re-crossed them the other way. "Beadie, over at the drug store has a big mouth. I don't want to go in there."

"Well, hell, I'll go in and buy it."

Angie was shaking her head with her eyes closed. "No, that won't be any better. Everyone knows everything in this damn town."

"Criminy, I'll drive down to Salmon and get it."

Angie's eyes popped open. "When?"

"Now, right now." Alex checked his watch. "It's only four thirty. I can make it to Salmon before six." He jammed his fist into his pants pocket searching for his keys. "You want to come along?"

Angie reconfigured her hair back behind her ears, both hands coming to rest on her neck. "I might see somebody. I better not."

"I'll be back before eight. I'll bring it over to your house."

"No, no, tomorrow morning will be fine."

"I'll bring it over to the café."

Angie was breathing in sharp puffs. "God, Alex, you make me feel like nothing when you talk like this."

"Like what? What do you mean?"

"You're scared to death, aren't you? Well, how do you think I feel?"

Alex flinched. "I can leave it in the truck?"

"You don't care much about me, do you?"

"Sure, sure I do. Of course I do. I care a lot."

Angie turned around like a soldier and walked away fast.

Alex called after, "I'll leave it in the truck, right on the seat," then added, "I'll put my jacket over it."

Ten yards away Angie turned around, eyes full of tears, "You just do that. You cover it up real good!" She was crying as she ran, ran fast all the way past the corrals and the fire warehouse.

Alex quietly called after, "Don't worry. It'll be all right." But he didn't believe it.

42

"Fear has many eyes and can see things underground."
Miguel de Cervantes

Alex stalked into the Salmon Rexall Drug Store with fifteen minutes to spare. He was damp with sweat, as if walking through the door had required all his strength. Now he was looking lost and perplexed in the aisle of feminine products: two long rows of brightly colored foams, lotions, and spray bottles, all attractively packaged, most phallic shaped, with upbeat, sunny names. The plethora of private products both fascinated and embarrassed Alex. "What do women do with all this stuff?" he wondered.

Within this bounty of bottles and boxes, Alex could not seem to find the pregnancy kits. His nervousness attracted the middle-aged woman druggist behind the counter. As she approached slowly, Alex moved away just as slowly. She followed him around the far side of the aisle. Alex checked his watch; ten to six. Time was running short.

The big woman in the white coat outsmarted Alex by staying put as he stumbled around the corner. "Can I help you find anything? We're about to close up, you know."

Alex grimaced and forced out the words. "I'm looking for one of those pregnancy testing kits." He quickly added, "It's for a friend of mine."

"Well, I should hope so," the horned-rimmed-glasses lady said. "Here, follow me. We keep them right up front with the prophylactics."

Alex followed, red-faced and sheepish, soon surrounded by a sea of condoms. He couldn't help looking at the boxes, with all the happy couples in silhouette facing fading sunsets, anticipating the lurid pleasures associated with the ultra-ribbed, special spermicidal-tipped, magnum-sized, ultra-thin latex personal protection devices in the little boxes on the shelf.

"Do you know what kind you want?"

"They come in different kinds? Oh, I don't know, just give me a good one."

265

"They come with different types of applicators."

"Just the regular kind of applicator is fine with me."

The woman in white reached for a bright blue box. "This is one of our biggest sellers." She placed the softball sized box into Alex's slightly shaking hand.

Alex held the box, wondering what was inside. Just his entire future life, he thought. And with that thought came the funny feeling that preceded a big freeze-up, as Alex stood still and stared straight ahead. He didn't speak or even move for a minute or more.

The drug-store lady seemed to think that Alex's hesitation was due to a careful and calculated consumerism. "I particularly like this model. The application is quite simple."

Alex willed his eyes to move and was able to glance at the directions on the side of the box. He immediately wished he were dead.

"It's the most expensive brand, but I have never had a complaint or a return."

"I'll take it!" Alex puffed out the words, startling the druggist two steps backward.

Alex nervously stood at the counter, sensing someone behind him. Even though the person was standing close, too close behind him, he didn't turn around.

"Just doing a little impulse shopping, or stocking up before the hoarders get here?"

It was Sandy Spotts, smiling as she looked gleefully at the bright blue box. "What's the matter, Tiger, cat got your tongue?"

"Oh, ah, Sandy, hi, what's happening?"

"Evidently not much compared to you."

"Oh, I'm just doing a favor for a friend, that's all." Alex knew he was red from forehead to collar.

"Oh, well," Sandy drawled. "What are friends for, anyway?"

Alex finally paid for the brown bag and said, "Yeah, well, I got to run, Sandy, see you later."

Sandy responded with her favorite, "Not unless I see you first," and pointed her finger like a pistol. But Alex was gone before she could cock her thumb like the hammer.

Back at the cabin on Garden Creek, Alex sat stoney-eyed, staring at the phone, hands clenched together, debating whether to call Angie. It was only nine o'clock. He wanted to, and then he didn't want to. The brown paper bag with the pregnancy kit sat on his kitchen table like a tombstone. Inertia took him to dark and finally to bed, where he wrestled his pillow and blanket to a draw, finally drifting off into fitful dreams of Nazis and large bears just before dawn.

The next morning Alex got out of his truck like he was exiting a funeral limousine. Three times he took in a deep breath, and three times he sighed. He looked at the bag on the truck seat, stared up at an empty sky, and sighed again.

Alex was the first one in the office. He closed his door, grabbed the phone and dialed Angie's number without even thinking.

Someone picked up the phone on the first ring. "Hello, Angie?"

"Alex?"

"I got it." His voice was quiet and conspiratorial. "I left it on the truck seat."

Angie didn't say anything right away, and Alex almost repeated himself before she said, " I don't need it."

"Ahh, don't need it? Ahh, why not?" Alex could hear his heart beating.

There was more hesitation, and then a guarded, "It took care of itself."

"It did?" Alex's voice rose to a high note.

"Yes, it did, so don't worry."

"Oh, God, Angie, that's great news." Alex leaned way back in his chair. "That's just wonderful!"

"Yeah, great news, great." Angie mumbled into the phone.

Alex started to laugh, one of those wild laughs like the people on the game shows. "Oh, man, you really had me scared there. Woo-boy, that's a relief. Am I glad that's over."

Angie audibly sucked in a long breath. "Alex, could you try to contain yourself? You're making me feel like a real shit here."

Standing now at his desk, bouncing on the balls of his feet, Alex forced himself toward a false calm, talking low and slow, but smiling all the while. "Angie, I'm sorry. Of course, I'm sorry it all happened."

"You don't sound too sorry."

"I mean, I'm sorry for the way I acted. I'm over it now, really." Alex couldn't stop smiling. "We'll just have to be more careful."

"You better be a lot more careful!" and Angie slammed the phone down so hard that Alex had to juggle the receiver to keep it from falling.

267

43

"POST COITUM OMNE ANIMAL TRISTE."
(After coition every animal is sad.)
Latin, post classical, anonymous

Deja vu swirled around the Plywood Palace like dust motes in sunshine. Alex could feel it everywhere he looked. He and Angie were back at the Palace for the Fireman's Brawl, this year being held a little later on the weekend before Memorial Day. Alex was enjoying the fit of the day and where the evening was headed. Around the table sat most of his friends from work: Fast Eddie, Harmon, Argo, Teffonie, Howie and Nedra; and, of course, Angie was sitting close, rubbing shoulders with Alex.

Howie brought over two more pitchers of beer. "Full Sail Ale at the Plywood Palace; now what could be better? Sunbeam, Idaho, one of the special places, a toast!"

They all raised their glasses and Howie went on, "To good friends, good gear, and good times."

"Hear, hear!" Harmon said, stamping his feet.

"Oh, Howie is so eloquent," Nedra said. "He made the same toast at the end of our awareness camp on Maui. It was so touching. Our awareness counselor was just in tears."

Alex leaned forward and just had to ask, "What's an awareness counselor?"

"Oh, he's like our yoga master. He was like, great, and could awaken all this energy that was dormant within us. We were, like, aware."

"Yeah, I see, aware."

Argo rubbed his downy red beard. "Were you able to get in touch with the core essence of who you are?"

"Well," Nedra said, "I don't know about that, but we were really, like, aware of it."

Far in the back of Alex's consciousness, a warning bell began to toll, barely audible; on the edge, a distant sound on a far-away shore. He tried to ignore it, not to look over his shoulder, but he kept feeling it coming toward him at a measured pace.

Finally, Alex had to look and turned toward the door just as Shaulane walked into the Plywood Palace looking like Princess Di and just filling the room, arm in arm with a carbon copy of the guy Alex had seen her with in Salt Lake.

Alex noticed that Angie was shifting restlessly in her seat and had been doing so ever since she returned from the female pilgrimage to the restroom. Alex thought maybe it was too much yoga talk and tried to change the subject. "So, how's Lazlo?" he asked.

Nedra jumped to the question. "Oh, Lazlo is just perfect, as usual. He just loves his latest Cabbage Patch doll we got for him on E-bay."

Fast Eddie joined the conversation. "Doesn't he just tear them up? Like every time?"

"Yeah, well, but it seems to make him so happy," Nedra explained.

Argo steered the topic back to yoga, his interest in Teffonie showing through clearly. "So Teffonie, do you practice yoga? You look like you do."

Teffonie seemed somewhat embarrassed but said, "Yeah, I'm sort of a beginner, though."

Argo stroked his beard once more. "I practice Kundalini Yoga."

"Really? I've read a little about it. I like the breathing part, sounds relaxing."

"You must mean the breath of fire, or the Bellow's Breath."

"Yeah, that's probably it," Teffonie said somewhat hesitantly. "I think so."

Alex could see that Angie was getting more agitated and more fidgety. He didn't know what it was about, but he could see it wasn't just the yoga. She seemed a little distant. Perhaps it was the difference in alcohol consumption. Most at the table were already on the edge, and Angie hadn't touched her glass.

"Angie, you want something else to drink?"

"No thanks, maybe later."

The Letgo Brothers were tuning up and getting ready to play. It sounded like a slow dance number coming up.

"Care to dance?" Alex asked.

"I don't think so, not yet."

Alex began to start up the worry meter, but he wasn't sure. Maybe it was

269

just the time of the month, or something like that. He moved his chair closer and put his arm around her.

Angie stood up quickly and picking up her purse, said, "I'm going to go outside for a while."

Now Alex felt the storm clouds approach. It was a full gale; warning flags, red and black, flapped furiously in the back of his mind. Alex stood up and watched her leave through the front door of the Plywood Palace, in a hurry about something.

Alex sat through the song, wondering about Angie. Helplessly hoping for a harmless, logical explanation, he excused himself and followed the path that Angie had taken.

At first he didn't see her. He expected to find Angie waiting outside the door. Scanning the parking lot, he found her sitting on the hood of Howie's Range Rover. Alex wandered over slowly.

"Angie, what's up?"

She laughed a short, strange laugh, more like a cough. "Well, to tell the truth, I was thinking about taking up smoking."

"Hey, don't you want to come in and dance? The band is just starting to get going."

"I don't know. Just don't feel like dancing is all."

Alex shuffled his feet in the gravel, like a little kid. "Well, hell, I guess I don't feel like dancing either."

Angie gave him a threatening look as she pushed herself off the hood of the Range Rover and stood, shoulders square, facing Alex. She seemed to be looking somewhere far in the distance and said, "Why don't you go back and ask your friend Shaulane to dance?"

The lightning flashed and big red warning lights went off. She knows, he thought; how? Trying to think of some way to defend himself, Alex said, "I want to dance with you."

Angie stopped stock still. "Oh, you do, huh?"

Alex waited a moment before answering, "Yeah."

Angie took a step closer and looked him full in the face. The light from the Plywood Palace danced in her eyes. "You fucked her, didn't you?"

Alex made a little noise, a breathing mistake that came from deep in his diaphragm. He was freezing up again fast. In his desperate search for an idea, he turned to the presidential defense and blurted out, "Angie, I swear, I never had sex with that woman."

270

Angie was shaking a little bit - he could see it - and was staring intently into Alex's eyes. A thin curl of a smile started at the edge of her lips. His hands tried to reach out to hold her, and Angie responded with a short, savage kick to Alex's crotch.

Alex hit the dirt hard, his hands cupped between his legs.

"You lying bastard," she said, and turned away, back toward the door of the Plywood Palace.

For the second time in less than thirteen months, Alex lay face down in the dirt in the parking lot of the Plywood Palace; and this time, he was pretty sure, it was going to hurt for a long time.

44

"The day breaks not, it is my heart."
John Donne

The normal spring rains never arrived that year in central Idaho. June was usually the wettest month of the year, followed by May, in most parts of the region. But that year, something was going on with the jet stream, and it moved north into Canada leaving most of the intermountain west, and particularly Idaho, high and dry. Goldburg only received an average seven inches of moisture for the entire year, and the loss of May and June were hard on both plants and animals. Spring green-up came and went without notice, and the landscape started an early move towards summer brown. The range started out poor that year, and unless summer thunderstorms brought some rain, the ranchers were looking at light calf weights in the fall. By mid-June, Alex couldn't even remember the last cloudy day. It was as if he lived under a cerulean blue dome instead of a living sky.

Like the effects of the drought on the landscape, the breakup with Angie had taken something out of him, an important missing part, and he couldn't seem to get it back. In the early morning, when the sun came over the high ridge, the time of day he always liked best, Alex now barely noticed the sunrise. The drive down Garden Creek past all his favorite rock outcrops that he previously so enjoyed, he now barely gave a glance. The days began to fade into each other, and it was as if he left his house, went to work, and there was nothing else of much merit left to do. Work was about the same. Now the papers sat on the edge of his desk in several piles that he stared at off and on during the day.

Then on yet another blue-sky June day, Alex was walking across the District compound toward the fire warehouse, when he stopped in his tracks. It was Angie, carrying a fire pack and balancing a yellow hard hat on her head. Alex sidled over quickly to intercept her path.

"Hi, Angie, what's going on?"

"Oh, hi."

Alex understood the meaning of the fire clothes and wondered why Buck had not told him anything about this, but he asked her the question anyway. "Are you working for us, on the fire crew?"

Angie smiled that wonderful smile of hers, but it was clear it was not directed towards Alex. "Yeah, I'm working for Buck on the fire crew at Indian Creek."

"Indian Creek, huh. I didn't know that." And now Alex really wanted to know why Buck hadn't said anything to him about this. Alex was quickly running out of things to say and Angie wasn't helping him one bit.

She repositioned herself to stand with her side facing Alex. "You didn't know?"

"No, no, must of slipped Buck's mind." Alex looked up at the sky. "So what happened to your waitress job?"

Angie took off the heavy fire pack and set it down at her feet. "Oh, I was tired of it. The money stinks, and anyhow, I thought I could do better."

Alex noticed her brand new smoke-jumper boots. "So you're headed to fire school tomorrow?"

"Yeah."

"Well, this is a surprise, a nice surprise."

Angie took her sunglasses out of her breast pocket and put them on. "Alex, don't get any ideas. I'm just working here so I can save up some money and get out of this town."

"I didn't know that." Alex's spirits sank to the depth of ground water. "When do you plan on leaving?"

Angie spread her hair behind her ears. "This fall, right after fire season." She was all business now. "Let's not make this any more difficult than we have to. Let's just stay out of each other's way for three months, and then I'll be gone."

"God, are you sure?"

"Yeah, yeah, I'm sure."

"If that's how you want it to be, I'll do my part. It's okay, really."

"That's good, I want it to be okay."

"Well, I'm sure I'll be seeing you down at Indian Creek."

"I'm sure you will."

"Okay, well, take care of yourself."

"You too."

"Angie?"

"Yeah?"

273

"I just want to say that I'm sorry, sorry for everything."

"That's okay, it really is." She picked up her fire pack and Alex watched her stride self-confidently over to the fire warehouse.

His chance meeting with Angelica had not gone unnoticed. When he returned to the office, Buck said, "You see we hired Angie Kowalski?"

"Yeah, I see."

"Good kid. She'll be a good worker."

Alex let out an involuntary sigh. "Yeah, I'm sure she will be."

And for the next week, Alex seemed to see Angelica Kowalski everywhere he went. The District held its yearly fire school in mid-June. Alex saw Angie at the office, at the fire warehouse, at dispatch, and on the day when he had to teach wilderness fire suppression techniques and no-trace fire camp, he looked at her sitting in the front row from morning until quitting time. All this Angelica Kowalski didn't seem to be good for him. He was having trouble sleeping, often waking up at three o'clock in the morning, wide awake, tossing and turning, and falling back asleep just before daybreak.

After work it was a different story. Angie was nowhere to be seen. Alex tried to scheme and plan and position himself to be near her at the end of the day, but Angelica seemed to sense his movements and easily eluded him. He checked out the café, the bars, even drove all way to Salmon once on a hunch, but Angie was nowhere to be seen after working hours. Alex imagined her working on the ranch, hot in the evening sun, sweating in her T-shirt and stretching her back and wiping her high forehead with the back of her hand. He decided that those types of thoughts didn't seem to help at all.

When he ran out of ideas for reconciliation, he decided to try to push her out of his system through exercise. He became an exercise Nazi; running Garden Creek at daybreak, bicycling the seven miles to work and back, push-ups and sit-ups five times a day, sets of forty and fifty, right at his desk during work hours, pull-ups at dispatch during lunch hours, three sets of ten. He stopped going to The Wild Bunch and gave up alcohol entirely. If he'd been a smoker, he would have given that up, too. He shaved off his mustache, got a crew cut, lost weight. He got so thin the folks at work thought he might be sick. His life resembled basic training, except with a desk attached. He was so tired that he sometimes fell asleep at the lunch table, face down on the wax paper from his sandwich. But no matter how hard he exercised, how many miles he ran, bicycled, or climbed, at the end of the day, he found himself sitting alone with thoughts of Angelica Kowalski.

Alex seemed to have lost his groove and was having trouble finding it again. He began to make small mistakes and errors in judgment.

One Saturday afternoon, Alex was helping Kloyd frame a tack shed that Kloyd was building onto his barn. Alex was working with a twenty-two ounce framing hammer, driving sixteen penny nails in one after another with no more than four or five blows of the hammer. From all the push-ups and pull-ups, his arms looked like Popeye's. On the last wall, the last stud, and the last nail, Alex flattened his thumb with the last swing of the hammer. He let out a stream of invective as he ran an exaggerated injury dance around the barnyard, holding his throbbing thumb in his hand.

"Oh, son-of-a-bitch! Mother fuckin' whore from hell!" Alex danced on one foot then the other. "Clum dummit!"

Kloyd tried to calm him down. "Here, let's get some ice on that thumb. Maybe that'll help."

"Oh, son-of-a-bitch, this hurts!"

Kloyd fixed a bowl of ice and Alex put the now blackened thumb in, feeling every beat of his pulse in the injured digit.

"I don't know," said Kloyd. "This here don't look like your garden variety smashed thumb. Maybe I should run you over to the clinic. Doc Dime should be in."

"Do you think he can do anything to help? Christ, this thumb hurts like hell!"

"Don't know, but let's not worry about it. It's a long way from the heart."

Alex gritted his teeth. "I'll try to remember that."

Kloyd felt the heavy weight of responsibility and insisted on driving Alex over. He checked him into the clinic and then sat in the waiting room, reading outdoor magazines.

Alex didn't have to wait long to see Doctor Dime.

"Smashed your thumb, eh?" Doctor Dime stated the obvious. "Well, I've got just the thing to take care of this baby. A little trick I learned in the Army."

Alex thought he caught a whiff of whiskey on Doc's breath.

"Perlene!" Doc called to the nurse down the hall. "Get me my butane torch, would you? And those red pliers too."

Alex tightened up at the words "butane torch and pliers". He felt he needed to ask, "What's the torch and pliers for?"

"Well, you see, most of your pain is being caused by the pressure of the blood trapped behind your thumbnail. Like I said, I've done this a hundred times in the Army. Set you right in no time."

Alex watched spellbound, thumb in hand, as Doc Dime took one of those heavyweight paper clips and began to unfold it.

"You see, I'm going to use this paper clip to burn a small hole in your thumbnail, to let the pressure out." Perlene brought in a shiny red pair of pliers and a yellow plastic box containing a portable torch kit. Doc fiddled with the torch, trying to get it assembled, and Alex noticed that Doc's hands were a little shaky. Finally Doc Dime got the torch working and soon had an inch long blue-white flame zipping out the tip of the torch. He held the unraveled paper clip in the pliers with his other hand.

"I'll get this paper clip red hot and Perlene will hold your hand still." Alex watched the wire of the paper clip begin to glow. "All you have to do is just tell me the moment you first feel the paper clip, and I'll pull it out and the blood will flow out the hole."

It all sounded logical to Alex, and he figured that Doc Dime knew what he was doing on this one; but the thought nagged him that it seemed a somewhat industrial-strength procedure for family practice work.

"Okay, I let you know the second I feel something, and then you pull it out, right?"

"Right as rain."

"The second I first feel it?"

"You got it."

The tip of the paperclip glowed red and white.

Perlene clamped down Alex's hand on the stainless steel table in a wrestler's grip.

Alex watched the slightly wobbling white-hot tip of the paper clip settle into the center of his black, swollen thumbnail. The smell of burning hair filled his flaring nostrils, the smell of his melting thumbnail.

After three long seconds, Alex felt a tingle in the center of his thumb. "Okay, I feel it. I feel it."

Doctor Dime blinked and pulled on the pliers. Unfortunately, his grip on the pliers had loosened sufficiently so that when Doc pulled, the pliers slipped off the paper clip, leaving it embedded in Alex's thumbnail and producing a thin column of blue-black smoke.

An involuntary noise started from deep within Alex, a single long syllable, expressed as "Ahhhhhhhhhhhhhhhhhh!" and quickly ascending in tone and volume.

Either a bad day or a previous night with too much medicine had dulled Doc Dime's reflexes to the point that he kept missing the paper clip with his snapping pliers. "Hold still, dammit!"

But Alex could no more hold still than he could fly by flapping his arms. He fiercely tore loose from Perlene, grasping his left wrist with his right hand and screaming "Ahhhhhhhhhh!" as he began a strange walk-and-dip type of dance. He hyperventilated his way around the examining room, just catching his breath long enough to scream an even louder "AHHHHHHHHH!"

Alex's screams filled the clinic. Kloyd stood up and dropped his magazine right on the floor. "Jeez-o-Friday," he muttered.

Finally, Perlene body-slammed Alex into the corner and pinned his arm against the wall. Doc Dime rallied one more time, and with the odds against him, finally clamped the pliers on the paper clip and just tore the hot wire from the bloody stinking mess of Alex's thumbnail.

Alex collapsed on the examining room floor, blowing like a racehorse.

Doc Dime dropped the paperclip onto the stainless steel tray, smoothed his thinning hair back, looked at Alex, and panted, "I told you it would work."

Kloyd led Alex out to the truck like an invalid without the wheelchair. Doc Dime had given Alex some painkillers and sent him home, saying that he would be fine tomorrow. As Alex sat in Kloyd's truck, his bandaged thumb elevated and now even more swollen, his pulse beating a bongo rhythm in his thumb, Alex realized he had reached a goal. His mind was clear. There was no room for anything other than the pain in his thumb, and any thoughts of Angie Kowalski would have to wait.

Two days later, Alex dragged himself to work with a bandage on both thumb and heart.

45

The bad vibrations from Alex and Angie's breakup seemed to flow outward in concentric circles of anxiety, like ripples from a rock thrown into a small pond. Other couples subconsciously felt the subtle strings of stress and magnified them into "issues." These negative vibes ran right into and over the always tense relationship between Big Stanley and Sandy Spotts.

Big Stanley didn't do his drinking in Goldburg but rather ran a trap line of taverns all within happy-hour driving distance from the office. Generally it was in a clockwise pattern, from Salmon to Mackey, from Arco to Clayton. Big Stan was careful not to be seen as a regular booze hound but imagined himself more as a traveling statesman who occasionally enjoyed his cups.

Sandy Spotts, his regular designated drinking buddy, sat close to his side that warm June evening at the Plywood Palace. Big Stan was enjoying the scenery, looking out the window through the whiskey in his glass.

"Stan, don't you ever get tired of this?"

"Tired? Tired of what?"

"Just sittin' here drinkin' and talkin'."

"No, not really. I sort of think of it as my hobby. You know, instead of golf or gambling, or something self-destructive like that."

"But you're wastin' your life, just sittin' there on that old barstool."

"Ah, Sandy, that smarts. Smarts like cheap aftershave on a nicked chin."

Sandy sort of squirmed on her seat and said, "Aren't you ever gonna settle down, get married?"

Big Stanley's bulldog mouth dropped conspicuously. "You know I tried it once, and it just didn't work out. Hell, marriage and me just didn't agree. That's all that ex-wife of mine did was complain about how I acted. Everything that I did was wrong. She had that marriage counselor's advice damn near tattooed to my forehead.

278

"Did she believe in what the marriage counselor had to say?"

"Believe what he had to say! Hell, if that bastard shit on a paper plate, she would swear that it was escargot on the Queen's own china." Big Stan let out a heavy sigh. "Do we have to go over all this again? Can't we just have a good time and leave it at that?"

Sandy didn't say anything, just sort of pouted in Stan's general direction.

Big Stan decoded the body language and swiftly tried to change the subject. "Why don't you have another drink. Make it a fancy one, you know, the kind with the little umbrellas and such. What's that you're drinking now?"

"A diet Coke."

"Nothing in it, just plain?"

"No, nothin' at all in it."

"No kidding?"

"Stan, I went to a meeting last night."

"A meeting? By yourself? What kind of meeting?"

"One of those AA meetings."

Big Stanley sat up straight and made the sign of the cross.

"I was thinkin' you might like to come and join me for the next one. You'd like it. A lot of your old drinkin' buddies are there. It was like the good-old-boy Forest Service retirement club."

"Sandy, you got to understand, I like drinking. It's how I socialize. Anyway, I'm not a drunk. I can slow down or even quit any time I want to." Stan swirled the brown liquid in his glass. "I just don't want to right now. If you've seen the light, that's fine with me. Just don't plan on taking me with you."

"This is just for me. I'm done drinkin'."

Big Stan sort of smirked. "We'll see how long you stay up on that wagon."

"What, are you sayin' I'm some kind of lush?"

"Of course not, of course not. It's just you're like me. You enjoy life and liquor, and it's not your nature to be an ascetic."

"Don't you say I don't believe in God.'

"No, no, an ascetic is someone who practices self-denial, someone who does without."

"Well, Mr. Smarty Pants, I know someone that I can do without, and that's you!" Sandy was using both hands, digging furiously through her purse.

Big Stanley sort of stiffened up, watching the tissues and crumpled-up

279

dollar bills fall on the table. "You're not carrying a gun in there, are you?"

"No, I got a hell of a headache, and I can't find my pills."

"Oh. I'm sorry I said that."

"You're just lucky I don't have a gun. I've had enough of this happy horse shit! I'm sick of your belly achin'. I'm so tired of hearing you say, 'I just need my own space,' and 'I'm not ready for marriage.' And I am so especially tired of those stupid skunks of yours. I wouldn't marry you if you were the last cowhand in the last corral in hell!"

"Please, people are starting to stare."

"Let em stare!"

"Now, calm down."

"I'm not calmin' down." She stood up and grabbed her purse like a weapon. "I don't ever want to see you outside of work, ever! You don't talk to me again until you deserve me." Sandy turned quickly and her wide hip caught the edge of table, spilling Stan's Irish malt down over his pants.

Sandy Spotts turned her too-tight skirt around right at the door and, with head held high, yelled at Big Stan - but also to everyone in the Plywood Palace - "I'm not one of your Russian whores!"

Big Stan cringed as the door slammed hard behind Sandy. He shook his head and said slowly,

"Somebody ought to name a drink after that woman."

46

"The mind has a thousand eyes
And the heart but one;
Yet the light of a whole life dies,
When love is done."

F. W Bourdillon

Alex's mood had mutated to a virus, seemingly infecting everyone he worked with. Others on the District began to have troubles with careless mistakes and embarrassing moments.

Buck was giving his annual horsemanship lesson to the new seasonal employees, going over basic horse use, safety, loading and unloading. At the end of the session, Alex anticipated that Buck would perform his horse trick, the old Hollywood cowboy stunt of running at the horse from the rear and vaulting into the saddle. Buck was pretty good at it. Alex had seen him perform it before, and the trick was a real crowd pleaser. Buck played the odds pretty well by using the shortest and gentlest horse in the string, an old white horse named Floatie, a short, fat, bombproof quarter horse that was usually reserved for packing dudes. One thing about Floatie: she didn't shy at anything, just pretty well stood still most of the time.

Today's performance hit a bit of a snag. Alex was watching as Buck doffed his black hat and turned toward Floatie in a track-star crouch, sizing up his short dash to the saddle. Buck scratched gravel with his boots and licked his lips. At some inner starting gun heard only to Buck, he leaped out of the starter's gate in a full sprint, everyone's eyes catching the sudden movement and involuntarily turning to watch. Just as Buck reached out his hands to time his leap, his spurs became entangled, grabbing him in a shoestring tackle that sent him into a spinning, headlong, full-speed crash right into Floatie's rear end. Buck crumpled up, knocked out of breath, right under Floatie's hindquarters. Floatie, being a good old girl, did not stomp Buck to pieces but rather just turned her head toward Buck with a look of surprise, wrinkled her horse lips, and

281

grinned, showing both uppers and lowers. Nobody watching dared to launch even the slightest giggle as Buck pulled himself to his feet, dusted himself off, and limped over to the tack shed.

Kloyd was also embroiled in inner turmoil. Bronda, his devoutly Mormon wife, had become even more religiously inclined when her brother Levi, became the new Bishop at the First LDS Ward of Goldburg. Now she was again trying to drag Kloyd to every Mormon function in town. It seemed that there was something good for Kloyd to go to every night of the week and, of course, all day on Sunday. The one night a week he had free for himself was Monday, and Monday family night at home was putting a real crimp on his outside activities. The biggest family drama centered on Kloyd's proudest possession, his newly acquired beard. Kloyd had never before encouraged facial hair until Alex prodded him into growing a winter beard. While Alex's beard remained at best a downy, beginner's beard, Kloyd's beard and mustache grew on a fertile face. Brown and thick, with straight smooth hairs, it was not the spiral, curly type of beard. This was the kind of beard that grows right up solid to the cheekbones and forms a tight oval about the mouth. It was the perfect beard, and Kloyd knew it. So when Levi had a revelation that the congregation should shave off all facial hair as an example of clean living, Kloyd balked. This latest revelation of Levi's seemed to stir up Kloyd's latent jack-Mormon tendencies. Kloyd constantly made excuses to work overtime, and escaping Bronda's and Levi's straight-laced Mormon admonitions became his primary short-term goal.

Big Stanley also was on a downward trend, with a bad case of tick fever. The story was all over the office. Alex heard the second-hand version, again from Kloyd. About three weeks ago, while riding Stain up in the Soldier Lakes country behind Seafoam, Big Stan had dug a tick out of his side, just above his belt. Stan didn't think much about it then, having had numerous tick bites every year; but he certainly thought about it as he sat in his rocking chair, wrapped in a blanket, staring at the bottle of codeine on the elk-antler coffee table and trying to gauge how long he would shiver before he took another swig.

Sandy Spotts was just plain tired. Alex could see it in her eyes. He wondered about it for a while and then figured she was tired from running the office by herself and worrying about the mail. Just last week she had intercepted another Russian-lady letter, but this letter was from Pocatello and was something completely different. It seemed that the Russian mail-order-bride people, in an interesting display of business prowess, had sold their mailing list to local Russian prostitutes. This particular mailing from someone named Tanya had no return address on the manila folder, only a short letter of introduction, an extremely revealing eight-by-ten-inch photograph that lustily displayed Tanya's personal attributes, and a copy of Tanya's travel schedule, motel by motel, as she traveled a long-distance love circuit through eastern and central Idaho. Sandy crumpled up the letter and photograph, stuffing it in her purse, the first conscious criminal act of her life. Torn between fear of the federal government and career-ending mail theft charges and the thought of Big Stanley surveying the market and trading up, Sandy had chosen the low road; and the constant vigilance was wearing her down.

This strange blue funk even drifted down to the seasonal employees on the District. Fast Eddie and Harmon had gotten into a ferocious argument about the previous presidential election and were no longer speaking to each other outside of work. Since neither of them had bothered to vote in the last election, Alex thought this unusual behavior even for Eddie and Harmon.

The oddest relationship casualty was the non-starter between Teffonie and Argo. Teffonie was definitely interested, but all Argo seemed to want to talk about was physics. The result was that Teffonie was frustrated and Argo was confused. Teffonie was sick to death of hearing about low entropy, that extra electron of every millionth or billionth or trillionth of matter versus anti-matter, and the continuing erosion of symmetry in the universe. Teffonie was bored to tears hearing about leptons, neutrinos, quarks, and quantum mechanics. She was especially weary of Argo's annoying habit of blurting out the obscure James Joyce quotation, "three quarks for muster Mark!" whenever he sensed it needed saying; she thinking, like it meant anything to anyone, anywhere. Teffonie wanted to play ball and play ball with Argo, but Argo didn't seem to know the rules of the game and couldn't figure out why Teffonie seemed so tense all the time.

In an unusual display of awareness, Howie confessed to Alex that he and Nedra were having problems. Not only having second thoughts about their yoga master; but they were involved in their first marital disagreement, and it was all centered on a new concept. Howie had independently developed the idea that he would like to take up bird hunting, a solid, gentlemen's pastime, as he cultivated an improved image of aging. The problem arose when Howie thought of including Lazlo, figuring that his golden retriever would make an excellent duck hunting companion and could join him in his hunting pursuits. Nedra was thoroughly and immediately aghast at this proposal. It was not so much the idea of Howie slaying innocent ducks and geese that bothered her but rather the

283

thought of Lazlo taking part in such a ruinous enterprise that made her break out in shingles.

It seemed that the only person on the District spared from this cycle of inner turmoil was Angelica Kowalski. She walked through the work day confident, satisfied, and with her head held high.

47

"Oh as I was young and easy in the mercy of his means,
Time held me green and dying
Though I sang in my chains like the sea."

Dylan Thomas

Alex recorded the best time of anyone on the District on the pack test. At least all that exercise was paying off on something, he thought. His time of just under thirty-eight minutes for the three miles put him more than a minute faster than even Fast Eddie. It was a pass/fail test; the only requirement to carry the forty-five pound pack over the three mile course in less than forty-five minutes. Other than bragging rights, it didn't really matter how much less than forty five minutes you made the trip. Alex did notice that Angie came in with the main group at a little over forty-three minutes.

As June passed on and faded, the weather became hotter and drier and each day the relative humidity sank lower and lower. Goldburg recorded almost no precipitation that June, only one brief shower that barely settled the dust. The long-term fire-weather forecast predicted July and August to be significantly below normal precipitation in the entire region. The winter snow pack was almost gone, even the high snow. The alpine lakes had melted out almost a month early and the river and stream levels were dropping quickly.

As the grass browned and dried, people began to speak of drought, the great fear of the west. The ranchers holding court at the Y café were the first to talk of the cutoff of high-water rights by the first of June and the concerns that the 1876 water rights would be next. The western irrigation doctrine of "first in time, first in line" was dogma and not subject to interpretation. Any reductions in water resulted in reductions of hay. If water was cut in early July, many ranchers would only get one cutting of alfalfa, the hay that was their winter lifeblood .

The Sleeping Deer Ranger District also had drought worries, and they all revolved around wildfire. The drought indexes were already high for so early in the summer. Heavy fuels, the down and dead trees, the fuel that really feeds an intense fire, were drying out rapidly. The top three or four inches of organic duff under the pine and Doug fir were bone dry, and it wasn't yet July.

Alex knew that Big Stanley had seen his share of wildfire in his time with the Forest Service, and Big Stan was worried. It was a similar story for Buck. Alex saw the hefty responsibility Buck took on as Fire Management Officer for the District. It was Buck's job to have the unit ready for fire suppression, and it was a big job; getting the employees trained and outfitted, contracts in place for the helicopter, agreements for mutual aid from other agencies and the state of Idaho, having the fire cache stocked and equipped - all this and a hundred more little things to do, watch, manage and worry about.

Alex had initiated and maintained a cease fire with his emotions for almost a week now. He still followed his exercise regimen, but not with the frenetic intensity of a few weeks before. It both thrilled and bothered him greatly to see Angie waltzing around the compound on a daily basis. For some reason he could not define rationally, Alex still entertained dreams of getting back together with her. When they did chance to meet on Alex's frequent wanderings in the work center, it was a polite, plaintive hello or a friendly wave, and Angie responded the same. It was a stasis condition, with no end in sight. Angie still drove her dad's truck back to the ranch right after work, and Alex did not see her on the street or in the Wise Buy or post office. He thought if she was trying to avoid him, she was doing an excellent job of it.

A ribbon of darkness seemed to follow Alex like a cloud.

Walking back to his truck after work, his head held down and full of thoughts of geography, Alex walked right up to and bumped into Angelica Kowalski. They knocked shoulders firmly, and Angie dropped her handful of papers.

"I'm, I'm sorry," Alex said as he helped Angie pick up her papers. "I didn't see you."

"I didn't see you either. No need to apologize."

Alex noted both the time and the fact that they seemed to be alone in the parking lot. In a fit of inspiration he said, "Angie, I've been thinking about it, thinking about it a lot. How about we give ourselves another chance? What do you say?" The words had come out without prior thought or preparation, like his innermost thoughts had formed and blurted out at the same instant without his conscious mind's consent. He lowered his eyes and scuffed his shoes in the gravel.

Angie looked surprised, but managed to keep her thoughts corralled safely inside. "I don't know if that would be a good idea."

"But, it all ended so badly."

"A lot of things end badly."

"But don't you see? They don't always have to. We could change that if we wanted."

"I don't think I want to try. You know, you made me feel like nothing. Like nothing at all. Like I wasn't even there."

"I didn't mean to, really I didn't."

"But you did. You did. You ran around on me with that slut from Sun Valley, and then you lied!"

"But . . ."

"But you gave me your promise."

Alex took in a deep breath but couldn't put his thoughts into any logical order. He just stood there.

Angie's eyes seemed fixed on his face, as if she were waiting for him to say something. She collected her anger from where it had fallen to the ground. "I don't think it's worth the effort. You can't change some things, especially the past."

Her words stung Alex deeply, effectively silencing his inner voice. Angry now, he said, "Fine, if that's the way you want it," and turned and crunched across the gravel.

Perhaps if the relative humidity had been lower, or perhaps if even the papers and garbage at the Goldburg landfill had been covered and backfilled as was required by state health department regulations, Alex might have seen Angie at the Mackay Rodeo, sitting there with a tall young fellow in cowboy hat and jeans. He might have noticed that this cowboy was a bit too drunk and a bit too loud. Alex definitely wouldn't have missed the heated exchange between Angie and her cowboy friend near the beer tent, because apparently no one missed seeing Angie use both hands to push the handsome young stranger into and over the rope fence next to the grandstand. If Alex had been at the Mackay Rodeo, he most certainly would have been watching Angie afterwards, sitting high in the grandstand next to Teffonie, watching the wind push her hair, watching Angie as she continually scanned the crowd. Perhaps he may have even done more than watch. But this scenario never materialized and remained just another potential reality that never happened, all because of a bottle rocket set off at the landfill by some high school kids that caught the dump on fire.

287

The Goldburg landfill was a hideous place, a dry gully in the sagebrush east of town, developed without site design or forethought. Some minimal earthwork had created a flat spot where you backed up your pickup to the edge and threw your unsorted, un-recycled garbage over the bank. On windy days the sky over the landfill was full of papers that floated across the landscape like strange white birds. Regulations required that all garbage be covered by a layer of soil at a minimum of once a week. The locals treated this regulation as more of a guideline or even just a suggestion. The community bulldozer had been broken down so long that small birds were nesting in it. About the only redeeming aspect of the dump that Alex could come up with was that it was home to a population of seagulls that floated on the wind and forlornly called out in almost musical notes, having traded their life at the sea and a sandy beach for three squares at the local landfill.

Alex got the fire call just as he was prepared to step out the door on his way to the Mackay rodeo. They needed another body on the engine, and Alex was quick to change into his fire clothes.

As wildfires go, the Blue Mountain, or Dump fire, wasn't much. By the early afternoon of July Fourth, the fire had run from the landfill, across the sagebrush and into the timber, torching trees on Blue Mountain. Everyone in town had an excellent view of the air tankers from Boise dropping retardant, six loads in all. The big bombers came low across Round Valley. As if in slow motion, their bellies opened up in an orange burst of retardant. The smoke billowed black each time a tree burned. What wind there was blew away from town, so no one had to eat any smoke. The Blue Mountain blaze was an exceptionally well-behaved fire, perfectly suited for a Fourth of July celebration. It was considered by most to be the best fireworks in Goldburg history. By that evening, the fire was contained on its eastern flank with a good hand line that extended from a dozer line across the sagebrush flat and foothills all the way to a solid rock outcrop. By nightfall, Alex had led a squad up the east ridge of Blue Mountain and tied off the fire line at a rocky prominence near the top. The wind was light and so was the fuel component. Alex anticipated that this particular fire was not going anywhere soon, and with a couple of days of mop up, this case would be closed. He came off the mountain just after midnight, unaware of the sad, disappointed eyes of a certain tall red-haired girl just back from the Mackay rodeo.

48

With a full moon so bright you could have read a book, unusual happenings were taking place in Goldburg.

Just before it got dark, Big Stanley went out in his yard and started laying a trail of popcorn, Cheese Puffs, and Cheetos all the way from his cellar entrance to where he had carefully placed a long plank across Garden Creek. From there, the tasty treats ran through almost two hundred yards of big sage to where he had previously placed a large metal box trap. He heaped the remainder of the popcorn and cheese puffs inside the trap, remembering to tie a long length of rope to the trap before he uncoiled it. Big Stan had the box trap rigged so he could open it safely from a distance. He admired his handiwork for a moment before he walked back to the house, singing softly under his breath a few verses of "Pretty Pamela Brown."

Other strange happenings were underway in Goldburg that evening. Buck drove his pickup around and past the post office parking lot three times before he was satisfied no one was in the lobby. He crept up to the mail drop, carefully looking both ways before he pulled a long white envelope from his jacket. Buck checked the address once more, debating whether he needed another half ounce stamp just to be sure. He set the envelope down on the table next to the mail slot and carefully lined up one more stamp exactly in line with the two Elvis Presley's already in place. Buck held the envelope up one more time, looking at the woman's name and checking the neatness of his lettering. Hoping, and almost saying a little prayer, Buck dropped the San-Diego-bound letter into the outgoing mail.

While Buck was trying to sleep, rolling first one way and then the other, his brain fixated on a San-Diego-bound letter, strange events continued to transpire out in the almost dark. You would have seen, if you had been there,

289

Big Stanley riding Stain through the moonlight, a long rope tied to the saddle horn, towing a metal box on a little sled at least sixty feet behind him. If you had been there, you would have smelled it, too. For Big Stan was embarked on the first of three trips that night, transplanting skunks from his house to a small meadow about two miles up on Keystone Mountain.

49

"Now a promise made is a debt unpaid, and the trail has its own stern code.
In the days to come, though my lips were dumb, in my heart how I cursed that
load.
In the long, long night, by the lone firelight, while the huskies, round in a ring,
Howled out their woes to the homeless snows, oh God, how I loathed the thing."

Robert Service

Two days later at the office, as Alex was watching Floatie out in the corral swatting flies with her long tail, Big Stanley lumbered into Alex's small office and sat down heavily.

"Alex, I need a favor."

"Sure, whatever you need."

"Well, you best think about this one, it's a big favor."

Alex nodded and didn't say anything.

"The Forest Supervisor, Riddles, wants to go on a raft trip. Normally, when Chester visits the District, I'd be the one to squire him around. But this damn tick fever just keeps hanging on, and I just don't think I'm up to runnin' the boat."

This was a big admission, as Alex well knew. Few in the Forest Service, especially Big Stanley, would readily admit to physical weakness. The desire to "suck it up" and keep going was somehow universal throughout the service. Nobody, absolutely nobody, wanted to be considered a "candy ass".

Big Stan looked forlornly out at his horse trailer, empty and still sitting on the jack. "Just last night it came on again. It comes and goes. I was sitting in that rockin' chair, gritting my teeth and staring at that bottle of codeine, just sweating and shivering and rocking, trying not to have to take it. Finally I gave in and took a swig, washed it down with some Jack Daniels and went to bed."

"You want me to take Riddles down the river?"

"If you can do it, I would sure appreciate it. He only has time for a short trip, two days, one night camping. We were planning on starting at the Flying B and just push the last thirty-five miles out to Cache Bar in two days."

"Sure, I can do that."

"Are you feeling confident on the lower river?"

"Well, pretty well, that is, I think so."

"This low water can be tough at Redside and Weber."

"How about Rubber Rapids?"

"No problem, it just turns to nothing at low water. Anyway, you'll have Eddie and Harmon with you, and they can worry about the river. Your main task is to shepherd Mr. Chester M. Riddles carefully around, keep him happy but don't encourage him. If he starts getting nosey, just watch yourself. You know what I mean?"

"Like if he starts to ask too many questions?"

"Yeah, sort of. I like to be careful with the Forest Supervisor. There's an old ranger saying that goes, you had a good year if you only saw the Forest Supervisor twice, and he only saw you once."

"I won't let out any state secrets."

"There you go. Anyway, just take it slow and easy, because Riddles is sort of a different breed of cat and we don't want to upset him."

"Like what kind of different?"

"Let's just say that sometimes Riddles can be a little hasty, and we don't want to encourage that."

The upcoming Chester M. Riddles float trip galvanized Alex into action, giving him a short-term mission of importance. He checked and rechecked all the logistics, planned and re-planned the schedule, then held meetings with Fast Eddie and Harmon trying to anticipate any possible contingencies, determined to make this a blemish-free trip. Other than Alex, everyone else quickly became tired of hearing about Chester M. Riddles and his Middle Fork float trip.

"Christ," Fast Eddie said. "It's only an overnight float trip. He flies into the B, we pick him up and take him down the river. How much simpler could it be? I think you're beating this thing to death, if you ask me."

"I just want to make sure we avoid any mistakes with this one," Alex said. "How about we go over the schedule one more time?"

Fast Eddie and Harmon both rolled their eyes and sighed.

Old Rolly and his Cessna 206 took Alex into the Flying B a day early, just to get everything set up in time. Alex was so enamored with his planning that he forgot to worry about Rolly having that long overdue heart attack and the plane spiraling down to his doom.

Fast Eddie and Harmon had dead-headed the boats down from Indian Creek all in one long forty-mile day, and they were already there waiting for Alex at the Flying B.

Fast Eddie told Alex, "Man, the upper river is really low. I've never seen it this low this early. Tappen Falls was a bear, and I was glad we were real light and just cruised the rafts down here without skimming too many rocks."

"What do you think of the rapids down river?"

"Oh, I think we've got it made. I guess we'll have to watch out for Redside, 'cause it can be tricky at low water. But other than that, should be a piece of cake."

"Now, I've heard that piece of cake story before."

"No, no, really. I don't anticipate any problems. By the time Mr. Chester M. Riddles gets to the take out, he will be suitably impressed. I guarantee it."

Alex scratched his chin, still wary of Fast Eddie's guarantees. "Well, let's hope so."

"Alex, you worry too much. That's your problem, you know?"

Maybe he wasn't worrying about it, but he most certainly was concerned. That night after the rafts were packed and repacked, Alex bought Fast Eddie and Harmon some beers. With cans of Budweiser, they lay on the lounges on the irrigated lawn at the Flying B under the Black Locust trees. Alex was still planning. He was trying to slow down his mind as he watched the shadow line of the sunset creep up the basalt cliff across the river.

"It don't seem to be coolin' off," Harmon said. "Goin' to be a hot one tomorrow."

Alex nodded. "Good day to be on the river. Just be glad you're not on the trail crew buckin' out logs with a crosscut."

"I don't even want to think about using one of those misery whips again. Why on earth won't they let us use chain saws in the wilderness anyhow?"

"You know how it is, the camel's nose under the tent and all. If they let us use chainsaws, they'd have to let the outfitters use chainsaws. Next thing you know, we'd be authorizing private helicopter use."

"But they let us use helicopters for fire all the time."

"But that's different. We can easily pass the red-faced test on fire, if we ever need to."

"But it would be so much cheaper to use chainsaws."

Fast Eddie smirked. "You idiot, the government's not in the business to

293

save money, the government's in the ideology business. What are you, simple or something?"

"Hey, it was only an opinion," Harmon said. "Don't get bent out of shape about it."

Fast Eddie seemed to turn serious when he said, "You got to watch what you say, especially about saving money and stuff like that. The next thing you know, you'll be under investigation or something."

Now Alex interrupted. "Hey, do me a favor, will you? Don't go pursuing this line of thought with Riddles? I'd like to keep my job awhile longer."

Eddie said, "You got it, boss. When Chester M. Riddles gets here, we'll be nothing but business."

"I can only hope."

The next morning Alex awoke relaxed and ready. As he scanned the sky for Old Rolly and his Cessna 206, Alex felt surrounded by physics. It was a relativity kind of morning, the way the sun dapples moved across the water in waves, the light refracting in crystal forms. In a quick daydream of parallel universes, Alex imagined himself in one where he hadn't fucked up and was still with Angie. It was a harmless, Star Trek kind of a daydream, with just enough cosmology in it to be interesting; but it didn't last too long, as Alex heard Rolly's plane coming over the ridge.

"There he is," Harmon pointed. "Coming in over Aparejo Point."

Alex jumped off the lawn chair as if he were headed to battle stations.

Making a slow circle around the Flying B, Old Rolly dropped the 206 down smoothly on the dirt airstrip and taxied up to the lodge.

"That's Riddles, huh?" Harmon asked, nodding toward the small man getting out of the plane. "I've never seen him."

"Well, then, you are in for a treat," Fast Eddie said. "That is himself, Chester M. Riddles."

If there was ever a man comfortable with his role as a minor but powerful public bureaucrat, it was Chester M. Riddles. From his small round glasses to his bristly shock of snow-white hair, Riddles was every inch the bureaucrat. A natural born critic, Riddles found fault with everything and everyone, and he let you know it in a caustic, demeaning manner.

"Kynwulf, I noticed your uniform, your badge, it's crooked," were the first words out of his mouth.

"Oh, sorry, Sir."

"And don't call me 'Sir'."

"Sorry, uhm, Chester."

Alex carried Riddles' water bag down the beach where the boats were waiting, careful to walk three steps behind the diminutive man.

The rafts and the crew looked neat and sharp that morning, and Chester M. Riddles nodded appreciatively at how quickly they got underway. Alex ran the sweeps with Riddles on board and kept Fast Eddie and Harmon at a distance in the Avon trailing behind.

As the Flying B drifted back in the distance, Riddles unpacked his pipe, the one with the elephant head and ivory tusks on it, and carefully tamped some Bugler tobacco down into the bowl as he began to hum. Alex couldn't quite make out the tune, but thought it might be "Maxwell's Silver Hammer." Alex was well prepped for any questions, but Riddles seemed content to just float and watch the scenery. He didn't seem to have much of an agenda just yet.

Riddles hardly said a word until they stopped for lunch at Rattlesnake Cave. There was a thin smile on Chester's lips when he recounted, "I was down here several years ago and we found a big rattler, true to its namesake, right here in the cave."

Alex nodded, said, "What did you do?"

"Oh, I killed it," Chester said nonchalantly, and went back to humming, this time something military in nature, possibly a Sousa march.

Alex winced when Fast Eddie started to recount a Middle Fork adventure, but Riddles just seemed to ignore him. It was like Eddie wasn't even there. Riddles just kept puffing on his pipe and humming.

The afternoon slid by like the river, smoothly and quickly. An occasional grunt from Riddles was about the extent of the conversation. In the mid-afternoon heat, Chester packed up his pipe and took a nap, leaning against the pile of water bags on the deck of the sweep boat.

This was not what Alex had been expecting. His limited experience with Riddles and Big Stanley's careful preparation had led Alex to expect a Jeopardy-like repartee of quick questions and answers; but so far, Chester didn't appear to be interested in river management in the least.

The boating group stopped at Veil Falls in mid-afternoon, getting out of the rafts and climbing the narrow goat track up into the granite amphitheater behind the falls. The grotto had a wondrous form, curved rock polished by eons of water falling over the one-hundred-foot lip of the falls. The water, backlit by sunshine, fell in silver beads that drilled and splashed in the small pool of bare

295

rock and sand, beating a staccato rhythm as it moved around the cave with the shifting breeze.

Once again Riddles didn't say a word, just kept puffing on his pipe and humming.

Alex couldn't stand the suspense any longer and finally said, "Beautiful the way the falls have created this grotto, don't you think?"

Riddles took the pipe from his mouth, his eyes scanning the expanse of Veil Cave as if noticing it for the first time, and said, "Yes indeed."

Alex looked out from the bedrock-enclosed space, looking down four hundred vertical feet at the green water of the Middle Fork flowing over car-sized boulders, so clear you could see the bottom like it was glass. He thought that Veil Falls deserved more than a "yes indeed," but smartly kept his mouth shut.

Later that afternoon they stopped the boats at Waterfall Creek, tying up right under the trail bridge. The water rolled down in crystalline spray. They climbed up the bank and stood on the trail bridge, letting the spray from the falls cool them down with a fine mist of negative ions that sparkled in the sun. On the rock face above the first falls, monkey flowers were still in bloom, bright yellow against a deep green bed of fern. Above the bridge the creek stepped down the mountainside in a series of silver ribbon cascades, one after another, as far as Alex could see.

This time Alex repressed his opinions and didn't say anything to Riddles, and neither did Harmon or Eddie. They all stood there like a group of monks under a vow of silence, just staring at the waterfall, waiting for Riddles. Chester, finally realizing his position as perfunctory VIP on this trip, took the pipe from his mouth and said, "Very nice," and with that utterance, turned and headed back to the raft.

Fast Eddie and Harmon exchanged glances, and Alex just shrugged his shoulders and said, "Well, then, let's head on down to camp."

Near the mouth of Big Creek, they hit a stiff up-canyon wind that caught the sweep boat like a sail. Alex couldn't hold the big boat in the current, and the wind pushed them over to the shore right next to where Big Creek dumps into the Middle Fork.

Alex explained, "The wind's got us pinned in this big eddy. We might have to wait for it to let up some before we can get out."

This simple statement seemed to energize Chester M. Riddles. "Do you mean we're stuck here and can't get to camp?"

296

"No, no, we'll get to camp all right," Alex explained. "We just might be a little late is all. These winds in the lower canyon usually peak about this time of day. In an hour or two, I'm sure they'll let up and we can float down to Elk Bar without any problems."

But Chester M. Riddles wasn't buying any explanations. "I had planned to be in camp by seventeen hundred hours, and I would like to stick to the schedule."

"Don't know if we can do it, Chester."

Riddles looked Alex in the face and said, "But you can try, can't you?"

Alex blushed red in the face, biting his lower lip. Not saying a word, he began to work the oars for all he was worth.

It was blowing a gale, and it took Alex three attempts to break free of the eddy and get into the current again. He had to fight the wind all the way to Elk Bar, three solid miles, and it took almost two hours to do it. Luckily, there were no rock gardens and not much maneuvering, or they never would have made it in one piece. All the while that Alex struggled on the oars, Riddles just sat there puffing his pipe.

It was well after five o'clock when an exhausted Alex pulled the raft up to the beach at Elk Bar, just as the wind was dying off to a breeze. Alex straightened up, took a welcome breath, and said, "Welcome to the presidential camp. Jimmie Carter stayed here in the 70s."

Riddles puffed up and said, "All we needed was some strong management direction and we're here in camp at a reasonable time, not quite six o'clock. I make it a rule to always be in camp by five, and it distresses me greatly to bend my personal rules."

This was by far the longest speech that Riddles had made the entire day.

"Remember that, Kynwulf, strong management direction."

Alex nodded his head. Riddles purposefully walked over and sat down precisely in the center of the shadow cast by a tall ponderosa pine, leaving Alex and the crew to unload the rafts and set up camp.

"I'd like to give him some strong management direction," whispered Fast Eddie.

"Just cool it," Alex said. "It's only for one more day."

Harmon worked up a culinary masterpiece of Dutch oven cooking, with fresh biscuits, baked potatoes, and a steak on the grill. The meal was eaten mostly in silence, but the copious amount of dinner seemed to take the remaining edge off the day for Alex.

Riddles sat by himself around the small fire in the fire pan, sipping something from a private flask, not even thinking about offering any to the underlings. No liquor was permitted on administrative trips like this one, but Alex was not about to mention it. After repeated hits from the flask, Riddles turned in early, weaving his way to the tent that Harmon had pitched at the far edge of the beach.

Fast Eddie spoke first. "Man, this guy creeps me out. I'll be glad to get rid of him at Cache Bar. It's an early pick up, right?"

Alex responded, "Yeah, Riddles wanted to be back early, so the shuttle is set for noon."

"That's seventeen river miles. We'll have to be on the river by seven or so," Harmon said.

"No problem," Alex said. "Tomorrow is just eat up and go."

But a problem did develop. For some reason Alex overslept and so did Harmon and Eddie. Alex never overslept. He was always the early one. He checked his alarm, certain he had turned it on, and the clock read six-thirty.

The crew scurried about, with Alex cooking a quick breakfast and Fast Eddie and Harmon taking down the camp and packing the boats.

Chester M. Riddles was more talkative today. "I see it is nearing eight o'clock and we're not yet on the river. By my estimate, we're almost an hour late."

"Sorry," Alex said.

"Sorry doesn't cut it. I need to be at that boat ramp by noon, so you might want to think about bustin' some ass to make it happen."

Alex felt his innate distrust and fear of authority begin to surface, but he beat it back within himself and only said, "We'll try our best to get you there on time."

"Just remember, Kynwulf, strong management direction, or you'll never get anywhere in this outfit." And with that said, Chester M. Riddles turned on his heel and stalked over to the sweep boat.

Alex needed some vigorous outlet for his pent-up anger and jumped at the oars before Fast Eddie had a chance.

"You sure you want to run the sweeps?" Eddie asked. "We've got Redside coming up this morning."

"You bet."

Strange events continued to transpire. There was an up-canyon wind that morning, an odd occurrence so early in the day. Usually you could bank on calm

298

air in the morning in the lower canyon, but that day it was gusty and blowing sand on the beach before they even got underway.

Chester M. Riddles took his place on the front of the raft, put his face into the wind and sneered.

Alex worked hard on the sweeps against the wind, watching the sun climb down the knife-cut walls of the lower canyon. The castellated ridge line was set in flying buttresses of stone. He pushed the sweep boat almost by will through the big pool above Redside Rapids.

"You sure you want to take it through Redside?" Eddie asked.

"Yeah, I'm good."

"Just remember to pull hard off the wrap rock below the drop."

"Don't worry, I've got it measured. I take the drop and pull hard right."

Redside Rapids took a long while to develop. The pool leading to the rapids extended a good piece above the drop. Alex was ferrying the boat toward the two smooth boulders that guard the big drop just beyond, still fighting the wind for position. Normally, Alex and Eddie would have scouted Redside to check what the water level had done, but today Alex felt he didn't have the time to stop.

He could hear the rumble of Redside above the keening of the wind, but couldn't see it yet. There was just a horizontal line between the two boulders as he fought the wind to take the sweep boat up to the lip. Alex handled the sweeps well, turning the boat into the wind and lining up on the river right side of the near boulder.

Just before the sweep boat entered the V-slick of fast water above the main drop, a strong gust of wind caught the boat and turned it slightly out of position. It was only a little out of position, and Alex leaned on the sweeps to correct it; but he immediately knew it wouldn't be enough as they lurched into Redside with the sweep boat about ten degrees from where it needed to be. The boat took the drop clean and was rolling through the wave train directly toward the wrap rock as Alex fought to turn it away. He missed by a thin, thin margin, striking the rock at an acute angle but striking it hard. Alex had just a moment to brace for the hit, which was enough. He stayed on his feet on the boat as it lurched partway on its side. Fast Eddie saw what was about to happen and anticipated the collision. Chester M. Riddles, unaware of what was transpiring, did not follow the age-old advice of one hand for yourself and one for the boat. He sailed over the side of the sweep boat in a near semicircle, so quickly and so easily that neither Fast Eddie nor Alex saw him go overboard. Alex was busy muscling the sweep boat back into position in the fast water and Eddy was trying to help.

Alex was the first to notice. "Where the hell is Riddles?"

Fast Eddie jumped up and peered downstream. "There he is! Hell, he's halfway to Weber."

"Jumpin' Jesus Christ!" Alex panted fiercely and flailed away at the sweeps. "He'll never get out of the river before Weber."

There was less than two hundred yards of fast water between the run out of Redside Rapid and the beginning of Weber, another big class four, this one with huge waves and hydraulics. Alex and Eddie on the sweep boat and Harmon in the oar boat raced after Chester M. Riddles.

"He's in it now," said Fast Eddie. "Let's hope he keeps his mouth closed this time."

Alex didn't appreciate the black humor, but saw that Riddles was riding through the big standing waves of Weber like a cork. He figured that Riddles would probably be all right if he just didn't panic. Alex now had the sweep boat full in Weber Rapids and was fighting to retain his position on the left side of the river, where he hoped to catch up to Chester M. Riddles.

One hundred yards ahead, Weber Rapids tossed out Riddles like he was a bad taste in the mouth.

By the time Alex maneuvered the sweep boat alongside, Riddles had eddied out of the main current. He was lagging, but he was alive and apparently unhurt.

Alex reached down and grabbed Riddles's life jacket and easily hauled the small man on board the raft.

Chester M. Riddles lay on the deck of the sweep boat, panting for air, reaching to his mouth for his long-gone elephant-head pipe. His eyes were glazed with terror. He caught his breath long enough to murmur, "Kynwulf, that was fucking bad management."

50

"I am of that temper that if I were underwater
I would scarcely kick to come to the top."
John Keats

Alex limped back from the Chester M. Riddles raft trip with a sore neck and a severely wounded psyche. He figured he was finished as a Forest Service employee. In three months, when his probationary period was over, Alex anticipated that he would be let go and never made permanent. He was already dreading the trip back home to Pennsylvania, hearing his dad tell him that he told him so; almost felt the hot sun on his back as he shoveled asphalt behind the paving machine. Alex had the blues three times over: career–love–life, a three-time loser.

Big Stanley tried to assure Alex that there would be no repercussions from Riddles' swim through Weber Rapids. After Chester had calmed down, Big Stanley had talked with him and carefully explained what had happened. Assuring him that all safety procedures had been followed, he had painted a picture of a narrow escape and a daring rescue for Riddles to think over. Big Stan told Alex that Chester M. Riddles, as was his nature, was still angry, but no longer solely angry at Alex. It was more of a universal anger now, directed at everyone who worked for him.

Alex was moping around the office, sighing deeply, rolling his neck from side to side, trying to shake the kink out. Buck was getting annoyed with his behavior and more or less told Alex so.

"Big fuckin' deal, so you dumped the big boss in the river. Who the fuck cares anyhow?" This was Buck's attempt at empathy. "The bastard deserved to get tossed in the drink. Maybe we should give you a medal for it and you'll stop draggin' around here like you was gutshot."

Alex tried to make an excuse. "It's not that, it's my neck." He rubbed it some more for emphasis. "I can't straighten it out."

"Why in the hell don't you go take your neck to the chiropractor and get the damn thing fixed?"

"I didn't even know we had a chiropractor in town."

"Yeah, and he's pretty good. Onslow is his name. He fixed me up when I was stove up after that fuckin' Appaloosa horse of Kloyd's rolled over on me."

"When was that?"

"A year or two ago, just before you got here."

"How come I've never heard of him?"

"They call him 'The Hippie.' Not been here much longer than you."

"Oh yeah, I have heard that name in town."

"Anyway, he keeps a pretty low profile. Spends most of his time in Sun Valley I hear. You know, birds of a feather an' all."

Alex thought for a moment and said, "I'll check him out."

Alex wasn't the only one moping around the office. The empty feeling seemed to be spreading. Sandy Spotts hadn't spoken to Big Stanley for over a week, not since Tanya, the Russian hooker from Pocatello, had stopped by the office for a get-acquainted visit. Big Stan wasn't doing so well in the personal department either, avoiding Sandy as best he could in the small office. Even Buck was more irritable than usual, which Alex found hard to imagine, but it seemed to be true enough. Sandy had told Alex that Buck was "pining for his long-lost San Diego girlfriend."

Alex had the feeling that he made everything around him turn to dog shit.

As Alex rubbed his neck, he thought about the chiropractor some more. Alex had only been to a back-cracker once before, but he remembered it sort of gave him a nice mellow feeling of wellbeing for a while after he'd been worked over. Maybe it could work for this, he thought.

"Hey, Sandy, where is this Onslow guy at? I don't see him anywhere in the phone book." Whenever he had questions about Goldburg, Alex always asked Sandy first, for she knew all the dirt on everybody in town.

"Onslow? He's a different sort of character." Sandy walked over to lean suggestively on Alex's doorframe. "He's one of those new-age types, got crystals and pyramids and such. He probably don't have a phone. He used to be in the Clinic, but for some reason he had to move. Anyways, he's got a little office of sorts right behind the Western Auto store."

"Funny, I don't remember seeing it."

"Well, it's easy to overlook. It's actually right in the Western Auto building, and there's a little door in the back alley. If you look, you can't miss it. This door is a shiny-bright green."

After work Alex walked up to the post office, picked up his mail, and then went looking for the green door. Walking around Western Auto, he found it right in the alley where Sandy said it would be, a bright green door. It looked to be painted barn wood. Above the door was the astrological zodiac emblazoned in candy apple red. On the side was a small hand lettered sign that read, "You are home now, time to slow down." When Alex walked up to the door, he saw a seagull foot hanging on a string that went right through a hole in the wooden door. Hesitating for only a moment or two, Alex grasped the seagull foot, pulled the string, and heard a melodious bell toll. He liked the sound so well that he pulled the string again.

Alex heard footsteps coming his way and presently a short fellow in purple bike shorts, yellow high-top sneakers, and a blue tie-dyed T-shirt opened the door. He had a graying beard, a pony tail, and a friendly, Jesus-looking type of face.

"You must be Onslow," Alex said.

"Yes, yes, come in, come in. I've got the teakettle on."

Inside, it looked more like a head shop than a chiropractor's office, Alex thought. Everywhere he looked, there seemed to be a Buddha staring back. Some tarot cards were on the floor and there were books, lots of books, books everywhere. On the walls, it was an eclectic delight: an original poster of the Grateful Dead at the Fillmore; a buffalo head, a big one; a large piece of whale baleen; photographs of killer whales and puffins; a framed picture of the Dalai Lama; and a wonderful R. Crumb poster showing the history of America in nine panels.

"Would you like some green tea?" Onslow asked.

Alex accepted the offer, feeling all the while like he was walking in the house of Tom Bombadil, right out of the Hobbit. Alex was trying to remember the rhyme of description for Tom Bombadil and remembered it when he looked toward Onslow again. "Bright blue his jacket is, and his boots are yellow."

Tea was served in a white pot with wings, black-tipped like a snow goose.

"So what seems to be your problem?"

Alex thought to himself, which problem? Finally he answered. "It's my neck. I think I jammed it last week when we had a bit of a raft wreck on the river."

"You work for the Forest Service, then?"

"Yeah, I do."

303

"Then you must know Argo, a friend of mine."

Alex thought that he should have expected that one. "Sure, he works for me."

Onslow seemed suddenly satisfied. "Oh, I have heard all about you. Welcome again."

Alex felt strangely at ease here in the little room behind the Western Auto store, in the house of Tom Bombadil, behind the green door. It felt like really returning home after being on a long trip, and Alex was now in no hurry to leave.

After tea and some English butter cookies, Alex was led off to an even smaller side room where he was directed to take off his shirt and lie on an examination table. Quiet music was playing, some Celtic kind of thing, and Onslow spread warm oil on Alex's back and began to massage. The smell of burning incense filled the air with the scent of rose petals. Alex noticed the Chinese writing on the wall about the same time he saw Onslow tapping on a small wooden box and extracting a long needle.

Realization came with the sight of the box of needles. "You're not the chiropractor?"

"Oh, my goodness, no, that's my brother, Fletcher. He's moved his practice to Sun Valley."

"So what are the needles for?"

"I practice acupuncture."

"Acupuncture?"

"Yes, I studied in China for two years." As if sensing Alex's anxiety, Onslow asked, "Do you wish to continue?"

Alex looked at the diplomas on the wall and noticed the English word, "acupuncture" several times among the Chinese characters. He already felt stupid enough for one day, and since he'd already had the massage, he figured he had to go through with this.

"No, I mean yes, I want to continue, I guess."

Onslow walked back behind him, still holding the needle. "I think I can help your situation. The neck should be relatively straightforward. Are you sure that there isn't something else that is bothering you?"

Alex felt a sudden strong urge to tell him all about Angelica Kowalski, what had happened and why, every last bit of it; and he almost did, only fighting back the impulse with a struggle. "No, just the neck please."

"I do sense some significant negative energy at your source."

304

Alex was a bit embarrassed now. "Don't worry about the negative energy, just work on the neck, please."

"This won't hurt," and Onslow placed the first needle with a solid "whack" of his hand.

And it didn't hurt. All Alex felt was a slight pricking and a warming sensation as Onslow expertly placed the needle into the center of his back.

Onslow continued with six more needles, all in the back, roughly describing an arc across the shoulder blades. "Are you sure that nothing else is bothering you?"

This time Alex let part of the truth slip out. "Well, I've been feeling a bit down lately."

"A woman?"

Alex dreamily answered, "Yes."

"It shows somewhat. Let me try a few more." Onslow set three needles, this time in a row, high on the left side of Alex's spine. "Now, try to relax. Listen to the music, and I will return in a short while."

Alex did more than relax, he almost fell asleep. He felt very calm and dreamy; not drugged, but with a hard-to-explain feeling of waking from a pleasant dream but not remembering much of it, just bits and pieces; but all the bits and pieces seemed to fit together into something pleasant and peaceful. Alex wanted to stay and sleep on this table all evening, but Onslow returned all too soon to pull out the ten needles.

Sitting up on the side of the table, his feet dangling, Alex felt different. His neck was still sore, but with a different kind of soreness. "I don't get it," he said. "I feel sort of better, but it doesn't make any sense at all to me why I should."

"That's your bodily energy moving more efficiently. Your neck should be fine in a day or two."

"So, while I was lying here, I was looking at your chart showing all the needle locations. I was wondering, why not just fill me up with needles like a pincushion and cure me of everything at once?"

Onslow laughed this time, the same way one might laugh at the utterances of a child. "Oh, no, it doesn't work that way. Your energy would be confused and much too diluted. It has to focus to heal."

Alex followed Onslow back to a desk covered in papers. He paid his bill and negotiated his way around the Buddha and piles of books back to the green door.

Onslow followed him out. "And as far as the other problem, I hope that works out also. I have a feeling that perhaps it will."

"Well, I'd like to share your optimism, but this is one problem that won't have a happy ending."

"If not happy, then hope for reason."

Alex shrugged, and the pleasant feeling along his spine continued to spread across his back as he walked toward his truck parked on Main Street. As he stepped off the curb, he caught a flash of red hair in a pickup truck parked across the street. It was Angie. She was sitting next to the passenger-side window of a new Ford, across from some guy Alex had never seen before. She certainly looked good. Alex watched her through the window as she talked and laughed that happy smile where all her teeth showed. Alex's eyes cast down to the license plate, saw the 8B prefix for Pocatello and wondered who the guy might be and what he was doing in town. But most of all, Alex was wondering at Angie's smiling face as he watched without her noticing.

If Alex went to get in his own truck, Angie could not help but see him, and Alex didn't want to get into yet another embarrassing situation. He watched a moment more, turned around, and then slipped into The Wild Bunch without being seen.

51

There is a tradition of sorts in The Wild Bunch that one table, way in the back, is reserved for the lonely hearts of Goldburg. Affectionately dubbed the "Sad Boy" table by the locals, it had a regular clientele of broken-hearted cowboys drinking away their sorrows in singles and doubles. Gender was not a barrier, and many an ex-wife or ex-girlfriend spent time sitting around the Sad Boy. The most common denominator at the sad boy was being unlucky in love. Alex noticed that Harmon sat alone at the Sad Boy on this late Friday afternoon, and from the look of him, he had been sitting there for quite some time.

Alex hadn't been in The Wild Bunch for over a month and had not had an alcoholic drink in almost two, but today he thought he would break his self-imposed fast and join Harmon.

Harmon was pretty well tanked, and the conversation between the two was somewhat stilted from the beginning and continued to follow the same pattern. Harmon had an odd habit of blurting out just a few lines, sometimes only one line, from old rock-and-roll songs that he felt had deep meaning to his own life. If Harmon had any alcohol at all, this habit became accentuated to an unusual degree.

Harmon hung his head low and said slowly, "In a coffee house the bastard sat."

Alex had to think a minute on this one. "No, I don't think that's right. It's not 'bastard.' It's somebody's name, some famous folk singer guy I think."

"That doesn't feel right. I liked the lyric better, 'in a coffee house the bastard sat.' Now you went and put a stain on my aura."

"Sorry."

"That's all right, my aura wasn't doing too good today anyway."

Harmon took another drink from his long-necked bottle of micro-brew. "You know, the first time I came out west, I was hitchhiking. You know, I went more than five hundred miles out of my way just to stand on a corner in this town in Arizona, called Winslow."

Alex sipped his first taste of beer after his long alcohol sabbatical and smacked his lips in appreciation. "What in the hell did you do that for?"

"Way back then there was this famous song; had a line in it about Winslow, seeing a girl in a pickup truck slowing down to just to look back at this fellow. That one line of that song so caught hold of me that I couldn't get it out of my head. You know how a song can do that? Well it went on and on, until I was singing it in my sleep. Figured I had to go out to Arizona and check it out for myself. Might turn out to be prophetic or something."

Alex did remember the song. "You really did that, because of that song?"

"Yeah, I did."

"So what happened? Did you see the girl?"

"Not really."

"How about the flatbed Ford?"

"Nope."

"Bummer." Alex had to ask. "How long did you stand on the corner?"

"I must of stood there for hours. It was so damn hot, probably over a hundred. You know, after I got dropped off in Winslow, the weakness of my plan became apparent."

"How's that?"

"Winslow's one of those western towns all built up along a long strip of highway, sort of like a giant strip mall that just goes on and on. The trouble was, there were too damn many corners. I just felt like I was standing on the wrong one."

Alex nodded, "I know the feeling."

"Anyway, I stood on that fucking corner until I almost got sunstroke. Finally a couple of Indians in a van saw me looking like near death and asked if I needed a ride. So much for Winslow. Ended up riding with those Indians all the way to Colorado."

"Colorado?"

"Yep, Colorado." Harmon drained his beer bottle, holding it in place to catch every drop before he swallowed. "I tell you though, that took care of that song stuck in my head. Every once in a while I think about how crazy that was to go all that way just for a song."

"It was a good song though."

"Great song. It was poetry, that's what it was."

"Yeah, poetry."

Harmon got a far-away look in his eyes. "You know, Feodora loved poetry."

It was the ex-wife blues, Alex thought. "Hey, you didn't know."

Harmon cut him off. "Damn, I did know. Deep inside, I knew, I knew what I should of done. I was just too scared or proud or something."

Alex wrestled with his thoughts like they were alligators. "Angie's such a great girl," he blurted out.

"She's an exceptional girl," said Harmon. "One in a thousand, maybe one in a million."

Alex felt that the current trend of this discussion was not favorable to his continued mental health and just said, "Yeah."

"So what's the problem?"

Alex tilted his beer back in a long swallow. "I still love her. That's the problem."

52

"Tis the last rose of summer
Left blooming alone;
All her lovely companions
Are faded and gone."
Thomas Moore

July continued hot and dry. Temperature records were being broken all across Idaho. On the nineteenth, at five thousand two hundred and eighty feet elevation, Goldburg recorded its first-ever one-hundred-degree day.

On July twentieth, the weather service issued a red flag warning. There was little chance of significant moisture from this storm but high potential for dry lightning.

Alex sat sweating in his uniform. The small double-hung windows in the office limited the air circulation and made the building feel as if you were in a furnace.

Buck pensively looked at the print-out. "This could be the real deal comin'. The drought code is over four hundred and the Haines Index is off the chart. We get any lightning out of this here storm, and it's Katie bar the door."

"Do you have the fire crew pre-positioned at Indian Creek?" Alex asked.

"Yeah, and I got a type two crew from the Leodore District over at Little Creek. Everybody is out and everybody is available. You got your fire pack ready?"

"Yeah, all set."

"Well, I wouldn't stray far from dispatch. I'll be needing you for initial attack from here."

It was too hot to eat inside the little cabin on Chipmunk Hill, so Alex ate his supper out on the deck, watching gray clouds begin to darken over White Mountain to his west. The sunset was lost in a jumble of gray and black and heat lightning jumped from cloud to cloud.

310

The wind rose at dark, with the bulk of the storm passing to the south over the Middle Fork. Alex sat on the floor of his cabin, the lights out, watching the lightning cracking on Twin Peaks. Great jagged bolts drilled into the mountain so fiercely he swore he could hear it breaking rock and splitting trees. The sky was full of thunder. Long, thin tails of virga streaked toward the ridges. At times the lightning was so intense the landscape was lit up as if it were day. And among all the thunder and lightning, only a smattering of rain reached the ground.

Alex was at fire dispatch at zero six hundred, dressed in his Nomex fire clothes, his fire pack ready in the pickup. Buck had a worried look. The automatic remote lightning sensor had detected over one hundred and fifty strikes in the Middle Fork. When the smokes started to get called in, Buck would have to decide which fires to staff and which ones to monitor. There wasn't the personnel to staff them all. Just after daybreak the calls began to come in from the fire lookouts. Buck was particularly interested in any fire that was smoking deep down in the canyon near the river, as these fires had more potential to develop into a project fire. Any fire, high or low, near the Middle Fork Lodge or Indian Creek, would be staffed immediately. These were areas of critical concern, with thick, dense stands of fir and pine and heavy fuels and major improvements and investments to protect.

Augie, the Forest Dispatcher, took a radio message from the fire lookout on Greyhound Mountain just before seven. Augie immediately relayed the information to Buck, giving him the legal description of two smokes, and Buck pushed two colored pins into the big fire map on the wall.

"The one fire, the one in the bottom, looks to be heating up already," Augie said.

Buck looked again at the pin he had just placed. "It's down here, in the bottom of Dome Creek. I think we'll have to go after this one; can't let it climb out of there and into Artillery or Mortar Creek."

Alex felt the familiar excitement beginning to buzz in his insides. He knew what was coming next.

Buck said, "Alex, I want you to be Type Four Incident Commander on this one. I'm going to send you and Eddie and three more. I think Henry can get the helicopter over onto the ridge to the west. If not, we've got a helispot just under Greyhound, and you can hoof it from there. Give me a size-up as soon as you get on the ground."

"Right." Alex jumped up to get the manifest ready for helitack.

311

"And don't be afraid to call in retardant drops if you need them."

In less than fifteen minutes, Alex and Fast Eddie were being loaded on the blue-and-white Jet Ranger. Henry had the rotors turning. Teffonie, Harmon, and Howie were scheduled on the second load out. Dalton, the new helitack foreman from Salmon, loaded the fire tools. Then he led Eddie and Alex, hard hats secure, leather gloves on, and heads bent down, across the front of the ship and within full view of the pilot and loaded them up.

Alex clipped on his microphone and fiddled with the volume control. "Hey, how's it going, Henry?"

Henry's voice came back somewhat modulated and sounding far away. "Just great. Listened to the cash register dinging all night long. That was some thunder and lightning storm."

"You're gonna be a busy boy the next few days."

"You know it," Henry said, switching channels and then powering up. The Jet Ranger vibrated and rose in little lurches, rising above the helispot to nearly sixty feet, dipping the top rotor and pushing over the compound. Henry squawked back on the radio, "Forest Dispatch, this is helicopter four three zero, with four souls aboard, bound for Dome Creek."

It was helicopter assisted deja vu. Alex had been here before and knew the geography quite well. They flew down Warm Creek to the confluence with Big Loon, down Loon and over Falconberry and all the way to the Middle Fork. Heading south along the river, Alex saw rafts floating far below on the shining green water. Then it was over Little Creek and the Middle Fork Lodge. As they passed over Indian Creek, Alex thought of Angie and looked for a speck on the airstrip that might be her. Past Pistol Creek, low on the mountainside on the west side of the river, Henry pointed and said, "There's your fire."

Alex looked and saw a tendril of white smoke rising from a small bowl full of green trees. It looked like mostly Doug fir, he thought. The smoke rose straight up and then flattened out in a small pancake in the early morning weak inversion.

"Give me a fly by," Alex said into the mouthpiece on his helmet.

Henry dipped the ship and circled the fire several times.

Alex studied the terrain, searching for potential safety zones and anchor points in the vegetative pattern and the topography.

Henry pointed again. "We've got a helispot location just on the ridge there. Won't be much of a hike down to the fire."

From a helicopter it always looks like an easy hike, thought Alex, but this time Henry's prediction seemed to be reasonably accurate. Alex thought that he and the crew would be able to drop off the ridge and hike across a big scree slope that traversed the hillside and led down into the basin. From there they could side hill into the base of the fire. The scree slope would serve as a good safety zone on the southwest flank of the blaze.

The opening on the ridge was a natural helispot: flat, bereft of trees and brush, dropping off steep to the south, and big enough to land on and move people and gear out of the way. Henry circled twice, came in from the south, and landed smoothly, his skids level on good gravel.

Dalton reversed the order in unloading the aircraft. First he led Alex and Eddie from the ship, repeating all the safety protocols and keeping well out of the range of the whirling rotor blades. Henry kept the helicopter powered up while Dalton returned twice for fire packs and tools. Dalton gave Alex the bye sign as he climbed back in the ship. Henry pushed the motor hard. A moment later the helicopter rose and hovered above the ridge, and then bird-like, dipped and slipped over the ridge on the way back to Goldburg. Alex listened to the "thuck, thuck, thuck" noise recede and dwindle down to nothing.

As his first task as Incident Commander, Alex asked Eddie to take out his belt weather kit and get temperature, relative humidity, and wind readings. Alex called into Dispatch with his size-up report. As IC, Alex got to name the fire, which he gave the intuitive name of "Dome Creek."

"The Dome Creek Fire is located in the northwest one quarter of the southwest one quarter of section seven, township fifteen north, range eleven east, Boise meridian, break... Elevation six thousand two hundred feet, very near the drainage course of Dome Creek." Alex waited for a radio break and then continued. "The Dome Creek Fire is currently class B, near two acres in size, approximately thirty five-chains in perimeter, break... Fire is currently located on a relatively steep slope, southeastern aspect. Fire has topographical potential to the west and northwest, break... Best access is from helispot on ridge immediately to the north. Helispot is identified and marked. No special hazards identified and no additional resource needs at this time, break... At zero eight hundred, at base of fire, temperature is sixty-seven and relative humidity is forty-six percent, wind speed of three to five, out of the northwest, break..."

Buck got on the radio. "What's the country look like? How about safety zones?"

Alex spoke back into his radio mike attached to his fire web gear. "From the fly over, it looks pretty good. We've got a nice rock slide to the west and an

313

area barren of trees to the northeast that should make good safety zones."

"Just watch the grass," Buck radioed back. "Don't establish any safety zones in grass."

"I hear you. The barren area is almost all rock, just some scrub but no continuous fine fuels."

"How does it look for direct attack?"

"It looks pretty good to go direct. I see a slide rock area we can tie into at the bottom of the fire and then flank it."

"Just be careful when that inversion breaks, Twiddle clear."

Just as Alex finished with his size up report to dispatch, Henry was returning with his second load of firefighters. Dalton quickly unloaded Teffonie, Howie, and Harmon and their fire tools and fire packs.

"We've got smokes all over the Middle Fork," Dalton was telling Alex over the noise of the idling rotor blades. "There won't be any hot suppers or lunches for a while."

"Okay," Alex shouted back. "We've got two extra cases of MREs here with us, and that'll do us fine."

All five stopped what they were doing to watch Henry and Dalton lift off and power out, holding their hard hats down. The helicopter wind blast hit them just as the ship went over the ridge.

Alex briefed his crew on the strategy for attacking the fire, taking extra time to talk about communications, escape routes, and safety zones.

'Hell," Fast Eddie said, "I'm getting anxious. Let's just go over there and put the damn thing out."

As they hiked down the rock scree slope and into the basin, Alex caught the scent of burning wood, a pleasing, almost home-like smell. Dome Creek was socked in with smoke from the inversion. Before they walked into the timber, Alex looked up at the bare face of Artillery Dome, the talus heaped into an ice-cream-cone shape of rock on the summit.

On the way in to the fire, Alex flagged the two chosen safety zones, again explained to everyone the color and pattern of the flagging, and walked them all down the escape routes so they could see the safety zones. They dropped their fire packs at the base of the fire near the rock shelf where Alex planned to anchor the fire line construction. Stashing the chain saw and the water containers, they adjusted their web gear, adding canteens, checking their radios and tools. Alex and Eddie had shovels and the other three were using Pulaskis.

314

Alex peered as if he could see through the smoke at something. "I'm anticipating that the fire behavior will pick up when this inversion does lift." Even as Alex spoke the words, he felt the first hints of a coming breeze on his cheek.

The crew started hot line construction at the bottom of the burned area. Howie was lead Pulaski. Except for Alex, he was the strongest of the crew and worked like a bull, digging his Pulaski deep to form the basis for the roll trench. Teffonie followed with her Pulaski, then Harmon and Eddie. Alex cleaned and checked the line construction, making sure the trench was all the way down to mineral soil, that it had a good roll edge on the downhill side to prevent embers and rolling cones from getting beneath them. He was busy processing information on everything he saw, heard, smelled and felt. The safety of the crew was his responsibility and he took it seriously. After his one season of firefighting, Alex had a healthy fear of wildfire and what could happen under the wrong conditions.

The wind didn't come up that morning and the fire stayed down, the flames lengths remained small. The crew had a rudimentary line scratched around the fire, pinching off the head, before the inversion began to lift.

There was a small grove of subalpine fir right in about the center of the fire that had not yet burned. Alex was watching it carefully. He pulled the crew together and discussed mop-up procedures.

"I'd like to take care of that upper line and work in towards the center, try to get to that subalpine fir and cool that off, drop some of those snags," Alex explained.

Howie had the saw, and had just finished dropping a fir snag that could have threatened the fire line "Need to cool that off," he said. "If we were closer to Dome Creek, we could call for a pump and hose."

Alex looked over the lay of the land. "It's a long hose lay, but we might yet. With the elevation difference, we'd have to use a porta tank or a series of Mark- 3 pumps. But it's too far and it would take too long to set up. Right now, we'll use our bladder bags if we get the chance." Alex looked back across the basin. "Now they're calling for wind this afternoon. If we're lucky, we'll have this thing knocked down before then. Let's go for one hundred percent mop-up on this. It's small enough."

Looking back over Artillery Dome, Alex saw a lens-shaped lenticular cloud pasted over the peak, mares' tails streaming high above. The sky was showing wind, but there was nothing at the surface yet.

315

Howie had dropped the last large snag and was approaching the copse of subalpine fir. Alex was alongside when he noticed a small whirling dervish of dust and wind, coiled up like a miniature tornado, rising over the basin and headed directly for them. The dry duff erupted into flame right in front of Alex's shovel and leaped into the prostrate branches of the subalpine fir to his left, the fire climbing the low, lateral branches like a ladder and up into the crown.

"Shit!"Alex shouted, as the lone subalpine fir turned into a torch, shooting firebrands into the air. "Watch for spots! Watch for spots!"

All five scampered toward the glowing firebrands as they settled like snowflakes on the wrong side of the fire line. They stomped, smacked, and dug out seven small spot fires. Alex sent Teffonie up on a pile of rock to look for more.

"Kynwulf, VanWinkle on one," the radio crackled.

"Kynwulf here."

"You better get up here. We got fire in the basin, starting to torch trees up ahead."

"Shit!" Alex said. He ran the short distance and scampered up on the rock pile like a goat. He saw five or six trees on fire, all subalpine fir, all tossing out firebrands in the breeze. Ahead of the spot fire, the fuels were nearly continuous, and Alex knew they had lost it.

"Shit!" Alex said again. He called on the radio to Eddie to bring the squad back to the rocks to regroup.

Alex had his squad around him and was thinking out loud. "More fuel and increasing flame lengths. What do you think, Eddie, six to eight feet?"

"Yeah, we've got six to eight-foot flame lengths easy."

"Get me a temperature and relative humidity," he told Eddie.

Fast Eddie twirled the thermometer above his head, checked the wet bulb and dry bulb charts twice before he said, "Temperature is eighty-four degrees and an RH down to twenty-two per cent." Eddie held the pocket anemometer up to the breeze. "Wind speed ten to twelve from the southwest."

Alex mused, "Too hot to direct attack, and too dangerous to go indirect at the head. Maybe we can get some retardant in here and build a wet line, keep the fire off the steep heavy fuels, and prevent it from climbing over the ridge and into Artillery Creek and the really heavy fuels."

"I think it's worth the shot," Howie said. "It's about all we have to work with."

"That damn subalpine fir." Alex grimaced as he spoke. "We're gonna

316

have to expect some aberrant fire behavior this afternoon and more firebrands when that subalpine shit torches."

Alex radioed dispatch and told Buck the news, discussing his plan at length: to build an indirect wet line of retardant across an area of lighter fuels of grass and scattered trees. The retardant line could be anchored to some rock scree on the east ridge, and the tankers could work downhill and into the wind. Alex felt that if they kept the fire off the steep, timbered slope, they still had a chance.

Augie sent out the fire order to the McCall air-tanker base.

It was mostly wait and watch then. The tanker base was a good forty-minute flight away. Alex didn't know what else was going on, but with all the smokes and this wind, he suspected the worst. He hoped he could get five or six loads of retardant on the fire before it got dark.

Alex had Teffonie, Harmon, and Howie carry the gear and hike back to the helispot while he and Eddie worked their way beneath the fire and up on the rock-scree anchor point on the eastern ridge. The talus field extended all the way down into the basin and was large enough to be an excellent safety zone no matter what, Alex thought. The rest of the crew at the helispot was also in a good, safe location, with plenty of rock if they needed it.

Alex heard the air tanker before he saw it. There was no air attack lead plane for the single tanker, so Alex figured that a lot more was probably going on other than his own Dome Creek Fire. The Douglas Super DC-4 was coming in from the south, high up, circling the fire in a left-handed pattern.

Alex flashed his signal mirror at the slow-moving plane and then made radio contact. He explained his plan to the tanker pilot.

"The target area is right at three o'clock from you. We want to build a progressive retardant line from this rock talus slope, across the head of the basin right before where it gets steep, on the gentle southwest facing slope, in that area of grass and light fuels."

"I got it," came the reply.

"Right across the lower third of the slope face on that good ground," Alex repeated. At almost six thousand dollars a load, Alex wanted to get the retardant where he needed it.

"Right, I got it."

Alex added, "I'm over here on the scree slope, right at twelve o'clock from you, two of us."

The radio crackled, "I've got you marked."

"The rest of the crew has pulled out to the helispot on the southwest ridge. They're out of your way."

"I've got them marked, too."

"I'd like to start right from here with that wet line and work dead west," Alex emphasized once more.

"Can do," the pilot said. "I'm going to make one more pass over, and then come in right over you."

"We'll be moving out of your way, then. Kynwulf clear."

Alex and Fast Eddie dropped below the rock-scree slope and into the edge of the timber, where they had an unrestricted view of the retardant drop zone. They watched the bomber make a long, lazy circle as it lost elevation and then disappeared from view behind Artillery Dome. The sound of the plane engines began to fade away.

Just as Alex became certain that the pilot had decided on making another fly over, the air tanker burst over the ridge directly above them, with only two or three hundred feet elevation clearance from the trees. Alex and Eddie froze and watched as the heavy plane opened its belly doors and a deluge of red erupted into a cloud of spray, orange at the edges where the sun caught the color. The pilot gunned the engines and the air tanker rose up above the timber.

"God, that was great," Eddie said.

"Yeah, it always grabs me the same way, by surprise, even when I'm expecting it."

Alex radioed the pilot and told him that the drop was right on target.

As Alex had predicted, the fire behavior became more erratic as the afternoon lengthened. Trees torched with each down-burst of wind from the clear sky. Alex had the crew watching for spot fires on the west flank, well within reach of the safety zone. He watched the hours creep by. The air-tanker base at McCall was busy, and Alex was able to get a retardant load approximately every hour and a quarter. It was always just one plane. At six o'clock, Alex anticipated that if they could hold the fire for another hour, the southeast slope would start to move to shadow and the relative humidity should start to go up. Maybe the fire would start to lay down then, he thought. He was still two retardant drops from completing his wet line, and the fire was moving steadily uphill in fits and starts.

Alex heard the wind coming before he felt it, a long, low rolling moan from across the ridge. He watched as the Douglas firs dipped their crowns away from the wind, pointing into the basin where the fire waited as a living thing in

318

the bottom of Dome Creek.   When the downdraft hit the fire, there was an explosion of flame from a group of subalpine fir, sending up a blue-black column of smoke, dense with firebrands sparkling like firecrackers in the swirling smoke.

"Holy shit!" Eddie said.

Alex hung his head and said, "It's going over the hill for sure."

The whole crew sat together now and watched the fire move rapidly up a chute of timber and brush as it blew past the unfinished retardant line, noisily and steadily moving up the west flank of Artillery Dome.   Spot fires smoked white ahead of the main flame front.

Alex radioed to dispatch.   "We have lost initial attack.   The Dome Creek Fire is moving now at an estimated speed of ten chains per hour, flame lengths of ten to fifteen feet, estimated size sixty acres and growing rapidly."

53

"Bring me my bow of burning gold!
Bring me my arrows of desire!
Bring me my spear! O clouds unfold!
Bring me my chariot of fire!"
William Blake

Big Stanley and Buck completed the Wildfire Situation Analysis and declared the Dome Creek Fire a type two project fire. Stan ordered a Type Two regional team and got prepared to manage the fire on extended attack until the team arrived.

Buck flew in to the fire and took over as type three Incident Commander. He ordered six more crews and a medium helicopter. Two crews arrived at daylight, the Forest Type Two Crew and the Union Hotshots, a Type One crew from Oregon that was passing near Goldburg on the way to Montana.

They had a hot time of it as the temperature climbed and the relative humidity dropped. The fire made a big run at mid-day, ripping off six hundred or more acres of fir with fifty-foot flame lengths and a mushroom cloud of smoke that could be seen from Goldburg.

The central Idaho Type Two team began work as soon as they arrived in Goldburg and continued working through most of the night. The team arrived with computers and communications and made the District office their incident command post. It was a full team, with an Incident Commander and separate staffs for planning, logistics and operations, fire behavior, safety, public affairs, supply, and contracting. Most of the night was spent reviewing the Wildland Fire Situation Analysis that Buck and Big Stan had prepared the night before. They agreed with the plan's merit and proposed no significant changes other than in ordering fire resources and splitting the Dome Creek Fire into two divisions. The decision was quickly made to order more of almost everything, which set the money meter running on high speed.

Buck was taken off the fire that morning, being replaced by two division supervisors, and flew back to Goldburg on the first helicopter flight of the day. His duties now were the protection of the rest of the District and the initial attack and suppression responsibilities for any new fires that might break out.

The team also asked to keep the Forest Type Two Crew on the fire, and Alex and the rest became part of the new fire organization on the Dome Creek Fire. Alex and his squad were assigned over to Kloyd's crew, and it didn't take long for Alex to notice that Angie Kowalski was part of the forest crew.

Kloyd was a good crew boss. His main objective on any fire was to bring back all of his crew and himself, home, safe and sound; for Kloyd had seen too many acres burned and too many mistakes made to waste any time worrying about how big a fire was going to get. His feeling was that the only thing that stopped a big fire like this one was the weather, and he often said, "All the trees in this country aren't worth the cost of one person getting burnt up." Kloyd had also seen too many big-shot overhead teams come in and screw things up royally, and a distrust of out-of-town authority was almost an automatic response for him.

Kloyd was also a safety zone fanatic. He had almost been burned over when he was on a Forest Service crew just out of Goldburg High School. It was a small fire that blew up in grass and light fuels when a thunderstorm downdraft hit. Kloyd had to run for a rockslide, not a very big one; and he never forgot the heat that small fire put out and how he had wished for more rock, a lot more rock. So Kloyd was constantly hounding the crew about safety zones as they progressed up the fire line. He made doubly sure that everyone understood the striped flagging that identified the escape routes.

A new spot weather forecast had identified the potential for local, blustery winds, and Kloyd took Angie from Alex's squad and positioned her as a lookout, watching for changes in weather and fire behavior. It was funny, Alex thought. He missed standing near the girl, even though they hadn't said more than a few words, and all of it was about work. Alex spent the rest of the day lost in thoughts of rocks and dirt, snags and safety.

The winds never materialized, and the fire progressed slowly but steadily. There was enough heat now in the smoldering heavy fuels in the center of the blaze that the fire began to be more fuel driven, preheating and drying the already parched fuels ahead of it, then making short runs uphill. Even without wind, the fire front had burned an additional six hundred acres by the end of the burning period that evening. It wasn't until Artillery Creek was in full shadow that the fire began to lessen in intensity. Alex thought that the crews made great

321

progress, so he was starting to feel some confidence growing inside himself again, thinking that maybe, just maybe, if the wind held back a couple more days, they could shut this fire down.

Alex said as much to Kloyd as he walked behind him in the dark on the way back to spike camp. "Looks like this fire could be contained in a few more days. It doesn't look too bad."

"Oh, I don't know. I think this case is a long way from closed. We got lucky today. The wind never showed up."

Up on Artillery Dome the Hotshot crews were working late, burning out portions of the line to create a buffer, a barrier of burned ground to keep the fire confined to Artillery Creek. The small fires spread out along the fire line looked like sparklers of red and yellow firelight, pulsing with the heartbeat of the fire-dependent landscape.

Kloyd said, "We still got a pile of unburned fuel down in the middle of Artillery Creek. I don't know what the team plans to do about it, but it's got my worry muscles workin' overtime."

Alex tried to peer down into the dark smoke in the Artillery Creek basin, staring as if, if he looked long enough, his eyes could force a way through the darkness. All he could make out was a sea of snags silhouetted against a strange yellow alpenglow.

"Do you think they'll try to burn it out?"

"That's what got me worried. I've seen this country burn when it's dry like this. It's like the country just wants to burn, and needs to, or something. When it's ready to burn, it's gonna burn, and all the helicopters and air tankers in the world can't stop it. And believe me, we do not want to see this fire come out of that canyon with a head of steam behind it."

Alex had seldom heard such a sense of certainty and urgency in Kloyd's voice, and it caused him again to look into the dark, smoldering basin and try to see what Kloyd was seeing.

"Do you really think this fire will get up and climb out of there?"

"Just pray the wind don't blow and the team don't blow it."

Back at spike camp, with the breeze so calm you could have lit a candle, Alex smelled hot food. The team had flown in a hot supper, large metal tins of fried chicken, mashed potatoes, mixed vegetables, and pie. After fourteen hours on the line and his sack lunch long gone, Alex was famished, his stomach growling. His first taste from the overstuffed tin plate confirmed the Y café touch, the unmistakable fried chicken, and Alex wolfed down his food like a happy dog at a kids' picnic.

The short time between food and sleep is traditionally a time of stories among the fire crews, and all the stories are about fire. The usual gist of the story line was how this particular fire pales in comparison to the fire assignments of the past. It didn't matter what the specific topic was, flame length, acres burned, food quality, overtime hours, or even how many days without a shower, everything was of greater scope and duration in the past tense.

This was truly Harmon's element. No Hotshot story, no matter how true, could compare to one of Harmon's yarns of fire and mayhem that, if only partly true, would have been a career high point for any Smoke Jumper. There may have been a few lies that Harmon left out of his fire story - but not many. The lies that Harmon did tell he told well, and soon he had a crowd gathered about his feet like the proverbial wise man.

Alex was sitting off to the side, only partly listening to Harmon tell of yet another narrow escape from the flames, when one of the Union Hotshots came over and sat next to him.

"Hi, how ya doin'?" the Hotshot said.

"Fine, a little tired."

"Hey, I was just wondering, who's the red-headed ground pounder on your squad? She's quite the fire-line kitten."

"You mean Angie, I guess."

"Angie, huh?" The fellow sat still in the dark for a time. Alex could barely make out his eyes on the soot-blackened face. "She got a guy here, on the crew?"

Alex paused, said, "She might."

"And I'm guessing that might be you?"

"Yeah, off and on." Alex nodded his head and added, "But hey, it's really only wishful thinking on my part."

"Sorry, man, just checking out the territory." The fellow slapped Alex on the back and stood up to move over into the dark toward his own crew. "Be safe."

"Yeah, you be safe, too."

Alex played with a ball of dirt in his hand, letting the pressure go and feeling the dry grains of decomposed granite slip through his fingers. He thought about the term "fire line kitten" and sort of liked it. He glanced over to where Angie sat with Teffonie and thought he caught her watching him in the dark. Alex smiled to himself and said out loud, to no one in particular, "Time to hunker down for the night."

The next morning was full of smoke, the sun blood red. The entire basin below Artillery Dome was socked in with a dense layer of brown-gray smoke. Kloyd, as crew boss, attended the morning briefing that the team conducted by a radio conference with the division supervisors, crew bosses, and safety officer at the spike camp. Yesterday had been a good day. The Hotshot crews on both divisions had pushed the fire line through some difficult ground, and on Division One, they had made the ridge overlooking Mortar Creek. If the wind didn't come up, the team hoped that the Hotshots could tie together with Division Two ahead of the fire and tie off the line. Burn-out operations last night had gone well, and there was a good buffer of black line on the western flank almost to the ridge. If they did encircle the fire, the shot crews could conduct burn out operations that evening to remove the fuel in front of the fire, effectively cutting off its head. Kloyd's crew's job was once again, to follow the Hotshot crew and continue to improve the line, mopping in a hundred feet into the fire, paying careful attention to any snags that could fall over and threaten the line. The safety officer gave a good presentation and warning about snags, beating in the fact that these trees are half burned and can fall without wind and without warning. Because of this falling snag potential, there was no night shift scheduled. The fire weather forecast was a better one, with only a slight chance of any local wind events, and just the usual up-canyon breezes in the afternoon. Temperatures were forecast to remain high, in the high eighties on the fire line, and relative humidities were forecast in the eighteen-to-twenty-percent range. The fire behavior specialist called for flame lengths and fire behavior similar to yesterday, with the fire continuing today to be mostly fuel driven. Tomorrow's weather looked similar, so they might have a good two day window of opportunity on this fire. The big news came from the planning shop, all about how, if good progress was made today, plans were being made for a burn-out operation in the Artillery Creek basin. The sizeable block of dead fir and subalpine fir on the north flank was too big of a risk to let go. The longer term weather forecast, out three to five days, called for a high wind warning, and the team was reluctant to take a chance on holding the fire in Artillery Creek if they had a major wind event.

Kloyd had come back from the morning briefing as nervous as a cat, dancing on one foot and then the other as if he had to piss real bad and nobody would let him. He said to Alex, "If we get the fire contained today, they're gonna bring in a helitorch operation tomorrow and try to burn out the rest of Artillery Creek."

"So what's wrong with that? We can't just leave all that heavy fuel to smolder down there. You just told me yesterday how that stuff can burn."

"I know, I know. It's just a feeling that I got. I never had any faith in helicopter operations. They always start late or somethin' breaks down. The worst part is, once the team gets their heart set on doin' a helicopter show, nothing on earth can sway that decision. It's like carved in stone. Fish gotta swim and helicopters gotta fly."

"They're planning on doing the burn-out early in the morning, right?"

"They better be. I'll know more tonight at the evening briefing."

"As long as they get right on it early, it shouldn't burn too hot."

Kloyd became animated, waving his arms, which he only did when he was really nervous or upset. "That's the trouble, right there. With helicopters, you're always dickin' around and never on time. All I know is that it's drier than I've ever seen it. The thousand-hour fuels are in the single digits for fuel moisture. Ain't no time to be messin' with a helitorch."

"Well, maybe we'll get this line tied up today and take care of the thing tomorrow."

"If not, we could have a major rager on our hands."

The winds did stay light. It was a good day to drop snags, and all the sawdogs were busy. Howie and his swamper were working behind Alex's squad, dropping small fir snags along the fire perimeter.

If you were to look at the fire in plan view, the fire line resembled a snake as it circled around the fingers of fire following the contours of the topography. Where the fire line went indirect, it was much less convoluted in shape. It marched in long curves from rock field to talus slope, trying to form an effective boundary that the crews could burn out from, a big black line to repel the expected attack if the fire came out of Artillery Creek. More than a half mile of green trees separated the head of the fire and the indirect line being constructed on the ridge between Artillery and Mortar Creeks. The fire in Artillery Creek had burned in a mosaic pattern. Black burned trees and bare ground alternated with green trees and lightly burned brown-needled ones. More than a third of the timber in the basin was either unburned or brown needled and ready to re-burn, with one large stand of unburned heavy fuel in the bottom of the basin under the north flank of fire line.

Kloyd was even more concerned about safety zones today, constantly checking on the time and effort needed to reach one if the crew had to. As they progressed around the north flank of the fire, Kloyd stopped the crew from proceeding until a better safety zone could be found. He didn't like the open area that the Hotshot crew had been using as a safety zone and ended up getting into a bit of an argument with the Division Supervisor.

"Too damn small," Kloyd told him.

The Division Supervisor was obviously getting a bit tired of Kloyd's preoccupation with safety zones and just sort of urged him to follow the Hotshot crews and everything would end up fine. Kloyd stuck to his guns, not moving the crew until the Division Supervisor and the Safety Officer found and established a big enough safety zone for Kloyd's liking, a large area of rock and short grass that could quickly be burned off if it was needed.

Afterwards Kloyd told Alex, "Them earthpigs wouldn't know a safety zone if it bit them in the ass. These teeny tiny safety zones won't hold if the fire comes out of that hole."

"How big do you need?"

"Well, I seen a hundred foot flame lengths and more comin' out of this subalpine fire when the fire runs through the crowns. You got to have four times the flame length, minimum, separating you from the flames."

"You need four hundred feet all around you?"

"Minimum, unless you're talking a shelter deployment. I ain't never popped one of those brown-and-serve bags, and I'm not anxious to start now."

Alex did some quick math in his head. "That's like ten or twelve acres?"

"That's what I been trying to tell you. You follow Hotshot crews too close, you're gonna be the one in trouble if there's a blowup."

By mid-day the inversion had lifted and the smoke moved upriver in a

325

ghostly cloud.   Not trusting the weather, Kloyd posted a lookout as soon as he felt the first air movements.   But the wind was a no show, and the shift went well; the line completed around the head of the fire before the first shadows fell on Artillery Creek.   As Alex hiked back with the crew that evening, he watched the burn-out operation on the head of the fire perimeter.   A glowing string of fire, a yellow-red moving line of flame, draped over the ridge line like a necklace.

The crew trooped into spike camp worn out and dirty.   The word was out that the weather looked good for tomorrow and that the overhead team back in the puzzle palace at the District office was bringing out the helitorch for some real fireworks the next day.

The news made Alex excited, a nervous excitement that was hard to define, an excitement that began down in his tired legs, setting them twitching.

Fast Eddie came up to him in the dark.   "Man, did you hear?   They're going for the whole shitaree tomorrow.   Should be fun to watch."

"Kloyd doesn't think so.   He doesn't have much faith in helicopters."

"Hey, neither do I.   But whatever happens, it'll be over fast.   If we had to burn this all out by hand and baby-sit this fire, we'd be here until September."

It was just getting dark enough that Alex had trouble making out who was who.   He finally saw Angie walking with Teffonie.   If he could only catch her alone, he could talk with her.   Nothing serious, just talk with her.   One thing about being on a fire, he thought, you were never alone.

"This is the way the world ends,
Not with a bang, but a whimper."
T. S. Eliot

Alex awoke early to the thick smell of smoke. Tendrils of smoke curled under diffused moonlight and fire glow, almost obscuring the moon setting over Artillery Dome. The smoke burned his eyes. He coughed in an echo to the sounds and coughs of the sleeping firefighters. Something was wrong, and in his half sleep he couldn't seem to place it. He had been dreaming of Dugout Dick, of all people. In the dream Dick was trying to show him something, but it was so smoky in the dream that he couldn't make it out, just a large form, a heart-shaped mass of something that sat motionless behind Dick and some woman in a long white dress. Whatever it was, it had scared him. Dick kept telling him to look, but Alex just couldn't see.

Since he was already up, Alex decided to forgo the extra half hour of sleep and joined Kloyd at the morning briefing. As he stumbled getting dressed in the early morning darkness, Alex could now see the zephyrs of smoke that swirled around him. That must be it, he thought, the smoke in spike camp. There must not have been an inversion during the night. He turned on his headlamp and headed for the large tent that served as headquarters, still dogged by feelings of predestination as he hurried to outrun the dawn.

Alex had his coffee in hand, like all the others except Kloyd, and stood next to him as the crew bosses received their assignments from the division supervisor. Alex noted the morning temperature on the fire, sixty-one degrees at zero five thirty, almost ten degrees warmer than yesterday, and wondered if it had importance or not. There were no surprises in the rest of the briefing. The fire weather forecast was for a repeat of yesterday, with light winds, low relative humidity, and temperatures in the high eighties on the fire line. The fire behavior was predicted for a slow expansion at the head of the fire, with the potential for torching of individual and groups of trees. There were no predictions of unusual fire behavior or extreme flame lengths.

Then came the operating plan for the day and all the specifics of the helitorch burn-out operation. The division supervisor carefully explained what each crew would be doing during the burn-out. Kloyd's crew was assigned to watch the northern flank of Artillery Dome, where not much was expected to happen. Their assignment was to hunker down on the line and watch for any slop-over or spot fires across the line. The Hotshot crews' assignment was to guard the head of the fire where they had conducted burn-out operations the day before. If there was trouble with spotting, this area was where it was most likely to happen. The Hotshots had a good burned area to escape to if they did hit some heat coming out of the basin, and there was a good secondary escape area and safety zone on the ridge separating Artillery and Mortar Creeks. The biggest concern expressed at the meeting was that the fire column caused by the burn-out could float some stray firebrands over the line in this area and into Mortar Creek. The burn-out would progress in strips from just inside the black at the head of the fire and then work in towards the center. Hopefully this would cause the smoke column to draw in on itself and curve inward into the center of the fire, drawing the firebrands in with it, keeping fire intensity and flame lengths within manageable parameters. The burn-out was supposed to start promptly at zero seven hundred, and all the crews needed to be in position and ready. If all went well, the unburned island of fuel should be consumed by mid-morning.

The Safety Officer gave the standard pep talk, ending with a watch-out for snags. "Remember," he said, "death comes from above."

The Division Supervisor ended the briefing with a jocular, "Be safe," and the crew bosses went to rejoin their crews, to get them watered up and on the fire line.

Alex fell in step behind Kloyd, who was muttering under his breath. Alex just caught a quiet "son of a bitch".

"You worried about the helitorch?"

"Yeah, I am." Kloyd stopped walking. "Once they start dropping those Ping-Pong balls, damn near anything can happen."

"So how does the helitorch work, anyhow?" Alex had been thinking about it for some time but was hesitant to ask the question. It seemed that any firefighter should know all about it already.

Kloyd stood still and pointed up to the smoke-red sky, as if it was already happening. "Well, they got this here little machine, you take the side door off the helicopter and it fits right in there. And it runs sort of like one of those machines that packs eggs, and you got a bunch of Ping-Pong balls full of this stuff called potassium permangatate, or somethin' like that. This machine takes these juicy Ping-Pong balls one at a time, and injects them with regular old antifreeze, and then spits them out, lickity split, out the door of the helicopter. Now the antifreeze causes some kind of chemical reaction, and it burns like hell, but it's funny, it takes about thirty seconds or so to start."

"So, they like, lay down a line of these burning Ping-Pong balls?"

"Yeah, but they ain't burnin' right away. The helicopter is seeding em down, and the fire sprouts out a couple of minutes behind it."

Alex understood now. "They lay out a carpet of fire just where they want to."

"That they certainly can do. The trouble is, they can't stop it."

Kloyd gathered the crew together and explained the helitorch plan. Most everyone on the crew was excited about it. With the promise of not much work to do, it would be something really interesting to watch.

Alex didn't share the general enthusiasm. The strange dream of warning from Dugout Dick still lurked in the back of his mind. The blood-red sunrise seemed full of portent. He saw that Kloyd was worried, and that bothered him.

The crew gathered their sack lunches and water and soon were marching down the fire line, tools in hand, filled with expectation. Alex and the rest of the crew hiked through thick smoke, tendrils snaking through the burned trees like will-o-the-wisps. He was behind Fast Eddie, with Angie just ahead, so he had a chance to watch her without being ready to look away. Angie, like the rest, was dirty with sweat and pitch, her ponytail more black than red. But Alex thought her beautiful. Even the soot smeared across her forehead, a lampblack streak above the bump on the bridge of her nose, so fit the role that she was playing that it made Alex ache inside. He wondered what she was thinking and tried to catch her thoughts as he once could, but there was nothing there for him to link to. Any doors that Angie might have had were closed tight now. Alex decided that it was a futile gesture. He might as well try to catch wild birds with his hands.

The crew was at its assigned position by zero six thirty. Kloyd's body language expressed an unusual nervousness, and he paced back and forth, then alternated by wrapping and unwrapping his arms around his shoulders. By zero seven hundred, there was no sight or sound of a helicopter. Kloyd asked Alex to take the weather. The temperature was sixty-eight degrees, with a relative humidity of twenty-eight.

"Looks pretty good for this burn-out, I think," Alex said encouragingly.

"If they ever get the Clum Dum thing started, it will be. I tell ya, it drives me nuts, these helicopters. They never get started on time."

At zero eight hundred, a radio message was received that explained that there was a mechanical problem with the Ping-Pong ball machine and the helitorch operation had been postponed to ten hundred hours.

"It's like bein' in hell with pigs," Kloyd said.

There wasn't much to do, and Alex hunkered down with the rest. Fast Eddie was trying to set up a private trip on the main Salmon River for when they all got back to Goldburg. He asked Alex if he wanted to come along. This set up a long discussion of logistics and dates and times and all that sort of thing that goes with planning a river trip. Alex had a fantasy about asking Angie if she wanted to go, but he didn't take the dream anywhere.

He took the weather again at zero nine hundred. The temperature was seventy-four and the RH was twenty-two. Far down in the fire, Alex saw a small fir candle with fire and thought it unusual so early in the morning; but he forgot to mention it to Kloyd.

At ten hundred hours, the sky was clear and very, very quiet.

"Where in the beejeezus are those rotorheads?" Kloyd fumed. "It's gettin' late already."

Alex watched the horizon as if he expected something dramatic to happen. The rising pall of smoke colored the view of the far mountains in a false glow of sunlight.

There was another radio message, and the helitorch show was moved back to noon. This time Kloyd didn't seem surprised. "See, I told ya," was all he said to Alex.

By noon there was still no helicopter, and Kloyd accurately predicted the message before it came over the radio. "One o'clock," he said.

Kloyd had the crew up and ready at thirteen hundred hours. He had two lookouts, Teffonie and Howie, posted high on the hill where they could see down into the bottom of Artillery Creek. The rest of the crew was broken into four squads and deployed along the fire line. Alex's squad of Argo, Fast Eddie, and Angie was stationed at the low point where the fire line dipped down into a small ravine before it began climbing up the western flank of Artillery Dome.

Before they broke off into squads, Kloyd went over, one more time, the escape routes, safety zones, and communications. If there was any problem, Kloyd wanted everyone to move into the big open area on the short ridge leading up to Artillery Dome.

"It must be twenty acres or more," Kloyd explained. "We can sit out anything there."

Kloyd decided that the last resort would be the safety zone that the Hotshots had designated during their first shift on the fire. It was marked with red-and-white striped ribbon.

"I think it's too small, but just in case."

Kloyd came over and talked quietly with Alex. "Now, you take special care, 'cause we've got a lot of unburned fuel between us and this fire they're gonna touch off. I'm not buying that the big concern is the head of this fire. If we get any wind, this fire could pick up and move our way." Kloyd stopped for a moment to tie his bandana into a sweatband under his hard hat. "This is crazy, doin' this so late in the day. I don't care how calm it is or what the weather forecast says, this is just plain, stinkin' nuts. Alex, your squad is the furthest down in this hole. If I tell you move, you move out fast, you got that?"

"Sure, Kloyd, I got it." Alex didn't know why, but the hairs on his forearms stood on end with goose bumps as a sudden chill ran through his body.

At thirteen thirty hours, Alex heard the drone of the Long Jet Ranger. He watched it power into view, and make two passes around the basin below him. Up somewhere near the head of the fire, Alex could just see the helicopter hovering over the tree line. On the edge of his field of view he saw a thin, dancing flame in the tree canopy.

"They're doing a test strip," Fast Eddie said. "Seeing how it burns."

The man-made fire began to creep up the branches of a tall subalpine fir,

330

and brown-black smoke curled straight into the air above. The helicopter moved in slow arcs barely over the treetops. When the helicopter slipped from view behind Artillery Dome, Alex saw a manageable flame front stretching north to south across the head of the fire. The trial burn must have gone well, he thought. Now the helicopter began a slow north-south passage, back and forth, from the head of the fire inward towards the last large patch of unburned fuel directly below the crew.

The fire began to grow slowly, and as it grew the smoke began to curl back into the burned area in long, sensual curves. A small fire plume bent back over itself into the basin of Artillery Creek. There was still no wind, no wind at all. Firebrands in the red-brown smoke floated up and landed back inside the line, almost like it was planned, starting a group of small fires in the unburned fuel island. The fire burned in designer strips, a man-caused pattern on the landscape that coincided with predicted results.

It was burning just like they said it would, Alex thought. He watched the helicopter working directly below him, far down in the basin. He couldn't see the Ping-Pong balls falling, but he could chart their progress by the line of fire following behind the ship, like a shepherd leading his flock.

All this while, the radio was almost silent.

Alex was running the eighteen watch-out fire situations through his head when he felt the breeze on his face. He quickly undid his weather belt kit. Argo and Fast Eddie noted the wind and looked at Alex with wide-open eyes.

"Spurr, this is Kynwulf. We've got a breeze out of the south, five to seven miles per hour, temperature eighty-six, relative humidity sixteen percent."

Kloyd immediately responded. "Kynwulf, this is Spurr. I see the smoke plume starting to tilt toward us. Time to pull back. Bump your squad up to the ridge line."

Alex wasted no time. "Eddie, Argo, Angie, let's pick up and move up."

"What's going on with this wind?" Argo asked. The breeze suddenly freshened in gusts.

"It's time to get the hell out of this hole," Eddie said.

Far down in the basin, Alex heard the fire before he saw it. A roar far down in the canyon that made him immobile. The wind hit his face hard. A stray limb on the branch of the jet stream had descended and raced down the Middle Fork and toward the saddle below Artillery Dome. It rolled like water in a rock-choked river. The air mass seemed to accelerate. It moved through constrictions and around obstructions. The wind brought the fire to life, and it grew in logarithmic terms, faster and faster on a deadly curve.

Alex saw the flames the same instant as the rest. A wall of fire, higher than a house, yellow and red far down in the bottom of the basin, moved toward them. He felt the hair on his neck stand out straight.

The radio crackled. Kloyd's voice sounded strange and distant. "Alex, get out of there now! Run! Run! Run!"

331

They dropped their tools and began to run uphill, faster than they could have ran downhill at any other time: Fast Eddie in front, Argo, Angie, and Alex right behind. Nobody said a word. They just ran, adrenaline surging. Heedless they ran, like they were on a level field instead of a choked mess of downfall timber and brush. Alex hazarded a glance back. The sky was cherry red. Burnt fir needles rained down on them, and Alex felt the convection wind hot on his back right through his fire shirt.

They ran up the fire line, kicking up dry black dust. They could hear the others in the crew. Alex caught a glimpse of yellow fire shirts.

Just a step ahead of him, Angie tripped over a root and rolled over hard on her side into a sawn log. Alex piled into her and rolled over against a snag.

"Get up! Get up!" He grabbed Angie by the arm, jerking her upright as if she were weightless, so quickly it looked as if she had leaped into the air.

"My leg!" Angie screamed. "It's jammed in there!"

Alex turned and lifted her at the same time. Her leg came free at a strange angle.

Angie took two steps and fell down again. "Oh my God!" She struggled up for a moment but fell with her first step.

"Get up!"

Angie bolted upright, swaying. Almost slipping, she caught herself against a tree. One foot bent terribly to the side. "No, no, oh my God!"

Alex saw the twisted foot but his brain couldn't seem to process it correctly.

Angie tried to move, a horrible uphill hop with Alex pushing, spasms of movement, her right leg still held high. "I can't walk! Oh my God, oh my God, no, no, I can't, I can't!"

Alex could sense the flames even without looking behind.

"I can't walk! Get out of here! Run! Get out!" Angie yelled.

Alex felt fear, felt its icy grip as he started to freeze up. His legs were as heavy as lead. In an other-world-like slow motion, he was able to see himself as a bystander. He watched himself in a smoke-filled movie, taking root in place as the fire advanced, trapped in a mirror of a mirror of himself. He couldn't break out. His eyes fixed on the flames, the terror holding him. A strange spell held him in place, a spell that mocked and shamed him motionless.

"Alex, for Christ's sake, get out of here, run!"

The words broke his ten mile stare. He looked down at the growing flames, and then into Angie's eyes. He saw her total absolute aloneness. Alex found his breath, breathed deep once, then again. The fear began to be replaced by a growing anger. Only one thought now; clear, what he had to do. "Like hell I will! You're coming with me!"

"No, you can't do it!"

Alex's gray eyes flashed fiercely, his long teeth baring in a rictus of rage. A low sound grew in his throat, an instinctual growl that turned into a roar, a long monosyllabic howl directed at the fire, a primal anger daring the flames to come closer.

The hate-filled scream froze Angie, her right leg held up like a damaged statue.

In wolf-like movements Alex grabbed her by leg and shoulder. Angie tried to pull away, but he had her in a death-grip. He easily picked her up and over his shoulder in the one-man-carry position.

"Put me down! You'll never make it!"

The adrenaline rushed through Alex in a spasm of intensity, and his legs moved in bursts up the fire line. "Shut . . . the . . . fuck . . . up!" he managed between clenched teeth and bellowing breaths.

His hatred of this fire fed the power of his body. His legs worked like pistons. Eddie and Argo were already gone. His one thought was movement, the herd instinct to follow, go up the hill to the safety zone. He was blowing like a race horse. His muscles burned. He thought his chest would burst with the effort to breathe, but he kept climbing without slowing.

"Oh, Christ!" Angie screeched. "We're not gonna make it!"

Alex glanced to his left, to where the fire line leveled out to the west, the route to the safety zone. All he saw was fire, a crackling red wall of flame.

"We got, we got, we got to go to the other one," he stammered between pants without stopping. His legs moving faster now on the level fire line. He saw the white-and-red striped ribbon that the Hotshots had tied up two days before. Seventy-five yards, fifty yards, twenty-five. The roar behind him bellowed into a crescendo, the air hot, too hot.

Alex burst into the rock scree like a demon from the netherworld. His eyes scanned the boulder-filled field. His legs never stopped. Grunts and squeals emanated from his air-deprived lungs. He saw two boulders in the middle of the scree slope, one rock much larger than the other, as big as a truck, and shaped like a heart. Like a heart. The thought moved through Alex's brain without finding context, but he struggled toward the rock anyway. He felt his strength begin to fade, first in step-like stages. Then, like dust in the wind, it was gone. His legs turned to jelly. Alex collapsed in the dirt just behind the boulder, his lungs squealing for air. Angie rolled right over his head, wide-eyed with terror, and pulled herself against the heart-shaped rock. After a long moment, Alex was able to say, "Fire Shelter!" He tried to pull the shelter free from his web gear. Angie heard and understood. Frantically she began to unravel the tightly folded aluminum foiled fire shelter. Alex was up on one elbow, still struggling for air. The onrushing flames had created a convection wind, and the fire shelter billowed like a sail in Angie's tight grip. Alex stumbled to his knees and was able to say, "Where's yours?"

Angie slapped her side and realized "It's in my fire pack!"

"We can both fit!" Alex yelled to be heard above the onrushing roar. He grabbed the shelter and forced it down on the ground behind the rock. The wind roared above the rock, wild and unearthly. The air filled with smoke and burning needles swirled like sleet. Before Alex dropped beside Angie, he looked down Artillery Creek one last time. Deep in the cherry-red flame, he saw a fire storm, a tornado of flame, a vortex spinning madly upward into a black, mammary-shaped cloud. Lightning flashed, thunder rolled. Red as blood, the image of the firestorm met the reflections in his eyes. Alex knew he was about to die.

He snuggled into the fire shelter on his side next to Angie, facing her inches away. It was too narrow for both to lie face down. They still had their hard hats on, chin straps tight. Alex had lost the glove on his left hand. He remembered the training films. "We have to keep our airways clear and away from the superheated air," he recited as if it were a catechism prayer.

"All-allright," Angie stammered.

Even in the lee of the boulder, the convection wind rocked the shelter, threatening to rip it from the ground. Alex had one foot firmly wrapped through the back loop, his left hand in another. Through small pinholes in the fabric, he saw the reflections of flames.

"Oh, Alex, we're gonna die!"

He tried hard not to panic. "No, no we're not. Just hang on." But he didn't believe his words.

"We're gonna die." She started softly crying.

"No, we're not! Stop saying that!"

It was hot in the shelter and getting hotter. He tried to estimate how long they had been there. Five minutes? Ten? His sense of time was lost in terror.

Alex opened his eyes and stared at the reflections of the flames through the pinholes in the shelter. A memory came to him, clear, strong; of being on the carousel at the amusement park as a little kid, the painted sky on the ceiling as blue as the lake. His mom and dad watched him and waved with each turn of the carousel. He was riding a white wooden horse with a painted mane and tail, up and down, holding onto the golden pole, up and down. Why was he thinking about this? A terrible sadness for his parents came over him. They would never see him alive again.

"Protect your airways!" Alex yelled in Angie's face.

"Oh God, I'm protecting them. I am. I don't want to die. I don't want to die."

Alex held Angie tightly with his right arm wrapped around her. "You're not going to die," he lied. The fire shelter assumed the total dimensions of his life as he struggled to protect his center. The fire wind keened high above the heart-shaped rock with a moan that was growing in intensity as the fire storm moved closer.

"It's like the dream! The dream. It's like the dream! Oh God, no, I don't want to die, not yet. Not yet!"

A profound sadness crushed Alex so he could barely breathe. "Oh Christ," he said. "I'm sorry, it's my fault, everything." His mind raced through all his failures that had funneled this girl to this space and time. Lost, no hope, lost forever. He began to cry in soft measured sobs. "I'm sorry. I'm sorry. I really am. If it wasn't for me, you wouldn't be here. It's, it's all my fault."

Angie was shaking as she let out her breath in a long, long sigh. "D-D-Don't be sorry," she stuttered. "It d-doesn't matter now." She spoke the words like a priest giving absolution. "It doesn't matter."

Alex cried as he tried to speak. The fear of death enveloped him completely. The leering face of the raw, painful nothingness so horrified him he couldn't speak. He held Angie's hand, held it tight, looked into her terror-filled eyes. He saw himself in the pupil's reflection, now glad not to be alone, accepting death as inevitable, hoping it would be quick.

He heard the fire storm getting closer. The tornado was almost upon them. It was too loud to speak, to hear, too loud for anything except fear. Alex closed his eyes. His tears mingled with Angie's. It was so hot. Again, the thought of the blue-painted sky on the ceiling of the carousel came to him unbidden, as he rode his wooden horse up and down, up and down.

55

"To die will be an awfully big adventure."
J. M. Barrie

Buck stood in the gravel parking lot in front of the fire warehouse. He watched the cumulus cloud of smoke reaching like a hand into a totally clear sky, almost forty air miles away, and he knew that something had gone terribly wrong.

Ten minutes later he was in the Jet Ranger and Henry was starting the rotors. The fire net radio was just a jumble of noise. Constant fire traffic kept cutting one person after another out. Buck couldn't make any sense of it, other than something had happened during the helitorch operation.

Augie, over at dispatch, never heard Henry's message that helicopter four three zero was leaving Goldburg bound for the Dome Creek fire, with two souls on board.

The two were silent. Henry pushed the helicopter at top speed, flying straight at the growing dark mass of cloud, billowing and growing in cauliflower-shaped explosions of smoke. Even from a half-way distance of twenty miles, Buck saw lightning in the cloud.

In less than thirty minutes, Henry had the ship over the fire, hovering to one side over the Middle Fork while the smoke rolled over Artillery Dome.

"Spurr, this is Twiddle on one, do you read?" Buck squeezed the receiver button hard.

The message came back almost immediately. Kloyd must have had the radio in his hand. "Twiddle, this is Spurr."

"Thank God," Buck sighed. "Kloyd, what is your status?"

"The crew has retreated to the north ridge."

"Are you all okay?"

There was no answer.

Again Buck asked, "Kloyd, are you all accounted for?"

Another long pause; Buck felt his chest constrict. He held his breath, then heard the message from Kloyd. "Two of the crew are missing."

"Who?"

A shorter pause, "Alex and the Kowalski girl."

"Oh, Jesus Christ!'

Neither he nor Kloyd said anything for over a minute as Henry kept the helicopter in place.

Buck asked, "Where was Alex's last location?"

"He was last seen right behind Eddie and Argo, just below where the fire line dips down. Where the alternate safety zone was."

"Do you think he headed there?"

You could hear Kloyd breathing over the radio. "I hope to God."

Buck looked over the mountains of billowing black and red smoke coming from Artillery Creek. "There's no way," he said, forgetting to take his finger off the radio transmit button.

Kloyd told Buck how he had led the crew into the big safety zone. Then, seeing the blowup was headed up the chimney toward the saddle, he worked the crew all the way to the top of the ridge. The crew stood safely on a sea of solid rock on the ridge line, like birds on a wire.

Buck didn't know what to do next. The smoke was too thick. The cloud moved up and over Artillery Dome. Buck looked out on a strange garden of spot fires sprinkled in Mortar Creek and growing like sprouts.

Whatever genie had released the wind from the jet stream and sent it packing down the Middle Fork had put it back in the bottle somehow. As the wind backed, the fire began to shrink in intensity. The great effort of burning had exhausted almost all the fuels that could carry the flames, burnt them so clean that all that was left were silver snags and smoking ash. Where the fire storm had raged, the tornado-like winds had windrowed the trees in circles and arcs, laid down smooth in a repeated geometric pattern. The fire had removed all vestiges of life from Artillery Creek and left behind just smoke and white ash.

Buck and Henry started a search with the helicopter as soon as they were able to begin to penetrate the smoke. Buck started to talk, saying, "Alex and that kid are somewhere down there . . ." He couldn't finish the statement, choking on his words, silent sobs wracking his body. He started to make a quiet wailing sound, a slow series of notes that rose up and down the scale like a funeral dirge.

Henry respectfully said nothing, just held the stick and guided the helicopter in a slow, looping curve.

Buck took a deep breath. "The smoke is starting to clear," he choked out. "Let's go over every inch of this fire until we find them."

Flames danced in small patches of down logs and dead snags. The landscape was black or white; black trees and logs and barren ground, white ash deep in the remains of the heavy fuels. The fire had burned so hot that even the limbs of the green trees had been burnt off, leaving only dark spikes piercing out the side of the trunks. Swirls of whirlwind trees littered the basin wherever the firestorm had touched down.

A light downhill breeze began to clear the smoke, moving it down river, and the firescape became visible in a series of on and off moments, like the flicker of a television set.

Buck was the first to see the crumpled-up fire shelter behind a large strangely shaped rock. From the air, the boulder almost looked like a heart. Henry moved the ship closer in a slow downward spiral.

That was it, Buck thought, that's where Alex made his last stand. Buck started to cry again, this time in quiet measured beats to match his breathing.

Henry turned the helicopter to the right; and there, right there where a low ridge of rock jutted out into the landscape like dinosaur bones, were two small figures in yellow shirts waving frantically, the larger one jumping up and down like a marionette on strings.

"Jumpin' Jesus Christ!" Buck shouted in disbelief. "They're alive. They're alive!" And then he began to laugh and cry at the same time, with tears so large and so hot you could have brewed a pot of tear-water tea.

Henry took the helicopter in close enough so even through the swirling ash from the prop wash, Buck could see the smile on Alex's face.

"Dispatch, this is Twiddle," Buck said into the radio, laughing with great happy tears streaming down his face. "Helicopter Four Three Zero will be returning to Goldburg with four souls on board!"

EPILOGUE

"Come live with me and be my love,
And we will some new pleasures prove
Of golden sands and crystal brooks
With silken lines and silver hooks."

John Donne

It was the third Saturday in October, and it was a Polish cowboy wedding at Our Lady of Angels Catholic Church in Goldburg. Alex stood outside on the church steps, waiting for his bride. The fall equinox storm had already come and gone, dusting the high peaks with snow. The Lost River Range ran like a line to the southeast, white-topped and lonely looking.

"It's bad luck to see the bride before the actual wedding," said Kloyd. "And marriage is hard enough without having bad luck trailin' you down the aisle."

Harmon struggled with his tie. "It don't count if he's in the church."

"Technically, he's on the steps," Howie added.

Fast Eddie countered, "Last I checked, these steps are part of the church."

Alex wasn't paying any attention to the current argument of his wedding party. He was busy singing, just under his breath, the Hesitation Blues:

"Tell me, how long do I have to wait.
Can I get you now, or must I hesitate."

The best way to describe Alex's wedding party would be to call it a mixed lot. Goldburg was a bit small to have a tuxedo rental, so suit and tie was the standard. Kloyd was best man, and he looked reasonable in his brown polyester western suit and cowboy boots. Howie, as always, was dashing in the latest fashion, wearing a suit that cost almost as much as a lower-end used car. Fast Eddie and Harmon, even cleaned up, still looked like a couple of river rats stuck in some cheap suits that fell off the rack, their ties obvious refugees from the thrift store.

Alex still had a bandage on his left hand, which was burned when he lost his glove. The skin grafts had gone well, with only minimal scarring, and he had lost no mobility in his hand. As he waited on the steps, he slightly shook his head in wonder at how things had worked out, not just for him and Angie, but for the rest of his friends. After he and Angie were rescued, it was like the pendulum had started to swing back, undoing some of the excesses and righting a few wrongs all by itself.

The trickle of good things happening turned into a flood.

339

Chester M. Riddles avoided the career-ending result of an employee death on the job and forgave all of Alex's and Big Stanley's past indiscretions. Alex's appointment to a permanent Forest Service employee was assured.

Buck's lonely initiative to look up a girlfriend from his Navy days had worked. From what Alex had heard, the romance was looking pretty promising. Buck's past girlfriend, Frieda, was recently divorced and was more than interested in seeing how the years had treated her old cowboy flame. She was there at the wedding: sort of foreign looking, dark-haired, in her late thirties, with strong features, an almost Persian look to her. She sure was a beauty, Alex was thinking, and what a dresser, giving Sandy Spotts a good run for her money in the tight skirt department. Buck looked happy, too, with an uncharacteristic smile plastered on his face that would have scared you if you didn't know him.

Another unlikely office development was that Big Stanley and Sandy Spotts had, despite the long odds, somehow gotten back together - and really together this time. Big Stan had made the first conciliatory moves. He had stopped drinking altogether, even went to a couple of AA meetings. The skunks had never returned from the cheese-puff relocation project. Big Stan carefully explained again that he didn't know how these Russian women found him; but he promised to swear off all Eastern European hookers, escort services and massage experts, so help him God. Even though he had never actually asked her, Big Stanley started introducing Sandy as his fiancée. Sandy didn't say anything to the contrary.

Argo and Teffonie were a bit of an item, and it all came to be because Argo felt guilty about leaving Alex behind on the fire line. He visited Alex about every other day the week that Alex was in the Salmon hospital for his skin grafts. Since Argo had never had a car, he borrowed Teffonie's old Crown Victoria police car that her dad had bought her at some auction in Philadelphia. After the first trip, Teffonie started to join Argo on the drive. Somehow, after hours of natural history discussions, the talk turned once again to plate tectonics. Alex actually heard most of the good part one evening in his room. Teffonie evidently had spent some time in the Goldburg Library, ordered some geology texts on interlibrary loan, and looked up some current research papers on the Internet. Armed to the teeth, she once again engaged Argo about the ancient continent of Pangea. From there it was only a short walk through the geologic epochs to an arm-in-arm walk down the Main Street sidewalk in Salmon. Teffonie just sort of grabbed Argo around the shoulder; and he reciprocated around her waist. Alex saw it happen, right outside his hospital-room window.

Harmon, too, was working on some life changes. After two long weeks on the Dome Creek Fire, watching the fire burn out Mortar Creek, jump the Middle Fork, burn all of Little Loon Creek and most of Rapid River, Harmon was both physically and mentally worn out. What both excited him and distressed him was that the Dome Creek Fire was such an incredible natural event. It burned more than ten thousand acres in one burning period, then the next day burned eighteen thousand more, creating a smoke column that rose so high you could see it a hundred miles away. The fire made its own weather, with heat lightning dancing in the giant cloud, and downdrafts that turned into firestorms and fire tornados – a flaming front with two-hundred-foot flame lengths that consumed an entire mountainside of trees in a thirty-minute run.

Harmon had seen it all; but he knew if he tried to tell anyone the true story, they wouldn't believe him, just think it was more tall tales. This strange paradox of being caught with the truth bothered Harmon to no end. He got to thinking of Feodora and Toby when it started to rain. A two-and-one-half-inch, three-day August drizzle, a month-early fall storm, just slowly turned out the lights on the Dome Creek Fire. Harmon sat next to Fast Eddie, both in makeshift garbage-bag raincoats, both cold, watching some stumps smolder. Harmon had decided that he would call Feodora as soon as he got off this never-ending fire assignment.

As soon as he hit Goldburg four days later, Harmon made the telephone call. He was surprised at the warm reception, almost as if she was expecting the call. The relationship was a long way from fixed, but Harmon figured the trend line was positive all the way.

Perhaps the strangest Goldburg happening was the recent change in leadership at the LDS First Ward. It seemed that brother-in-law Levi had gotten a little carried away with his marriage counseling role, and a burgeoning scandal with an admiring lonely housewife was nipped in the bud with his quick relocation to Utah. The surprise choice for new bishop, a real dark-horse candidate, was Kloyd's brother Payson, a facial hair advocate and an all-around light-hand-on-the-throttle type. Kloyd stroked his handlebar mustache and smiled every time he thought about it.

Looking out over Round Valley and the empty sky, Alex had a deja vu experience right there on the church steps. It was just an ordinary occurrence, an everyday kind of thing, when the noon whistle on the roof of High Country Builders went off. Its slow wail froze Alex on the church steps, standing still in his new five-hundred-dollar suit, looking up at the small angel carved above the door lintel of Our Lady of Angels, certain that he had seen this all happen before in a dream. The shivers worked down his arms.

Kloyd ushered Alex inside the church just as the Kowalski pickup truck with the stock rack came into view. "Let's go, Alex, got to keep the tradition. You never know, there might be somethin' to it."

Alex and his attendants waited in the vestibule. He was still humming "The Hesitation Blues" but now in a more nervous-tic sort of a way. Alex looked out at the crowded church, his mother and father in the front row looking like expatriates lost in a foreign land.

Alex had a spur-of-the-moment thought and just asked Kloyd straight out, " Kloyd, now tell me true, do I have a town name?"

"Well, Jeez-O-Friday, what makes you ask a question like that at a time

341

like this?"

"I don't know, it just popped in my head. But I think I need to know."

"I don't know. It just don't feel right."

"Why not? You're my best man and all. The way I figure it, you have to tell me, as I'm asking you right here in the church."

Kloyd scratched his head. "I don't know if that sticks, as I ain't Catholic."

"Just tell me what my town name is, Kloyd, and get it over with."

Kloyd dipped his head down in despair. "The Kid," was all he said.

"The Kid?" Alex was thinking, it could have been worse.

"Yeah, The Kid."

"The Kid," Alex said again in a firm voice.

Alex remembered the wedding ceremony in moments permanently ingrained in the Vermont granite portion of his mind. Sandy Spotts did a blues riff on the church organ before switching to the wedding march. His first view of Angie coming down the aisle gave him a wonderful feeling. Her veil covered her face but he could still see her long red hair done up in two braids by her mother, a Polish tradition for the maiden moving to becoming a married woman. Angie walked straight and tall and didn't limp, even though the walking cast had just been removed the week before. She wore her mother's long-sleeved wedding dress, old-fashioned in lace, and Alex lifted the veil and saw her full face looking right at him. Then Kloyd almost dropped the ring. All these things just seemed to roll themselves up into a wonderful ball of happy thoughts.

Father Domenico read the vows. Tears were shed. Alex and Angie were standing on the church steps, with rice in their hair.

Alex stood still for the photographs and he wondered again at his long, strange trip to Goldburg, Idaho. He was thinking about probabilities; how two snowflakes, like Angie and him had somehow gotten together in this constantly expanding universe, how all the collections and combinations of atoms evolving all the way from the big-bang singularity, ended up with him and Angie standing on the steps of Our Lady of Angels Church on a Saturday afternoon.

"It can't be thought," Alex said out loud.

Angie looked at him funny. "You're not thinking about physics again, are you?"

"Just a little bit."

"Well, maybe we can experience the big bang later tonight," Angie whispered to him.

Alex decided right then that he loved having a classical education.

Alex had rented the American Legion Hall for the wedding reception. The building was full to bursting with people. Buck was bartender and Big Stanley the unofficial bouncer. As in some strange opera, everybody seemed to have a role, and all enjoyed playing it.

Of course there was music. The Gold Dust Twins' old dad was an accordion player, and a good one. His big accordion had rhinestones on the side that spelled out his name, Jerome, in sparkles.

Then it was Alex's turn on the dance floor with his bride. The Gold Dust Twins and Dad played a lovely Obedek, a Polish dance number, and Alex swept up Angie and her long gown and confidently moved her all around the dance floor. There was a hush in the crowd as they watched.

"I forgot how well you dance," Angie told him.

"I've got happy feet, you know."

Then were toasts and Alex drank and smiled and drank again.

Big Stanley displayed his usual eloquence, stating "I just want to say how happy all of us at the Forest Service are for Alex and Angelica. Alex came to us just about a year and a half ago, from back east, and look how well he's done for himself." There was general applause. "Anyway, welcome Angelica to the Forest Service Family."

Buck had evidently decided that it was necessary to sample all of the liquor in his role as bartender, and his toast was short and sweet. He stood there in front of the bar, glass held high, and then couldn't remember what he was going to say. The crowd waited and Buck hesitated until finally he just said, "Clum-Dummit, the Kid got himself a bride," and leaned back and finished his drink as the wedding crowd applauded.

The best man, Kloyd, was taking every opportunity to indulge his jack-Mormon tendencies with alcohol. He enjoyed this part of the wedding reception tremendously. Kloyd, already red faced, stood up behind the wedding-party table, glass in hand, and said, "Here's to Alex. Came here a year and a half ago, not knowin' nothin' at all, and corralled the prettiest gal in Goldburg as his own cowboy angel." The whole Legion Hall erupted in laughter, which surprised Kloyd, as he was not trying to be funny.

The Gold Dust Twins and their old Dad played and played, only stopping long enough to suck up alcohol. In one of those rare moments of life, Alex truly did lose track of time and just danced without forethought or care.

Just as the party was starting to lose steam, Teffonie rounded up the rest of the wedding party and formed a tight circle around Angie. Alex knew his part in this play, as he had seen it once before at a friend's wedding in western Pennsylvania, where a buddy of his had also married a Polish girl. Alex was expected to try to break into the circle, and the wedding-party was expected not to let him in. This went on for a good while. Alex was hamming it up quite well, expressing his disappointment in an exaggerated display, like an actor on a stage. Everybody in the American Legion Hall was on their feet and formed another ring around Alex as he wandered around the wedding party circle, trying to get in to Angie. There was clapping and yelling and all sorts of carrying on. When Alex sensed the timing was right, he made a big display of taking his wallet out and held it over his head, so that everyone could see, and then tossed the wallet over the wedding-party circle right at Angie's feet. This act symbolized that

343

Alex gave all he had, surpassing all the gifts, to claim his bride. His next attempt to push through the circle was successful, and all you heard was cheering and clapping as Alex swept up Angie in his arms and carried her out of the Legion Hall.

Like the bursting of a dam, everyone in the place just flowed out the door of the American Legion and out on the sidewalk to watch Alex and Angie drive away on their honeymoon.

In the bed of Alex's old Chevrolet, a large carefully crafted and painted plywood "Just Married" sign had been nailed together and bolted right into the box of the truck.

"Christ, would you look at that," Alex said, still holding Angie in his arms. "Not getting rid of that any time soon. I hope I'm not dragging a couple of old saddles."

Angie clutched him tightly around his neck. "No saddles, but lots of beer cans."

Alex placed her down lightly next to his truck and opened the door for her. She slid right over into the driver's seat. "I'm driving," she said. "I'm probably the only one in the place over fourteen that's not over the limit."

Alex mumbled through the residue of too much alcohol consumed, "No complaint here."

He was surprised that it was dark outside, for the reception had started immediately after the wedding. As Angie put the truck in gear, Fast Eddie and Harmon set off a series of bottle rockets right on Main Street, lighting up the sky in green and yellow star bursts.

"It's just like the Fourth of July at the rodeo," Alex smiled. "Only better."

He rolled down his window and hung his head out, happy like a dog, as Angie drove down Main Street, hearing the car horns honking behind them.

It was Alex's turn in the middle seat, sitting tightly against Angie as she negotiated the curves of the Salmon River Road on the way to Sun Valley.

The stars were dancing and following the moon reflections in the Salmon River as they drove along. Alex and Angie didn't say much to each other, just sort of let the intense feeling of anticipation grow.

As the effects of the alcohol started to drift away, Alex's head began to clear. He thought about Angie and remembered only blue skies. He thought about Buck, Kloyd, Big Stan and Sandy, riding old Major, packin' into the Middle Fork. High mountains surrounded his thoughts of Arlo, Harmon, and Fast Eddie. Pictures of the The Wild Bunch shared the stage with Teffonie, Howie and Nedra. He even recalled a quick memory of Yellow-Glasses Bob at Boundary Creek. Alex smiled a special Goldburg smile and decided that he was a good match for all of them.

As Angie drove over Galena Summit, Alex caught a glimpse of a shooting star out of the corner of his eye and had an idea. A vision of time as a river floated into his mind. Like a raft in the rapids, he was being pulled downstream, towards the mouth of a dark canyon. But now Angie was on his boat. In a daydream that he constructed right then, he pictured himself on the sweep boat, Angie there next to him with her red hair flying in the wind, Haystack Rapids dead ahead; but then, instead of continuing down river, he calmly spun the sweeps and turned the boat into a side eddy of smooth, deep, clear water, a wondrous sandy beach tempting them to stay awhile. There was plenty of time left to float through the rapids.

Maybe, just maybe, it was that easy.